Song of the Ëan

EMILY NORDBERG

Copyright © 2016 by Emily Nordberg

All Rights Reserved.

This book or any portion thereof may not be reproduced or used in any manner whatsoever without the express written permission of the author except for the use of brief quotations in a book review.

ISBN-13: 978-0692752210 (Eon Publications)

ISBN-10: 0692752218

Chapter 1

William hated boats.

This fact was gravely unfortunate, as not only was he on a boat, but on a passenger ship. He had been stuck here for over a week, and they had still not reached land. In his twenty-two years, his only previous sailing excursions had involved one-day journeys upriver to the King's vacation palace outside the capital city, Ossia. That had at least been a pleasant destination, worth the voyage.

No, this was not a pleasure cruise. The prince had not volunteered for this voyage, but there was no one else for the King to send on this errand. William's elder brother Arthos could certainly not go. He was the King's heir—he had more important duties. The King insisted that his youngest son should go on this particular voyage. He wanted someone more personal than the ambassador. It wasn't just a question of collecting the annual tribute this year. King Eduar Tellor had something more important on his mind, something William did not like to think about. He had tried to forget it a long time ago. When he was a boy, all he wanted was to drown his memories. His father could not. Now they were digging up everything again.

William preferred to have nothing on his mind at all. Not obligations. Definitely not diplomatic missions or the painful past. And not, absolutely not, boats.

Of all places, it had to be Belond. Belond was the only province of Edenia not connected to the continent. All other provinces could be reached from Ossia by overland travel. Belond was an island in the eastern sea. It was one of many islands in the ocean, but this was the largest and one of the few Edenia had thought valuable enough to colonize. The territory had been acquired for economic purposes, as it had a thriving mining industry, but it was largely ignored due to its distance and relative insignificance to the Empire as a whole. Edenians were generally not fond of the sea.

William rolled over in his bunk, moaning. He had recovered from his awful seasickness of the past few days tolerably, but he still felt queasy. What was almost worse was being stuck in this little room. This was a huge ship, part of the King's royal fleet. It was well-manned, with fifty of the King's Guard and as many sailors. No pirate would dare attack this ship. It was state of the art, the best vessel available besides the King's personal ship. Even with all this, the ship still had this tiny little chamber for its illustrious passenger. Whoever had designed this ship, William decided, did not anticipate having to live in this little room for days on end.

He climbed out of bed. Yes, he had to *climb*. The bunk stood above the floor, for some odd reason, and could only be reached with a ladder. Apparently that left more space in the room, but it only meant that a tall man, which he was, would hit his head if he sat up in bed.

He decided to go up on deck. He hadn't been out of this room in days, and at this point it was just making him queasier. It was also *very* dull. That was yet another thing he disliked about sailing: there was nothing to do.

He stepped outside the door. Even the servants and guards, normally loitering to wait on him at his call, had completely abandoned him to his bad temper. Typical. He set off anyway.

He got lost in the hallway only once, and a kindly sailor (rather shocked at encountering the son of the most powerful man in the Edenian Empire wandering around alone) pointed him in the right direction with a bit of confused stammering.

The prince climbed the stair that led to the deck. As he emerged, blinking, into the fresh air, he was buffeted by a fierce sea wind. He hesitated, gaining composure.

Everyone noticed his presence abruptly. All activity temporarily halted as the sailors hailed him and performed a rather boisterous salute. The servants and attendants—so *that's* where they all went—swarmed him immediately. The ambassador, along to perform the ordinary yearly diplomatic duties to Belond, also approached.

"Greetings, my lord," he exclaimed, bowing. "You have joined us at last! Is not this sailing glorious! Truly, there is no ship that can tame the waves like one of Edenia's own. Do you not think?"

The ambassador, Lord Elber, was among the many nobles in the Edenian Empire, most of whom were descended from the ancient families of a previous age—before the Tellors had claimed the throne. The vast majority of these titled families no longer possessed much influence—just the power of a name. This was the age of the businessman. Since the Tellors had taken over Edenia some few hundred years ago, the common man had gained more power. The nobles were still, however, the leaders of the political world. Ossia was filled with them, in varying degrees. Most royal positions were filled by men of lineage who could barely manage to trace their ancestry to some illustrious personage but still claimed the name.

Elber was one such noble. His family tree was questionable, but he claimed to be related to the Rainauldts, a very old name indeed. William's mother, Queen Sylva, had been a Rainauldt. The relation was obscure, so Elber's position was, too. There were few people who were willing to sail to Belond. Elber was willing to do anything to ascend the Edenian bureaucratic ladder. Ambassadors were generally fairly prestigious, even if he himself was not. He hoped to distinguish himself and eventually attain a higher position. In twenty years, he'd had little success. Having the King's own son on board and traveling with him offered him a golden opportunity. If he did well, he hoped to earn a recommendation and, consequently, a promotion.

This reasoning led him to annoy the prince with obsequious flattery and over-enthusiastic ejaculations such as the one he had just made. He made a show of being pompous and official, meticulously proper, and always loyal to the

King's person and to the prince. William did not like him at all, but Elber persisted.

"Mmm," the prince mumbled skeptically in response to Elber's effusion. "How much longer until we reach the island?"

"Two days, your majesty," a sailor chipped in, "if the weather holds. There's a storm brewing; we hope to beat it."

"Two whole days?" the prince grumbled.

"Come, your highness," the ambassador soothed, "look over the railing. It is beautiful scenery, and we have only a short time left to enjoy it. What a sight we saw yesterday! There were dolphins leaping out of the water by the boat! It was incredibly beautiful! But it is lovely even without them. You will agree, I am sure."

"I do not think so, Elber," William grumbled, but he accompanied him anyway. He leaned his arms on the railing, peering into the water below.

He had to admit, it was rather beautiful, but in a fierce, not altogether friendly way. He was not about to sing the raptures of the waves like Elber. He turned his eyes upward.

A black speck against the bright sky arrested the prince's sight. He shaded his eyes to examine it more closely, pushing his dark hair out of his face. It was very, very small, almost indiscernible. He thought for a moment that he was imagining things.

"Elber," he asked, "do you see that black spot in the sky?"

Elber peered. "I confess I do not," he replied.

"I see it," one of the attendants piped up. "It's moving."

"I see it too," another declared.

William glanced at them, checking to see if they were serious. Many of these lackeys, seeking to please their lords, agreed with whatever they thought their superior wanted to hear, regardless of truth. It was a rather annoying behavior, but then, it is dangerous to offend a powerful man. In this instance, it seemed they were in earnest, as they watched the skies intently.

It grew larger. Soon the whole group of people was

discussing it.

"It must be a bird," said one servant.

"Birds don't fly so far from land, do they?" asked another.

"We have not seen one yet! We must be getting closer to the island."

Soon even the sailors were noticing the commotion. One old, weathered sailor declared, "That's an eagle! Eagles are not often seen in Belond—and certainly not this far out to sea."

This started low murmuring. The sailors all made a gesture against evil. "A bad sign," another sailor mumbled.

"It's only an eagle," the prince said, taking his eyes off the bird for the first time since he saw it. "What's so frightening about that?"

"Have you not heard the stories, my lord?" the sailor asked wide-eyed.

"What stories?"

"Be careful," Elber broke in imperiously. "Do not believe him. Sailors are known to be a superstitious lot."

The sailor protested, "No, this is true. Everyone has heard of the haunting of Belond."

"Haunting?" William asked, captivated. He did not believe any of this—it was just an eagle, after all—but it was the first thing he had heard about the whole business of the voyage that was remotely interesting. It was all just a boring diplomatic excursion on a tedious ship to land at a backwoods, uncivilized island to collect tribute, perform his father's onerous and unpleasant task, and go home—the sooner the better. A ghost added a little vitality to an otherwise dreary voyage. Edenians, though they were highly civilized and far too modern to credit such tales, enjoyed stories of the supernatural. They believed in one God, El, but he was a rather distant and uninvolved figure to all but a few religious dogmatics. Science and civilization impacted their lives far more. There was still, however, an unaccountable interest in tales of fantasy, perhaps left over from the days when all the people roamed in ignorant, superstitious tribes before they were united a thousand years ago into the Empire. William was not sure what it was about these stories that was so fascinating, but they held his and other Edenians attention readily.

"Yes," another sailor spoke up. "They say the island is inhabited by a goddess."

"Goddess, not ghost?" he questioned, surprised. This was a twist. "Please, continue. You interest me."

The first picked up the tale. "Deep in the forests of Belond," he began dramatically, "The goddess Auria dwells in hiding."

Auria, according to ancient tribal legend still vaguely remembered by the now more enlightened Edenians, was the queen of the gods. She was the goddess of war, the mightiest being in existence, according to the story. She possessed unrivaled power. She had hair made of lightning and storm clouds for eyes. But what explained the sailors' sudden fear was the tale that spoke of her symbol: the eagle.

"I see," William said, smiling.

"No, my lord," the sailor declared, "we are in earnest."

The second sailor picked up the tale again. "She is a very spirit, they say. She haunts men's houses, and she can walk through walls. Nothing happens that she does not know about. She lurks in the shadows to ensnare any unwary man who dares trespass in her territory. She possesses ten thousand voices which echo in the air. All men in Belond fear her wrath, which is swift and falls hard."

"Enough," Elber cut him off. "This is nonsense. There is no such person. Auria does not exist. The goddess is a mere legend."

The sailor mumbled something testily, but he bowed and backed away. William, irritated at the interruption of a good story, turned back to look at the eagle. It was certainly strange, he admitted that. It was no wonder the simple souls were fearful.

He was surprised how large it had grown. It was nearly above them now. Its white-feathered head could be espied.

Its wingspan was wide, even viewed from a great height. The knot of people still murmured. Elber announced, "I see him now, Lord William."

The prince rolled his eyes. "Yes, Elber," was the most civil response he could manage.

The bird soared above them. Suddenly, his flight changed. The bird dropped rapidly into a dive, as fast as lightning. A collective gasp arose from the people on board. Everyone began to exclaim and point.

The old sailor shouted, "It would not dive unless it was hunting!"

The story-tellers said together, "It is Auria, come upon us!"

William watched in fascination. The bird's flight was almost mesmerizing. It seemed to grow larger and larger.

It unleashed a shrill scream. With a flurry of wings, it alighted on the railing. William's hand had rested there only a second before.

He found himself face to face with a huge bald eagle. He had seen eagles before. This one was bigger than *any* bird he had ever seen. The prince's heart beat rapidly, suddenly afraid. For all that he did not believe in ghost stories, this bird unnerved him. It was a wild creature. Who knew what it would do? Its yellow eyes examined him ruthlessly. He could not hold their gaze. He backed away, slowly. Everyone stared at the bird in fixation.

The bird flapped its wings on the railing, cawing again.

It suddenly sprang off the railing, flying straight at the prince. The crowd began shouting, some afraid, some angry, some confused. William's guards rushed to his side.

The eagle soared upward again, leaving William. He clutched his hand. The bird's razor sharp beak had ripped the skin on his finger. The talons had briefly gripped his arm. It might bruise, but he was not seriously hurt. He was surrounded by people, all asking him a thousand things at once, but he stared silently skyward at the bird that had just attacked him, heart beating fast.

The eagle was still shrieking wildly, circling around the ship. It finally landed on the mast, the very highest point on the whole ship. It screamed its angry cry. It looked down on them imperiously, examining the tiny figures below. Then, once again, it took off. It dove at the flags flying on the mast just below it. One was purple for Edenia, marking the ship as one legally allowed to sail and belonging to the empire. The second was red with the Tellor emblem, declaring the presence of a royal person on the ship. The bird aimed for the Tellor flag, and, flying through it, ripped the fabric and tore the flag away in its claws. It screeched one last time, and then the bird soared away, toward Belond, carrying the red flag in its talons.

William stared after it, breathing hard. Nothing so strange had ever, ever happened to him. It was enjoyable to hear stories of unnatural happenings, but he felt quite differently to encounter them himself. For once, no Edenian rationalization could explain to him what had just happened. Doubt crept over him. The sailors could not be right. Auria did not exist. So what exactly had just happened?

"My lord! Answer me!" Elber exclaimed. "Are you all right? Did that blasted creature hurt you?"

He looked down at his right hand, which he still cradled in his left. There was blood on his fingers, but it was not a serious cut. (Elber, however, nearly fainted.) He looked closely at the scratch, still confused. Why did the beast attack him, and why did it gouge his hand?

Then he realized. His ring, bearing the Tellor insignia, was gone. The bird had stolen the proof of his identity. The ring, the flag. The eagle had taken the two most obvious things that proved that a son of the King was on board.

Had it been a man who had stolen his ring, William's confusion would be abated at once. But why would a *bird* care that there was royalty on board the ambassador's ship?

Elber was bustling about, making himself a nuisance. "You there!" he pointed to a guard. "Bind his lordship's hand!"

"Yes, sir!" the soldier said smartly, obeying his orders. He ran for bandages.

"You," he said to a sailor. "Get another flag up there!"

"There is no other Tellor flag," the man stammered fearfully, still rattled by the whole incident.

Elber harrumphed. "There must be another one! The prince of Edenia cannot arrive on Belond without proper announcement!"

"It does not matter, Elber!" the prince snapped. He was not normally so sharp with Elber, but the man was exasperating, and the prince's emotions were rattled. "Just go! You're not helping!"

Elber stopped abruptly, an injured expression on his face. He bowed coldly, saying, "Sire," and then he departed.

The soldier came back with a bandage, but the prince waved him away. He shouldered his way through his attendants, not talking to any of them. He still cradled his hand as it continued to bleed. He did not tell anyone about the ring. The flag was strange enough.

He heard the sailors murmuring. "Horrible." "A bad omen." "Ill luck follows that one." "Auria has some wrath in store for the prince." "That must be so."

He did not listen. He walked briskly toward the stairs, leading below-decks. Suddenly, his room did not seem so cramped or insufferable; rather, it was a safe haven. Even the boat did not strike him so badly. He did not mind sailing. He would not have minded sailing another two *weeks* to reach their journey's end now.

Anything was better than reaching Belond. The island had taken on a new light for him. While he hated to admit it to himself, he was afraid. The island was too unknown. It represented a threatening, ominous destination.

All the rumors he had heard about Belond returned to him. There were reasons other than distance that Edenians shunned the island. It had a wild, dangerous, and even unnatural reputation. It was nicknamed the Isle of Death. Many who went there never came back, and those who dared undertake the journey were few enough. The king's delegation and a few merchant ships were the only traffic to the province. It was strange, isolated, and dangerous. The eastern sea was treacherous for all but a few weeks in the spring and summer, and even then, sailing was hazardous. Pirates were known to roam the seas.

The island itself had an ominous reputation. Even the most desperate of lords looking for power would not have consented to be Governor of this province. It had a long history of unrest, whether by human or natural cause. Early in the history of Edenia, a thousand years ago, it was said that the island, then inhabited by ancient tribes, was bitterly fought over, and even with the might of Edenia as it was then it was barely won. The province was not well colonized, so it was still predominantly wild, and those Edenians brave enough to live there were often rather wild themselves. It was an unsavory place, even without this strange phenomenon that William had encountered.

At this moment, he felt he would do anything rather than set foot in Belond. He wished his father had not insisted on this action, that he could have stayed home. If the King was not so wrapped up in the emotions of the past, the prince would not be on this ship.

No. The King would not let go. William had tried to forget, because it was too difficult to remember. The King could not forget. Even after all this time, he was still grieving.

Among other things it could claim for itself, Belond had one dark distinction.

A long time ago, the King's heart had sailed to Belond, but it never came back.

William wondered if he, too, would never come back.

Chapter 2

While those first few days on the ship seemed to take ages, the last two went by like lightning. Go figure. When a person wants time to pass, it crawls along; when he doesn't want it to pass, it flies.

Belond was close now. The prince had emerged onto the deck again, though he wasn't enthusiastic about it. He had regained control of his emotions—at least to a casual observer. He still could not shake the feeling of foreboding that the island inspired, but he was a better master of his trepidation. He had convinced himself that there *must* be some explanation for what had happened to him, despite the rumors that surrounded Belond. It was all a coincidence, surely. He was perfectly safe. Yet some part of him, deep down, remained unconvinced.

He was still afraid of the island.

It loomed ahead. The day was dark because of the impending storm. The wind was bawling in fitful blasts. A haze lay over the island, which appeared as only a large, misty green blotch on the sea. It was bigger than he had thought it would be but still a very small island in comparison with the vast expanse of the Edenian Empire. There was very little territory in the entire world that Edenia did not control, and that was either wasteland or barbaric tribal holdings. Not even this tiny island had been overlooked in the Empire's thirst for territory.

As they drew nearer, he could make out the city, Belo. Not a city in the true sense of the word, of course. It was barely even a town. It was probably just a collection of huts and cottages, he surmised, judging by what he had heard. Belo was, however pathetic, the largest settlement on the island. There were a few outlying farms, but the main industry was mining, and the miners lived in the town, traveling up the mountain each day to their labor. The rest of the populace was craftsmen. Not skilled craftsmen, of course—those were limited to truly civilized regions, like Ossia. No, all these villagers did was refine the raw materials so that they were actually valuable enough to ship off to the capital.

He had few hopes of civilized accommodations. While Elber tried to assure him that the place was not so bad as he thought, he viewed the whole island as backward and unrefined.

The Governor, however, was a different story. He was the man William had been sent to see. William had known him in Ossia—years and years ago, before he had foolishly, but dutifully, taken on the burden of the governorship of Belond. In those days, he had been very close to the King and his family. He was once accounted as the King's closest friend. It had been a blow for the king to lose him to Belond. Tragedy surrounded the Governor now, both for his circumstances and the losses he had suffered. The prince would not be unhappy to see him again—it was only the dark memories and the strange dread of Belond he feared.

"We are close," Elber said at his side, with far too much enthusiasm. "We will pull up to the dock in just a few minutes."

William silently wished the man would cease to state the obvious, but he merely nodded in acknowledgment.

Nearly the whole party attending the two noblemen was assembled on deck, whether soldiers or servants, ready to begin the disembarking process. They were eager to beat the coming storm, and a prince's retinue took time to unload.

William looked around him as they drew alongside the dock. He could see the town more clearly now. It was just as he had anticipated: a quaint little country town. There was a large square in front of the docks, which themselves were rather small. Along this square were some huge warehouses, well-built and impressive. Further back were a bunch of pitiful smithies to supplement the miners' industry, and behind those, some ramshackle houses which extended to the fringes of the town. Some streets ran between these, but one wider lane led down to the barracks, or that was what William guessed. This was a very large stone building, surprisingly well-maintained. It was located in the distance at the far end of the town. That was all he could see. In all, it did not impress him. He had seen the wonders of Ossia, a bustling, thriving metropolis. This was a pitiful excuse for a city in his eyes.

Despite the foul weather, there was a small crowd assembled in the square to see the ship. Peasants, mostly. Dirty, poor, and insignificant. They craned their necks to get a look at the ship. It was probably one of the highlights of their dreary lives to see an Edenian ship pull in. Elber commented on them. "Ah, the old welcoming crowd," he soliloquized. "Such jolly citizens." In truth, they didn't look jolly at all; rather, they appeared lean, hungry, and rather desolate. William did not like the look of them.

There was also a crowd of men in uniform, proudly wearing the Edenian purple. They were in tight formation and looked striking in comparison to the peasants. They surrounded a small group of people on horseback, in the center of the square. William could not see them clearly, but this, he assumed, was Governor Whitefeld. He noticed one woman in the party, which he guessed to be the Governor's daughter.

The ship drew alongside the dock, and the sailors hastened to make it fast and lower the gangway. William drew away from the railing. He would be among the first off the ship, as was proper. It was time.

Elber led the way. The prince moved mechanically behind him. He tried to believe this was all just a bad dream. He wasn't really here. He wasn't about to set foot on this island. He would wake up in a minute back in his own bed in Ossia.

The ramp having been lowered, Elber walked pompously down onto the dock. The Governor's greeting party, having dismounted, was standing on the dock to meet them. William could see them clearly now, standing on the ship above the gangway.

It was indeed the Governor. William would know him

anywhere. It had been almost fifteen years, so his memory might be dimmed, but there were only a few Edenians with golden hair. The Whitefelds were distinguished as one of the few families who possessed the trait. They were also known for their striking green eyes. The Governor's eyes were not as bold as he remembered, but it had been many years. He looked older, certainly, and more weathered, but he was still in his prime, only in his forties. He did not give the impression of having caved to his trouble at all.

Lord Andel Whitefeld was a strong man. When he had lived in Ossia, he had been known for his generosity, honor, and devotion to duty. He was brave enough to take this position, one all other lords had shunned. It had traditionally been governed by a Whitefeld, a fact which had driven Andel to accept it. William could see the confidence in his demeanor, like he had nothing to fear. This must be the Andel he had once known. So many things flooded back he had forgotten. The way he had laughed, the way his father used to smile—that last year. Things had never been the same after the Whitefelds were gone.

"My Lord Elber," Governor Whitefeld said with polite enthusiasm, bowing at the waist. He was of a different sort than Elber. He was not condescending. One did not have to wonder whether he was genuine in his manner.

"My dear Governor," Elber said pretentiously. "It does us good to return once more to your fair island."

"Not so fair at the moment, I'm afraid," he said congenially, "with the weather. I hope the journey was not difficult."

"It was glorious!" effused Elber. "As always, it afforded a great pleasure."

"I am glad of it," the Governor said. "Well, let us—"

"Forgive me, my lord," Elber interrupted, "but I must introduce you to a most illustrious personage who has attended me on this voyage. You are acquainted, I'm told, but it has been some time since then." With a wave of his hand, Elber announced dramatically, "Allow me to announce to you

Lord William Tellor, son of King Eduar Tellor and Prince of the Edenian Empire."

William descended the ramp. There was no turning back now. He felt a thrill run through him as he set foot on the dock. He approached the party, all eyes on him.

The prince was a bit surprised by the Governor's reaction. Lord Whitefeld looked absolutely aghast. His mouth had dropped slightly, and he stared in astonishment. While his surprise was understandable, since he had received no warning, even by the Tellor flag, the prince had hoped he would be glad.

The Governor recovered his surprise quickly. He went down on one knee. "Your Majesty," he said swiftly. The rest of the party, a lady and two other men, did the same.

"Please, rise," William said.

The Governor did so. "I... I confess I am shocked," he stammered. "We had no word of your coming, Your Highness."

"I did not know myself, until a few weeks ago."

"Yes, of course. Forgive my lapse. If I had known we expected royalty... But I digress. Uh..." He seemed at a loss. He began again. "I scarcely recognize you, sire. It has been a long time."

"Yes, it has," the prince said.

"You have grown into a quite a young man," he said, his voice fond. "Are you well?"

"Well enough. The sea did not agree with me."

"I am sorry to hear that," he said. "But we are glad—very glad—that you have come! Welcome, my lord, welcome to Belond!"

"Thank you, Governor."

"Andel, for you, sire. We are old friends, you know."

The prince smiled. Governor Whitefeld had the engaging manners he remembered as a little boy. Though the meeting was awkward, he was beginning to feel a little more relieved.

"Oh!" the Governor exclaimed. "I am forgetting. You would not know my daughter, Anjalia."

The young woman in the party stepped forward. The prince regarded her for the first time. She was just a girl, only fourteen, he remembered. She was pretty enough in appearance. She did not have her father's gold hair. Hers was a light brown, arranged elaborately, but not strikingly beautiful. She had the typical womanly charms but nothing that particularly stood out from other girls. She was dressed finer than the occasion warranted, giving her a pretentious air, quite unlike her father. She had a pinched look about her otherwise pretty face that added to the impression.

He greeted her civilly enough. As she was a lady, decorum demanded he speak first. "A pleasure to meet you, Lady Whitefeld." He dipped his head politely to her.

She giggled girlishly and curtsied, batting her eyelashes. "The pleasure is all mine, Your Majesty."

The young lady was not impressive. Indeed, the servants' gossip back home was unwarranted. She was far too young for him, and she was too untutored. Despite his opinion of her father, he knew she could not possibly be a refined lady in this place, despite all her acting to the contrary. In Ossia, the royal servants had whispered about how pleased the King would be for his son to marry into the Whitefeld family. They claimed it had been loosely intended for William to marry Lord Whitefeld's daughter when they grew up. He had not been told this by his father, but he had only been seven years old. Anyway, it didn't matter now. It had not been Anjalia he would have been intended for. Besides that, it could not have been a serious plan. The King had been too busy planning his own marriage in those days.

The Governor continued his introductions. "This is my captain of the guard, Zoc. He maintains the excellent peace we have in Belond."

"Your Majesty," the captain addressed him, bowing.

"A pleasure," William said again.

A loud thunderclap sounded above them. Lady Anjalia jumped perceptibly.

"Oh, dear," Elber moaned. "What a tragedy. It *would* rain

on our arrival."

"We must get you indoors," the Governor urged. It will not do to stand in the rain all day talking. We will finish our catching up later. Let us go."

"Bring the horses down. Quickly!" William ordered to the servant standing next to him. The man bowed and swiftly darted off.

"Bailan," the Governor said to the third man in the party, "take Lady Anjalia home, before it rains."

"Yes, sir," he said quickly. He offered Anjalia his arm. She curtsied quickly to the prince, with a coy smile. She flinched as a raindrop hit her cheek. She walked with improper speed back to her horse. Bailan helped Lady Whitefeld onto her horse and they rode away, down the main road toward the barracks.

The horses were brought down carefully. William's own, already saddled and ready, was a huge black horse, impressively well-bred, one of the best in Edenia. The groom led him to the prince, handing him the reins. "Hey, there, Blazer," William murmured to the horse.

"That is a fine animal," the Governor said admiringly, looking at the horse calculatingly.

"Thank you." William called him Blazer because of the star-shaped white splotch on his forehead, the only part of him that was not solid black. His father had given him Blazer as a colt a few years back. Blazer normally resided in their upriver vacation home, but William had sent for him especially to come on the journey. He loved this horse.

He swung easily into the saddle. He waited while the others mounted. Elber's attempts were rather pitiful. William tried to ignore the embarrassing scene. Elber, like most older noblemen, was not exactly trim.

The Governor had no such trouble. He seemed fit enough to take on an army, even though he was no longer exactly young. He jumped easily into his saddle. The horse he rode was nothing special, but it was a well-bred animal. He was clearly not an avid rider, but he looked downright impressive in comparison with Elber.

"I apologize, my lords," Elber wheezed when the servants finally had him mounted. "I am unused to riding."

"Think nothing of it," the Governor said grandly, but William had seen him smirking behind his hand. He was glad Lord Andel was not taken in by the ambassador's ridiculous airs.

Captain Zoc mounted a horse at the head of the contingent of soldiers. He was an older man, more grim than any William had ever seen. He did not blame the man, keeping order in a place like Belond. He was tough and wiry but tall and strong. William would steer clear of such a captain if he were an outlaw. At the head of the group of soldiers, he looked commanding and even intimidating. In such hands, he felt safer. His own guards were certainly superior, being the King's personal soldiers and the most elite group of men in the Empire, but they did not have the grim confidence that these men did.

Once the party was all mounted, they began to ride. "The servants will see to your belongings," the Governor assured. "The Felds, my estate, is just a short ride away. I am glad it is situated outside the town. It would be burdensome to live right in the middle of it. I have more space this way. You will see, my lord."

In fact, William could not see much at all. The rain had begun in earnest. He was not yet soaked, thanks to his thick red cloak, but the rain was dripping into his eyes. He pulled his hood over his head. As he did so, he glanced at the sky.

He stopped cold, halting his horse, eyes, no longer minding the rain, fixed to the sky.

The Governor and the ambassador stopped also, regarding him closely. "What's wrong, sire?" Lord Andel asked, confused.

The prince did not at first hear. The blood was rushing through his ears. He forgot all notions of feeling safe. All the dread returned in an instant. He felt he was trapped in some nightmarish ghost story. Even if he thought he was safe for a moment, it was all a lie.

"My lord!" exclaimed the Governor, clearly confused. "Are you all right?"

William breathed hard. He finally said, "The eagle."

He was close to the Governor, otherwise he would not have seen the sudden change in his countenance. He grew angry, even fierce. His eyes narrowed. He scarcely looked like the same man. He mumbled, "Curse her meddling—this is her fault." Had he not heard those words, the Governor's next, now consoling, might have abated his fear: "Come, William, what is the harm in a bird? It is just an eagle, nothing more."

"It is not likely to be the same one we saw before, Your Majesty," the ambassador reasoned. "It is a mere coincidence. That incident was just a strange occurrence, nothing to dwell on."

"What *incident*?" the Governor said, his countenance icy again. In all their words thus far, William had not heard such a tone out of their host. It jolted him.

Elber answered, not noticing the change. "A strange bird flew at us while we were on the ship. It dove at his Majesty, foul thing, and then tore the flag right off the mast. 'Twas the strangest thing I ever saw, but nothing to worry about, I daresay. Just a freak of nature."

"*Indeed*," the Governor growled under his breath. Elber did not hear it, but William did. Louder, the Governor said, "I am sure you are right, Ambassador. Come, your Majesty, do not fret about something so trivial. It was just a strange creature, and probably not the same one as this. You are perfectly safe. Let us go on, we will get soaked if we stay out here."

William could do nothing else. It would do him no good to stand out here in the rain like a fool. He prodded Blazer forward, mastering himself, but he could not again shake his dread.

The Governor knew something about this. There *was* a reason for what had happened to him. He did not believe in goddesses. He did not think this island could be haunted by a ghost or any other such creature. So what *did* haunt this island? William felt a foreboding he could not alleviate.

What bothered him more was that the Governor was hiding his suspicion. William had caught the Governor's remarks under his breath. He saw the significant glance he now cast at Captain Zoc, who now looked not only grim but decidedly angry—or perhaps irritated was a better word, as if someone had seriously inconvenienced him. For some reason, they were not voicing anything—they were trying to convince their visitors that the eagle meant nothing and that there was nothing wrong.

William did not believe that. There was no such thing as a coincidence, his father used to tell him. There *was* an explanation. Something was going on.

The eagle screamed somewhere in the clouds above him, but the rain now obscured it from view. Every single person in the procession flinched. He knew the attendants, more superstitious than he was, probably believed there *was* a ghost. The trouble was, he didn't know *what* to believe.

"Come, my lords," said the Governor, "pay it no mind. Put it from your minds. It is a bird only. Nothing more."

William did not think it was nothing. Actually, he was certain it was something serious.

Chapter 3

William fidgeted in his chair, still brooding. It didn't help his disposition that the chairs were the height of Edenian style—that is, beautiful, tasteful, and incredibly uncomfortable.

He would have preferred to stay in his feather bed. *That* was comfortable. He had spent the whole of his first day in Belond in it, claiming fatigue. He had suspected some degree of relief in his secretive, if welcoming, host at being rid of him when Andel had agreed without the slightest argument. Lord Elber had made himself useful in impeding the unpacking process, and so the prince had been left to himself and his thoughts.

He had put it off as long as he could, but now his questions must be answered. He must delve into the dark memories of the past for his father's sake, in one last attempt after fifteen years to find King Eduar a measure of peace.

The prince loved his father more than anyone, but he wished to heaven that the King could have sent someone else.

Tonight's dinner would bring everything out. Hospitality had extended this far; now the Governor would want to know why he was really here. It would take more than a casual visit to drive the son of the King to Belondian shores. Curiosity would wait only so long.

He had foolishly hoped to talk it over with only Lord Andel without everyone else listening. He didn't relish the idea of reliving the past under the eyes of countless servants, Lord Elber, the other officials, Captain Zoc, and his own guards, including the impressive Captain Tiran who looked after the prince's security, all of whom graced the dining room with their presence.

Lord Andel sat at the head of the table as the host. He spoke to the ambassador on his left, patiently exchanging meaningless pleasantries with the insipid nobleman. William pitied him. For all this time as Governor, he had been forced to deal with this simpering toady and even conduct business with him. It had been Elber's duty for twenty years to inspect this province, seeing that her citizens were satisfied, and to conduct, with the help of the officials, the yearly approval election. If the people were unhappy, they could vote to recall the King's appointed Governor and the King would appoint another, subject also to their approval. It was a procedure introduced to the Empire by the first Tellor, King Kellian, who had led the Peasants' Revolution and ushered in a new age some two hundred years ago. The Whitefelds' fame had begun at the same time. Valan Whitefeld, a man who had come from the province of Belond to Ossia as a mere commoner, had become Kellian's closest friend during the rebellion and his first supporter. The Whitefeld line had remained unusually small, but the family retained a close relationship with the Tellorian house, as seen in Andel's friendship with King Eduar all those years ago. The family's origin was also the reason why they always governed Belond, and it had been the reason why Andel had been the only real choice for the Governorship of Belond. He was the only Whitefeld male left when his uncle, Lenad, had died, vacating the position. It had been a blow to him, his family, and the King, and Eduar had tried to find someone else, but Andel did not think that there was any choice. He was devoted to his duty, and he pursued it. The King had lost his friend, but far more than even that.

Andel had enjoyed a strong approval from the people according to Elber. His elections each year had yielded unanimous results—not a single dissenting vote—which was a miracle even in a province so small. There were several thousand people on the island if the soldiers were included. The ambassador brought back a glowing report each year of internal affairs. The mines, the most profitable in the Empire, created by a long dormant volcano, sent back their tribute without fail. While few merchants sailed the dangerous waters, those who did were well rewarded for their trouble. By Elber's account, little Belond and its Governor were nothing but happy and prosperous.

But Belond had a contradictory reputation. No one wanted to travel to the island. No new settlers were drawn to it. Even fortune-hunters avoided Belond, despite its reputed wealth. Its name, "The Isle of Death," told a different tale.

The King had sensed something was strange. Perhaps it was just the distance, but he felt his old friend was somehow different. His letters lacked warmth, and their communication through others felt too formal and not genuine. The King missed his old companion, and he worried after Andel. He wanted Lord Whitefeld to return and visit, but Andel had refused to ever set foot on a ship again after that first disastrous voyage to the island.

That was the heart of the matter. The King was still grieving, and he could not find any peace. He had not received any assurance from Andel to help him, other than formal word of the tragedy. The King was broken-hearted himself, but he also needed to know how his friend fared. He hoped that sending his son to Belond might offer a resolution.

William didn't want to think about it. He didn't want to talk about it. Let the dead stay dead. Let the memories be buried with them. It was so much easier.

Andel had clearly not been broken by grief. He must be a strong man. He had lost as much as the King, yet he seemed to remain happy. He did not succumb to his loss; he remained as steady as ever. Eduar put on a professional and dutiful face to the world, but he was not truly happy. The two men could not have reacted more differently to their troubles.

William broke off his musing as the steward announced the last member of the dinner party, Lady Anjalia. She glided imperiously into the room as all the gentlemen rose and bowed. She was once again overdressed, but it seemed slightly more appropriate in this setting. The Felds was the equal of any noble house in Ossia, tastefully decorated and fashionable. It had all the latest advancements, including a heating system and running water. The Governor had clearly poured a great deal of his vast wealth into it—and into his daughter. Her dress was fancy enough for an Ossian noblewoman at a royal ball, and she had lavish jewelry and hair. She only looked foolish, like a girl playing in her mother's clothes. Elber, however, sighed, "Ah, Lady Anjalia, you grow more beautiful each year. Your loveliness is incomparable."

The girl giggled, looking flirtatiously at William as if he had been the one to say it. He resisted the urge to roll his eyes. Too many women had tried to approach him before. None of them cared a whit about him; they only liked his title and his good looks. He had the kind of features that made girls fawn over him: blue eyes (a bit rare among the dark-eyed Edenians), fair skin, and dark hair, which was cut above his ears but not close-shaven. That wasn't who he was. His brother was the one who knew how to handle women. William had never liked all the superficial attention he received. Anjalia clearly found him pleasing, but he hadn't even really met her. Besides, she was eight years his junior anyway.

"Come, be seated, my dear," the Governor said, indicating the seat next to Elber, but he spoke absently. He was frantically trying to catch Zoc's eye, much to William's confusion. It was hard to tell because he kept his face calm, but Andel seemed near to panic. Zoc only looked grim, but that was an unchanging expression for this man.

A whine from Lady Anjalia caught his attention. She was berating her attendant who had followed her in. The servant was a middle-aged woman, well-dressed, clearly a lady-in-waiting of sorts. She was remarkably beautiful although her face was worn. She had dark hair partly tucked under a modest cap. When he had looked up, this woman had been staring at him with something like shock, or perhaps horror was a better word. When Anjalia scolded her, it was because she had been too busy gawking to pull out Anjalia's chair, so the young lady was kept waiting. The woman became flustered at the rebuke. Anjalia's temper rose. She did not shout, but rather hissed at the woman, "You idiot! You're ruining everything, L—"

Before her name was said, the woman interrupted, her voice trembling. "I am sorry, my lady," she murmured, and she pulled the chair out. Anjalia sat down with a huff.

Zoc had risen without William noticing, and he now returned to his seat. Seemingly without prompting, Bailan came forward, taking the errant attendant by the arm. "I offer my apologies," he said, steel in his voice. "You will not be disturbed again."

The Governor nodded seriously at the steward, and the odd light faded from Andel's eyes. Elber, however, said magnanimously, "'Tis no disturbance. Servants are commonly troublesome, lowborn as they are. Think nothing of it."

With a tight nod, he acquiesced, and then he left the room with the woman in tow.

"Well," Governor Whitefeld said with a forced smile, "now that we are all settled, let us eat!" He turned to a kitchen girl standing at the far door. "Aggy, please tell Yalke to send in the meal, please." The girl dipped her head and obeyed.

William returned to musing as the food was brought. He reconsidered his first evaluation of Andel. Maybe things weren't as they seemed. There was a certain tightness about his eyes that belied his words and manner, and there were those occasional glimpses of something that William could not define in his eyes. Andel Whitefeld was not telling them everything. A vague feeling of danger surrounded William, beginning with rumor and ending with suspicion. To reason, everything seemed innocent enough; however, his gut told him otherwise.

He longed for the safety of that feather bed upstairs.

An attendant served him food on his plate. The cook, Yalke, had created a masterpiece of Edenian-style food featuring chicken, vegetables, and the King's favorite pastry. The prince murmured thanks to the servant, only to then notice that the Governor had failed to observe the blessing of the meal. The prayer to El was made more out of tradition than conviction, but its absence felt strange. He wondered at the reason for it but had little time to consider the matter, for the governor chose that moment to draw the prince out of his silence.

"I hope you find my home to your liking, Lord Tellor," he said formally. "I strive to make Belond feel as much like home as possible. I hope you will enjoy yourself."

"It is quite excellent, sir," William responded with as much enthusiasm as he could muster. "I can see you have spent a great deal of effort on it."

"Indeed," he replied. "I have enjoyed improving the Felds." He paused to take a bite of food. "It serves to remind me of Ossia. Elber tells me something of home each time he visits, but I am eager for your news, sire. It has been many years since we were together."

He was once again lapsing into those easy, engaging manners that had reassured the prince at their first meeting, but this time, William was more wary. He felt guilty for being suspicious of Andel—he was an old friend, and he was doing his best to welcome his surprise visitor. William's presence likely brought to mind old grief of the Governor, too, so it was understandable if the man was a bit unsteady at times. William softened under this reasoning, but the tension in his insides remained despite himself.

"It has been a long time, yes."

"Elber had mentioned most of the general news, but please tell me of your father, the King, if you would. I am eager to hear of my old friend."

This was a subtle way of asking why he had been sent here, but William didn't want to talk about it. He was avoiding it as long as possible.

"My father is of good health, and he enjoys all of his old strength." The Tellors were known for their prowess as warriors, and Eduar was no exception. As for William, while he was tall and had the build to become a soldier if he had tried, he had never put much effort into athleticism. He was decent with a sword, but he didn't have the desire to get better. What was the point of it? Eduar was a master swordsman; William was content to be mediocre.

"I am pleased to hear it. But—*how* is he?"

"He misses you, of course."

"I wish I could go back and see him, but I cannot sail."

"He knows, and he wishes the same. He would be happy to see you. As it is, he enjoys his subjects' approval. They call him the greatest King since Kellian."

"That is good sire; I am glad. But—does he remain unmarried?"

All subtlety abandoned. Oh, Andel had already guessed why the King had sent William here.

"Yes, sir; I think Elber would have mentioned it."

"That is a pity. I had hoped he would find a way to fill his heart again. The loss is hard to bear still, is it?"

He didn't want to talk about it.

"You have not remarried, my lord," he countered.

Andel's face darkened. "No. No woman for me but my Seyenne. I will not remarry. I am just happy to have my daughter, Anja." He smiled at her, and she simpered.

"Was it hard for you?" William didn't want to talk about this, either, but better Seyenne and Karia than *her.*

"It was. The death of my little one was enough, and with Elissana, too—I curse those pirates every time I think of them—and then to lose Seyenne in childbirth the next year...." He trailed off.

Elissana. It had been a long time since he had heard her name spoken aloud.

William closed his eyes, pushing it all away. He had loved her as much as his father had. She could have been the mother he never had.

"I am glad I have Anja. She is my consolation. I imagine you were much the same for your father, William."

He *didn't* want to talk about it.

He was conscious of eyes on him, so he replied, "He has said so."

"It is hard for you, too, I know. You *and* Arthos. He probably remembers more than you. You were only seven."

"I remember enough."

"Life is hard. We can give in, or we can fight back. I know your father understands this."

William could avoid it no longer. "He sent me here."

"I thought so, but even so, I am very happy to see you again, William, and I hope you will convey my sympathy to your father."

The Governor's tone was kind, even friendly, despite the subject. (And how had Andel maneuvered him here so easily? William understood manipulation—he lived in a world of politics—but Andel had trapped him before he could wriggle out of the conversation.)

"That is what I am to do," he said dully. "Along with delivering the same from my father. He wanted me to see that you were well and try to gain some measure of understanding about what happened."

"You want the story? But I told him, fifteen years ago, hard though it was." Andel seemed confused.

William sighed. "I know the story. You sailed with Seyenne, your wife, Karia, your daughter, and Lis, your sister, to take the Governorship of Belond. You were attacked by pirates just three days from the island. The guard fought them off, barely, but most of them died and the ship was damaged. Your sister, Elissana, died standing over Karia, who was only six. You and your wife survived. A year later, Seyenne died giving birth to Anjalia." He concluded with a sigh.

No one but Andel would meet his eyes. Everyone knew the story. It was the greatest tragedy ever to befall the King.

When Eduar was a child, his little sister, Princess Marri, drowned by accident at their country vacation home. It had nothing to do with Eduar, but his father blamed him for not watching over the little girl, and the old King hated him ever after. His mother cared for him, but she died when he was a teenager.

Eduar's father died early, leaving Eduar a newly married

twenty year-old with a pregnant wife arranged for him by his father, to take the burden of the throne. Sylva had given birth to Arthos, then she had conceived again and given birth to William. She died in the aftermath of the second birth, leaving the King alone with two infant boys.

Only a few short years later, he met Elissana, the woman he loved, and lost her before he could marry her. At the same time, the comfort of his best friend was denied to him.

The King was a man who knew grief. William did too. He could not dwell on the dark past. It was too much to bear.

His father had asked it of him. He steeled himself.

"What more do you want, William?" Andel asked gently.

"My father," the prince responded tensely, "wants to know *why*. How could it happen?"

Andel did not console him as William expected, like the man he remembered. His voice hardened into iron. "I have told you," he answered. "Life is cruel. If there is a God, he cares nothing for our suffering. Terrible things happen to people, William. That's all the why there is."

"That's not enough!"

Silence stretched for a long moment.

"I am sorry, my lord," Andel spoke. "It *is* all there is."

He opened his mouth to change the subject, but William interrupted. "I need to see her grave, Lord Andel."

It was the first time since the conversation began that William saw genuine emotion cross the face of the Governor. The expression he saw was not at all what he expected. It was not grief, apology, or sympathy—it was fear and panic, pure and plain.

The Governor looked to Zoc, stammering. "That—that is not possible."

William's grief gave way to anger. "What? Why not?"

The Governor made frantic gestures, looking at Zoc. All eyes were on him now, curious. The Belondian servants looked afraid, but the Ossians looked confused. It was a simple request, was it not? No need for such a reaction.

Zoc stood. "It is forbidden, my lord. You cannot see it."

William rose also. He was growing angry. Even the harsh figure of the captain failed to intimidate him.

"The two of you," he growled, "had better explain. I have had my fill of your secrets. Start talking. *Now.*"

Chapter 4

"Now, my lord," Elber protested. "There is no cause for such ire. Think of decorum, for heaven's sake." Elber had risen along with everyone else, and he spoke for those shocked by William's behavior and sudden vehemence.

William didn't care what they thought. "Shut up, Elber," he snapped. It was the rudest he had ever been to the man, and Elber gaped in astonishment. William didn't notice his reaction. He was too furious. He *needed* to know what they were hiding. This was too much for him to handle, which was the reason he hadn't wanted to come here in the first place.

"Peace, my lord," Zoc boomed. "This ill becomes you."

"You owe me an explanation. I have seen the two of you together, and I am sick of your secretiveness. I was sent here for explanations—I have had *none* from either of you whatsoever! I was told to find answers, and that is what I want! *Why* can I not see her grave? Tell me *that!*"

The Governor, still gaping in his chair, looked to Zoc in desperation.

Zoc was silent for a moment, as if considering, then his face resolved slightly, although it still did not soften. He spoke, but with a little less anger this time. "Her grave is on the north side of the mountain. It is impossible to get there now, and it is forbidden to try."

William noticed obvious relief on the Governor's face when the captain said this, but a measure of wariness remained, and Andel looked furtively at the ambassador.

"I don't understand," the prince growled, not placated in the least.

Here Andel finally spoke up. "The Whitefelds are traditionally buried in a graveyard in the northern meadows." He sounded calm and charismatic again, more himself. "Access is denied us now, however, and it cannot be reached anymore. You cannot see it, William."

"Why not? Why can it not be reached?"

Andel looked sideways at Elber. Then, as if decided, he sighed and nodded to Zoc.

Zoc took up the conversation again. "There is a band of outlaws that has arisen in the forest. They hold most of the territory beyond the town and mine, including the road to the north side of the island. My men and I are still attempting to put down the insurrection. You cannot go, my lord. It is far too dangerous, especially for someone of your importance. It would be foolishness to enter such lawless territory until it is made safe again."

Elber, proper as he was, put in his opinion. It was his duty as royal ambassador to inspect the island, and this admission put the nature of his report in a different light. If it was serious enough to endanger free travel, Elber might have to recommend that the Edenian guard be sent to help the effort. Though this may be an unwanted intrusion, he insisted that it would be necessary if it was found that the current government could not put down such a little rebellion, and he even insinuated it might hurt their standing with the King. Rebellion against the government of Edenia was a serious matter.

Zoc responded that he could and would handle the problem without help, but it simply hadn't been handled *yet*. At the current time, it remained unsolved. The captain's grim words clearly intimidated the ambassador, and a little of the pompous man's indignation faded, but he was not satisfied and continued to pursue it.

William, however, was not sure they were even telling the truth. Everything in their behavior indicated deceit to him. Outlaws in the forest? Maybe, but it sounded like a childish fabrication to him—comparable to the sailors' ridiculous assertions of the goddess Auria haunting the forest. *Something* was going on here, that he knew, but he was certain this was not the explanation. It was just another evasion of the truth.

"I don't care," he said, interrupting the argument. "My

father asked me to do this, and I intend to try." He did not believe their assertions of danger. He would get to the bottom of this.

"As Zoc says, my Lord William, it is quite impossible," Andel said, attempting a placating tone. William looked from him to Zoc, who still looked grim and even defiant. His fierce aspect may have served to daunt those under the law, but William refused to be intimidated. He was the prince of Edenia. He would not be cowed by anyone, nor would he be swayed from his course. He *was* going to see Lis's grave. It was the only thing that would satisfy him now. He *would* complete this task for his father.

"Do not think to tell me what I cannot do!" William shot back at him.

"Enough, my lord," Elber said to him again. "You are not yourself. Rebellion against a province of the Edenian Empire is a matter for the state to handle. Let me take care of this, and keep your private concerns for later when these issues are resolved."

"Write all the petitions and make all the protests you want, Elber," he snapped. "I don't care."

"The matter must be settled—immediately. Rebellion cannot fester; it must be crushed!" This was said to the room at large, with considerable bravado from the fat nobleman, and it received many appreciative nods from members of the Edenian party. William could have smacked him in frustration.

"*I* will settle it," Zoc replied. "My men are attempting to root them out even now. It is a dangerous business."

"I don't care if it is dangerous," the prince yelled at him. "My guards are certainly capable of protecting me!"

Andel interrupted again. "They are not. No offense to the Tellorian order," he said with a nod to Captain Tiran, "but they do not know the territory or the ways of the outlaws. They are cunning, and they use everything to their advantage. They are difficult to anticipate unless you are familiar with their ways. Even so, our men have difficulty combatting them."

"That doesn't matter. I don't understand why you are

evading me at every turn!"

"It is for your protection!"

"For El's sake!" William practically screamed, hitting the table in front of him. *"I don't care!"*

"Look," Andel said quietly. "We are not getting anywhere. Calm down and let us think this through. William, I know this is important to you, but you must understand that your safety is important to me. I would not do anything that was not in your best interest."

William glowered at him, unmoved by his attempt at soothing him. "I am under orders from the King," he countered. "Would you deny that?"

"I doubt your father would ever wish to endanger you," Andel answered.

"Are you afraid?" asked William.

Zoc raised a dark eyebrow. "You would lecture *me* about bravery, my lord?" he asked coldly.

"Can't you protect me?" he asked, his tone biting.

Zoc glanced at the Governor, who looked wary. But he answered stonily, "Perhaps we can come to some arrangement."

"Zoc!" exclaimed Andel.

The captain met the Governor's eyes for the briefest of moments. Andel looked apprehensive, but he said to William, "If Zoc thinks it can be done, we will try, for your sake. But do think on our warnings, William."

"Either you help me, or I'll go on my own," he replied, "but don't take too long."

He stomped away from the table. Before leaving the room, he turned to give a slightly mocking bow. "Good night, my lords—and lady. I have had my fill of company." Without waiting for a response, he stormed up to his room, trailed by his guards and a few servants.

The next morning, William saw things in a different light. The magic of a night's sleep had helped to put things in perspective. (El's enormous blessing be on feather beds!)

He was not taking back anything he said. It was still too sensitive an issue for that. He was still going to insist on seeing Lis's grave, rest her blessed soul. He still wanted answers—real answers, not evasions that looked like explanations. He refused to take no for an answer.

He was, however, sorry about the way he had behaved. He had let his temper run away with him, and Andel was likely hurt by it. William had behaved abominably to his father's old friend, and he knew the King would not be pleased to hear it. He was frustrated with the Governor, but he realized Andel had only been trying to help. Lord Whitefeld had not wholly done right, but the prince had not either.

As such, he was prepared to do everything in his power to make it up to him. He was not compromising, but he *was* going to be contrite.

He came promptly to breakfast where he made his apologies to everyone—making it clear he apologized only for his temper, not his statements.

To his relief, everyone was very gracious, even eager to forgive him, the Governor most especially. Even Anjalia's flowery expression of pardon made him feel better. Zoc was not there to hear him, and the prince wondered why, but he *was* a captain, and he was most likely on duty.

The Governor was even a bit more divulging this morning. He said to the prince, "I have been pondering your—um…request—and I may have come up with a way to keep you safe and see you to the gravesite. That is, if you are still determined?"

"I am, my lord; I must be."

"Well then. It will take a bit of planning—Zoc will have to plan your route and assign guards. We hope to be ready by tomorrow. Does that suit you?"

"Yes! Thank you, Andel."

"It is still very dangerous, my lord," he cautioned. "I do not think it is wise. I do not want you to get hurt. I am not happy to be taking any risk where your safety is concerned, not as your host and your friend. Belond has an unfortunate tendency toward tragedy. It is not called the Isle of Death for nothing."

"That is just superstition, surely," William protested weakly. He had seen some *superstition* in the past few days that defied his ability to explain. The secrets this place held surrounded him at every turn, whether the Governor's or the island's.

"Maybe," Andel said without conviction, his face serious. "I have lived here for fifteen years, and I am not convinced that it is. Please, William, trust me. Give this up."

"You would do well to listen," Elber put in. "You are too important to risk. Let the King send the Edenian guard in before the summer is out, and then see." William hoped to be long gone by summertime.

Even Anjalia had something to say. "You don't want to fall in with *that* rabble. They'll kidnap you for sure. Those outlaws are devils! Stay here with *civilized* company." Here she smirked flirtatiously, and William considered for a moment that he'd rather be with the outlaws—if they existed, which he seriously doubted. He didn't believe that he was in any danger from that little piece of nonsense. There were other things he feared more.

"I won't be satisfied until I go," he declared. "Maybe not even then." He cast a significant glance at Andel, but the Governor acted as if he had not noticed. The man was impossible to draw out. What was he hiding?

"So," was all Andel could say. "Zoc and I will look to the arrangements.

"In the meantime," he continued brightly, clearly changing the subject, "you shall see Belond at its finest, my lord. Let it not be said I did not suitably welcome the King's son and my own friend. You and Elber shall attend me on a tour of the province—Elber may perform his yearly inspection, and you may merely enjoy the tour. The royal officials may begin the election and tribute collection of course, with the help of my steward, Bailan.

"The weather has cleared magnificently; it is a beautiful

day. We shall all do quite nicely."

"You are the soul of hospitality, Lord Whitefeld," Elber beamed. He was eager to be in everyone's good opinion after his humiliation at William's hands the night before.

"We shall ride through the town, and then we shall go to see the mine," the Governor informed his guests. "On another day, we will also see a bit of the countryside. I am sure you will also wish to make a report of the farms, Lord Elber."

"Of course. The state is nothing if not thorough. Never let it be said that I neglected my duty."

"Certainly not, my lord. Is that agreeable to you, William?"

He smiled with as much enthusiasm as he could manage. "Yes, my lord." The last thing he wanted to do was traipse around the Isle of Death. He would not enjoy a minute of his tour of Belond. He hated the whole island and the secrets it held. Let it keeps its ghosts hidden. He didn't want to see them all.

He had promised himself he would make it up to his host. He *would*.

"Good, then," Andel seemed pleased. "Let us get ready to begin. Norn, run down to the stable and tell the groom to saddle our horses."

If nothing else, at least he got to ride Blazer.

He had changed into something more suitable for riding. He wore a blue cloak edged in gold against the cool spring air. The day was clear and even beautiful, but it was not warm. Spring was just arriving in Belond. There were flowers beginning to bud and green leaves slowly starting to show.

It made William sneeze.

He was relieved they weren't walking. Not only would it be horribly undignified, it would require squelching through the mud from last night's thunderstorm. He wasn't thrilled about even the small walk off the porch to where the horses were waiting.

He had to admit, however, that the view was spectacular.

The Felds was on top of a rise overlooking Belo and the bay. The land seemed to sparkle in the sunlight, and the water appeared sapphire blue. The proud royal ship lingered just offshore, like a watchman.

The prince failed to be impressed by anything. The island was still just as backwater and dull as ever. Not to mention the reputation it held. Even in its beauty, the place had a masked glint of danger, as if the landscape was the sheath of a knife.

Elber and Andel followed him out, each accompanied by a servant. Elber had donned a ridiculous orange riding outfit, sharply contrasting Andel's dark green attire, which showed his strong figure to good advantage. Elber was still babbling on about some obscure point of his enthusiasm. It was not contagious. William caught the ambassador's servant rolling his eyes.

"Will Lady Anjalia be joining us today, my lord?" Elber asked after his effusion subsided.

"No, Lord Elber. As I'm sure you recall, she has little taste for this sort of excursion. It taxes her delicacy."

"Oh," he replied, crestfallen. "That *is* disappointing."

William considered Elber's interest in Anjalia a little overenthusiastic, but then, they were kindred spirits. It was stranger to him to think about Andel's affection for his daughter. Andel was noble in the true sense of the word, while Anjalia was shallow. Two more opposite people could not be imagined, yet the Governor maintained his overwarm affection for the girl.

The prince mounted without waiting for the groom's unneeded assistance. Blazer tossed his head, clearly pleased. The prince did not often ride him at home. The horse at least would enjoy Belond.

"Your horse is just marvelous," Andel said. "I do not have any that are half so fine in my stables." He reached to touch Blazer's nose.

The horse's demeanor changed abruptly. He bared his teeth and flared his nostrils. He gave a low, threatening whinny.

William pulled him a step back in surprise as the Governor jerked his hand away. "I'm sorry," he exclaimed. "He isn't normally like this." He stroked Blazer's neck in an attempt to soothe the horse, but Blazer would not be calmed. He eyed Andel warily like he was a threat.

Andel's face darkened. "It is a small matter," he said, but his expression showed otherwise. He strode, muttering, to his own horse.

The incident rattled William even further, but he was not given time to dwell on it. The Governor mounted his horse, and then they were off.

They went first to the village, Belo. Entering it from the Felds, they encountered the barracks first. In a clearer light, they were much larger than he had first thought. He couldn't help wondering why little Belond needed all these soldiers. And since they had them, why would they be unable to flush out a little group of outlaws? It didn't make sense.

The barracks were arranged as a fenced-in compound at the rear of Belo. They rode into the gate to better see them. They had obviously been expanded recently. There was a forge to one side, and next to it, the heavily guarded armory. When they dismounted to look around, he saw that the weapons (in great variety) were as high quality as any he had seen in Ossia. Andel had clearly put a lot of Belond's wealth into building up his military.

There was a large cookhouse and dining hall, but nothing much was going on in these at this hour. Everyone was in the training hall (or on duty). Here the visitors saw dozens of men sparring with various practice weapons, practicing the bow, performing strengthening exercises, or running formations. Elber enthused about the discipline they had, but William felt like he was in a war zone. What was it all *for*, anyway?

They briefly looked in on the soldiers' living quarters, skipping the prison in the basement of the building. After this, they departed the barracks. The visit left William unsettled, and despite the show of the power that would provide his protection, he only felt more endangered.

They rode fairly quickly through the town. It was not much to look at. Miners and unskilled craftsmen, these people were not exactly wealthy, despite Belond's prosperity. It was not surprising. The peasants were always divided from the upper class in any society, and that was not about to change. Despite the idealism in Edenia after the Peasants' Revolution, there would always be poor people.

They took a quick look at the storehouses. These were the products of the famous Belondian mines, just a few miles up the mountain and to the southeast. No matter how far down they went, there was always more to be found. Belond had been, in ancient times, a volcano, home to fiery explosions that had built this island, but there had not been an eruption since long before the empire began—which was over a thousand years ago. The fire of the old mountain had, however, borne fruit still collected today. The mine held gold, diamonds, and other valuable metals. These raw, unrefined, yet priceless materials lay under lock and key in the warehouses, heavily guarded, awaiting the summer merchants—those few that braved the seas. Some, of course, would return as crown tribute, but that was for the officials to coordinate. The amount of wealth in these warehouses awed the prince. He had heard of the prosperity of the Belondian Province, but he hadn't quite credited it.

Another thought occurred to him. Wealth drew people to it. Belond should have five times the inhabitants it did, and merchants should flock to this island. What was keeping them away?

They went back to the Felds to eat and then spent the afternoon at the mines. It was a slightly longer ride this time, as the mines were in the south of the island. The road from Belo to the mines ran through the extensive swath of fertile farmland, but the road from the Felds to the mines ran right between the forest and the farms, as the Felds bordered on those wild lands itself. The Governor ordered more guards for the ride. Half a dozen of the Tellorian guard flanked him, only making him more nervous. Every time a twig crunched he jumped, and every time a bird called he could have fainted. He saw a hawk overhead and at first wanted to panic, thinking the eagle was back again, but nothing happened. In truth, that in itself seemed ominous.

The mines were nothing impressive. They did not even go in, as it was hazardous. All they saw was the entrance, with a few begrimed workers, heavily surrounded by guards, loading ore onto a wagon. It might be profitable, but it was hardly clean. The dust was worse than the spring pollen. No wonder nothing grew to the south of the mines.

Elber being satisfied with what he had seen so far and promising a good report, they returned to the Felds. Upon arriving, they dismounted and handed their reins to the grooms. Elber waltzed inside, but Andel caught the prince's arm.

"You've seen the island now, my lord. Are you still sure you want to make the journey?"

A bird called from overhead, making both of them jump, but twilight now obscured the sky, so they could not see it. William swallowed hard.

"I have to go, my lord. My father asked me to, and so I must."

The Governor nodded. "Well, we will get you ready for tomorrow, then."

He led the prince back inside.

Chapter 5

The day dawned clear again. Deceptively so.

The feather bed had not been quite so magical last night. William had barely slept at all. For one thing, there was a mouse somewhere in his room, and it had been chattering all night. For another, he kept thinking he heard whispers. Finally, he was tormented by wondering about all the secrets Belond held. He had to admit, despite his skepticism, that he was nervous for today.

He walked out to Blazer after a quick breakfast. Andel and Zoc awaited him, despite the early hour.

"Good morning, Lord William," Andel greeted him, but his voice lacked warmth. He was not happy that William was doing this. Zoc said nothing to him.

The prince nodded in response to his host's greeting.

"Let us explain the plan to you," Andel said. "It is half a day's ride to the gravesite—the northern meadows, that is—so you will not have much time there if you want to get back before dark."

"You want to get back before dark," Zoc informed him dryly, but there was steel in his words. William nodded, growing steadily more nervous.

"Benjen is your guide," the Governor continued.

"He is my lieutenant," Zoc interrupted again. "Treat him as if he were me."

"You aren't coming?"

"It would be foolish for me or the Governor to attend you," Zoc stated as if this fact were obvious. "You are a very desirable target. It would be unwise to add any further to the value of the travelling party. The outlaws will only be more motivated to attack, despite the guards."

"We have assigned thirty of Zoc's men to be in your party. He spoke to Tiran, your Tellorian captain, and arranged for four of your private guard to attend."

"Why only four?"

"They don't know the island," Zoc said factually. "More would get in the way. Your captain tried to add more, but I convinced him otherwise. Four was the number we agreed upon."

"Mine are the finest soldiers in the Empire—surely their protection is better for me?" William reminded. He didn't like the idea of going with so many of Zoc's men and so few of his own. The visit to the barracks had unnerved him, and he trusted Tiran and his men better.

"Mine are the finest in *Belond*," Zoc retorted, "and they will serve you better than anyone else. They know what to do."

William wasn't pleased, but there was no arguing with the captain about this, so he conceded. "What else?"

"You will be preceded by four of my guards, flanked by two of your guards on your right and left, and followed by the remainder of yours and then mine," Zoc said. "Benjen has arranged the formation."

William thought about it. He was not trained to military strategy, so although something seemed fishy, he did not have the knowledge to figure out what. He could detect neither fault nor advantage in Zoc's arrangement.

Zoc went on. "You may stop for brief rest, but only on Benjen's word, and you cannot break formation. That is the time the rebels would be most likely to strike." He saw William's look of indignation, so he added, "It is only for your protection. Do not disobey me; this is my area of expertise."

"Fine," the prince muttered.

"All right, then," Andel sighed. "You had better go so that you can be back in time." He stepped back to let William mount, and then he approached Blazer to speak again.

The horse reacted the same way as before, with a threatening rumble. William had to pull him away.

The Governor didn't like the reaction, but he still said what he had intended to. "Are you sure about this William? I had rather you stayed safe."

William didn't like the way he said that, as if it was a feeble hope too slender to have any merit. He nodded and moved to join his guards.

As they came into formation and began to ride, with a little difficulty from the horses, William realized what was wrong with Zoc's arrangement.

It made him feel like a prisoner.

They had been in the forests forever (about two hours).

If he had not been so nervous, he would have been utterly bored.

No one said a word during the journey. Maybe they were concentrating on the road which grew a little rough and rocky in some places. Maybe they were nervous. Maybe it was some other reason. In any case, it did not contribute to a friendly atmosphere. He felt like he was part of a funeral procession.

What's more, it seemed the entire forest was silent. The only sound in the whole place was their horses' hooves. Not a bird, not a squirrel moved in the trees—just emptiness. The huge, ancient trees created yawning shadows on either side of the path. He fancied that these trees were the woods that had inspired the old tales of goblins, elves, and the rest. They were certainly ominous enough.

More than once, they paused for the lieutenant (at the back) to listen and look around. There was never anything to be heard or seen, but the impression that they were being watched remained.

If Auria did exist, this would be her haunt.

They rested once, quickly, and moved on. Benjen was as grim and implacable as his superior—in short, impossible to reason with or even to talk to.

William sighed for the millionth time, pulling his cloak closer to him. It was not very warm. He would have preferred his red one, but he had been persuaded that blue attracted less attention. Anjalia had added that it better suited his eye color, to his embarrassment.

Blazer gave a low rumble. William leaned close over his

neck to give him a reassuring pat, but he wasn't in much of a place to give anyone reassurance.

Off to his right, a twig snapped.

Behind him, every one of Zoc's men drew their weapons, whether swords or bows. It was uncanny how quickly and simultaneously they had done it, as if it had been planned beforehand. He turned in the saddle, his heart racing, looking in fear for Benjen. He had no idea what was happening. His guards, to his dismay, looked equally confused.

Then someone shouted a strange word, and pandemonium broke loose.

All the horses except his own began to rear and buck for some unknown reason, throwing their riders in terror. In less time than William would have thought possible, he was the only one left on his horse. The rest of the horses turned and flew back down the road, trampling more than one man as they went.

The instant they were gone, a rain of arrows flew onto the men, who were still down. Shrieks rang out as the barbs found their marks. William could only stare as the carnage unfolded before him. He didn't even have the sensibility to draw his sword.

The soldiers put their shields up over their heads, buying them enough time to get to their feet. Benjen shouted something, and they advanced toward the prince, swords still in their hands somehow.

They did not get far. A score of men, masked and cloaked, emerged from either side of the forest, weapons in hand. There remained perhaps twenty soldiers standing, and all were forced to engage.

William could not believe his eyes. *Outlaws.* There really *were* outlaws in the forest.

He should have listened to Andel. He was going to die for his stupidity.

The next thing he knew, a bolt from a crossbow came flying at him. He did not see who fired it. The instant before it hit, a huge bird snatched it out of the air, blinding him with a flurry of feathers.

Someone shouted a loud curse. Once he could see, he observed a wolf leap onto a man bearing a crossbow a few paces away. The man went down. He blinked. Had he just seen that? He shook his head.

The prince drew his sword at last. Only just in time. A figure in a dark cloak and mask was running toward him, shouting something in an unintelligible language.

This one was not like the others. There was a marked tone of authority in his voice.

This was the leader. William was sure of it.

He rushed at Blazer, a long knife whirling in each hand. Inwardly, William laughed at the man's foolishness for charging a mounted swordsman, even if the prince lacked his father's talent. But he could not laugh in battle. He swung his sword toward the attacker.

Without knowing how, he suddenly found himself flat on his back, the wind knocked from him, unhorsed. The sword had not even come close to finding its mark. His adversary was on top of him, one knee driving painfully into his chest.

The outlaw rolled off as one of the Tellorian guards aimed a stroke at him. He engaged the guard with a flurry of knives. Faster than William could follow, the outlaw stepped inside the guard's defense and, with a twist of his arm, flipped him over completely so that he landed on his stomach. The renegade knocked him out with a blow to the head.

William barely had time to get to his feet before the outlaw came at him again, knives flashing. He tried to block the blow aimed for his chest, but he was not fast enough. The outlaw's fist slammed into his chest, knocking him once more onto his back. A crossbow bolt whistled just next to him. He may have imagined it, but he thought he saw his attacker slice through it with a knife, faster than seemed humanly possible.

The outlaw kicked him hard as he tried to roll away. His thick boot crunched into the upper part of the prince's arm. He screamed in pain and panic, unable to escape the man.

He was about to die.

The outlaw hissed, "For heaven's sake, be still!"

With confident speed, his fist came down toward William's head, the knife's pommel falling first.

William's last thought was that it was strange that the outlaw wouldn't kill him with the knife pointing down—why carry a weapon and not use it?

Then the world went black.

The next thing he knew was the feeling of cold water being splashed in his face.

He spluttered, choking. He moved a hand to wipe his eyes but found he could not. As his awareness returned, he realized he was sitting down tied to a tree, his hands pinned to his sides.

"Yes, we tied you up," a deep woman's voice said. "I imagine if we hadn't, you would be flying at us again. If you behave, we might let you loose."

He opened his eyes. One of the outlaws stood above him, hands on her hips. The look of disdain could be read clearly on her face despite the leather mask which obscured all of the upper half of her face except her eyes. She was taller and more muscular than any woman he had ever seen and would have been a match for any of the fiercest warriors he knew. The thin, hard line of her mouth, high cheekbones, and defined chin gave her a tough, determined look, as if she was willing to take on anyone or anything—and win.

What surprised him most, however, was her hair, which was no longer covered by a hood. He had seen a few rare golden-haired Edenians, but never anyone with hair so pale, almost white. It was cut short and gathered back by one band of red cloth. Her eyes were icy blue, unlike his own, which were a deeper color, and different from any he had ever seen. She had very pale skin, almost translucent. No Edenian could look as she did. He realized with a start that she was a barbarian. He had never seen one before. There were few remnants of the old tribal ways left.

"*Ona*," she called behind her, turning. The strange word

and the lilting way she spoke betrayed her for a foreigner. "He's awake."

He looked behind her. A whole crowd of the outlaws was milling about: polishing weapons, eating, or tending wounds. There were twenty or thirty of them, all well-armed and dangerous-looking.

He was in the middle of nowhere. The road was not in sight. They were in a clearing, so it was not terribly dark, but it didn't need to be for a coil of fear to surround the prince's heart.

He was alone. There was not a guard in sight. He was completely surrounded and helpless.

He had no idea what was going to happen.

At the barbarian's call, a couple of other outlaws walked up. One was a man who was well over six feet tall and had all the accompanying muscle. He had removed his hood and mask, revealing brown hair and a smiling, open face half obscured by a short beard. He had a jagged scar above his left eyebrow that marked him as a man experienced with war. He was not young, but not old either—probably forty. He had the look of a formidable fighter, but somehow a warm-hearted man, too.

The other he recognized instantly as his attacker.

The knot of fear tightened in his gut. His heart pounded.

The leader, as it seemed he was, spoke to the barbarian woman. "Thank you, Szera."

Szera said to him, "Don't expect much. I'm sure he'll at least be *entertaining*."

"Mm-hmm," he agreed. "We'll see if he's worth the effort."

Szera sniffed and walked away.

The leader turned to the prince, the larger man behind standing with his arms crossed.

"Welcome to Belond, Lord Tellor. I hope you have been *enjoying* your stay."

Chapter 6

"Please," the prince pleaded, his voice desperate. He found it hard to speak past the lump in his throat, and his head was pounding from the blow he had received earlier. "Don't hurt me. Whatever you want for ransom, you'll get it, I promise." He knew his voice shook, but he couldn't help it.

To his dismay, the outlaw laughed.

He was the kind of person who was intimidating by mere presence. He retained his mask and hood, so it was hard to see his features, but William could see his brilliant green eyes which were stern despite his laughter. He was moderately tall (Szera had been larger), not above six feet, but he gave the impression of towering height even so. The way the other outlaws, fearsome themselves, deferred to him told William that this man was a formidable presence among them.

He couldn't keep the trembling from his limbs, despite the ropes that squeezed him against the tree at his back. He'd never been in a situation this dangerous and he was near panic.

"Aw," the outlaw said, still laughing. "Are you frightened, poor thing? Not in Ossia anymore, are you? You don't have your daddy or your nursemaids to take care of you anymore, love. Welcome to the real world."

His mockery bit William's pride. He was a Tellor! No one had *ever* addressed him in that manner—not even his own father. His position should afford him some respect. He felt resentment rise hot in him. The outlaw's sarcasm steeled him where he could not steel himself. He drew himself up, his shaking stilled.

"That's better, love, but save me your royal indignation. Your pride is worthless here."

"Do you know who I *am*?"

Now the big man laughed too, but he put a hand to his mouth to hide it.

The leader rolled his eyes. "For heaven's sake, William Tellor, haven't you been paying attention?"

He blushed, his ego taking another sting.

"If you don't have any wits about you, maybe I shouldn't have bothered to rescue you," the outlaw said in exasperation.

What?

William didn't understand. "Sir, I have already said, that my father will ransom me. Whatever you want, you'll get it."

The big man chuckled openly now.

"All right, love," the leader said. "Let's clear a few things up, since you don't have the mental capacity to figure things out for yourself."

He crouched down so he was face to face with William. "One," he said slowly, his voice dripping with sarcasm, "I have no intention of collecting ransom, so get that idea out of your head. Two, I would prefer you not call me *sir*. If you would call me anything, you can call me *ona*, or—"

Here he paused, pulling back his hood and taking off his mask.

Not his. Hers.

William's jaw dropped.

The leader was a woman, with braided golden hair and the most beautiful face he had ever seen. She was slim but strong for a woman. She was surprisingly young for such a leader, not more than about twenty, but the air of authority suited her.

"—or," she continued, mirth dancing in her green eyes, "you can call me as the people do: Auria."

Ten thousand thoughts raced through his mind. The one that came out of his mouth he knew was stupid before he even finished saying it. "But... you're not a goddess!"

The big man laughed heartily at this, but Auria just arched an eyebrow. "Did you expect there to be a real live goddess haunting the woods, love? I thought you'd be a little smarter than that. That's just the sailors' superstition. The citizens fuel it by their stories, and they come to their own conclusions.

The only one haunting this island is me—and the Eagle Flight behind me."

Surprisingly, this actually made sense. The ignorant were known to idealize and fantasize until fact became fiction. A woman *called* Auria made much more sense than the goddess herself.

But the reference to eagles unnerved him.

"Eagle Flight?"

"My loyal brothers and sisters." She indicated the other outlaws scattered around the clearing. Our true name is the Ëan, by the way. It is them you have to thank for your life."

"What? You attacked us! Why should I thank you for *that*?"

She turned to the outlaw behind her. "Why do I bother, Ovan?"

"Because you are good, *ona*," Ovan answered. "Think of your aunt, and think of what he could do for us. You know the reasons, *ona*, better than anyone. This was *your* idea—you told this to *us*."

She sighed. "Right, then." She turned back to William. "Well, love," she said resignedly, "it appears you still lack the wisdom to discern who your real enemies are, so let me explain.

"You had the stupidity to walk right into an assassin's trap, but the assassins walked right into mine. I spent the morning tailing you. The moment they drew weapons on you, they were finished. They should have known better than this. Their whole plan was perfectly idiotic. I think they knew it at the end—one of them thought they saw us so they moved too fast. Like that helped. They failed miserably in their charge. The last thing they wanted was for me to actually reach you—and me in the flesh, no less! As it is, your would-be murderers are even more dangerous to you now, because you already know too much for their comfort."

"I don't understand," he said in a small voice, but he almost thought he did. If her words meant what they seemed, it meant he was in *really* deep trouble. He didn't want to be in really deep trouble.

"You mean you don't believe me," she countered, reading his face well. "Well, I may be many things, love, but I am not a liar."

"You're saying Captain Zoc and Governor Whitefeld tried to kill me?"

"That is precisely what I am saying. If not for the *Ëan*, you would have been dead long before now. Zoc's guards would have killed you and run back to your pitiful ambassador blaming me. The fool would have believed them of course. But then we stepped in. Had we not done so," she said slowly, "not only would it be gravely unfortunate for you, but it would have caused yet another damaging lie to be packed off to the Edenian authorities."

"I don't believe you. Andel is an old friend of mine—and my father's—and he is a good man. There is no reason for him to kill me—he wouldn't," he said this last with vehemence, daring her to contradict him.

"Believe it, love. It's time to start using that brain of yours, if it's in there."

"He's my friend. Andel Whitefeld would *not* try to assassinate me."

Her sarcasm suddenly changed to coldness. Her expression became unreadable and her eyes grew far away. Her mouth hardened. "You're right," she conceded stiffly. "*Andel Whitefeld* never would."

"Ha! You see, it cannot be true!"

"Examine what I have said!" she snapped. "*You* said *Andel* would not, but *I* say that the *Governor* would."

William tried hard to digest what she was saying, but it made no sense. He had so desperately wanted answers to the questions he harbored in his mind, but if this was the way he was going to get them, he didn't like it.

"Are you saying that the Governor is *not* Andel? That's ridiculous! No, it's impossible. I know that he is—no usurper could take the Governorship of an Edenian province. The government would not let that happen. The King's messengers and the election would take care of that." He dismissed this idea outright.

Ovan looked grave. Auria, on the other hand, looked irate. "I'm not saying anything, she retorted sharply. "I'm merely pointing out the facts. If I tell you what *I* think, you won't believe me, even if I'm right—and I can assure you, I know what I'm talking about. I suppose I can't expect you to trust me enough to take my word for it, though it would be easier for everyone. You have to figure it out yourself for it to mean anything to you. But by all means, love, hurry it up! Your life, and others' lives, depend on it."

"All I want is to understand," he whined, and he winced at how petty it sounded. "That is why I was sent here."

"Well, then, figure out who your friends and enemies are, boy!" He had to be older than her, yet she addressed him like a child! He fumed inwardly. "I can't trust you until you do."

"Why should I believe you? You're an outlaw—a rebel against the crown."

"*I* am the one *supporting* the crown. I saved your life, William Tellor!"

She still seemed angry, but oddly enough, he no longer felt that she was threatening him. He was still afraid of her, but he had the odd sense that she wouldn't hurt him.

He decided to humor her.

"Please, my lady—"

"Mm-mm," she scolded, "don't call me that. Ëa ona or Auria. I won't have this 'my lady' business. I am not titled, love, and I don't want to be."

"What does that name even *mean*?" he asked skeptically. "It sounds like a barbarian tongue."

"*Ona* is Djoran for leader, or chief, or captain. There really is no direct translation. It implies leadership, but not superiority. Ëa means eagle, and Ëan is plural, so Eagle Flight. I am the Ëa ona."

"Djoran?" he tripped over the strange word.

"The Djorn are the native inhabitants of this island. They have lived here since before the empire even began."

"Barbarians—you consort with barbarians? And you call yourself an Edenian?"

Both of them looked offended. "They can hardly be called that," Auria lectured. "They are as civilized as any Edenian I've ever met—and more intelligent. They remember more about the roots of humanity than we do. And I'd watch what you say about the Djorn, love. Szera can be very temperamental. The others probably wouldn't care what you said; for the most part they are gentle and forgiving, which is lucky for us. But you don't want to get on Szera's bad side. She's the most ungentle Djor I've ever met—a bit of a lucky exception."

"Point taken," he replied, but he was repulsed by the idea of barbarians. He hadn't even known that there were any left aside from the few on the far western wastelands of the continent. But he would let this point go.

"So, *ona*," (he said the word deliberately and slowly), "supposing what you've told me *is* true, why would anyone want me dead?"

"Isn't it obvious?" she asked. "Oh," she answered herself at his expression. "I guess it's not. They don't want you to talk."

"Talk…" he prompted.

"You are the only direct link to the King that has been on this island in all the fifteen years the Governor has held control here. He has kept secrets from the crown for an impressively long time. You could be the end of him if you carried them back to the King. He would prefer those secrets stay secrets."

"Why is Lady Elissana's grave a secret? I only wanted to see it—it was something that bothered my father: he never got to see her grave. He thought it would give him more of a sense of finality."

She ignored the emotion in his words, continuing in her brusque manner. "Your insistence on seeing the grave is what got you into trouble in the first place. You might have been allowed to return home without trouble if you hadn't been so stubborn."

Well, he realized that now. He wished he'd never set foot on this El-forsaken island.

"Instead, you presented him with a dilemma," the *ona* continued. Here she leaned closer, her green eyes boring into his. Heaven, she was beautiful, despite all the dirt and roughness, but William could not let himself concentrate on that.

"He could not stop you from going to see it, but nor could he show it to you—because what he will never tell you is that it doesn't exist."

"What?"

If William had been shocked before, he was thunderstruck now. This pronouncement hit him like a physical blow.

His would-be mother, fifteen years ago, wasn't dead?

The King would move heaven and earth to find her if he knew. He had been broken-hearted at her loss. If this was true, then the King would be more than overjoyed.

"She's alive?" he asked.

"You've seen how the Governor has been acting," she stated. "What do *you* think?"

If it was true, the whole of what he knew was turned upside down. Nothing was impossible anymore.

"Where is she?" he pleaded.

"I'm not telling you," Auria replied sternly.

"Why?" he asked, his longing making him surly.

"Because I don't trust you. You don't know half of what's going on here, and you've already proven that you have a penchant for rash behavior. If I tell you where Lis is, you'll probably do something stupid that will expose the both of you to your enemies and get you killed. There's already the likelihood that *you'll* be killed anyway, but you're not bringing *her* into it. She's already walking a fine line with you just *being* here, let alone seeing her."

She was not taking any argument. He wanted to scream with frustration. After fifteen years, he might see his mother again, and this woman would stand in his way?

"How can she be alive? They told us—"

"They lied," she said simply. "Now you know, and the Governor will never let you return to tell the King if he finds out that you know. He will kill you first, as he already tried to do when he thought you would discover his secret."

Hopelessness came over him. He just wanted to be back home, away from this. But he also wanted desperately to see Lis again—and to bring *her* home, so that things could be the way they used to be.

"Why should I believe you?" he asked again, but it was a weak protest.

"I am your only friend on this island, love. Either you can accept that—and my protection—or you can take your chances with the Governor. I can't force you; you have to choose your side. This is war. You can help me, or you can hate me. But your blood is on your hands. I can't protect you if you don't want to be protected."

"Protect me?" he asked. Protection was good.

"Yes, love. If not for my friends, you'd have had several arrows and a sword or two in you by now. Blazer is a very intelligent horse, but he didn't trust me enough to throw you when I told him to. I wish he had. It would have made you a less obvious target. They could all see you easily to fire at you. Talon had to snatch that arrow out of the air, and I got another one. The Ëan took care of the other archers for you. But you're lucky Talon was hanging around."

"The eagle?" he said tremulously.

She grinned. "So, you remember Talon." She turned, standing, and called behind her, "*Ara*, Talon! Come say hello!"

A few seconds and a flurry of wings later, the eagle landed on her shoulder. He gave a light croak, but he did not seem threatening; rather, he seemed very pleased with himself. He preened as Auria stroked him gently. "William, meet Talon," she said, still grinning. "He's a friend of mine."

"You have a pet eagle?" he asked, nervous. Those yellow eyes were not tame, even if they were happy. This bird was still a predator. If he could have backed away, he would have.

"Not a pet," she corrected firmly. "Friend. He's not tame.

He just listens to me and does me some favors. I do the same." She threw William a sideways glance. "He says you don't like him much. You panicked whenever he came around. He seems to like you, though. You shouldn't be so flighty." She laughed at her own pun.

"But he attacked me!" William protested. "And how would you know what he says?"

She unloosed a string of Djoran to the eagle. The bird gave a long croak in reply. She looked back at William. "The Djorn still remember the language of the forest," she explained. "And the animals that of the Djorn. I can talk to almost any animal on this island."

"That is—creepy," he said as the implications reached him.

She laughed. "Yes, love, I know, but it makes for a very efficient spy network. I wouldn't have known about your assassination if not for them. I am quite able to protect you, William Tellor."

"You stole my ring," he accused, suddenly realizing why the bird had taken what he did. He was the Ëan's reconnaissance.

She laughed at the suddenness of the accusation. "Did that upset you? My apologies." She reached into a pouch at her belt, withdrew the ring, and tossed it to his feet. "Here you go. I didn't mean to keep it, and I don't need it anymore. I just needed to know who was on that ship. Elaon, the leader of the dolphins, told me it was larger than usual. Talon wasn't supposed to hurt you; he was just looking for information on the passenger. And he didn't do *that* much damage—for an eagle. He was pretty careful, if a bit dramatic. He's a theatrical bird. I think it comes with the territory. But in any case, you're lucky. I knew you were coming; the Governor didn't. I had time to prepare for your arrival; he didn't. If not for that, you might not be alive right now.

"Yet I have to keep protecting you," she said. "We are not finished yet. I need you to cooperate. I need to know if you are on my side, love."

The finality of the statement scared him.

According to Auria, the outlaw in the forest, Andel was not Andel and was trying to kill him; Lis was alive; and the only way for William to survive was to accept the protection of a strange but dangerous woman who was the friend of barbarians and animals. Yes, that summed up the insanity of her assertions.

Either she was crazy, or she was telling the truth.

"Why are you doing this?" he asked quietly.

"It is simple," she responded. "The Ëan fight for the people of Belond. The Governor's injustice has oppressed us for fifteen years. He has stolen our land, our possessions, and our lives. I would fight a lifetime to win back even a tithe of what he has stolen. I believe you can help me."

The eagle cawed and lifted away dramatically from her shoulder. She crouched down to look him in the eye again. "What I want is *justice*, William Tellor. You will help me get it."

There was no denying her.

Every line of her showed her conviction. She could not be more different from what he had seen of the Governor and Zoc, always evading and scheming. She was completely open and honest with him. And it was that, perhaps, that convinced him.

He had no choice but to believe her, terrifying though it was.

"What do you want from me?" he asked in resignation.

She smiled. He liked her better when she was smiling, but he did not feel more comfortable in her presence. She might be beautiful, but she was cold as ice and just as dangerous.

"That's really the question isn't it? Now we're getting somewhere," she said with satisfaction. "I will explain your options.

"This is your dilemma. The Governor wants to silence you; I want you to talk. If you help me, you help justice. If you help the Governor, you stay alive. Maybe. You have to decide.

"You have four choices, really. The safest would be for me to take you prisoner and keep you under the watch of the

Ëan." She noted his reaction with amusement. "Perhaps you would not enjoy our hospitality, love, but it would only be for your protection. You would be better off under my watch than many a prisoner in Edenia. And your second option would be to stay with me willingly—I can't quite see you wanting to do that. Both these options keep you safe, if not comfortable. This is the easiest option available to you."

"What else?" he prompted.

She laughed again. "We are not such disagreeable people, love. No need to be so eager to get away from us. I think you might find we are better than many Ossians. You nobles are a pretentious lot. We are more humble, but happier in what we do."

"How would *you* know what *we* are?" he grumbled.

"Because I know *everything*, love," she answered.

He raised an eyebrow.

She chuckled. "Just kidding. I only know *almost* everything."

Ovan found this hilarious. It was a few seconds before either regained their composure.

"But," she continued more seriously, "maybe you have no stomach for an outlaw's life. In truth, that would not best serve either of our purposes. I think we both want you to get home and tell your father what I've told you. If you stay with me, you might be stuck in Belond for a long time, with the King none the wiser that you're still here. Elber would report to the King that you are dead, that lie courtesy of the Governor, and no one would know any better. I would have to find another means of getting a message to the King—and I've already exhausted most of my ideas.

"So, as a third option, you could go back to the Governor. If you wanted to die, you would tell him everything about your encounter with the Ëan, including what I've told you. It would be the height of idiocy. He would kill you where you stood."

"Or, as a fourth choice," she continued, a devilish light coming into her green eyes, "you could play his game.

"Pretend that you know nothing and that you want to know nothing. Play dumb. (It shouldn't be too hard for you.) It is much less trouble for him to ship you back home, secrets unsuspected, than it is for him to murder you. He might buy it if you act like you're still ignorant. You could get back to Ossia and tell the King what he has been hiding.

"It is risky, but if it worked, the reward would be great. You could save Belond, William." She looked expectantly at him.

He didn't really want to save Belond. How about saving himself first?

"Would he be so easily fooled?" William asked skeptically.

"I didn't say it would be easy. He is a suspicious man. You would have to play it perfectly, but it is possible."

"Why would he think that you would pass up the opportunity to tell me what you know?"

"Because," she explained, "if I was solely interested in keeping you alive and getting you home safely—which it is plausible I might be—I would keep you ignorant so that he would have no reason to kill you. I would have to make it look like I just rescued you and then let you go without talking to you or you even understanding what I was doing.

"If he buys it, he will probably stall your return, just to be sure. Zoc will never buy anything. They're extremely careful that no wind of this gets out. If Edenia knew how far the Governor's actions have gone, he would be done for."

William was terrified. If a usurper had displaced Andel and stolen his authority, Edenia needed to know. If Elissana was alive, the King needed to know. It was not a question of comfort; it was a question of duty. But why did it have to be him?

His father had sent him for answers. Despite his reluctance to go, he loved his father, and he would never want to fail him. The King *needed* to know, both as the King and as a man.

If only it could be someone else.

He sighed, and then he made his decision. "I'll do it, *ona*."

She smiled. "Good decision. Maybe you do have some steel in you, love, but we'll see."

"Fine," he retorted. He wiggled his entrapped limbs, which were beginning to go numb. "Can you untie me now?"

She had the nerve to laugh at his discomfort. She waved Ovan forward. He untied the knots behind the tree and pulled the rope off the prince, coiling it in his hands as he did so. He slung the finished coil over his shoulder.

"Just a formality," she apologized, extending a hand to help him up.

He hesitated. "I don't bite, love," she promised. He took her hand.

She had a strong grip, and an even stronger arm. He was on his feet as quickly as she'd thrown him down a short while ago.

"So," she invited, "let's see about the plan, yes?" A devilish smile lit her features. He didn't like that look—it meant trouble.

Chapter 7

"Now," said the *ona* in the kind of tone an adult uses on a child, "listen carefully, love."

They had walked a little farther toward the center of the clearing, where the rest of the outlaws were sitting. Ovan had left them after untying William, so the prince stood alone at Auria's side. He was much taller than she was, but standing beside her made him feel small. A number of curious stares greeted him from the rest of the *Ëan*, ranging from amusement to hostility. But, to a man, they came to attention when the *ona* looked their way—faster and with greater respect than the Tellorian guard did, which was an impressive feat. These men (and more than a few women, surprisingly) were all unfailingly loyal. The *ona* was clearly the kind of leader that inspired devotion.

Not inattention, as William discovered when she flicked him lightly on the nose with her gloved fingers. "Pay attention, love," she scolded mildly. "This is important."

"Sorry," he mumbled, rubbing his nose, but his pride stung more. No one had ever dared to humiliate him the way she did.

"Right, then," she continued in the same tone as before. "This is what you're going to do—and without deviation, understand? First, you'll wait here with a couple of men I'll leave behind, just for a few hours."

"Why can't I just leave now?"

"Already wanting to leave us, love?" She clicked her tongue. "A poor guest you make." He grimaced. He would have been more than happy to leave her. He was tired, confused, and frightened, and her sharp tongue was grating on him.

"You can't leave now," she continued, "because your *friend* the Governor is going to think you've been wandering lost in the forest for the whole afternoon."

"But won't he know you captured me? The guards escaped, and they would have gone right back to him."

"Yours did," she conceded. "We only knocked them out. *They* were sincerely trying to protect you, but they were misinformed—and outmatched. There were only four of them. Zoc planned well. They would have died right along with you. As it is, they woke up a short time ago, back at the edge of the forest where you started. We tied them to their horses so they wouldn't get hurt, then my *Ëan* left them there. By now, they'll have run back to the Felds and raised the alarm. There'll be a search party out before long, but none of them have any idea how to navigate this forest." She smiled mischievously. "It will be thoroughly entertaining."

He felt sorry for Captain Tiran, his head guard. The loyal soldier would be beside himself with worry, and it was cruel of Auria to derive *entertainment* from his situation. "They've never found your hideout?" he asked wonderingly, gesturing at the clearing.

"This?" she said in surprise. "This is just a resting place, and we don't use it that often. No, love, they don't even know the *general* location of the Nest. They think we live in the forest. We don't. We just happen to own most of the island, and that includes the forest. They were foolish to mount an attack on our turf. It never works. I assure you, our 'hideout' is quite safe."

"Oh," he said simply. He was suddenly glad he hadn't taken up Auria's offer to go to their headquarters.

"Back to the matter of your guards," she continued. "Benjen escaped—rogues always seem to, and the leaders have enough experience to get themselves out of a scrape—and two others went with him. The rest are dead."

At his shocked expression, she gave him a simple defense for her actions. "I do not love war, William Tellor, but if that is what it takes to protect the innocent, I will kill an army of soldiers—though pitched battle does not usually work in my favor. But every one of those soldiers had orders to kill you and your guards, and they would have happily done it if I hadn't stopped them. Besides even that transgression, they have been instruments of oppression since the day they signed on. They take the lives of the innocent for their own gain. I do not regret my actions, nor should you blame the Ëan for unleashing death. I, unlike them, do not kill merely to serve my own interests. See that you remember that."

He could only nod at this speech, which was quiet but firm. Still, he felt sick to his stomach thinking about all those men killed. He was not a soldier. He did not relish the thought of killing anyone, even if it *was* right to do so.

"What about yours?" he asked.

She seemed surprised he cared. Indeed, he didn't know what made him ask the question. "I did not lose an Ëa," she replied. "I have not in a long time. We are skilled—though war is always risky. We protect our own, and we are cautious. We fight battles to win them. In any case, there are a few cuts and bruises, but no lives lost."

This remarkable fact attested to their talent. Their numbers had been evenly matched, if not a little larger on the Edenian side. The outlaws were lightly armored, wearing mostly light leather and a few bracers here and there, and they were not in formation, while they faced an organized force in full combat armor. William knew little of the Ëan's training, but he had seen the impressive skill of the soldiers they had faced. To defeat them so easily without casualties told William that their fighting skill must be honed to a formidable level. If the men were even the least bit like the *ona*, they were formidable indeed.

"So," she continued, "Benjen and your guards will know that you were caught. Therefore, we must invent a story for your escape."

"No one will believe I escaped, though—will they?"

"Is that a compliment to the Ëan, or an insult to yourself?" Her eyes twinkled. "But you're catching on. No, the Governor certainly won't—but let me explain."

"You'll tell them you woke up, tied to a tree, a short distance from our camp."

"So far, so good," he muttered. That's what actually happened. He was still stiff from that treatment, and he rather resented it.

She smiled as if reading his thoughts. She seemed good at doing that. "The Ëan were all busy, not looking, and not paying attention to you. You were tied next to a pile of supplies, and there were weapons in the stack. Using more cleverness than you actually possess, you managed to grab a knife with your feet and pull it close enough to reach with your hand. It was miraculous you did not chop off a finger in the process, but you sawed away at the ropes we used to tie you up. This you did with uncharacteristic stealth, and, by uncommon luck, no Ëa noticed (not that you know that name). You got up and slipped away, somehow managing to avoid tripping over your own feet, and you escaped into the forest, where you wandered hopelessly (and helplessly) lost for the rest of the day."

William would tell the story a little differently, when it was his turn to tell it. His ears burned. He desperately wanted to find a way to put her impertinence in its place, but he could not think of anything to say in response. She didn't give him much of a chance, anyway.

"You saw nothing of the Ëan—a name you do *not* know—but their backs. You never saw me, you don't even know I exist—you do *not* know *who* the leader is, or that the leader is a woman. You absolutely *never* spoke to anyone. The whole story rests on that point—if he finds out what you know, he'll kill you without a second thought. If there's doubt—there'll be hesitation. He never did have much conviction except when it came to saving his own skin."

The threat chilled him afresh.

"I hope you are a talented liar," she said, "but then, most noblemen are."

That did it.

"What is your *problem*?" he snapped. "You don't even *know* me! What have you got against me?"

He knew the other Ëan were staring at him, and his ears

burned, but he was fed up with this woman deriding him at every turn.

"That's right, love," she said dryly, not rising to his anger at all. "Grow a spine. You'll need one."

"Answer me, woman," he growled, his hand resting on the dagger at his belt. "I am the prince of Edenia. I am through with your disrespect."

Several Ëan drew weapons and advanced toward them. Auria only waved them away.

"Oh, for heaven's sake, take your hand off your weapon. You're annoying the Ëan. You *don't* want to annoy the Ëan. Besides, you know perfectly well you would never stand a chance against me, even without their help." She was right, but he was not placated in the least.

"Answer me!" he demanded again.

She smiled darkly at him, as if enjoying his indignation. "In this forest, love," she explained, "you are only a man. In your world, a noble is born to respect. In the real world, the world the Ëan and I live in, he earns it. You have earned nothing from me, *Lord William*. I do not pander to arrogance. If you wish to be honored, you must be worthy of honor. That is what your kind does not, and never will, understand."

He couldn't frame a suitable reply. How often had he had the same thoughts of Elber? Was that who *he* was? The thought disgusted him completely. His irritation faded into shame.

She was right.

He hated that she was always right.

"Back to the plan," she said calmly. Her voice had not risen at all. "It will be obvious to the Governor that I *let* you go, but as long as he thinks *you* believe you escaped, you are safe. Is that clear? Your life—and Belond's future—depends on how well you play the story."

"I understand."

"Good. Then I have only a few safety precautions to arrange. I *will* do my best to protect you if something goes wrong, as long as you cooperate."

He nodded, feeling a bit numb. He had been thrown through a whirlwind of emotions, from fear to anger to longing. He didn't know what to feel anymore.

"All right. So, I have a friend who lives in your closet."

He started at how casually she said this. "What?"

She laughed. "A mouse. His name is Harry. He's been watching out for you. He's one of the animals that told me about the Governor's plan to kill you. He's a very nice little fellow. I saved him from a mouse trap in one of my other expeditions into the Felds. He would have been food for Anjalia's cat—if the girl could stand seeing her cat eat a mouse. Heavens, but that creature is a devil. If you see it, don't pet it. Run the other direction first."

Her familiarity was creepy, but *expeditions*, plural, surprised him. "You can get into the Felds?" he asked.

She laughed again. "I can get almost anywhere, love," she said significantly, "with no one the wiser."

"But the guards!"

"Never see me," she stated simply. "I have better ways of getting into places."

William had seen how many soldiers guarded the Felds. Was this woman a sorceress?

"Anyway," she said, returning once again to the point, "Harry will watch out for you. If you need the Ëan," she paused to hand him a smooth, reddish stone about the size of his thumb, "put that on your dresser. He'll see it. I told him to look for it."

Another thought disturbed him. She used the past tense. "You knew this would happen?"

"I guessed. I have become a good guesser, love—and I planned things to happen this way."

"But you didn't *know*."

"No one can ever be quite certain of the future, save El. And *he* has a strange sense of humor."

Her reference to a supreme deity surprised him, especially since it seemed sincere. He would have thought an outlaw godless.

"Back to the point," she said, with a hint of exasperation, "(you certainly get sidetracked), my friends will tell me if the Governor buys the story. If he does, wonderful. If not, we will have to get you out in a hurry. I will do my best to keep you safe. But do me a favor: make sure your guards stay *outside* the door at night, okay? It will make things simpler. I hate bashing people in the head. It makes so much noise."

He didn't want to think about the implications of *that* request.

She pulled back her cloak to reveal her belt, into which were tucked four knives, all long, tapered, and elegant blades. He remembered them well. They'd been used on him. He still had that knot on his forehead.

She pulled one from its sheath and handed it to him. "Tell them this is the knife you found and used to untie yourself. It will lend you more credibility, and it will make them think. He'll know I mean business, sending you back. The Governor will recognize it, I assure you. But please don't lose it. I'll want it back. I hate having an odd number of knives. They don't balance as well when I wear them."

He fingered the blade. The craft was finer than any he'd ever seen. He wore a small dagger of his own, tucked into his belt, but this knife was far superior. It was made of a metal he did not recognize, and the pommel was a smooth white material. There was a strange design etched in both the blade and the hilt, but he could not make it out.

"Where did this come from?" he asked, curious. "I've never seen anything like it."

"You don't need to know," she informed him curtly.

He was disappointed, but he held his tongue.

"So in a few hours, you'll let me take Blazer and go?" he summed up. "Then I tell him the story, feign disinterest in any more revelations, and sail home."

"More or less," she answered. "With one small problem. You go on foot. I said nothing about a horse."

"My horse," he growled, "comes with me, or the whole thing's off. I'm not about to abandon Blazer to *you*."

Understanding, if not empathy, dawned on her face. She softened ever so slightly. "So you *do* care about something other than yourself."

If he cared only for himself, he would still be in Ossia, but at least he had a chance of convincing her. He *couldn't* give up Blazer, not even to save himself. The horse meant everything to him.

"Look," she said, with less sarcasm, "It wouldn't fit the story if you came back with Blazer. It would ruin the credibility of the whole thing. I'll take good care of your horse, William. No one better. You can have him back when things are right again. I'm sorry, but that's the best I can do. Don't worry; I know how to care for animals."

"That's not good enough," he retorted. "I'm not leaving here without my horse."

"Your horse will be fine with us," she informed him. "He's already made friends with Kata."

She pointed over to where the very horse in question stood tethered lightly to a tree. One of the barbarians, Djorn, Auria had called them, stood by Blazer. This one was as small as Szera had been large, and as slight as Szera had been muscular. She was probably about eighteen or nineteen, but she looked younger. She put William in mind of fairies, with her wispy pale hair, pretty blue eyes, and pixie-ish features.

"Ekata is our healer," the *ona* told him, "and the gentlest among us. Our forest friends trust her best of anyone, aside from perhaps Torhan and Yewul."

He did not know the others she spoke of, but the lilt with which she said their names indicated that they were also Djorn. He could not discredit her description of Ekata. Blazer nuzzled her with a trust that stung the prince with jealousy.

"He's *my* horse," William asserted. "I'm not letting you keep him."

Auria sighed in irritation. "You are stubborn, love, and it gets you into trouble. Tenacity you need, but not foolishness. I've already answered you."

"And I'm not taking no as an answer."

"You're looking to kill yourself," she argued. "He'll know it's a lie if you return on horseback."

"So just bring him back later," William countered. "I don't care. But I'm not giving him up to you."

The *ona* considered this.

"I *could* do that," she pondered. "But it would have to look coincidental, as if he wandered off during the fight. You would have to act that way, and so would the horse."

"Fine, as long as I get him back."

She sighed. "The horse is important to you," she observed dryly. "I get it, love. C'mon, let's go have a talk with him."

She had a long stride. He had trouble keeping up. She reached the tree almost instantly. "What does he say, Kata?" she asked as she approached.

Both the woman and the horse turned to her deferentially. "He was telling me about his home," she replied. Her voice was soft and sweet, much more womanly than Szera's had been. Ekata seemed out of place in this crowd of warriors; she clearly was not a fighter. "Does he like Belond?" Auria asked Ekata.

"He's—ah—" Ekata was less than sure of the language. "*Ta cërt,*" she finished in Djoran.

Auria laughed. "Maybe you'll make up his mind." She glanced at William. "Your horse has more sense than you—funny how that works. In any case, he's certainly loyal to you."

Blazer had moved to nose the prince's shoulder, much to his encouragement. Ekata hadn't bewitched him, at least.

Auria looked Blazer in the eyes and unleashed a string of Djoran. He seemed unusually respectful to her, as if the horse were one of her gang. He stirred at times as he listened, tossing his head or stamping a hoof, but his attention did not waver. He watched her with intelligent brown eyes.

The *ona* concluded, and Blazer seemed to make some response. She turned to William, hands on her hips. "Well, he's certainly intelligent. He likes the plan, and he agreed to help. He'd rather stay with his master, it seems, even though he was polite enough to compliment our hospitality." She winked at William. "He'll stay with us tonight, then he'll run down tomorrow, in a bit of a lather, as if he'd been lost all night. He's agreed to do this on his own, which is quite generous of him. You will, of course, be convinced upon your arrival that he is lost, as he ran away after you were knocked off his back. Am I clear?"

"Yes," the prince replied. "Thank you, *ona*."

"Taking a lesson from your horse, I see," Auria laughed.

William didn't respond, but he ducked his head.

"Are you satisfied, now, love?" she questioned.

"Yes," he answered.

"Good," she said. "Then the *Ëan* will see to you." She turned on her heel, leaving him alone with Ekata and Blazer, not even bothering to say goodbye.

Ekata smiled uncertainly at him until Ovan came and led him to where he could sit down with a couple other outlaws. They were quiet, but fairly friendly.

"What now?" William asked Ovan.

"We wait," the tall man replied.

Wait they did.

Chapter 8

William could almost believe the lie he would have to tell, after the afternoon he endured.

He had seen no more of *Ona* Auria. She had not bothered any further with him after explaining her instructions. In fact, most of the *Ëan* had left with her, going he knew not where—most likely returning to that secret hideout of theirs.

Ekata, the pretty, pale-faced barbarian who had taken charge of his horse, had taken Blazer along with the outlaws, promising in her quaint accent to take care of him and send him back to the Felds in the morning. Blazer had seemed unhappy to leave his master, but he had responded easily enough to the gentle young woman's leading.

William had been left with Ovan and another outlaw, a dark young man named Baër. He stood well over six feet, near William's own height, but he had easily twice the muscle on his frame. Baër had the dark hair of most Edenians, but it was clear he had a bit of Merath ancestry in him somewhere from the deep tan skin and dark almond-shaped eyes. William wondered how his family had ended up way out here in the middle of the ocean, when Merath was about as far away as far could get. He was not quite handsome, but he had a sort of intensity about his person that some people might find appealing. Ovan was friendly to him, as seemed in his nature. There was no hostility between the two outlaws—as the *ona* had said earlier, they were all like brothers—but William sensed that these two were not the closest of friends.

Baër had ignored William entirely. He muttered in complaint about being ordered to "serve as a nursemaid to a worthless noble." It sounded like something Auria would say, but instead of teasing, he was entirely serious. Ovan reprimanded him gently, reminding him that the *ona* had asked it of them, and therefore it was their duty. After that, Baër had said no more to either of them for the remainder of the time they waited.

Ovan had been fairly quiet also. He spent most of the afternoon polishing his sword with meticulous care.

William grew bored very quickly, despite all the emotions raging within him. It was a long time to sit and do nothing, after all, so he watched Ovan's efforts. The whetstone ran with precision along the edge of the smooth metal. He studied the craft of the sword. It was a remarkably fine weapon for a mere outlaw to possess. The workmanship seemed familiar to him, but he struggled to place it. It was certainly Edenian, unlike the knives the *ona* wore. It even looked Ossian, which was saying something. How did an outlaw get an Ossian sword?

It dawned on him.

"How did you get a sword made for the Tellorian guard?" he asked the outlaw in surprise.

Ovan glanced at him as he spoke, his expression unreadable. "I *am* one, your highness," he replied simply. William noted that Ovan used his title while his captain scorned it.

His statement was ridiculous. A Tellorian guard was a Tellorian guard his whole life. No one who had worn the royal red would leave his duty, even if it meant his own death. Ovan could not be here, in Belond, if he were in fact a Tellorian guard. He would be with the king in Ossia.

"Impossible," William concluded dismissively.

Baër snorted in derision. Ovan just smiled, a bit ruefully. "Is it so, my lord?" he asked in a measured tone.

William thought about it. He could not offer an explanation for Ovan's assertion, try though he might.

"Yes. Why would you be here?" The Guard rarely left the presence of a Tellor, unless directly commanded by the King. Was this man a traitor? William knew he should be nervous under this reasoning, but for some reason, Ovan failed to frighten him. Though William did not doubt his warrior's skill, Ovan's friendly face and easy demeanor reassured him somehow.

"I see your thoughts," Ovan said. "But I am not a traitor. I am here because of orders assigned to me fifteen years ago. I have failed in many ways, but I still hope to perform my duty as I am able. It was not meant to be for such a long time. I was intended to return home after a few weeks, but fate decreed otherwise."

William tried to digest this information. He would never have expected to find one of the Guard here, but the explanation was almost plausible. The Guard was known for extreme devotion to duty. If one really did have some mission here, he would not have abandoned it even after all these years.

Ovan pulled his ragged brown sleeve up above his shoulder. "See?" he said, indicating a tattoo on the thick part of his shoulder. "I am not lying." Every royal Guard had one. It proved their identity better than uniforms could, and also made their service lifelong. It was a symbol of honor throughout Edenia. Only the best of the best joined the Tellorian Guard. Soldiers all over the Empire coveted their status.

Ovan suddenly appeared different to him. All the *Ëan* did. If they had a Tellorian Guard with them, and he really *was* pursuing his duty, they would be fighting for the King. But what was the duty he had been assigned? Fifteen years ago—William thought he could guess.

"Did you come with the Whitefelds?" he asked.

Ovan grimaced as if at a bad memory. "Yes, my lord."

"And you still say you're following your orders?"

"Yes, I do."

"But then—"

"Forgive me, but it is not my place," Ovan interrupted. "The *ona* prefers not to speak of it, so I think it is best if I do not, either—not yet, anyway."

William glowered. "You claim to be a Tellorian guard," he grumbled, "yet you'll follow that woman's orders above mine."

Ovan looked him sharply in the eye, then said quietly, "I

will always be loyal to the King, my lord. Please believe that. I am not trying to cause trouble for you. What we do is for the best." He sighed. "I have tried my best to serve the King as he ordered. I will protect you, your highness. All the Ëan will."

Is that what these outlaws really were? Glorified freedom fighters defending the King? That's what they all seemed to claim, but William was convinced that there was more to it.

He didn't want to think about it, though. He didn't like thinking about all these things. The sheer amount of information to ponder intimidated him. He didn't respond. Ovan continued sharpening his sword.

When dusk began to settle, Ovan had stood, saying, "Let's get going." He reached into his pack, pulling out a hunk of bread and some dried meat. He proceeded to wolf down this simple meal, then bundled his pack up and slung it on his back. Baër did the same.

William's stomach growled. He was repulsed by the pitifully poor fare, but he hadn't eaten all day, other than a light breakfast at dawn. He was hungry enough to eat almost anything.

Ovan glanced at him. "Sorry," he said. "The *ona* told us not to feed you. She said it would be more convincing that you'd been lost and alone all day if you were *actually* hungry." He shrugged in embarrassment.

Baër spoke for the first time that afternoon. "She also said," he added scornfully, "that it would do you good to be a little uncomfortable. Make you understand what our people feel. A leader should be the first to feel the pinch, our *ona* always says."

"We have to remind her to eat, sometimes," Ovan confided quietly to William.

"She's a better leader than anyone alive," Baër confided. "She'd give the cloak on her back to the least of the *Reben*. You wouldn't understand that, would you? You've never known want. Time for you to learn."

William didn't know whether to be angry or hurt. Auria was a hard woman. Everything was cruel practicality to her.

She might deny herself, but she was only too happy to deny him, too, it seemed.

"Let's go," Baër ordered, turning on his heel to the south.

Ovan hesitated, looking abashed. He reached to his belt and displayed a waterskin.

"Here," he offered. "I can give you water, at least. She said nothing about that."

William smiled. It was the kindest thing anyone had done for him so far on this island. "Thanks," he said, taking the skin. He took a few long sips, letting the water cool his throat. He was unused to drinking plain water, and he could taste that it was not entirely pure—probably taken from a stream somewhere—but it refreshed him nonetheless.

"C'mon," Baër urged. "We'll have to get back to the Nest, Ovan. At this rate, we'll be lucky to get there and back by dawn."

"I know, but it will be easier going home when we can use the Gnomi road." Ovan glanced awkwardly at William as he said this as if he'd made some slip, but William had no idea what he was talking about. Baër glared impatiently. "We're coming," Ovan assured. He took back the skin and headed after Baër. William followed.

They had walked for hours, until William could barely lift his feet his legs burned so badly. It was rough going, as it was very dark in the forest, and they did not use the road or even a trail. They plowed through fresh mud more often than not, and William wished he had worn better shoes. The outlaws were unfazed by anything. No matter how far they walked, they remained untired. William gasped for air and felt fatigue crushing him. They still looked perfectly fresh. It was irritating.

Finally, when it was nearly midnight, Ovan put up a hand, only dimly to be seen in the dark. He motioned for quiet. William did not at first see the reason, but he welcomed the rest. He stooped, trying to ease his aching muscles.

It would be easy to pretend he'd been lost in the forest all day. Every bone in his body believed it. He'd never been so tired.

He suddenly noticed the torches bobbing in the distance. They were at the top of a hill, overlooking a wide view below. There was a search party just below them.

Ovan crouched behind some bushes, though no one would have seen him anyway. He whispered to the prince, "All right, then. That's as far as we go. You go on down to them, as if you've been lost, remember? Stick exactly to the plan."

"That's it?" William asked. He didn't know how he thought he'd part from them, but he didn't think they'd just abandon him.

"Of course. We cannot go with you. We will watch, never fear," Ovan reassured, noticing his consternation.

"Oh," he said. These people were very prone to abruptness.

"El be with you, Lord Tellor," Ovan said softly. Baër did not speak.

When William opened his mouth to say goodbye, they had vanished. He looked about him in surprise, trying to figure out where they went. He had not even heard them go.

There was nothing else for it. He stumbled down the hill toward the searchers, hoping he was not falling from the frying pan into the fire. At this point, he felt too far gone to care.

Exhaustion overwhelmed him. He was hungry, thirsty, and aching with fatigue. He forced himself to continue on.

They were calling his name. He recognized their voices, though they were edged with panic. His own guards. His heart warmed. At last! He raised his voice and shouted as loud as he could, "Here! I'm over here!" Genuine relief colored his voice.

The searchers shouted elatedly in response, and they were on him almost instantly. He was surrounded by members of the royal guard. He was safe.

Tiran, his captain, came forward, catching him around the shoulders. "Forgive me, my lord," he pleaded. "This is all my fault. I failed you. I let others convince me to agree to foolery. My life is forfeit, my lord."

William had been one of those others, as had Zoc. It was not the captain's fault. He had done what he had thought best for the circumstances. He just didn't know how misinformed he was. William shook his head weakly. "You did nothing wrong," he reassured.

Tiran did not seem to hear. He continued on, his voice still plagued by guilt. "I can scarcely believe it. We thought we'd never find you again. Lord Andel insisted that you must be dead."

He observed William's fatigue and became the businesslike captain of the guard once more. He called to his men, "Bring my horse! His lordship must be taken home at once!"

"Yes, sir!" said one, darting away.

"It is not far, my lord," Tiran promised. "We will see you safe. No more harm shall come to you, my lord, if I have any say in it. I swear it on my life."

Tiran's sincerity reminded him strikingly of Ovan. The two men were a lot alike, despite their difference in circumstances. They were both defined by loyalty.

"How did you escape those fiends? Benjen said you were captured!" Tiran questioned.

"Later, please, Tiran," William murmured. "I just want to go home."

"Yes, my lord. Forgive me. You must rest first."

"Do you have any food?"

A little bread and some water were salvaged for the prince. "It is all we have, my lord," Tiran apologized. William ate it faster than he'd ever consumed anything.

Tiran doffed his cloak and placed it around William's shoulders, as the night was growing cold. They waited a few moments more, then the horse was brought. Tiran boosted the weary prince into the saddle, then took the reins to lead it himself on foot. It was his own horse.

Some guards were mounted, some walked, but all fifty formed a protective ring around the prince. Tiran arranged them personally. "Home!" he cried to his men, who shouted in triumph.

Their loyalty and welcome warmed him, but he knew that he was not going home, not yet. He might never get there.

"Now, wait a moment," the Governor interrupted.

It was the next morning. William had been hustled back to the Felds, where he had, before being swept off to his bed, briefly seen Lord Andel—no, not Andel. William could see the subtle difference now that he was looking for it. This man was startlingly similar to Andel as William remembered him, but the eyes and lines of the face were wrong. Also, there was a hint of something that lurked just beneath the surface of his countenance that did not fit his memory of Andel at all.

This was an imposter. Auria was right.

He was still in bed, refusing to get up. The Governor had been all sympathy, ordering everyone to see to the prince's comfort, but he also demanded to speak with him for an explanation. William had declined the invitation to the Governor's quarters, but the Governor would not be put off. He asked to see William in his own chambers. The prince found himself out of excuses. So, the Governor, Captain, Zoc, Tiran, Bailan, and several other officials from the royal diplomatic party crowded around his bed to hear his story. Elber was not there. William was glad of it. The dramatic sympathy of the empty-headed ambassador would have rankled. Instead, Elber was busy arranging something to do with his role as official.

It was easy to play the traumatized victim. He was, in a sense. What was hard was concealing his distrust of the Governor and his confused fear and doubt. He knew he had to be convincing or he would killed—which didn't help balance his emotions.

It was hard to tell whether the Governor believed him. Zoc was clearly skeptical. Bailan was impassive. Tiran was calculating, trying to reason the matter out. William would have to watch him. He was clever, and he might get too far in his deductions. The Governor was the only one William could not read—naturally. The whole plan rested on convincing him.

"You cut the ropes with a knife—which you just *found*? And no one noticed?" his interrogator asked.

"Yes," he replied, trying to sound indignant that at the Governor's doubt. "It was risky, but they were busy with something. I was quiet."

He asked for his cloak to be brought. When his servant retrieved it, he rummaged through the folds and pulled out the *ona's* knife. "See? I kept the knife." He showed it to them.

Zoc's eyes narrowed, and he made a wolf-like growl in his throat. The Governor inhaled sharply, stiffening. "Give me that!" he snapped, snatching the weapon out of his hands. The Ossians' reactions ranged from shock on the part of the officials to measuring on the part of Tiran.

The Governor examined it with Zoc. They both recognized it; that much was clear. Again, Auria was right. Why was the woman always right? It was endlessly irritating. He waited to see if the *ona's* gift would have the desired result.

"This was just *lying* there?" the Governor demanded.

"Yes—on top of some bundles of things. It was the only thing that was sharp I could reach."

They exchanged another one of those significant glances that William dreaded. He couldn't stop his heart from racing. He hoped no one would notice his agitation, or at least discern its true cause.

"What is it?" Tiran asked. He was no fool. He had noticed their behavior, too. The difference was that he, as yet, had no reason to mistrust them.

The Governor looked to Zoc. The captain grimaced, thinking what to say. "That knife belongs to the ringleader," he stated at last. "We've seen it before."

He rounded on the prince. "Did you see h—" he hesitated, "did you see the leader?"

"They wore masks, and none were ever near me, except those who attacked me. I was not looking carefully at them. I don't know who the leader was."

"No one spoke to you?"

He tried to appear confused. "No."

Zoc's eyes bored into him, disbelieving. The Governor, on the other hand, relaxed.

It had the right effect. For Auria to give him her knife proved to the Governor that she had *let* him go, even if William appeared to think he escaped. It offered the explanation Auria wanted to convey without William seeming to know. She had allowed him to get away unharmed without speaking to him, which meant that the Governor would have no reason to harm him. She'd left him her own knife to accomplish this, and she'd known they would recognize it. There was no way she would have simply left her knife on a pile of supplies. It was a message.

She was a smart woman.

It clinched the story.

William's heart slowed a little. Maybe the Governor *would* believe him.

"You were lucky," the man who was not Andel declared, as if satisfied. He still fingered the knife thoughtfully. "They are barbaric. They likely intended to kill you. We shall endeavor to keep them from following through on the intent."

"We certainly shall," Tiran argued. "But they would have killed him outright if that's what they wanted. Why leave him alive?" William hoped the canny captain would not uncover the plot. He needed the Governor's lies to appear unchallenged in order to escape Belond. The captain meant well, and he was a wise man, but blundering into discovering those secrets would mean their deaths.

William halted that line of inquiry. "It doesn't matter. I escaped. I am never going back there again. I should have listened to your advice, Andel. I was wrong to try the forest road. I will not pursue it anymore. I can do no more for my father. The sooner I see the open sea, the better. *You* handle the outlaws. I just want to go home." This last he could say truthfully, but his desire for answers was not abated in the slightest. Auria had not satisfied him. He just needed it to appear that way.

"As you wish, my lord," Andel acquiesced easily. "It is understandable. Such an experience would have proved beyond the measure of most men. I am horrified it happened under my hospitality. I had hoped your time in Belond would be pleasant."

"You warned me," William countered. "I didn't listen to you." He wondered if it would have been better if he had given up the idea of Lis's grave and hadn't learned the truth. He could have gone home—unsatisfied, but safe. Ignorance was not exactly bliss, but it was better than knowledge. Both created fear, but one was a foolish fear while the other was wise. He did not enjoy being wise.

"I am glad we can agree, my friend," the Governor said. If he was not Andel, he was eerily like him. He had the same sort of charisma. William remembered the way Andel had spoken to him as a child—it was the same voice that addressed him now. William was briefly tempted to trust him—it would have been easier—but Auria's warnings had all proven true. He knew better now.

"So am I," he said a little reluctantly.

The Governor stood. "Thank you for your help, sire, and again receive my apologies for this awful turn of events. Captain Zoc and I will pursue these outlaws with increased fervor. They will be brought to justice." His words were eerily like what Auria had said of *him*.

"I do not wish to hear of it, when you do," William sighed. "I never wish to hear of them again."

"As you wish, my lord," came the response. "I am your servant."

William gave a heavy nod, but he did not reply.

"I shall leave you to your rest, my lord. Lord Elber and I must continue official business to speed your return home, but you need not concern yourself. Rest and recover. You will be sailing home as soon as we are finished, which for your sake I pray will be quickly, though I will miss you."

The admission that he would be going home soon told William that the Governor had believed his lie. He breathed a slow sigh of relief, his heart rising. He would make it!

The whole group of visitors left him alone. After a brief visit from the healer who attended him, he was left entirely to himself, though heavily guarded. He enjoyed the comfort of his feather bed, and he allowed himself the pleasure of wasting the hours with food and sleep. Perhaps this plan would not be so bad after all. He was certainly enjoying it now.

After eating dinner in bed, he fell asleep. His fear had given way to triumph. He had made his escape good.

Chapter 9

William jerked awake with a muffled cry.

It was the second night since his return to the Felds, and he had not gotten out of bed the whole time. He had been sleeping quite comfortably when someone snatched at him in his sleep.

He tried to cry out, but a gloved hand clamped his mouth shut. He pushed at his attacker uselessly.

"Be still!" a voice hissed softly. "It's just me, love!"

In the dim light, he could barely make out the hood and mask of the *ona*. He stopped struggling, and she let him go. His breath came quickly. She had scared him, and now that he knew who it was, he was scarcely less frightened.

And... she was in his room. In the Felds. And no one had noticed.

Was he dreaming?

"Shh!" she whispered when he was about to speak. "Your guards aren't part of the Tellorian order for nothing. They're smart. If you're not careful, they'll hear us."

He sat up in bed, looking warily at her. He did not like the thought that she could just break into his bedroom anytime she chose. Or that she was a woman in his room well past midnight.

"Why are you here?" he asked with just the merest breath, resentment coloring his voice.

She smiled coyly at him. "Didn't you miss me, love? I thought you would be lonely." At his expression, she laughed softly. "Mm-hm. I know, love. Not funny. Noblemen have no sense of humor."

"I have a sense of humor," he countered.

"Of course you do. It involves tripping over your own feet to give everyone else something to laugh at."

"Do I *amuse* you?" he snapped.

"Of course, love. Naiveté is very amusing. Just

dangerous."

She sat on the bed. "This is nice, I will admit," she chatted. "But I think too much time in it would make anyone soft." He moved his feet quickly out of the way as she flopped backward. "Mmm. Feels good. I haven't slept in a real bed for years. I don't blame you for taking up a two-day residence in it."

He grimaced. She'd been spying on him.

She turned to look at him, that mocking smile still on her face. She laughed again. "C'mon, love," she laughed, "I told you I know everything. Besides, I promised to check up on you, didn't I?"

"Right," he muttered sarcastically, but she was always right.

"So," she whispered, sitting up again. "You've done rather well, so far. The Governor's willing to believe you, and he is planning to let you go, if possible."

He already knew that. "So why did you come?"

"Obviously," she said, "I *enjoy* babysitting defenseless lords who can't move a muscle to help themselves. Why else would I bother with you?"

Her sarcasm had not lost its richness. This was the most cynical woman he'd ever met.

"You didn't answer me," he replied stiffly.

"Keep your voice down," she hissed. "This isn't a game." She glanced at the door, poised to bolt. William heard a floorboard creak as the guards outside shifted. His heart hammered in his chest. He hoped the guards wouldn't hear *that*.

When nothing happened, she said, "Fine, love. Harry told me what you said to the Governor, and you acted the part well. Congratulations. I knew you'd make a good liar, even if you do wear your heart on your sleeve.

"Bits, however—"

"Bits?"

"He lives downstairs. Harry's brother."

"Do you name all the animals that spy for you?"

She shot him a mischievous glance. "Not all of them, no," she said lightly. "Just the ones that spy on *you*." She laughed at his expression. "Just teasing, love. Anyway, Bits heard that Zoc doesn't buy a word of it. Not that I'm surprised. For all he is a demon, he is difficult to fool. So, he still wants to kill you. It was his idea to kill you in the first place, and once he latches onto something, he doesn't let it go. Their most radical plans are the ones he likes best. They've been arguing about it, and I'm still not sure what they'll decide. Zoc has to convince the Governor, and *he'll* just stall until he decides. They may still try to kill you while you're here."

All William's confidence shattered. He'd hoped he was out of danger. The bluntness with which she spoke of his peril, with no more emotion than if she was talking about what she ate for lunch, terrified him.

"It would be more convenient but riskier for them to send you home. No trouble of explaining to the King why his son is dead and inviting the possibility of the Imperial army into Belond. Who knows what the King would do if you were killed here? But it would be dangerous to let you live and bust their whole story. They can't decide."

The thought of his father avenging his death did not make him feel better, although then Eduar might find Lis.

"So," Auria continued, "as I thought, he's stalling. He'll sabotage your ship tomorrow, but that will be presented as *my* fault, of course. I have a wonderful reputation for making things complicated. I tried to work a way around it, but I can't get my men out into the harbor without us being seen, and there's a good chance anyone I'd send would be killed trying to stop the Governor's men. It's not worth the risk. So, you'll be stuck here until he's sure of you or kills you. I still hope he'll let you go.

"But," she said. "I need to warn you. Don't go anywhere with them—like you did when you first arrived, going on that tour—and don't step one toe into the barracks or they'll have you like a mouse in a trap. Watch what you eat. I have arranged for a group of flies to warn you if they try poison. If you see flies near you when they bring your food, don't eat it. And for heaven's sake, whatever you do, avoid Anjalia."

What?

"Why her? She's just a girl. She can't be dangerous at all!'

"Oh, *she's* harmless enough, but spend time around her and it will decide matters. That will definitely make them want to kill you off."

"Okay..." he said, humoring her.

"I'm serious. If she invites you to visit her, say no. She's planning to. She has some pitiful infatuation for you, empty-headed female that she is."

"I'm used to it."

"Think you're attractive, eh? You don't have nearly enough muscle and you're not nearly smart enough, which is generally what women are interested in."

Thanks. "That's not what I meant. Noblewomen just like a title. I have a good one."

"A title never made a very good husband—or wife. I don't recommend marrying one. A *person* would be a much better choice."

He knew what she meant, and part of him agreed, but he disdained the idea of marrying a common woman. He was the prince of Edenia, and if he ever married, he would marry a woman worthy of being a princess. He would not marry some low-born, uncultured woman. He wanted an equal.

"Uh-huh," was all he said.

She stood up. "Well, I was just dropping in on you. I've got other business in the Felds. Things to do, you know, love."

"What things?"

She grinned mischievously. "Wouldn't you like to know?" With a laugh, she said, "Fine. I'm spying (obviously), stealing (my knife that you lost), and sneaking (past pathetic guards that don't even know to look for me). I'm a busy girl. The Governor will be rather upset when he finds out I stole my knife back. I'm a step ahead of him—again." She laughed. He actually sort of liked the sound, since for once she wasn't laughing at him. It made her seem friendlier. Almost. And it pulled at his memory, as if he'd heard that laughter before, some other place. He couldn't remember.

"I'll be back later, love," she promised. "I make fairly regular visits to the Felds."

She melted into the shadows, disappearing soundlessly. He strained to hear where she went, but other than a few soft sounds, he could hear nothing. Then it was silent, and she was gone, leaving him to his own thoughts.

Chapter 10

Unfortunately, William lacked Auria's talent for sneaking around. She could seemingly walk through walls, but all he could manage was walking straight into his guards.

The *ona's* visit had unsettled him to the point where he could no longer enjoy lying around. To ease his restless mind, he decided to get up. He knew, however, that he would still have to play the victim and act completely disinterested in those questions that plagued his mind.

He decided an unsuspicious activity would be visiting his horse (he didn't feel like visiting *people*, after all). They had told him when Blazer came back. He hoped a visit would not attract attention. His hosts would all be excited that he was "feeling better," anyway. His hope of stealth ended when he opened the door and ran right smack into Captain Tiran.

The captain apologized (loudly), coming to immediate attention. For heaven's sake. It was hard to skulk around as the prince of Edenia. His guards prevented stealth entirely.

"Hello, Captain," William sighed.

"I didn't think you would be getting up," Tiran explained. "Though I am pleased to see you are feeling better."

Mm-hmm. He'd thought so.

"A bit better, Tiran—but I don't think I'll venture out too far today."

"As you wish, my lord. Would you like to go down to breakfast? All the party is assembled."

Absolutely not! He was avoiding the Governor—and, apparently, he should also avoid Anjalia.

"Um—I don't think so. A little… taxing. I had actually wanted to visit Blazer. I haven't seen him since he wandered back."

"Certainly, my lord. The guards will accompany you." He nodded to the two Tellorians who had been posted outside his door. Had it been possible for them to come to more rigid attention, they would have done so.

Well, he hadn't wanted to sneak around anyway. He hid a grimace. Now *everyone* would know where he went. At least if anyone tried to assassinate him, he'd have loyal protection. He fingered the dagger at his belt, covered by his tunic.

"Thank you," he said to his captain. "But let's keep it quiet, okay? I'd rather not have a fuss." This was directed more to the two guards. They nodded and threw him a salute.

"Perfect," he muttered. "Let's go, then."

"I have some things I need to see to here—just routine security," the captain said, not elaborating further. "Come straight back, please, your Highness. I have no trust in this place anymore. I do not wish to fail again in my charge to protect you."

William was struck by a desire to tell him everything. It would shed responsibility, leave his safety in more capable hands. Besides, it was unfair to Tiran. The captain was entirely sincere about his duty—how could William keep such a secret from the one person he fully trusted? And if *he* was in danger, as his guards, so were they.

But a shared secret was no secret at all. He remembered the disdainful frown of the *ona*, and he knew he had to handle this himself.

"I will," he promised Tiran. "Thank you, Captain." A pang of guilt stabbed him, but he shoved the feeling away.

His guards followed him down the hallway. He thought better of this arrangement, and asked one of them to go first. He had no idea where he was going—another small flaw in his plan—but it was a big house.

The guard behind him was a friendly sort, despite being on duty through most of the early morning hours. He yawned prodigiously at times, but he chatted to his companions quite cheerfully.

"I don't blame you for wanting to see your horse, sire," the soldier said. "He's a beauty. I'd give a lot to own a horse like that. But he doesn't seemed to have fared any worse for his time astray. Captain Zoc and Lord Whitefeld went down to see him when they heard he'd wandered back, and they said the same. He flew into a panic at the sight of them, though. I hope you don't find him skittish after all that."

"Not to me, I'd think." William was not surprised by the information, but his enemies' interest in Blazer's reappearance still worried him.

"You'd know best, sire. Personally, I'm not much good with horses. I can ride, of course, but I fight better standing on my own two feet."

The foremost guard, named Elix, agreed. "We weren't trained to be cavalry, though, Hart," he added.

"True. We're watchmen. We were just trained to..." he yawned, "stay awake." The two guards shared a long laugh at this. William knew they were only joking. These were some of the most talented warriors in the Empire. For the first time, he considered how lucky he was to have such men guarding him. Then he thought that was silly. Luck? It was because of who he was. These men were the King's Guard. They served the Tellors, and only the Tellors.

"Just out of curiosity, did you hear anything last night, my lord, while you were sleeping? We heard some noises from outside a few hours past midnight, and we wondered."

William's heart raced at this. "What sort of noises?"

"Voices. Do you talk in your sleep, sire?" Elix laughed.

William responded, "I don't know; maybe I do. I didn't hear anything, though." He felt guilty lying, but what could he do?

"The captain said we should have checked, but we didn't want to wake you up, seeing as how you weren't feeling well. He's worried about everything now, the Captain is. He's even double-checking whether your room is secure."

"He *should* worry," Elix pointed out. "We failed in our duty. Our lives are already forfeit when we go home." That sobered Hart. Elix shot a furtive look at the prince, but said nothing more.

"It wasn't your fault," William told them. "It was mine. And I'll tell the King that. If I have any say, you all will be fine.

Anyway, it doesn't matter. I'm all right now. I won't be venturing out into the forest again." He hoped this would prove true. He didn't want to deal any further with the *ona* than he had to.

They were quiet after this. They reached the side of the house and walked outside toward the stables, their shoes crunching the gravel path. William was glad it wasn't mud. He'd had those blasted riding boots burned—they would never have come clean.

They entered the stable without any fuss. It was still fairly early, so there weren't many servants about. Most were busy feeding the many horses that resided in the stable. The Governor's stables likely served his militia.

Elix asked one of the grooms to show them to Blazer's stall. The man bobbed his head in assent, but he didn't seem to realize who William was. Maybe he didn't expect the prince to be up, but the lack of deference pricked William's pride nonetheless.

He escorted them to Blazer and then left. William was happy to see Blazer. The big black horse seemed quite pleased himself. He responded enthusiastically to William's touch. The prince smiled.

"Hi, Blazer. Nice to see you, too, boy. Glad you made it back okay." At least he knew Auria kept her promises.

He paused as he heard two grooms walk by, talking softly to each other. They were a few stalls over.

He knew it was bad, but he had developed a keen ear for eavesdropping over the course of his life. He told himself he was just in the right place at the right time, but really, he *wanted* to listen. Maybe it was because no one was ever honest if they knew he was listening and just told him what they thought he wanted to hear. He wanted to know what they *really* thought.

So he immediately tuned in to their conversation.

"Did you hear about Lam?" one asked.

"No, what about him?"

"He's going to *dissent*."

The way he said that drew the prince's attention. The man sounded aghast, even terrified, like dissent was another word for suicide.

"No!" the other responded vehemently. "He wouldn't!"

"He says he will. No one can convince him otherwise."

"What about *Auria*?" This was barely a whisper. William strained to hear. Blazer tossed his head.

"I don't know."

"He can't! No one has dissented for five years! You remember what happened to Reelif! They killed his whole family."

"Lam's fully set. He's a widower now; he has nothing to lose. His children fled to the Nest two years ago."

"It won't do any good! Doesn't he know that?"

"Of course he does. He just can't lie anymore, he says. He's a fool. They'll kill him."

"What decided him?"

"The prince, I think. It's different seeing a royal actually *here*. He says he's tired of lying to his King. And there's the raids this morning."

"The King never hears any of it. Curse that stupid ambassador! He's a fool! Were they as bad as last time?"

"No one was killed, and no homes were burned. They have to be careful, at least, when the ambassador is here."

"Did anyone talk?"

"What would they say? No one knows anything about her anyway—she brings us food, shows up to protect or comfort us, then she's gone. We don't know where she is. Even those who run to the Nest don't know where they're going until she finds them. The Nest could be anywhere."

"Ewen might know. So might Ayel."

"They targeted Betta. Poor girl. She'll not be working this next month. And for what? She didn't know anything."

"It's just because of her brother. Poor girl. It's hardly her fault."

"Dero was never the subtlest lad. He should have taken her with him."

"She wouldn't go. My Aggy told me."

"Poor lass."

"They'd have beaten her to death if the Ëan hadn't showed up. Then the devils were too busy trying to follow an invisible trail—bless Auria."

"But what about—"

They stopped abruptly as a shout rang through the stable. One of Zoc's men barked an order for the hands to get back to work. The two servants ran off immediately. William stepped behind Blazer, hoping the soldier wouldn't notice him. He didn't want to attract attention, especially after what he'd just heard. The man, impressive in his black uniform, paused to regard those in red. Elix and Hart, sensing William's desire to remain undiscovered, acted natural enough to dispel the soldier's suspicion. He passed them by, to William's immeasurable relief.

The Tellorian guards turned to William. Elix looked seriously at him. "My lord," he asked, "what was that about?"

They had heard the servants too. It was all over their faces. They looked as appalled as he did, but more confused.

"Please," he answered quietly, "don't ask me. Forget you heard anything, all right? And don't tell Tiran." If he couldn't hide the truth from his own guards, how could he hide it from the Governor or Zoc?

Hart and Elix glanced at each other. They were smart. They knew something was going on. If they nosed too far, they would overturn the whole plan. Worst case scenario, they would be killed and lies sent back to the King. Best case scenario, they would end up stuck in Belond, enjoying the hospitality of the King's most loyal outlaw, and lies would still be sent back to the King. William wasn't even sure the best case was much better. He didn't relish the thought of living in the Eagles' Nest.

No. He had to get back home.

"Please, just trust me," he pleaded. They remained as stoic as before. He sighed. "Let's just go," he said. He couldn't do this anymore. It was too much pressure on him. If the

Governor was willing to slaughter peasants to further his schemes, why not princes?

They walked back up to the house and ran right into one of the prince's absolute favorite people.

Lord Elber was going out again with the royal officials on who knew what diplomatic procedure. William hadn't seen him since before that dreadful day in the forest, and he didn't want to. The man was exasperating.

So much for any secrecy. The whole island was going to know he'd been out.

The Edenian party erupted into greetings when they saw him, congratulating him and asking him a thousand things at once. All at the same time, they empathized with him about his terrible experience. He put them off, claiming fatigue. It was hard to escape them, but with the help of Elix and Hart, he managed to scare them off, much to his relief. In his current state, those empty-headed nobles were the last people he wanted to talk to.

He practically ran back through the house to his room. Funny, a few minutes ago, his room was the last place he'd wanted to be. Now, it seemed like the safest, most comfortable place he could go.

"Slow down, my lord," Elix pleaded. He and Hart were struggling to maintain their dignified decorum and still walk quickly. William just told them to keep up.

He got lost. It was a big house, after all! He ended up in a strange hallway that he'd thought was the one to lead to his room. He should have reached it by now. He stopped, near panic.

For some reason, he felt terrified. He had grasped something of the Governor's real nature for himself, with more evidence than Auria's word alone. If this hadn't seemed real to him before, it did now. This wasn't just superstition or a children's story. It was really happening. People were suffering, dying—and he might be next.

Hart caught his arm, steadying him. "Calm down, sire. Everything's perfectly all right. You're just overexcited." Hart had no idea. "Come, we're just a bit turned around. We'll get back to your chamber in a minute."

"We'll find a servant to escort us back," Elix reassured. "You just need to rest. You're not thinking clearly."

That was true enough. He again pictured Auria's disdainful frown, and his pride helped him regather his demeanor.

"Sorry," he murmured.

"It's quite all right, sire, but come along now."

They took the lead, looking for a porter. His guards were lost, too, which was not encouraging. The hallway was strangely empty. They could not find anyone.

They wandered down the passage, soon growing all the more confused until they weren't sure where they'd come in. It was a strange corridor, unlike any of the others they'd seen in the house. It was out of place in the brightly decorated, stately house. There were odd objects affixed to the walls, like old tarnished weapons or pieces of wood and cloth. It looked more like a dungeon than a palace.

The guards were already worried by what they'd heard and William's reaction to it. They grew increasingly grave as their surroundings grew more ominous.

Finally, they heard low voices drifting from a room near the end of the hallway. Elix started eagerly forward to ask them for help, but William grabbed his arm and pulled him back, shaking his head furiously. His hands shook. He knew now why the hallway was empty.

It was the Governor and Zoc, clearly holding some sort of council together.

He wanted to run, to flee as far away as possible. But he couldn't. Not when he heard what they were talking about. Instinctively, he leaned forward to listen.

"I'm telling you," Zoc said, "He's lying."

"And I told you—you have no proof."

"I shouldn't have to prove it. Guilty until proven innocent, my lord, and the guilty must be disposed of. It's too risky not to kill him—you agreed to that in the first place. What if she got to him? I think she did. He's been acting suspicious."

"He's an idiot. The fool is little better than a child. He hasn't got an ounce of fight in him. Maybe she thought it would be little use trying to send a message through him. And if she wanted to keep him alive, she wouldn't try."

"But what if she did, and he talks? It would be your head. All of our heads. We've been safe for fifteen years; you can't let your guard down now! You have to kill him!"

"It's not that easy this time! It's a lot more trouble to kill the son of the King than it is to kill any other nobleman. It would draw the King's attention, and then what? If he doesn't know anything, just pack him off home."

"It's too dangerous! Who knows what he knows?"

"The girl is the only one who does. She's been playing us. I told you, I want her caught. Then we can find out once and for all. The ship will keep him here long enough for us to get to her."

"*Really?* After six years, you think I can catch her in a couple of weeks?"

"You have eight-hundred men! She has less than a hundred!"

"I'm trying! It's not that easy. No, in fact, it's impossible! We've tried everything, but even when we catch sight of her, we can't get close. She just disappears! I'm beginning to believe what they say about her. Maybe that niece of yours *is* a goddess!"

Niece?

That word snapped William out of his reverie. He had wondered from their first meeting who Auria really was, but she had never told him. And she'd also never told him *who* had taken Andel's place.

He had never suspected the two were *related*.

He couldn't go on wondering. He needed the truth, the whole truth. He needed to know what he was facing. The Governor was ruthless, willing to do anything to have his way, including killing William.

Why? Who *was* he? What did he hope to gain?

There was only one person he could ask.

Conscious of his danger, he backed away, making as little sound as possible. He didn't need to hear any more of what they said. Hand trembling, he beckoned for Elix and Hart to follow him. They looked shocked, angry, and even a little afraid. They were only too willing to follow the prince.

They ran back down the hallway. They wandered for a terrifyingly long time, still lost, until they finally found a chamberlain. They enlisted his help, and he led him back to the prince's room. The three men burst into the bedroom and shut the door behind them.

"My lord," Hart stammered, "what is going *on*? Did we just hear what I think we just heard?"

"We've had it backward," Elix said angrily. "And you knew, sire. Why didn't you tell us that Lord Whitefeld was a traitor?"

William wished he had, but it was out now anyway. Maybe they could help him.

"I was scared," he confessed. "Now you know."

"What's happening?" Hart asked.

"I don't have all the answers," William said. "Auria was not exactly forthcoming." They already knew enough. He would tell them the rest. There was nothing else to do.

"Auria?" they both said incredulously at the same time.

He nodded shakily. "The outlaw chief. She owes me more information." He fingered the red stone in his pocket, then he put it decidedly on the dresser. "And she'll give it."

He looked his confused guards in the eye. "And I owe you more, but first we should find Captain Tiran. We have a lot to talk about."

Chapter 11

William had never seen Tiran so furious. He was not angry at the prince, but at himself.

The honorable captain considered the whole situation an unforgivable lapse on his part. He was irate upon hearing how depraved the Governor was, and he promised to see Edenian authority restored, but first and foremost he was determined to protect the prince.

He favored hiding—any way to quickly distance William from such a threat. But William had to convince him that it was better for them to remain and act unsuspecting, that there was still hope of getting home.

Secretly, William wanted to hide, too, no matter how he felt about the *ona*. He was terrified, but he knew he needed to make it home.

He and Tiran both wanted more information, so despite William's better judgment, he allowed the captain to convince him that he should come along to meet Auria when she answered the prince's summons. Assuming she *did* answer, of course. He didn't think she'd be terribly pleased about it. Especially since he had told the captain what was really going on—but what choice had there been?

At Tiran's insistence, he spent the rest of the day in the captain's quarters, not his own. The captain didn't like the idea that someone could break into the prince's chamber. "If the outlaw can, someone else can," he stated. William got the sense that the captain didn't trust the *ona*. It was wise. William didn't entirely trust her, either. She was too dangerous and too unfamiliar to place unreserved confidence in her.

They were interrupted only by a few messengers. At each knock, William feared discovery, but nothing of the sort happened.

One brought word that the royal ship had been

sabotaged. It was leaking substantially and would take a long time to fix, though the workmen had not yet determined an exact prognosis. It was suspected that the outlaws were the perpetrators of this crime. William knew better, of course, but he displayed the proper reaction to the servant.

Another came to extend William an invitation to dine with Anjalia at noon. He declined, of course. He would have refused even without the *ona's* strange warning. The Governor's daughter, insipid though she was, made him nervous, as did most flirtatious girls.

Then one of Tiran's men, sent out in disguise to spy in the village, returned. The captain was nothing if not thorough, and he was a capable commander. The spy, named Eron, only repeated what the stable hands had said, but it was enough to corroborate William's account.

The day dwindled away under doubt and anxiety. After finishing their evening meal, Tiran said, "Well, sire... I suppose we must go and meet this outlaw friend of yours."

That wasn't quite how William would have described the woman, but he agreed without contesting the point. They reached his room without incident, walking quietly and flanked by two guards. It appeared no one suspected them of anything.

"You two stay out here, please," William requested. The two guards, named Rak and Pharin, nodded in acquiescence.

"I'm not sure when she's coming," William murmured to Tiran as he stepped inside, shutting the door behind them. "She could be here any time."

"Or she could be here already," a voice spoke.

William jumped visibly, and Tiran gasped, drawing his sword like lightning.

"Stand down, captain," the *ona* ordered forcefully. If William had thought the captain commanded an air of authority, this young woman made him look childish. "I'm in no mood for games. Besides, that sword will do you little good in a room like this. Not enough space."

She stepped forward as Tiran raised his lamp to shine it on

her. The brown leather mask obscured the upper half of her face, and the hood covered her golden hair. She looked every inch a roguish vagabond, not at all the image one would have conjured for a beautiful goddess. There was too much steel in her, and she did not bother with glamor—quite the contrary, as the dirt on her clothes and face attested. Her brow was lowered to give her a dark look, her mouth pursed into a hard line. She was not teasing tonight. Her green eyes were bloodshot, but they blazed with suppressed irritation.

"You are Auria?" Tiran asked quietly.

"Or Ëa ona," she added with a touch of pride. "Yes. And you are Captain Tiran. Another of William's many nursemaids. I pity you."

William blushed, but Tiran looked shocked. "How dare you—" he started to say, but she cut him off with a sound.

"Spare me," she barked at him. She turned to the prince, and he had to restrain himself from gulping. She was furious, and he did not enjoy being the object of her fury.

"What do you mean by calling me here?" she demanded. "I am not your servant to come at your every whim. I have important business to attend to! Do you think you are my only concern?"

She was entirely different from when he'd seen her last. Then, she had been playful, if mocking, but tonight, she was just angry. He didn't know how to respond.

"What happened?" he asked in a small voice.

She growled at him. "The Governor has stirred up a hornet's nest," she answered, "and I must collect all the hornets and take the stings. Yet I stand here talking to a blithering coward! Idiot!"

She was angry, all right. And from the look of her, completely exhausted.

"You mean the raids?" he ventured.

"How do you know about *that*? I told you not to go nosing around!"

"I wasn't trying," he protested. "It was an accident."

"Well then yes, love," she snapped. "He's pillaging and

beating the townspeople to get to me. It's happened before, but he's using renewed force this time. The people can't defend themselves, and most of the time they're too frightened to anyway. Threats are generally enough to get his way—they know he can back them up."

"You defend the people?" Tiran asked in admiration, though his spies had told him that was rumored.

She regarded him. "When I'm not cleaning up after the nobility, yes, Captain." She used *his* title. *Not fair*, William thought.

"It should not be," Tiran lamented. "None of this should be."

"That's Edenian justice, for you," she answered coldly. "If the King knew, it would be different, but the Empire has only ever cared what it can get out of Belond, not what is best for the island itself. And even if Edenia *was* paying attention, our communication has been effectively barred. The King has no idea what's going on here."

"We will help you," Tiran promised. "I am the King's servant. I will not see his name dishonored by these men."

"And you serve him well," she replied, softening. She was not quite as polite as Edenian etiquette would have demanded, but she treated Tiran with more respect than she did William. "I am different. I serve first Belond, then Edenia, then the King. But I think our object is the same."

"Consider the King's guard your ally," he stated, finally sheathing his weapon. For some reason, he'd decided to trust Auria.

"Wonderful," she replied. William couldn't tell whether she was being sarcastic or not. "But don't do anything drastic, all right? It won't help. Just stick to the plan. I already told William what he should be doing. He should never have dragged you into this. It's still possible it won't work."

"So far it is," William answered peevishly. He winced at how childish he sounded. It was a pitiful complaint. That was the idea, wasn't it? Even if he *was* miserable, she'd done her part well enough.

She glared at him, hands on her hips. "Why do I bother with you, love?"

He couldn't frame an answer that didn't sound as childish as before.

"Too late you learn restraint," she scolded fiercely. "You should have been so careful all along."

"I'm doing my best, *ona*," he said as placatingly as he could, "but I'm not used to this sort of thing. And you haven't told me everything I need to know."

Her frown deepened. "*That's* why you brought me here?"

"Yes?" It came out more as a question than a statement. Her mouth dropped open a little. He tried to make his voice firmer, summoning all his Tellorian dignity. "I need answers, Auria." For some reason, everything seemed different to him when she turned those blazing eyes on him. His concerns looked petty and inconsequential, even to him. His earlier resolve wavered.

Then he thought of the misery of his ignorance, and he knew he could bear no more uncertainty. If he was going to defy a murderer and make it home, he needed to know everything.

And in the back of his mind, he still wanted to see Lis. Just for a minute. Even a minute would be worth it.

"Please," he added after a moment.

She did not soften. "I told you. If I tell you the whole truth, you won't believe me."

"I will, I know I will."

"Ha."

"Everything you've told me so far has been true."

"I am no liar, love." The epithet was more an insult than a tease this time. "Yet there are some things I do not say."

"Why not?"

She glared at him.

"Who do you think you are?" he demanded. "I mean it. Who are you? Why are you doing this?"

"I am the *ona* of the *Ëan*. I fight for the people of Belond and for justice. That is all that matters."

"No, I mean who *are* you? I know that the Governor is your uncle!"

She actually looked surprised. "How do you know that?" she asked softly.

He grew sheepish. "My guards and I got lost. We overheard Zoc talking with the Governor. Zoc called you his niece."

"You did *what*?"

"I'm sorry, all right? It wasn't on purpose."

"You're a fool!" she fumed.

"You haven't said it's not true."

She sighed angrily.

"You are, aren't you? You're his niece." The thought repulsed him, but it was a paradox. These two were mortal enemies, yet they were close relatives. "Who *are* you?" he asked again. "Who is *he*? How did all this happen?"

She was stubbornly silent, though William and Tiran both looked expectantly at her. She drew her mouth in a tight line and crossed her arms. Her eyes blazed in anger.

As he looked her right in the face, it hit him, with all the force of a physical blow.

He knew her. He should have seen it before.

He'd been a fool. It was written in every line of her, from the stubborn determination, charismatic leadership, and fierce passion to her strong build, golden hair, and green eyes. He should have recognized her long before. Who else had such traits?

"Karia Whitefeld," he breathed. It was almost an accusation.

The way her jaw hardened confirmed his guess. He knew he was right. She was as much a Whitefeld as a Whitefeld could be.

"You survived," he stated incredulously. Even Tiran seemed shocked by William's pronouncement.

"You have a tremendous ability to observe the obvious, love," she mocked dryly.

"They said—"

"They lied. I have already told you. Everything the Governor told your father is a lie."

He reeled. He hadn't expected this.

"I need the whole truth. Please, Karia."

"Do *not* call me that!" she snapped.

"But that's your real name!"

"Not anymore. I ceased to be Karia Whitefeld fifteen years ago."

This statement made him feel sad. He had lost a mother; what had she lost? She should have been a noblewoman in Ossia, with wealth, opportunity, and a family around her. Now here she was, with next to nothing.

"I am not a pompous noble," she snarled, as if reading his thoughts. "I *earn* my respect. I have chosen my own path and made my own name, and I am who I am because I choose to be. Can you say the same, William Tellor?"

"Tell me the real story," he said quietly, not rising to her question.

She glared some more, but he was determined. She sighed. "Fine, love," she conceded. "You win." He opened his mouth to thank her, but she held up a hand. "But *I* won't tell you. You should hear it from the one who remembers it better. I think you'd believe *her* more readily anyway."

Lis? His face lit with longing. He would *see* her?

"You'll take me to her?"

"Not now. When I can return. And you'll follow *my* instructions and agree to *my* terms, understand?"

"Yes, *ona*," he said compliantly.

"It is dangerous," she warned, looking now at Tiran.

"Could you not tell him yourself?" the captain asked reluctantly. "I would not wish to tempt fate."

"It is better this way, trust me. I am nothing if not careful," she assured, "and I would do nothing to endanger my aunt. Anyone can make mistakes, but he ought to be safe with me, Captain."

Tiran considered, still reticent. He looked to the prince, who pleaded silently with the captain. *Please*, he mouthed. His mother! He had to see her.

Tiran sighed. "I suppose it will have to be risked. It is for the best."

William smiled with relief, letting his gratitude show through.

"She'll be happy to see you," the *ona* told William, an odd note entering her voice. "Though it makes her position complicated."

"I want to see her. More than anything."

"Mm-hm." The *ona* turned away. "I'll come back when I can, but I have to leave now. I have *important* matters to attend to."

"Thank you, *ona*," he said sincerely.

"Right, love," she answered.

"I am sorry to be a trouble to you, *ona*," Tiran apologized. "The king will thank you for this."

She nodded. "Just don't call me again unless it's an emergency, all right?"

She strode toward the far side of the room.

"Where are you going?" William asked in confusion. She couldn't get out that way, unless she jumped from the window—but they were on the third floor.

For the first time that night, a spark of that mischievous light came into her eyes. She cast him a devilish smile. "I have many ways in and out of this house," she told him knowingly. She opened the window, letting in a blast of cool wind. It was quite dark outside, as there was no moon.

She stepped onto the sill and leaned out. Both Tiran and William started forward, afraid she would fall. She just flashed that same wild smile back at them, laughing at their concern.

She gave a soft call, eerily close to that of a bird. After a brief pause, she looked behind her. "I'll be back," she promised. Then she threw herself from the window.

Both men gasped and ran to the window, only to be blasted by a flurry of wings.

Auria soared away in the claws of her eagle, Talon. No one in the house was any the wiser that she had visited.

Chapter 12

It was two days before she returned, but despite William's discomfort, the prince didn't blame her—that much.

Tiran's reconnaissance had determined that Zoc's men were conducting secret forays into Belo, the farms, and the mines, often brutally mistreating the people that fell into their hands. Their raids were always meant to bring out the Ëan, and without fail, they did. But the outlaws would rush to the rescue and then melt away into nothing before they could be pursued.

What Tiran told William, he always related with admiration. He had clearly grown to esteem Auria highly. Everyone spoke of her and her flock of followers with awe. She was their hero. Her name could not be spoken aloud, but it was whispered on every tongue at all hours. The Belondians depended upon her faithfulness to rescue them.

She hadn't lied when she said she was a busy girl.

Still, he awaited her return with impatience. His nervousness had not abated; his curiosity had not faded; but now, he was also filled with anticipation. He could not wait to hear those long-awaited answers, and he also longed to see Lis again.

Ironically, when she did show up, he wasn't expecting her. She once again shook him out of his sleep, well past midnight.

"Wake up, love," she hissed at him. He started awake in surprise, but soon he realized who it was.

"Why do you always do that?" he complained.

"I work around the clock, love. Now get up. If you want to see my aunt, you'd best get moving."

She threw him his clothes. He hoped she wouldn't see him blushing. He was wearing a nightshirt, but still. She turned her back while he got dressed.

"Let me tell you my conditions," she said while he pulled his clothes on. "First, you will follow my instructions to the letter. Do what I do, and remain silent until I tell you—or it's your head. Second, you are not to speak with Lis at any time other than when I take you. Should you see her elsewhere, you will act as if she doesn't exist. You do not know her. Third, you will not try to visit her without me. That would be inviting disaster.

"This is not only to protect you, but also Lis. She doesn't know we're coming. Her position is... *awkward* with you here. The Governor could easily decide she's too much of a risk to keep in the open. If you fail to agree, I'm leaving right now. Do I have your word?"

He could see her hand fingering her knife even in the dark. He'd seen what she could do with it. Only a fool would cross this woman. "I agree," he answered.

"Good. Are you ready?"

"Yes."

She turned around. "Here. Put this on." She tossed him something firm. He caught it, fumbling. It was a mask like the *Ëan* wore. "Just in case," she added. "And pull your hood up."

He did as he was told. The hood and mask made him feel like some hero out of a story, an unfamiliar sensation.

"Perfect," she muttered. It was hard to determine whether she mocked him or not. "Let's go. Remember, not a sound."

He desperately wanted to ask where they were going, but he didn't dare. He wondered whether he'd have to fly with the eagle. The idea chilled him.

But she didn't head toward the window. Instead, she moved toward the corner. There was no exit besides the window and doors—what was she doing?

Or was there?

She bent down, and though he could not see, he heard her move something. He suddenly realized what she was doing. He nearly laughed aloud.

The Governor had invested the money into giving his house a heating system. Now Auria was ruthlessly exploiting the product of his greed. If she crawled through the vents, she could get anywhere in the house.

But that still didn't explain how she got into the house.

"Follow me exactly," she whispered. Then she wormed her way in.

Though it made him nervous, William followed.

He didn't enjoy the vents at all.

They were dark, cramped, and dirty. It didn't help that he had to move soundlessly while keeping up with the *ona*, who had much more experience when it came to crawling through heating vents. She kept turning through the system without hesitation when William was hopelessly confused. He wondered how she could possibly be leading them outside.

At least he didn't run into any spiders' webs. If there were any, Auria would have plowed through them first.

At last, he saw a faint light bouncing off the narrow walls up ahead. He hoped this was a good sign.

The *ona* stopped facing a grate like the one in his room. She craned her neck to look back at him, and he could see her mouth form the word "stay" with a firm nod. Then she almost silently eased the grate off and slipped out of the vent. He crawled forward to look out.

They were obviously still in the Felds, but they had just passed over to another chamber. William had expected her to lead him into the village. Why were they *here*?

It was a small room. There was just a bed with a single occupant, a dresser, a few chairs, and a closet. Not as poor, certainly, as some might have, but nothing impressive.

He watched the *ona* move across the room. There was a candle burning on the dresser, but she was still hard to follow. She seemed to pick out the shadows and blend into them. Even looking right at her, it was hard to see her.

She reached the bed and leaned over the sleeper. "Wake up," he heard her whisper softly. "It's me."

Lady Elissana had been in the Felds the whole time? She *lived* here? He could have seen her at any time! How had he missed her? How had the diplomatic party missed her all these years?

He waited impatiently in the vent as Lis stirred and awoke in response.

"Ria?" she said sleepily.

"Yes."

She sat up and then swung her feet over the side of the bed. "I didn't expect to see you," she said in surprise. "I thought you'd be run off your feet!" She stood. "But I'm glad you've come, of course."

William's heart rose to hear her voice again. It sounded just like he remembered, warm and gentle.

"Let me look at you, darling," she said to the *ona*. "Take that awful mask off. I want to *see* my girl."

Auria complied, if reluctantly.

"Beautiful as ever," Lis said. "It's been a while, dear. How are you? You look exhausted."

"I'm all right," Auria brushed off the concern.

"Have you been getting any sleep?"

"Not really," she confessed.

"Food?"

"I'm fine, Aunt, really."

"But—"

"Listen, I only came because I brought someone to see you."

"What?" Lis asked in confusion. "Who? Ovan?"

Auria walked back to the vent. "Come on out now, love," she said, beckoning. "But keep it quiet." He crawled out eagerly.

Lis gasped as he got to his feet. He pulled the mask and hood off and looked straight at her. "William!" she exclaimed softly as she gazed at him. He suddenly found he couldn't move. Every concern or fear melted away as he stared back at her. All of a sudden, he was seven years old again on the day that his mother sailed away, remembering the way she looked, how sad her face had been. It was the same beautiful face staring back at him now.

He remembered those beautiful green eyes, once filled

with laughter, but now tears. He remembered the smell of her long dark hair when she would pick him up as a little boy. She seemed small to him now that he was grown, since she was a very slender woman, especially standing beside her tall niece. She was painfully thin and worn by the years, but she still possessed a queen's dignity, even without the fine jewels and clothes. She had once been the greatest beauty in Ossia, well worthy of the King of Edenia. She had the look of a Whitefeld, if not the golden hair.

He cursed himself for not having recognized her sooner.

She'd been Anjalia's attendant that first night at the dinner table, the one who'd stared at him in shock. The strange actions of the Governor and his captain made sense now, as did the *ona*'s warning to avoid Anjalia's company. How could William have looked right at her and not known who she was?

A silent tear traced her cheek. She extended her arms to him.

"Mother," he said softly and rushed into her embrace. He felt like a child again, but not the child he had been. How he had longed for a mother.

She held him for a while, every bit as overwrought as he was. It had been a long fifteen years.

"I didn't think I'd ever see you again," he said when they separated.

"I hoped. Truly, I did. Oh, I've missed you! How I longed to go home, son, but I am trapped here. I failed you—forgive me. If I could change it now, I would. Look at you! You've grown up without me! You're a man now, William!"

"He thinks he is," Auria muttered in the corner. She remained unmoved by their emotional greeting. Her hardness grated on him in that moment, but Lis acted like she hadn't heard.

"You look just like your father—in truth, I thought you *were* him that night I first saw you. You've grown so handsome! Just like a Tellor!"

He smiled, feeling as bashful as a child given a rare

compliment.

"How is your brother? And—your father?" She faltered on the last question, mixed emotion in her face.

"Arthos is fine—he's off in Svetana right now. He'll make a good King someday; he's a good leader. Father depends on him."

"How is your father?" Lis asked again.

"He still misses you," William answered plainly.

"He is unhappy?"

"He is not himself, as he used to be. He does his duty, but when he takes off the crown, he's just a man. There's no real life in him anymore, and he's gotten worse, not better."

"I think of him all the time," she said heavily. "It breaks my heart what he has endured."

"What happened?" William questioned. "We thought—I thought you were dead. I can still scarcely believe it, but how is it possible?"

"Has Ria not told you?"

"I told him what he needed to know," Auria answered.

"Ria!" Lis scolded.

"What? I know what you think of him, but I'll make my own judgment. I don't live in a world of sentimentality, Lis. I see things as they are. To me, he's a helpless little boy I can't trust to be quiet or act intelligently. He hasn't earned anything from me."

"Why do you focus so much on *earning* respect, darling?" Lis asked as severely as such a gentle woman could.

"Because that is reality," she responded coldly. "You can't be born into respect. The Ëan do not care whether you are young, old, male, female, dark, light, noble, or common. You are judged by your character and by your actions. Only that. I don't see titles, or family ties, or sentiment, just the proven worth of the person. That is all. William hasn't earned my respect. What I did for him, I did only so that he may help Belond."

Lis looked at her in silent disapproval. "And because it was the right thing to do," Auria added with a sigh. "I may yet live to see the King thank me for it. And I would not refuse what you ask of me, aunt. You can tell him; it doesn't matter anymore. Satisfy his curiosity, and then maybe he'll quit pestering me."

Lis's frown melted away. "I worry about you sometimes, but you've turned out well, Ria," she said with a smile. "Those people don't deserve all the effort you spend on them. They don't realize what it costs you."

"It doesn't matter," Auria said. "I'd do it anyway. Service isn't always about recognition. I am called. Besides, who else would do it?"

"They'd follow no one else, Ria." Auria didn't reply, she just shrugged.

There was a note of tension between the two women, but their hearts were in the same place. They were cut from the same cloth.

"I shall tell you the story, William," Lis said to him. "Though I hate to think of it. But we must see you safely home to tell your father, and then we can be happy again. The King will set everything right."

William noted Auria's tightened expression as Lis pronounced this hope with such faith, but she did not comment.

"Come, sit," Lis invited. He took one small chair, and she took the other. Auria walked over and flopped irritably on Lis's bed.

"If you don't mind," she said to them, "I'm going to take a nap. The spider on the wall over there will warn us if any of my friends see someone coming." William shivered at the mention of a spider, but she seemed unconcerned. "Talk away," she said to Lis, and then she turned over to go to sleep.

Chapter 13

Lis settled into her chair next to William. She pulled a shawl close about her shoulders against the cold, then she began.

"Well," she said, "you remember when we left for Belond fifteen years ago—no," she reconsidered, "I must go further back."

She blew a strand of her long hair out of her face and began again. William was all ears.

"When I was a little girl," she said, "I lived on the Whitefeld estate—just upriver from Ossia. I'm sure you know it. My mother and father would often sail to the city for months while my father was at court, so we children were left alone much of the time. Back then, I had two brothers." Seeing William's surprise, she added, "Not many people know that. They were both much older than me. Andel was six years older, Jeron four. Still, we were fairly close as siblings. Andel was more like a father to me, in some ways, because ours wasn't around much due to his work in the government. I think I rather idolized Andel. Jeron was a little more distant—he didn't get along well with Andel even when we were young.

"We lived next to the Arnaugh estate. It was only a few miles away, so we would constantly go back and forth. There were a few children in that family that we played with: two boys and a girl. They were all older than me, though. The youngest was Seyenne, who was four years older than me. We would all go romping around together, as children do. Seyenne was my best friend, despite the age difference—like the older sister I didn't have. Andel and Jeron both doted on her, too. She was a beautiful girl, so very bright..."

Lis cleared her throat after a moment's silence and continued. "We got older. My mother died of a fever when I was ten. Losing her changed the family entirely. My father grew hard and intractable, completely closed to us children. He was grieving, so it's understandable, but it was still difficult for us. He was gone even more often after that.

"It changed us, too. Andel grew more serious, wanting to take on responsibility and take care of everything. I think our mother said something like that to him right before she died—about taking care of the family and us younger children. It made him absolutely impossible to sway when it came to doing his duty. He was determined to make her proud of him.

"Jeron was just the opposite. He grew restless and wild. Nothing would curb his behavior. I won't even tell you some of the trouble he got into—he did awful things, sometimes. He hated Andel and his sense of duty. He just wanted to make himself happier. He couldn't.

"We tried to move on. Andel went to school and then to Ossia to work in the government, like all sons of nobility. He met your father there. Eduar always said that he liked it that Andel was so humble. He didn't flaunt his title or play up to Eduar's. He acted like a normal person, and he was proud of it. I think that's where Ria picked up her opinions." She added this last statement aside. "Don't mind her harshness, William—she really does mean well."

"I suppose," he conceded noncommittally.

Lis sighed, but didn't press the point. "Anyway—where was I? Oh, Andel at school. Well, when he came back, he went to the Arnaugh family to ask to marry Seyenne. Seyenne had told me in confidence that he'd asked her before, but they were waiting until he was in a position to make a formal offer to her parents. He was twenty-one; she was nineteen. Her parents were thrilled. Our name is a privileged one, I suppose, so it was an advantageous match, and Andel was responsible and already had a promising career. They arranged the wedding for the next year. Our father was pleased, too. He liked the way Andel observed protocol and decorum and how he advanced himself wisely.

"At this point, Jeron went utterly wild. He'd spent three

months at school, but he'd been expelled, so he was back home and a thousand times worse. Father despised him, constantly comparing him to Andel's spotless behavior. Father imposed punishment after punishment on him, but nothing helped. He only got worse. It was hard to watch.

"Andel and Seyenne's betrothal was the last straw for Jeron. Secretly, he'd always loved her, too. He had tried to win her, but what woman would fall for a man who doesn't even know who he is?

"He grew violent. He and Andel actually fought one time. Poor Andel—he felt horrible, but what could he do? Jeron was ready to kill him. They were both talented fighters, but this was just a brawl, a fistfight. I don't know who would have won if my father hadn't pulled them apart.

"The fight was what pushed my father to his limit. He took everything that belonged to Jeron except the clothes on his back and disowned him. Jeron was cast out with nothing, just like that. I have never seen such an uproar. My father told him he was a disgrace and never to come back.

"I have to say he deserved it, but I pleaded bitterly with Father to give him one more chance. He dismissed me completely, saying I should learn not to question my elders and betters. To put me back in my place, the next month, he arranged for me to marry Lord Wilifred Hollen, a man whose father mine wanted to appease. I was horrified, of course. I didn't even know him well. He was eight years older than me and a disgusting brute. Andel tried to help, but even he couldn't change father's mind. The wedding was arranged for my twentieth birthday, which just gave me a long time to be miserable.

"Andel married Seyenne, and they went to live in Ossia. I spent several awful years at home by myself, Lord Hollen coming to visit me at intervals. I liked him less each time. I saw Andel and Seyenne every once in a while. She came home while she was pregnant, so I was there when Ria was born. Ria's grandfather loved her dearly—spoiled her rotten. I think she softened his temper a little, but his health was already declining. He'd had heart trouble for years, and the stress was telling.

"Anyway, when I was nineteen, Andel convinced my father to let me come and stay with him, Seyenne, and Ria in the city. I was ecstatic. It was the loveliest idea I could have wished for. I had never been to court before.

"That's where I met your father," she said, blushing. "I remember perfectly." She paused. "I'm not boring you, am I? I know I can be a rambler."

"No! Of course not. I'm happy to listen."

"You're a sweet boy, William. Well, then, favor an old woman's sentimentality."

"You're not old," he protested. "You're what... Thirty-seven?"

"Mmm," she sighed. "Yes."

"Still in the prime of life," he told her cheerily.

She laughed. "If you say so. Anyway," she continued, "I met him at a banquet. It was for some visiting dignitaries from Svetana. Andel had been invited (he was the King's best friend!), and he contrived to bring me along. He insisted on introducing me to the King, even though I was a bit shy, and the idea of meeting someone so important scared me.

"He was... charming. I don't know what I expected, but he was just so real! He was friendly to me, not at all stuffy. Maybe it was because I was his friend's sister, I don't know. He was young and handsome, too, which always helps. He was just a few years older than you are now. He looked *just* like you.

"Andel had told both of us about each other, and with my brother there, it was hardly awkward at all. It was only when he asked me to dance that I felt nervous. He just laughed away my fumbles. I couldn't help liking him. He called me beautiful. That was quite a compliment for the King of Edenia to give to a nineteen-year-old girl. I was smitten.

"Andel was thrilled that I liked him, of course, but my father wasn't. Neither were all the ambitious ladies who flirted with the widowed King, many of them much wealthier or better-positioned than me. The Hollen family was especially displeased.

"I didn't care. I liked him too much to mind what other people said. I saw him many times, always with Andel, but my wedding date was approaching quickly.

"Eduar was as appalled as I was when he learned I was betrothed against my will. He married your mother the same way. I never knew Sylva, but I know they didn't really love each other. They were amiable enough and treated each other well, but it wasn't the same thing as love.

"Eduar didn't want that to happen to me, so he went to talk to my father. He didn't summon my father to see him in Ossia, he went himself. He was humble enough to speak reasonably to him without giving orders. He convinced my father to cancel the engagement. I don't know what he said, or what my father said to the Hollen family, but I never saw Wilifred again. Eduar was wonderful.

"He then asked my father's permission to court me. It was important to both of us that we take time to get to know each other after the experiences we'd had. I spent three years in Ossia living with Andel and Seyenne. The four of us had the happiest times when the men weren't involved in their duties. Sometimes Seyenne and I would go play with you boys and Ria. Do you remember that?"

He did. He darted a glance at Ria, now sound asleep. He remembered her as a fiery little girl, who, oddly enough, was better than him at *everything*, and didn't act like any other titled girl he'd ever met. Her proper mother would meticulously arrange her hair and clothes, and she'd tear the dress and put mud in her hair to make it stick straight up. Her aunt brought her toy dolls, but she ditched them and found sticks to make into swords. She was her daddy's girl, not a princess at all. When their fathers were around, they would all sword-fight. Ria had actually been good at it, unlike him. He'd never known what to make of her as a child.

He nodded. Not much had changed.

"I'm glad you do. Those were the best years."

"Yes," he agreed, "they were."

She threw him a sad smile. "Then you know what happened. My father and his brother both died within a month of each other, leaving the Governorship of Belond unfilled. My family was small. Andel was the only male heir to the Whitefeld name. He believed it was his duty to take up the Governorship, even though he had only been to Belond once. He had a promising career ahead of him in Ossia, but Belond *is* where our roots are. Besides, there was no one else who was willing to take the position.

"Eduar was devastated. Andel was his best friend, the only one he could really trust. He begged him not to go. Neither of them wanted it, but Andel was iron-willed when it came to his duty.

"Seyenne was upset, too. She didn't want to leave behind everything she'd ever known. More than that, she was worried about the journey. She'd just found out she was pregnant again, although she hadn't yet told Andel. She'd had trouble giving birth to Ria, so they hadn't planned to have any more children. She was worried about making the journey with her health, and she thought Andel would make her stay behind if he knew that. She dreaded being apart from him more than anything, especially in such a difficult time, so she didn't tell him. I don't know if he would have changed his mind if she had, but we'll never know. What's done is done.

"She asked me to come along to help her. Ria was always a handful for her to manage, and she was worried she wouldn't weather the trip well by herself. She was my best friend. What could I say? I certainly didn't want to go, but I had no choice. I couldn't deny her. We didn't think it would be long. I would go with her on the trip and return soon afterwards.

"Your father told me a flat no. So did Andel. They didn't understand, and although I was reticent about making the journey, I convinced them. I think Andel was secretly glad for my company.

"Eduar was beyond upset. He was losing his best friend

and his sweetheart at the same time. It broke my heart to leave him that way, but I promised I'd come right home. Not more than two months, if that. That's what we all thought.

"And so we left. Your father gave us one of his best ships and two squads of his own guards to accompany us. We had a few soldiers of our own and some servants. We took nearly everything from Andel and Seyenne's home in Ossia.

"It was a rough voyage. Seyenne was terribly ill the whole time, poor thing, but we all became seasick when a storm struck us in the middle of the trip.

"We had just pulled through the storm when we were attacked. A pirate ship came from the southeast. We guessed they had a base on one of the islands in that area. We didn't think they would dare attack a royal ship, but we were wrong. Two more ships emerged behind them, and we knew then that we were in trouble. It was horrible, William. I hope you never have to see a battle."

He'd already seen one. He thought of the ambush, just a few days past. He shuddered.

"They were stronger—though our men fought hard. The Tellorian guard was slaughtered. Only one of them survived.

"They caught us all and took us captive. I'd never been so frightened or horrified." She shivered. "Then their captain came on board."

"Jeron?" William guessed.

She nodded. "We never knew where he had gone. It had been seven years. He'd fallen in with foul men, but he was somehow successful enough to end up commanding his own force. He'd planned revenge all along. Seyenne thought he might have killed my father, perhaps poisoned him. I don't know. But he planned to usurp the Governorship of Belond when our uncle died. He said it was his birthright, or some such nonsense, and that Andel had stolen it from him. He wanted to take everything his brother had.

"He began to boast over us. Andel was furious, but he couldn't do anything. He'd taken a bad wound to his side, and we were all tied up, anyway. I remember Ria kicked Jeron when he passed her. She had knocked out two of his men, before, too—just a little girl. He learned not to underestimate her." She smiled, but it was a melancholy expression. "He wishes now that he'd killed her back then, I imagine. She has caused worlds of trouble for him.

"But he wasn't interested in us. Just Andel. He pulled my brother to the middle of the deck, and—" Here she broke off, trying not to cry. "Sorry," she apologized.

"It's okay," William soothed. "You don't have to say it." It had been pretty clear that Andel was dead, but now he knew for certain.

She steeled herself. "Right in front of us," she said angrily, "Jeron cut his head off. It was horrible. Seyenne shrieked endlessly. I was sobbing. Ria... she was steely silent. I've never seen a child react that way, but I know it broke her heart. I think it was the worst for her. She watched her father murdered right in front of her. What does that do to a child?"

William's gut twisted. How would he have felt? He saw Ria in a different light. Even after everything that she had lost, she still fought. That was not how he had reacted when he'd lost his mother. He'd never allowed himself to care enough to fight for anything ever again. Ria would fight to her last breath for justice.

But could she win?

William wanted her to. At that moment, he decided he would do anything he could to help. He thought of Tiran's promise. He could also take that vow. The Governor was a monster, who needed to be brought down.

"He decided to leave us alive," Lis continued. "Mostly because of Seyenne. He still wanted her, even after all that time. He agreed to spare me and Ria, too—but we would be servants, and no one could know who we really were. For his plan to work, we needed to be dead, or else the King would come looking for us. I became just 'Lis,' Seyenne's maidservant. Karia became just 'Ria,' my niece.

"Ovan was the only guard who survived—and that was because he joined them. Or pretended to. He told me he could protect us better from the inside. He would not fail in his duty by being uselessly killed. He handled himself well. The man is a saint. Have you met him? He's almost always with Ria."

"Briefly."

"He was our anchor. We were utterly bereft. I had no idea what to do. He looked out for me and Ria without fail. He gave us almost everything they ever gave him—food, money and the like. I don't think I would have survived without him.

"When we arrived, Jeron began a full-scale conquest. By pretending to be Andel, he secured the island by force and imposed his rule on it. He centralized all labor and wealth, making everyone practically slaves, and no one could leave the island. Zoc, his old first mate, was his chief instrument.

"He forced Seyenne to marry him. The poor girl was a wreck, understandably, and I could do little to help. She lost the baby. She didn't have the will to fight. But she conceived again, not long after. It was harder than before, and she was bedridden the whole time. She gave birth prematurely, and the effort killed her. I think losing her mother, though they weren't close, hurt Ria almost as much as losing her father. Seyenne didn't want to live anymore, and she was too distraught to care for her daughter. So was I. We both failed her. We were selfish. We should have done more for her instead of succumbing to grief, but we both blamed ourselves. Ria withdrew from me after that. She's completely independent now. She never lets anyone take care of her, me least of all.

"Anjalia survived, though, by some miracle. I helped care for her. That was how Jeron chose to employ me. I have stayed with Anjalia. At first, I had no choice, but now I choose to stay instead of hiding with Ria. Anjalia is my niece, too. The poor girl lives a shattered world of lies. She doesn't understand; she's just a child. I have tried to do what I can for her, but her father spoils her.

"He tolerates me, just as he had always done. I don't think he hates me as he hated Andel. I always loved him as my brother, even though he's done horrible things. I still hope he might come back to himself, but he's far gone. He's a greedy, cruel, selfish man—but my brother is still in there somewhere.

"I should have helped him all those years ago," she confessed. "I think I was the only one who could have. He was broken after our mother died, and there was no one to heal him. I tried, but it wasn't enough. I failed. I should have tried harder. It's still hard to remember it." She halted a moment, brooding, but then she went on.

"Ria is harder than I am," she continued. "She wants to see him brought to justice. She's determined to right all the wrongs he's done and heal Belond. I wonder if it will heal *her*, though. It won't bring her father back. She is the most unselfish girl I ever met. She's a hero. She's the only one who was willing to resist him, even when she was small."

"How did she go from being a servant girl to... *Auria*?"

"That is a tale I don't know well myself," she answered. "I scarcely saw her for those years. You'll have to ask her."

Nope. No way. He wasn't about to risk her yelling at him again.

He sighed. She smiled, sensing his reluctance. "Then you'll have to wonder. But now, at least, you know how all this came to be."

"Thank you, Mother. I know it's hard to think about. I'm sorry for what you've had to suffer."

"I am sorry for what *you've* suffered. I wish I could have been there for you. We should have been a family."

"It's not your fault, Mother. I'll go home and tell Father what's happened, and everything will be right again. You can come home, and Ria will have justice."

"Don't do anything foolish, William. You're in a dangerous position. He's ruthless. He *will* kill you. Don't make me bear that."

"I won't. But I *am* going to get you out of here." He *would*. He would bring his mother home.

She leaned forward to give him a hug. "Thank you, Son."

Chapter 14

They talked for hours, but William learned no more about her. Lis wanted to know about *him*. He told her, at her insistence, everything he could think of about Ossia. It had been fifteen years; there was plenty to tell. Lis hung on his every word—especially if he mentioned his father. She was starved for news of her home. She said she'd heard nothing of import in years. She was all ears for anything he had to say.

She was also a sympathetic listener. She actually appreciated the emotional trials he had endured in Belond, though he realized they were small in comparison. He tried to curb his complaining. After listening to her, he realized he was quite fortunate, and he felt honored to be the one to set things right. He *wanted* to help now. For his mother.

He was disappointed when Ria stirred, then sat up on the side of the bed. She yawned, gaining their attention. She stood and went to the window. She pulled the curtain away just a fraction of an inch to look out, then she turned back to William. "Sorry, time to go," she announced. "Morning is approaching."

He didn't want to leave.

Lis rose, smiling sadly. "It has done me more good than you know to see you, Son," she said to him. She did not question or protest her niece's words at all, like William wanted to do.

She spread her arms invitingly. He stood and embraced her. "I don't want to go," he murmured in her ear, hoping Auria would not hear.

She did, of course. "Sorry, love. If you'd like to get caught, you're welcome to stay. Besides, I think your loyal captain will realize that you're missing fairly soon."

"I told him to get some sleep," William said. "It took some convincing, but he did."

"Mm-hmm. I'd rather not alarm him unnecessarily, yes?"

He sighed. "All right."

"You'll be fine, William," Lis comforted. "You've got steel in you, Son—be brave. Ria will take care of you."

He hugged her close one more time, but it would never be enough. He sighed again and released her. "Goodbye," he said half-heartedly.

"El be with you," she answered softly.

William pulled his hood and mask back on. Ria did the same. The *ona* moved toward the vent.

"Ria!" Lis called softly.

She was the outlaw leader once more, but she still turned. "What?"

"Be safe, dear." She looked like she wanted to say more, but she didn't.

"I am never safe."

The words stung Lis. She pursed her lips. "I love you, Ria. Don't ever forget that."

Ria stiffened. Her jaw tightened, but she replied, "I know, aunt." She turned away, crouching to enter the vent.

William noted the tension between them, but was unsure of the cause. They'd argued briefly earlier, but was there more to the conflict between them?

"Goodbye, William. I love you," Lis murmured as he followed Ria.

He turned back a moment. "I love you, too." She smiled.

It wrenched him to leave her, but he had no choice. He had promised to see her home, and to do that, he had to follow the plan. He was leaving his mother behind, but he took new resolve with him. He entered the vents once more.

He emerged into his own room. He wondered how Ria managed to navigate the heating system with such accuracy, but he didn't ask.

He returned her mask. "Thanks, Karia," he said.

"I *told* you: don't call me that," she growled.

"But..." he protested, "it's how I used to know you."

"Used to, love. That was worlds away. My name is Auria

now."

"Can I call you *Ria*?" He liked the idea. When Lis had called her that, she seemed less frightening and more human. And he liked the sound of it when he said it himself.

She stiffened. Her face went flat. "That's what my parents called me," she informed him. "No one calls me that now but Lis, and sometimes Ovan."

He'd touched a nerve, but he kept going. "Are we friends?"

She arched an eyebrow.

"We used to be, when we were little." He said this without antagonizing. He understood her better now that he knew a little of her past. If she was hard, it was because she had to be. He no longer thought she was heartless. He loved Lis more, but Karia had once been close to him, too. He wanted to help her. He wanted to be her friend. "Are we friends *now*?" he asked again. He offered his hand. "I know you don't like me, but I want to improve. I promise to do whatever you ask to help you."

She ignored his hand, but she softened. "Help Belond," she said quietly. "Not me." She considered a moment. "Do that, and we will be friends," she decided. "But I'm watching you."

"Can I call you Ria?" he asked again.

She sighed. "Fine, love, but if you're among the Ëan or anyone else, I'm *ona* to you, understand?"

He nodded.

"Wonderful. All right, then. I'm off home, love. I'll come back soon, if I can. You'll have company in about two minutes, so I'd get back in bed. I'm sure you won't mind doing that, will you, love?"

He laughed. Her sarcasm didn't grate quite so much. "Bye, Ria," he said to her.

She only frowned in response. Then she stepped to his window and jumped out.

An eagle cried, and she was gone.

The next day, he actually left his room. Purely miraculous. It had to be a tremendous change in him to warrant such a transformation.

Well, maybe, but he was just restless. He'd gathered all this new resolve, but he didn't have anything to do with it, except wait.

It took some convincing to get Tiran to let him go. The captain was horrified that William had gone off who knows where with just one outlaw to protect him without his guards knowing. William assured him it was fine, but Tiran was still berating himself. He decided to sleep in William's room if he slept at all. William didn't think Ria would be very happy, but Tiran left him no room to maneuver.

"If she can get in, someone else can," the captain had declared. "I'm not taking chances. How does she do it, anyway?"

"The vents," William answered.

Tiran appreciated this. "Brilliant! That's brilliant!" Then he thought some more. "How does she get in to the house in the first place?"

"I don't know. She never said."

Tiran wanted to know. William didn't. It was too creepy to think about.

In any case, Tiran agreed to let him leave his chamber, but only when accompanied by Tiran and four other guards.

Hart and Elix were on duty again. William smiled at them, pleased to see men whose names he actually remembered. He would have to start trying to learn some names. He didn't know the other two. With fifty, it was hard to keep track of them all, but William had ignored them most of his life. He might as well try to treat them like real people instead of machines. They made little response, however. They just nodded grimly to him.

For lack of a better destination, the prince went to the breakfast table. He wasn't scared to encounter the Governor. Lis had made him feel brave.

When he appeared, he thought several people looked like

they were having a heart attack. Most notable was Elber. He was expounding upon the virtuous principles of direct election when the prince arrived. He was mid-sentence when he halted so abruptly that he fell out of his chair with surprise.

The royal officials, the Governor, and Anjalia were all present, though Zoc was absent (to his relief). Lis was attending Lady Whitefeld. It tore his heart, but he ignored her the way he did all the other servants.

"Good morning," he said to the assembled party. Echoes rebounded from all the guests. He moved to take a seat.

The Governor rose to greet him. "I am surprised, my lord, but I am glad you are well. We have missed you." He seemed ill at ease, eyeing Tiran, who looked intimidating and impressive in his captain's uniform.

William nodded, forcing a cheerful smile onto his face. "I am feeling better today," he declared, as if he'd just decided. He took a seat next to the ambassador, who was climbing back into his chair, smoothing his yellow tunic.

"It is the sun and stars to see you, your Highness," Elber effused. "I confess, all company seemed dark in your absence."

Elber should have taken up theater. William smiled thinly in response. Elber was a fool. He had no idea what was really going on here. That was good, though. If he did, he'd ruin everything and likely get them all killed.

"How is business coming, Ambassador?" William asked disinterestedly.

"Just fine, sire, just fine. In just two days we shall have finished the election. I have made my report, and the officials are nearly done finalizing the tribute. When accounts are settled, it shall be set aside to load onto the ship. Of course, no cargo may be loaded until it is repaired."

"How long will that take?"

"Your shipwrights evaluated the damage and made plans for repair. My builders estimate a month, my lord," the Governor spoke up. He shrugged in apology when he saw William's disappointment. "I'm sorry."

He put it aside. As long as he made it. But it gave a narrow window to sail. The seas grew risky after spring was over, and it was already mid-April. Not even pirates would sail in June. Too dangerous.

Ria would see to him. He had plenty of reason to believe she'd do anything to get word back to the King, if she could.

"Curse those outlaws," Elber said. "May El's wrath rain on them. How dare they interfere with the business of the crown?"

William's face reddened as he tried not to laugh.

"How did they form?" an official asked. "Rebels are usually after something."

William winced, mirth gone. This was dangerous territory. Leave the secrets alone, everyone. It was part of the plan.

But he was curious, too. He didn't expect the truth from the Governor, of course, but he wanted to know how Karia had become Auria and how the Ëan began. He looked to see how Lord Whitefeld would answer.

The Governor responded simply, "They are criminals. We attempted to administer justice, and they refused to submit. Most obtained illegal arms and fought their way into exile. They all received a death sentence—or most, at least. They are murderers, to a man. The lawless always want to cause trouble."

The Ossians all nodded their heads at this, but William didn't know how to react. Maybe there was a grain of truth in his words. Had the Ëan escaped their executions? It would explain their uniform hatred for the Governor. But what about Ria?

He decided to push it. He was supposed to be disinterested, but he couldn't help asking. "And the leader? What about him?" He hoped the pronoun would help throw the Governor off. He saw Lis look at him out of the corner of his eye, but she ducked her head an instant later.

The Governor paused, considering how to respond. All eyes were on him now. He looked calculatingly at William. Finally, he said, "Sentenced to death years ago. Escaped.

Disappeared. Came back and organized rebellion. The usual criminal story."

William noted the avoidance of saying *she*. "What did he do?"

The Governor grimaced. He wasn't enjoying this. Originally, he hadn't even wanted the Ossians to know about the outlaws. It had been provided as an excuse to dodge William's query about Lis's grave. He didn't want the embassy nosing about in his affairs. The royal army coming to the island was the last thing he wanted.

"Does it matter? Troublemaker even as a child. That sort is just destined for criminality."

Elber agreed. "The low-born will always be low," he declared. "They are nothing to us."

This from a man who praised democracy? William suddenly understood Ria's hatred of nobles. He thought about himself, and he wondered if he'd shown such disregard for his subjects.

He had. He knew he had. It disgusted him to think of it now.

An idea came to him. He would change. He would not be like them. Even Auria could not help but approve of an idea like that.

He turned to Elber, keeping his voice from betraying his disgust. His tone was that of a benevolent master. "Yet, Elber, those who rule may be generous. The people of Belond are Edenian citizens after all, and I am the prince of Edenia." He stood. "It is rare such a remote province receives a visit from its monarch's son. Therefore, I would like to mark the occasion."

He addressed the officials who arranged the tribute. "Arrange for me that a gift of money and food be apportioned to each family on the island—from the royal treasury. A gift from the crown to the people of Edenia." At their shocked and even horrified expression, he said sternly, "It is my wish. See to it."

The Governor looked calculating once more, measuring

him with surprise. Elber protested openly. "You are most generous, my lord, but it is wasteful to spend the King's bounty on such a frivolous—"

"It is my wish, Elber. That should be enough for you."

Elber had no choice but to acquiesce, though reluctantly.

The Governor said, "On behalf of my people, I thank you, my lord. You are a generous man. Allow me to arrange this for you. Put your gift under my care; I will see it is distributed fairly."

Oh, no, you don't. You're not cheating me on this one.

Elber opened his mouth to agree, but William interrupted. He said cheerfully, "Thank you, Lord Andel, but I would like to see to it personally. I will attend the delivery of the gifts myself."

Everyone looked shocked at this. Protests ranged from cries of indignation to warnings of danger. Even Tiran, who had at first smiled in approval of the scheme, now looked tense.

William wanted to go. He wanted to the see the people Ria so lovingly cared for, and he wanted to know what had been taken from them by the usurper. His mind was made up.

"We are stuck here anyway," he argued. "This is how I wish to spend my time. I am decided."

All protests were made in vain. That was that.

Chapter 15

William trudged tiredly back to his room. He'd spent the entire morning following up on his idea of a gift to the people of Belond. The royal treasurer, a thin, miserly man named Arnold, had been reluctant to coordinate the plan, but he had set to it. It would come out of the tribute money. The officials promised to apportion the gifts; then he and his attendants would oversee the distribution. It had proven surprisingly complicated, but they would start in two days.

He opened the door and walked into the room. Tiran followed, equally tired—he hadn't gotten as much rest as the prince. They sat down, William flopping onto his bed and Tiran taking a chair.

"Well, my lord, I admit that you surprised me. That was quite a scheme."

"It is that," a voice said.

Both men jumped, hands flying to their weapons. (William had to fumble to get his hand on the hilt of his dagger.)

"Be calm," the voice said placidly, betraying no alarm at their gestures. "I am a friend."

"Show yourself," Tiran demanded.

A cloaked figure emerged from the corner. An outlaw, but not Ria. The voice was male. What's more, his accent gave him away.

He was a Djor.

He threw back the hood, revealing hair so light it was almost translucent. He wore no mask. His electric blue eyes glowed out of his pale face. He was handsome, and not just for a barbarian. He was young, but perhaps a few years older than William. He had a calm demeanor that spoke of peace, quite different from Auria's intense personality.

Tiran did not relax. He remained threatening.

"Peace, Captain," the man said, holding his hands out placatingly. "I am a servant of *Aiael* and of the *Ëa ona*. My intention is not violence. You have nothing to fear."

"Who are you?" William asked.

He smiled. "My name is Torhan. The *ona* sent me." The smile faded a little. "She is not pleased, Edenian, not pleased at all."

A few moments later, when shock had subsided and Tiran had been convinced of Torhan's truthfulness, they were at last polite enough to offer him a seat before proceeding with his interrogation. Torhan remained calm and even-tempered, unfazed by their discomfort.

He continued easily. "*Vitha Inkosa*—"

William's confused look stopped him. "Our name for the Ëa *ona*," he explained.

"What does it mean?"

He hesitated, searching for words. "It is difficult to translate our language directly into yours... The best is 'brave one who stands alone.'"

"Oh." William wasn't sure how to respond to that.

Torhan smiled. "The *ona* is many things, friend of the Ëan. She has nearly as many names."

William believed it. She was already a confusing person without having half a dozen names.

"*Vitha Inkosa*," he resumed, "is at the present busy elsewhere. She sent me to talk to you."

"You can get into the Felds in broad daylight?" William asked.

Torhan smiled that same calm smile. He reminded William of Ekata. "The Djorn remember paths on this island that the Edenians never knew—except the *ona's* followers, now. The *ona* walks the road of the ancients, as do all the Ëan."

"What road is this?" Tiran questioned. He had long been curious.

Torhan looked at him directly. "In time, you may learn. It is not my place to tell you."

Both men showed disappointment, but he would not budge on this point.

"This is my message: she wishes to convey her anger (she had some interesting words, Edenian, but I am not so harsh as to repeat them to you). She particularly wished that I tell you it was foolish to expose yourself as you did. She did not think it good of you to give out charity to the people. I believe it good to serve our brothers in whatever way we can, but she may be right. The money will be useless; it will be taken from them immediately. The food will help, but the *ona* says she feeds her people. She does not let them starve. Even if the usurper takes their food, she gets it back. She is very accomplished at raiding the storehouses, and she does it with regularity. She takes care of her own, the *ona* does."

William felt annoyed. He was just trying to help! Why did she always criticize him?

"You must hold to your path now, of course, or arouse suspicion. But the *ona* says next time you must consider more carefully beforehand. Though this may work to blind the usurper to your connection with us all the better, I think. If you were under the *ona*'s orders, you would not have attempted such a scheme. *Aiael* works in mysterious ways."

"I just want to see them," William said. "Even if it does me no good. I want to help."

Torhan smiled kindly. William was glad it was not the *ona* who had come. Ria would have bitten his head off, but Torhan seemed almost sympathetic.

"You have the makings of a good man, Edenian," he said simply. "Do you follow *Aiael*?"

"Who?"

"Your people call him El."

The conversation grew awkward. "Um, I suppose."

"Either you do, or you do not." Torhan intoned. There was a sort of serene gravity in his voice that made his words seem powerful. He studied William intently. "I will pray you see him, friend of the *Ëan*."

He stood to go.

"You're leaving already?"

"Yes," the Djor answered. "I have delivered my message. I

pray you do not seek to cross the *ona* again, Edenian. There is a reason she is our leader. She is wise. She knows what she is doing. And she does not like it when people disobey her.

"I will tell her what you said. I do not know what she will do, but if she can come to you herself soon, she will."

"Where is she?" William asked.

Torhan seemed reluctant. "She is trying to prevent a death," he said simply.

"The dissenter?"

Torhan hesitated, surprised, and then admitted, "Yes."

"Will it work?"

"*Aiael* knows. I do not."

William sighed. The dissenter, whoever he was, was brave but foolish. He hoped Ria could persuade him.

"Thank you, Torhan." He bowed slightly, as did Tiran.

"Farewell," he replied, "until we next meet." He had quaint manners, putting William in mind of the past.

Torhan disappeared silently through the vent.

"Who knew there were still barbarians?" Tiran marveled. "I rather liked him, if he's a King's man. He was a nice fellow, perfectly civilized. Maybe Auria is not so foolish as I thought to consort with them, if they are such a gentle people."

William laughed. "Not all gentle. The first one I met had a temper to rival Ri—Auria's."

Tiran grimaced. "I fear the *ona* may be right, my lord, though it was a noble gesture."

She was *always* right.

"It's too late now," he replied. "Besides, it's what I wanted. I want to meet them, to do something for them. They must hate the crown, Tiran. I'd like to change that."

Tiran nodded, but he said, "We'll see, sire."

Chapter 16

She returned sooner than anyone would have predicted. William didn't even get a chance to try out his plan first.

He awoke that same night to the sound of the captain thrashing on the floor, where he'd taken up protective residence. *Typical luck,* William thought. *He's a restless sleeper. Won't I ever get a good night's sleep?*

Then he saw the shadow standing over Tiran, one hand clamped like iron to his mouth.

He struck a light. A flash of green eyes beneath a hood met his glance. They didn't look happy.

Tiran stilled, seeing who it was, but he looked irritated at being trapped so easily. Ria had managed to wrestle him into submission with little apparent effort. It rankled the captain. Not many people could have done that. He huffily got to his feet, still wearing his full uniform. William had gone to bed dressed this time, too. He sat up.

"It's you," he said in surprise.

"I have little time," she said by way of greeting. "You must come with me. Now."

He started up, bewildered. "Why? Is this about this morning?"

She huffed a sigh. "No, love. Had I the time, I would scold you for that scheme—you were a perfect idiot. *Ask me before you rashly go off and announce your hare-brained plans for charity.* But that's what I sent Torhan for. He was probably too easy on you. Runs in his family.

"No, I have other business. I need you to come with me—now, no more questions." She handed him a mask and hood.

"Wait, *ona,*" Tiran protested. "You can't just—"

"I think you'll find I can, Captain. Don't test me."

Tiran was undaunted. "Then I'm coming with you."

Ria frowned, but Tiran remained firm. William looked back and forth, measuring the impasse. "Fine," Ria sighed at last.

"You're probably less trouble than *him*, anyway. Just stay quiet, all right? Not a sound. Trust me."

"I trust you, *ona*." Tiran's faith was endearing. The captain was as loyal as a man could be. He'd be a truer ally than any Auria could have asked for.

"Let's go," she said. "Quickly."

They traveled through the vents, but not the way William remembered to Lis. Instead of twisting through the maze of tunnels, they climbed down. There were little rungs to use as ladders, probably intended by the builders for cleaning. It was certainly dusty enough to warrant it.

William desperately wanted to know where they were going, but he didn't dare ask. He and Tiran had enough on their minds trying to match Ria's remarkably silent movements, and besides, any word he spoke would likely echo through the whole house.

The further down they went, the warmer it grew. Finally they crawled out of an opening rather uncomfortably close to the furnace. William inhaled the cooler air with relief. They emerged into a damp, dirty room, lit only by the glow from the furnace. The men took a moment to catch their breaths, but Ria moved purposefully to the corner.

"Welcome to the cellar, boys," she whispered.

"Why are we here?" William hissed. If they were going out, why go to the basement?

She turned back. The coals cast her smile in a fierce light. "This is our big secret," she declared. She stooped to the stone floor near one of the larger stones. She worked at it with effort. After a hard pull and a grunt, it came free, and she lifted it.

Instead of dirt underneath, there was a hole.

So that's how she got in! A tunnel!

"You first, gentlemen," she said, a wicked smile on her face. "There's a ladder."

William peered down. It looked deep, but dim light reflected off the walls. What was down there? He felt nervous, but he tried not to show it. Ria already thought he was a coward. He didn't want her to think even less of him.

"I'll go first," Tiran offered, reading his reluctance. William smiled at him, relieved.

Tiran stepped into the hole, working his way down the rungs. William darted a glance at Ria. She was still smiling fiercely, challenging. "You wanted to help," her eyes seemed to say, "then do it."

He took a breath and climbed in. When he was far enough down, Ria followed. She pulled the stone back over the top with an effort, sealing them in.

They climbed a good while, as the hole went a long way down. Finally, it opened up into a large cavern. A few more steps down the ladder, and he was on the ground again.

He found himself face to face with a trio of outlaws, all holding torches. Tiran was tensely eyeing them, but he made no threatening moves. He'd befriended their leader, after all. He wouldn't go back on his word.

There were two men and a woman. One was Torhan—William could tell even with the mask. The others he recognized, but did not know their names. The woman looked a little bemused, but the men were stoic, attesting to the seriousness of their business.

Auria hopped down behind him. She smiled at the outlaws. "A little addition," she said to them. "This is Captain Tiran. You all remember the delusional noble, of course." *Thanks a lot*, he thought to himself.

The woman laughed. She had a hearty laugh, quite different from Ria's. She struck him as a wholesome, motherly kind of woman. She was thick in frame and looked like a good fighter. The second man looked young, but he was tall and well-muscled, with a pale face and sparkling brown eyes. He carried a bow over his shoulder.

"Tiran, William, meet Winna and Kerran. Torhan you know." The Ëan nodded to the Ossians.

"Let's go, then," Ria ordered, moving down through the cavern.

No, not a cavern. It was a road.

It was a wide lane, wide enough for ten horses to walk side by side, paved with smooth white rock, and perfectly shaped with straight walls and a high ceiling. The walls were covered with carvings, paintings, or designs of all kinds. Gemstones decorated these artworks liberally, but tastefully. The art was finer than any Edenian design William had ever seen, with an ethereal quality to it. He gasped in wonder, staring. Tiran reacted similarly.

Torhan stepped close and said to them, smiling, "Welcome to the Gnomi Road—the way of the ancients. It is trust indeed for the *ona* to bring you here. It is beautiful, is it not? And so well preserved! But come—we must not tarry." Ria was already moving at a fast jog up the road, the other Ëan following. The torchlight rebounded from the beautiful walls.

William withdrew from his distraction enough to follow, but he still asked Torhan, "How did this place come to be?" Clearly the Ëan had not built it, though it served their purposes. To think an underground road ran right under the Felds! No number of guards could keep the Ëan out. And, if it ran as straight west as it appeared to, it would go right under Belo.

Torhan smiled. "I will tell you as we go, yes?"

"Please!" William replied.

He began. "My people are the Djorn. You know a few of us, I think, but little of our ways. Our tribe has lived on this island, which you call Belond, since the beginning. Our roots are deep. We never lost our ways as a people, even in the great melting of tribes that led to the Edenian Empire. We have always lived in harmony with the will of *Aiael* and with nature. We make our homes in the forest on the high mountain. Before the invaders came, we dwelt throughout the woods, but we have since been forced into hiding. We live only on the north side, now. We are a peaceful people. We train warriors, but we do not love war. If we may avoid it, we do. So we hid. Your people never found us, except twice.

Once was long ago, the other only ten years. *Vitha Inkosa* was the first to call us from our solitude. On her rests the hand of *Aiael*.

"But I digress. We were not always alone. There was, a thousand years ago, another people on the island. They were called the Gnomi."

"Gnomes?" William wondered. "I thought that was just a story."

"Stories hold truth, sometimes," Torhan said, "twisted though it may be. But they were not gnomes, they were the Gnomi—a people, if strange. They *were* small in stature and their skin was grayer than most people. They loved to craft and build, as their road attests. They were the first to mine the mountain, even before the volcano ceased its activity. They did not hate the sun, but they preferred to live underground. They made beautiful dwellings for themselves, a city to last the ages. They built wondrous machines and inventions. They traded with the Djorn, the neighboring islands, and even with a few tribes on the continent. They built a network of roads all over the island, but two main roads to their ports: one from the center of the island due east, the other, due west. We are on the west road now, but the west port was destroyed. Belo was built upon its ruins."

"What happened to them?" William asked, saddened. Their loss seemed a grave tragedy indeed, if their mere road was this beautiful.

Torhan sighed. "The conquerors came, thirsty for gold. They had heard of the wealth of the Gnomi and desired it for themselves. The Gnomi fought, but it was not enough. The Edenians conquered all resistance. The Gnomi were killed, and the Djorn withdrew."

It struck William that to Belond, the Empire had always meant war, even from the beginning. Edenia owed the people of this island a tremendous debt. It had been abused and ignored too any times.

But Torhan was not finished. "But the Edenians never found the road. The Gnomi sealed the entrances of the ports before they were killed, and all other entrances were hidden. *Vitha Inkosa* was the first Edenian to see the underground civilization of the Gnomi—it was my people that showed her. The Gnomi would not have begrudged her, I think. She fights for justice, a cause dear to them—and she is not purely Edenian, anyway."

This last surprised William. It was a ridiculous notion. The Whitefeld name was as old as his own, and every bit as loyal to the Empire. Despite her uncharacteristic golden hair, she was Edenian through and through.

"I see your incredulity," Torhan said, "but I speak truth." Here he grew quiet. "Not many know this," he admitted. "I am one of only a few who even knows who the *ona* is among *your* people. Her family has an interesting history.

"Three hundred years ago, an Edenian hunting party stumbled upon a Djoran maiden gathering berries in the forest. She was defenseless, so they took her captive. Her name was Aleia. Because she seemed a novelty, the lord of Belo at the time took her for his slave. Slavery is an abomination to all humankind, but so it was in the Empire at the time.

"He had another captive, a man named Veld. He was a better man and a kinder one than most, and he took care of Aleia as he was able. He did not label her barbarian, as many others did. Though a slave himself, he provided for the desolate girl. Eventually, he married her, subject to his master's approval. They had a son, named Valan, who was nicknamed 'Whiteveld' for his pale hair and his parentage. Valan escaped his master and sailed to Edenia, where he met the first of your dynasty, Kellian Tellor. The *ona* comes from his bloodline, though few remember it."

The Whitefelds were descended from a Djoran woman? This would have scandalized the Ossian socialites back home. No wonder he'd never heard it before.

"Torhan," Ria called back, "enough of the clandestine historical discussions, please. We have a job to do, remember? And I daresay you're distracting our guests."

"I apologize, *ona*," he responded graciously. "I take too much delight in memories."

"Your people love the past," she said forgivingly, "but it is my lot to think of the present. Yes?"

"Of course, *ona*," he agreed peaceably, not at all offended.

"We must hurry," she urged. She pointed to a branch in the road on the right. "This way. Come."

They jogged for a long time. It was hard to measure the hours underground. William passed the time by watching the walls go by and counting the number of ladders marking the *Ëan*-built exits from the Gnomi Road. They kept turning onto different branches, all smaller than the last, but no less well-crafted.

William grew fatigued quickly. Each road was perfectly flat and straight, but he was not used to lengthy exertion. The others, Tiran included, seemed fresh as ever. They easily outpaced him. Pain lanced his sides as his body protested the exercise, and his muscles burned. He regretted that he had not devoted more time to his own fitness. It was taking its toll now. He dared not ask to rest, though he felt he could barely go on. The *ona* brooked no delays.

Finally, the *Ëan* came to a stop before a ladder. They all gathered to the *ona*. William's gasps for breath sounded loud in the quiet tunnel.

Ria addressed William. "Here," she said, handing him a pair of coarse boots, dirty with age and use. "Put these on." He took them, and she kept talking. "You must make no sound when we go up," she commanded. "We will be in an open field. There are no guards about, but that may change. No one must see us—you in particular. If you were recognized by the wrong person, we'd be done for.

"We are heading for a farmer's house. He lives alone except for a few helpers and his animals. We do not wish to wake *them*, only the farmer. He will be waiting for us—or should be. His name is Lam."

"The dissenter?" The reason for his journey suddenly became clear. She wanted him to help her convince the man to vote as the Governor's regime demanded. He was the King's son; his influence might be helpful just because of who he was.

"Yes. If he votes down the Governor, he'll be killed, and likely others with him. Last time, I couldn't stop it. I won't let it happen again. He said only the King could absolve him this time. You're not the King, but you'll have to do.

"You told Torhan you wanted to see the people. Here's your chance, William Tellor."

She would do anything for them, William realized. Anything at all. She loved the people of this island, whether Djoran or Edenian. She would do whatever it took to protect them.

"I will do what I can," William agreed.

"Good," she said, satisfied. She turned to the others. "You all stay here and wait for us. You, too, Captain." She cut him off before he could speak. "The fewer the better. I'll take care of him." Tiran hesitated, but he agreed.

"We will be back soon," she promised. "We must get you home before dawn."

With that, she began to climb the ladder.

"Be safe, my lord," Tiran cautioned. The Ëan gave him hopeful smiles of encouragement, desperately wanting him to succeed. He smiled weakly back. Then he followed Ria.

The cover of the hole was a pile of sticks hidden by a bush that grew near a clump of trees. It was well hidden. No one would have reason to examine such a place for a secret tunnel.

Ria replaced the sticks as soon as William climbed out, scratching his face and arms on the bush. He winced, but made no sound. Ria moved furtively, blending with the shadows. He tried to do the same, but he lacked her skill.

She darted glances over the field before them. The house—or cottage, more like—stood about a hundred paces away through a furrowed, muddy field. He was glad for the boots.

She moved forward, picking her way through the field. She turned her feet at odd angles to avoid leaving a footprint, and she wove through the furrows, taking unevenly spaced steps. Despite all these extra measures, she still moved furtively, almost invisible in the darkness. He tried to imitate her, but he knew he probably just looked clumsy.

They came to the cottage. Ria gave a light, almost inaudible tap at the door. A light appeared at the crack at the bottom, and the door opened softly.

"Come," a man whispered urgently. He shepherded them inside, darting glances back and forth. They came soundlessly in, and the door shut behind them.

The man was old, but not feeble. He had silver-gray hair, weathered skin, and brown eyes. He had a strong build, though of average height. He didn't look like the courageous, stubborn zealot William had envisioned. He wore an air of sadness and resignation, and rather than brave, he looked tired.

"*Ona* Auria," he said. "I didna think you'd really come back. I answered ya, didnai? I will not change me mind."

She removed her hood, but retained the mask. "I never break my word, Lam."

"That be true," he sighed. "Yer too good to us, ya are. Donnaya never sleep?"

She smiled, but it looked savage with the mask covering the whole upper half of her face. "I am always busy, Lam, but you have demanded my visit."

"I donna wish to trouble ya," he apologized, his simple accent slurring the words together. "But my mind's made up."

"I brought someone to see you," she said. "Lam, meet William Tellor."

The old farmer turned widened eyes on the prince as William removed his mask and hood. He smiled uncertainly at Lam. Funny, he'd never felt nervous in a peasant's presence before, but for some reason, he wasn't sure how to act. He glanced at Ria, hoping for guidance. She offered none.

"Hello," he said hesitantly.

Lam gaped, the hand which held the candle trembling. Then he sank to his knees. "Milord," he said shakily, "ye honors me, ye does." He was a pitiful sight: an old man in nightclothes, kneeling on the dirt floor of his cottage. But at the same time, there was honor in him, too. It was almost a pride in humility. He was happy to be able to offer even simple reverence to his lord, though he was just a poor man. His honor and loyalty to his King demanded it.

William had never been so touched by a subject's homage before. Normally he took it for granted. What had he done to earn devotion from this man? He was born; that was all. Ria was right. But Lam was kneeling anyway.

"Please," he urged, "get up, my friend. No need to bow to me."

"You are the prince of Edenia, milord, son of our great King. How cannai not?"

Ria crossed her arms but said nothing.

"You are a devoted subject of the Empire, I know—but please, Lam, rise."

Lam hesitated, still looking at him in awe.

I'm just a man, William thought to himself. He was surprised by the thought, but it was true. His name didn't make him superior to anyone else.

Lam rose to his feet. "What do ya wish from me, milord? I be at yer service."

William smiled at him. "The *ona* brought me here to ask you not to dissent, Lam."

An uncomfortable silence stretched a moment. Lam's face grew unreadable. At last, he said. "Ah. Then... Ya do know." He paused, turning to Ria. "Auria, ye be a smart one."

"If you won't listen to me," she replied, "listen to him. He's not the King, but he's the best I can do on short notice."

He sighed, turning back to William. "How cannai not, milord? I haff lied to my King for fifteen years—it dishonors me ta lie again. An' all o' the men tha' died to give us poor folks a voice."

"More men will die if you vote him down," William argued. "That's not the way to fight the Governor. Your *ona* is wise; listen to her." (She clearly liked that, but she didn't add anything else. She'd already said all she could say.)

He was still unconvinced. "But the King," he protested. "No one 'ere has the courage to tell 'im the truth. If we'd all voted against 'im, we'd be free now. It's cower-dice that keeps 'im in power."

"It is all you can do," William said. "*I am going to tell my father*," William assured. "When I go home, the King will hear of this outrage—I promise you that." He thought for a moment, then he added, "And I will tell him that Lam votes against the Governor, no matter what the record says. He will know the truth."

Lam's head rose at this. "Ye would do tha' fer me?"

He smiled, sensing Lam beginning to waver. He nodded. "An honorable man should not be ignored. I will tell him, Lam."

Lam gave a relieved laugh. "Ya make me heart lighter, ya do," Lam confessed. He looked at Ria. "I submit to yer judgment, milord, Lady Auria." William observed the use of a title for Ria, though she didn't approve of them, but she was too relieved to notice.

"Praise El!" she exclaimed. "Thank you, Lam!" she rushed forward to give him a hug.

"I wish t'were otherwise," he admitted, "but I surrender."

She beamed. "You've saved lives, Lam. That's what matters." She laughed, the scowl at last erased from her eyes.

Lam laughed, too. "Now ya can stop yer frettin'," he told her. "Go off and get some rest." He added, "Tell my Rose and my Leif that I love them, Auria."

She smiled at this. "Of course I will," she promised. "Someday I'll bring them back to see you, Lam."

His eyes misted. "It's too dangerous," he said. "Leave 'em be. I canna come to them, and they canna come to me."

The *ona* looked sad, but she nodded. "They will be happy at your decision," she offered.

"But cannai face 'em? A father canna appear a liar ta his children."

"You're not lying. William will take your message to the King."

He nodded, smiling. "Tha' is somethin'," he admitted.

"I'll come back soon," the *ona* said to him, replacing her hood.

"Don'," he told her. "Don' worry about me. We need ya strong, *ona*. Get some rest."

She grinned. "Deal," she answered, giving him another hug.

"Off ya go," he said, shooing her toward the door. Then to William, "Thankye, milord. Ye've blessed me, ye haff."

William smiled and nodded in reply. Then Ria motioned for him to follow. He said simply to Lam, "Goodbye."

Lam watched them go, then the door closed and they were out of the cottage once more. They paused on the doorstep, then Ria laughed softly and tackled him with a hug. He was astonished, not knowing how to react.

"I didn't think it would work, but you did it!" she exulted. "Maybe there's hope for you yet, love!"

She hadn't sounded this happy in all the time he'd known her. It was infectious. His heart rose. It was the first time she'd ever complimented him, even if it was teasingly.

And it was true. He *had* actually done something, simple though it might seem. What was better, she approved of him.

Maybe they could actually be friends. He liked the thought.

"C'mon, love," she said softly, releasing him. "Let's get you home."

Chapter 17

His plan wasn't working quite as he'd envisioned it, but that was okay. Ria fixed everything.

It had been two weeks since he'd visited Lam. The election had concluded, yielding unanimous results once again. No retaliation was made against anyone.

He'd seen Ria several times. Twice she'd taken him to see Lis, to his delight, but the visits were short, and Tiran went along. Ria seemed less angry once Lam had been convinced, and she became friendlier, almost playful, again. She introduced William to Harry, and the prince now called the mouse out of the closet each evening to give him a bite of cheese. She'd also woken him up one night by dropping a large spider on him, which set him to yelping and her to near hysterical laughter. Fortunately (or unfortunately), "Legs" was unharmed—but he disappeared somewhere into the corner, so William was still terrified of another encounter.

He lived a sort of double-life. In the day, he went through the motions of how everyone expected him to behave. He still had to evade the Governor's suspicion, but his completely un-Auria-like plan actually helped him in that regard. Ria still didn't like what he was doing, but she let it go. Eventually, he began to understand what she meant. His grand plan to give to the people ended up less grand than he'd imagined. He felt like a peacock strutting around rather than a human being trying to help others. He just rode the streets looking impressive on Blazer while his attendants distributed the gifts. He saw little more than the tops of the citizens' heads as they knelt to him.

And they didn't react the way he'd expected. Instead of heartfelt gratitude like he'd received from Lam, all he was given was cold acceptance. They took the gifts readily enough, but there was little personal interaction.

He asked Ria why this was, and she answered, "You're too

far away from them. To understand someone, you need to live right beside them. To love them, you must invest yourself in their lives. They accept your gift as one from a stranger. It may be heart-felt, but it is only pity, not love. That is why your gift seems cold to them."

"How do I change that?" he asked.

She smiled that devilish smile he'd grown to recognize, telling him she had a scheme. And so his midnight rambles began.

She decided he needed to see the people—up close and personal, the way she saw them. So she took him to see them.

Every night, one of the *Ëan*, usually Ria or Torhan, would come for him and lead him onto the Gnomi Road. He was never allowed to go alone, because Ria still didn't trust him not to do something clumsy and blow cover. So, he was always escorted.

Tiran wasn't pleased about this plan. He thought it tempted fate and was far too dangerous. Ria admitted the danger, but she thought as long as they weren't caught and the Governor didn't suspect, it would be fine. Not one of the people they visited would ever betray them. She also argued that it would be better for William to be able to tell the King about the people, not just Lis and Ria and the *Ëan*. Lastly, she said, "Captain, you are a leader. You know that any good leader must know the people he serves. The best leader comes from *among* the people. William has to learn this. It is worth the danger."

She convinced him in the end, though he retained his misgivings. Ria appreciated his concern, but she was not the kind of person who let others' opinions sway her. She liked to have her own way.

He wanted to come along, or at least send one of the royal guard with them, but Ria said no. The fewer the better, she argued. This point almost ruined the whole agreement, but Ria declared that if an *Ëa* could not protect the prince, no one could. William had seen her in action. No one fought better than she did. What she said was perfectly true. Tiran had to concede.

It was what William wanted to do. He sleepily drifted through the days, eagerly looking forward to the nights.

And the people! By day, they were cold faces staring out of a resentful crowd. By night, with the *ona* there, they were real people with their own personalities, desires, and struggles. It was hard to think of them as peasants now. They were human beings.

He met many of them....

Hanna, the old widow who lived on the edge of the town. She knitted almost endlessly, selling her goods to earn enough money to survive. Her home was barely livable, and she would have starved without the *Ëan*. She welcomed him in, insisting on making him a watery cup of tea. Despite her troubles, she treated him warmly, though her tongue grew sharp at the mention of the Governor. She reminded William of the nurse who'd raised him.

Lath and Vielet, a young mining couple. They both worked in the most treacherous lower mine, as the perpetual grime on their faces attested. They were fiercely devoted to each other and to their baby daughter, fighting each day for their survival.

Aggy, a servant in the Governor's household. She was probably only thirteen. Her father, Mort, was a groom in the Governor's stables. She worked in the kitchens and occasionally waited on Anjalia.

Xia and Laia, two sisters working as farmhands to Lam. They insisted on thanking him for his royal gift. They asserted that it had been a great blessing to them. They'd given it all to their aging father, who was dying from a lung disease contracted in the mines.

Robairt and Ellairt, a father and son who worked as smiths for the Governor's troops—against their will. They rued every blade they crafted, but they also secretly hid a cache of weapons, some for the *Ëan* and some for the people.

There were more, many more, all different, all touching,

and all interesting. He felt he was beginning to know them. They were no longer so cold to him when he rode through the countryside in the daytime, either.

But what he really enjoyed was getting to know Ria.

Granted, he was not always with her. He liked Torhan, too, but he always felt a twinge of disappointment when it wasn't Ria who came to escort him.

She was not an easy friend. She was so different than anyone else he knew, so it was hard to determine what was "normal" for her. She had unpredictable moods, and she rarely explained herself. She was stubborn, headstrong, and determined. She didn't show sympathy to *him*, even if she did care for many others. She still teased him with incessant mockery.

But there was something enchanting about her. Everyone she met adored her and devoted unreserved loyalty to her. It was hard to explain. Maybe it was how charmingly beautiful she could be. Maybe it was her frightening strength. Maybe it was her charismatic passion that made a person want to drop everything and follow her.

She was just good.

But cross her, and she would kill you without regret. The Governor and his men received not an ounce of her compassion. She hated everyone who swore allegiance to the usurper.

The Governor returned the favor. William observed him carefully, and Tiran still sent spies to check on his activities. He pursued Auria relentlessly without worrying who or what got in his way. She outwitted him at every turn. He wasn't even close to her trail.

This was the world William had stumbled into. Had his father known, he would never have sent him. But while he was still terrified, he no longer felt miserable. He wanted to go home, and didn't really want to come back, but he no longer loathed the island. It was not Ossia, and never would be, but it was a beautiful place in its own way. If he could help save it, he would try.

It was the lot he had been given.

Something wet and slimy hit his cheek. He stopped in his tracks, astonished. Ria laughed hysterically, mirth bubbling over into sound.

They were going on another midnight adventure, walking by moonlight along a fairly secluded pond out in the farmland. It was further than usual from the entrance to the Gnomi Road (or burrow, as Ria called the holes), but Ria had no fear of discovery. The nearest guards were miles away, according to the animals.

He wiped the mud off of his face, a bit annoyed, but it was hard to be angry when she was laughing like that. He found himself laughing, too, in spite of himself.

"Don't you remember how we met, love?" she laughed. "I don't—I was too little—but Lis likes to tell me."

He smiled. "Sure I do," he replied. "I was five, I think. Our parents introduced us and sent us off to play in the garden. We boys thought we were too manly to play with a girl, so we started building piles of mud, thinking you wouldn't join us." He laughed at the old memory. "You pelted us with mud, not caring if you got dirty. We were shocked!"

She laughed some more, grinning coyly. Then she stopped again and flung more mud at him, faster than he could dodge. He growled playfully at her, "Ooh, you're gonna pay for that!"

In no time, they were chasing each other around the pond, flinging mud at one another. She had better aim than he did, to his chagrin. He got much dirtier than she did.

They spent some minutes at this, but finally, she said breathlessly, "We'd better stop. Lou will think we're mud monsters."

He guffawed at this, but he put down his handful of mud. He dashed some water on himself to wash away the mud, but it hardly helped. Ria just laughed at his efforts. He cast her an embarrassed smile.

"Come on, love," she chuckled. "Let's keep going." Time enough for fun, but still the *ona* was business-minded. At least she was laughing. Even a few minutes was pure happiness.

He followed her eagerly, darting through the cover of the trees. They still had a ways to go. Who knew what else she might throw his way? She kept him on his toes every minute they were together.

As they walked through the fields, he couldn't help but admire the countryside. They were deep into the south of the farmlands, just below the third road that ran through the farms. It was a beautiful landscape, especially in the light of the moon. Every once in a while, he caught a glimpse of the sea. It was an enchanting scene even without the goddess who ruled it. *Her* aura made the island practically glow.

Ria paused as they came in sight of the road, ducking behind a bush. She looked around vigilantly, but it felt more like a game of hide-and-seek. Still, she was cautious. He followed her.

"It looks like we're in the clear," she breathed to him. "Let's—"

She stopped cold as a group of birds landed in the bush, twittering with agitation. If they could have spoken with human voices, they'd have been yelling her name.

"*Eta?*" she demanded in Djoran.

Chills ran over the prince at her tone. Gone was the playfulness. She was deadly serious, even horrified. Her hand had gone to the knife at her belt, and her knuckles were white.

Something terrible must have happened.

She listened to the birds, breathing hard and her face white. William desperately wondered what they said, but he didn't dare interrupt. Fear crept into him, displacing any pleasure he had felt a moment ago. If something was grave enough to daunt *Ona* Auria, it would be enough to petrify anyone else. Her expression showed in turn anger, fear, shock, and then determination.

She cut the birds off, loosing an urgent string of Djoran. The only words William understood were *Ëan*, Talon, and Luna, but the gravity of her commands was unmistakable.

They flew away in different directions, as fast as their wings could carry them.

Then Ria turned to William, her expression pinched with worry and also deliberation.

"What's happened?" he asked at last. "Are we in danger?"

"Not yet, but Dero is. The soldiers caught him trying to visit his sister. They're taking him back to the prisons of Belo right now."

"I have to rescue him. I've never let an Ëa be caught—they'll do horrible things to him. They'd try to break him to get to me, but no Ëa would ever betray me. They'll torture him for ages. I have to save him. They're on the central road, from the mines to the town. I'm the closest—my sentries will be too late to catch them. I can get there... but I can't leave you alone, either."

"I'll come," he offered. "I'll help."

She nodded to the first, but to the second, she said, "No, you won't. They can't see you, or even know you're there. You have to stay hidden, understand?"

He nodded, not daring to protest. In truth, it was actually a relief, though he hated to admit it. The idea of real combat terrified him. But it was cowardly not to want to help.

"Let's go," she barked, taking off at a run. "We have no time to lose."

It was hard to keep up with her. She was a seasoned athlete; he was a soft nobleman. He wheezed after only a minute, his sides burning. He could only try to avoid tripping and nod briefly to her rapid-fire instructions.

"I'll find a place to hide for an ambush, and you will *stay* hidden there. Do you have a knife? Good, but don't draw it. They'll see the glint from the moonlight. Do *not* come out, no matter what. Even if something happens to me. If I get caught, or worse, you stay until they're gone, then bolt back to the burrow—understand? No heroics!"

The fact that she thought she might get caught or killed terrified him. She was the invincible Auria, fearless, brave, and formidable. No one could hope to defeat her.

No. She was human, too.

Fear coursed through him, but he ran on. For the first time in a long time, he prayed. He didn't know if El would hear—but it couldn't hurt.

Let her succeed, he pleaded. *Please. I don't want to die. I don't want her to die.*

William crouched behind a clump of bushes, waiting beside Auria.

She'd picked a good spot. The road curved around the little hillock where they were perched, and she had a bow at the ready. (She carried all manner of weapons hidden on her person. She was prepared for anything.) She'd shoot some arrows and then follow through with knife work. William prayed fervently that it would be enough.

The group of soldiers appeared on the road, carrying torches to light their way. They were moving quickly on foot, clearly eager to secure their captive. They followed a mounted leader. They flanked a small man, pointing crossbows at his back. He was bruised and bound, but alive. Dero, she'd called him.

William's heart sank. There were at least twenty soldiers.

She pressed his arm, offering a weak smile. He tried to smile back, to encourage her, but it fell miserably short. His heart pounded with fear.

They came rushing around the bend unwarily. Ambush fell without warning.

Arrows rained on the soldiers with incredible speed, as if a group of archers stood on the hill. There was only one, but that one was worth an army. They shouted alarm even as four or five men fell, clutching their wounds. Ria had uncanny aim with more than just mud.

An arrow split Dero's bonds, and he wrested away from his captors. The bowmen had grown confused, but they were regrouping. The rescue would do no good if they shot Dero in the back.

Then Auria leapt on them, and William remembered why

she was named for the legendary goddess of war.

She was everywhere. There remained probably twelve foes, and she had little help from the struggling and weaponless Dero—but they couldn't take her down. She slashed her knives faster than sight, dodging and rolling out of reach of swords, moving in and throwing men onto their backs where they met her blades. It was a fluid, almost beautiful dance with death. His heart rose. She would do it yet!

Then he looked to Dero, and his heart froze. The unarmed *Ëa* was making a fairly good account of himself, but there was only so much he could do without a weapon. He was as good as any Tellorian guard, but he was not the *ona*. They were going to take him.

Two swordsmen attacked the young man. He tried to dodge, but they managed to knock him down. Auria screamed his name, but she had too many on her.

If they couldn't capture him, they'd kill him. One soldier raised his sword while the other held Dero down, despite his struggling.

He was going to die.

Time slowed down. To William, the stroke moved in slow motion. Ria screamed a frustrated battle cry, trying desperately to get there. Dero cringed, still struggling.

There was no help—except William.

He had a split second to make a decision.

Ria had been clear. If they saw him, the whole plan was ruined. He'd be lucky to survive, let alone save Belond. They needed the Governor to think him ignorant. If they caught him with Ria, he was signing his death warrant and destroying what was perhaps the last chance to save this island.

But he couldn't sit by and watch a good man die.

He chose.

His dagger was out, then in the air.

The red King's jewel embedded in the hilt flashed in the light of the torches.

It landed with a sickening crunch into the soldier's chest.

The man dropped the sword from his lifeless hand, a surprised expression on his face. Using the distraction, Dero broke free of his captor, grabbing the sword as it fell.

William breathed in relief, but only for a moment. Now they knew he was there. He heard shouts and saw them point. Ria uttered a mild curse below him, still battling her way through the soldiers. He ducked further into the bushes.

Then worse.

"It's the prince!" the leader cried, aghast. He pointed at the dagger.

How could he be so stupid? He carried a knife with his name practically written on it.

And he knew this man. Benjen, the leader of the men who'd tried to kill him.

"Fire!" Benjen screamed at the remaining bowmen, pointing at the bushes where William was hiding and ignoring the two outlaws who fought his way. Nearly all his other men were fallen.

The bowmen each fired one shot before Ria and Dero cut them down. One went high, sticking in the branches above his head.

The other landed with red hot impact in his side.

He screamed, unable to keep quiet. Everything blurred. He collapsed.

The rest of the battle seemed far away to him. He heard Ria shouting as she fought the last of the soldiers. He heard an eagle cry as Talon swooped in to help finish them off. He heard hoof beats as Benjen fled back to Belo, alone.

Then it was quiet.

He moaned, hands pressed to the wound in his stomach. It had sliced neatly through his abdomen and out his lower back. He had never felt so much pain in his life. The blood ran over his hands with sticky warmth. Sparks danced before his eyes as he fought to remain conscious.

Then Ria was there. "You fool!" she berated him.

"Sorry," he whispered, closing his eyes.

"No!" she shouted at him. "Stay with me, William!" Her

voice seemed distant, more like a dream than reality.

"Hurts," he moaned.

"Stay awake," she commanded. "Dero! Help me!" Then, "You're going to be fine, William, just hang on."

"Dying," he murmured.

"No, you're not. Not if I can help it," she promised, grasping his arm. "Fight for it, you idiot!"

"Can't," he groaned. She said something he couldn't understand. Everything began to swirl.

"Sorry," he breathed, then he blacked out.

Chapter 18

William awoke slowly, feeling lightheaded and dizzy. His brain struggled to discern where he was and why he felt so very cold and numb.

He heard voices bouncing in the air around him, a woman's and a man's. He couldn't place them in his memory or make sense of the words. He struggled against the fog in his mind. What were they saying?

Where was he? He discovered he was lying on his side, on top of something hard. It was difficult to move. He felt weak and tired—it would be so much easier just to sleep...

The woman spoke again. *Mother?* he wondered hopefully. He longed for her right now, as he had when he was sick as a child.

He forced his eyes to open, though it took all his effort.

Nothing was in focus. He caught an impression of gemstones and whiteness. *Gnomi.* The word drifted to him, but he could not place its significance.

A woman was kneeling beside him. Light hair. Ria?

"He's awake," the male voice said excitedly.

The woman turned to look, a smile on her face. Not Ria, he realized, blinking away the blurriness of his vision. It was the Djoran woman, the one who was good with horses. The healer of the *Ëan*, he remembered. Ekata.

The *Ëan*. Where had that word come from? It was important, he knew.

William looked for the male speaker. He crouched nearby, hovering over Ekata's shoulder. He was young and slender. He had short brown hair, a small nose, mouth, and face, but round ears that stuck out to each side, giving him an earnest appearance. His warm brown eyes peered down at him with concern.

"Careful, Dero," Ekata cautioned him softly. "Don't upset him."

Dero?

Memory crashed in on him, and with it the weight of his failure.

What had he done?

The plan was ruined, laid bare to their enemies. The Governor knew everything now. He couldn't go back—he'd be killed. He would not save Belond, or Lis, or anyone. If he even survived tonight, he'd be trapped on this island like everyone else.

Then he remembered Tiran, still back at the Felds, and panic swept through him. What would the Governor do to his guards? Or to the nobles, the servants, the sailors—everyone? And Lis—even she might be endangered.

He moaned as he tried to sit up, thrashing with his agitation. Pain blossomed in his side, and he gasped with the force of it.

Ekata pushed him gently but firmly back down. "Easy, friend," she soothed in her odd accent. "You are safe—have no fear."

"Have to—" he murmured, "have to warn—"

"Shh," she hushed. "Do not worry. All will be well. It is in *Aiael's* hands now. You can be no help. You must rest."

"Wha—what happened?" he slurred, not relaxing.

Dero answered this time. "We brought you down here, out of the open. The *ona* sent word to Kata to come and the *Ëan* to meet her wherever she was going—and El knows what else she told the messengers to do. She's been in a flurry, if not panic—but the *ona* is too canny to panic."

"Where is she?"

"I don't rightly know—but if anyone can set this to rights, the *ona* can. Don't you fear. She's clever. The *ona* won't let us down."

William sighed, still fearful. It was as if he'd kicked a giant anthill, and now Auria had to put it back together—down to the last ant. Even if she *was* a goddess, it seemed impossible.

"I'm a fool," he lamented. For once, he agreed with Ria's assessment of him. He had ruined everything. "But I had no choice," he argued softly to himself.

Dero heard him and grimaced. "I know," he agreed with quiet earnestness, "but you saved my life. I'd be dead if not for you. I thought I *was* going to die, you know—after they were finished torturing me in the prisons. I've never been so frightened in my life," he admitted reluctantly. "We have to be careful, because we *cannot* get caught—we know what will happen to us. *I'm* the fool. *I'm* the one who got captured in the first place. You should never have even had to rescue me. It's *my* fault."

William shook his head weakly, but Dero continued as if he hadn't noticed.

"I'd be an ungrateful wretch if I didn't thank you," Dero offered sincerely. "If I wasn't dead, I'd be where you are now. I should be," he lamented, berating himself. "I'm sorry."

"Don't be sorry," William whispered back, the words hard to form. "I don't... blame you."

Dero smiled gratefully. He squeezed William's hand. "Thank you, my friend."

The way he said he last word warmed William. *Friend*. That was something. His father had told him once that a King's true friends are few and far between. William was not a King, but he had found the same to be true for him. He didn't have any real friends in Ossia. Most people just flattered and simpered, not at all genuinely interested in him. Dero talked to him without guile, like he imagined a friend would.

"Enough now," Ekata remonstrated. "You need to rest, William." It was endearing the way she stumbled over pronouncing his name.

At her command, he closed his eyes again, emotions still roiling. Before he knew it, he was asleep again.

The next time he woke, he was somewhere else.

It still took a long time for him to fully wake up, but when he did, his mind didn't feel so fuzzy. His side was no longer quite so numb, so pain sharpened his thinking. His head ached and he felt exhausted.

He was lying on a bed. For a moment, he thought he was back home in Ossia, but then it would not have been so warm. He enjoyed the heat. It made the room feel cozy.

There were people talking. Women, both. He opened his eyes, hopeful.

"He's awake," Ekata said. "The herbs have worn off."

The other woman turned to look, but he knew her before he saw her face. Same weathered cloak, dingy green tunic and breeches, thick boots. She didn't look like a hero, she looked like a vagabond—and exhausted, at that. But the glint of intensity in her eyes belied her appearance, and no mask or hood concealed her face.

She moved to sit on the bed next to him. Her face was hard, but pity was hidden underneath. He had seen her sympathy before, but it had never been directed toward *him*. "Well," she sighed, but without anger, "you've made a real mess, William."

Had it not been so serious and had he had more energy, he would have laughed at the understatement. "Sorry," he murmured in response.

She did not acknowledge the apology. Instead, she slowly pulled away the blanket to look at his wound. They'd taken his shirt off, but his abdomen was wrapped in clean white bandages. He shivered as air touched his skin. She carefully began removing the bandages.

He wanted to ask her a thousand things, but the look on her face forbade him. Her forehead was furrowed with tension, but her hands were even gentler than the healer's.

She handed the cloths to Ekata. She probed the area with her fingers, the first time William had seen her not wearing her leather gloves. Her hands were the only part of her that looked clean and fresh.

He winced as she touched the stitched-up wound, but it didn't hurt unbearably. It was covered in some salve that mostly numbed the skin. He didn't want to look, but she just pursed her lips. "You'll live," she declared. "I've seen worse. Ekata did well, though it was a bit complicated on the inside, she said." She cast the healer a smile, then she waved Ekata forward again, and the small young woman darted nearer to reapply some concoction and wrap new bandages.

Ria rose as if to leave. William stopped her, unable to go on wondering.

"Ria," he asked, "what happened?"

"You should rest," she said sternly. "You can't be worried about anything but your health. I'll handle it, love. You take care of getting yourself well, and that's it."

"I have to know," he pleaded.

She looked hard at him. Then she sighed, glancing at Ekata. The Djor hesitated, then said something in Djoran. Ria nodded.

"Fine," she conceded. "But only enough to rid you of curiosity.

"Tiran's fine. I got to him and the guards in plenty of time. Two of your guards were injured in their escape but none killed. I led most of the sailors to safety, but the ship was burned. As for the nobles, none of them would listen to our warning. They're either dead or in prison. The whole island is locked down while the Governor looks for you. The Ëan will be busy a while yet."

As news went, it was mostly bad, but she said it almost casually, as if she did this every day. "How long has it been?" he asked.

"It's been two days since we rescued Dero—it's evening now. We'll be at this much longer than that."

He was willing to bet she had been out all this time without sleeping, and he felt yet another twinge of guilt.

"Where are we?" he asked.

"The Nest. Where else?"

"How did I get here?"

"The Gnomi Road. I presume some of the *Reben* came for you."

He didn't know what she meant.

She turned to go.

"Ria," he stopped her again. She looked back. "I'm sorry."

She glared sternly at him. "You disobeyed me, William. In the army, that's called insubordination—and it kills. We're at war. I'm your commander. You have to follow orders, William. I can't command if no one will listen to me, and if some listen all must. You have to trust me. I told you what I did for a reason."

"I had no choice."

"You always have a choice, William."

He amended his statement. "Then I chose right," he declared. "And I'd do it again."

She finally softened, laughing. "Maybe you do have a spine, love," she decided. "For my part, I forgive you—this time. You've paid the price of your actions, and what you did *was* for a good reason. But don't ever disobey me again—especially in battle. There *will* be consequences, and I might not always be able to clean up the messes you make."

She turned to leave again. "Enough scolding for now, love. Get some rest. You lost a lot of blood, and you'll be some time healing. Listen to Kata, and you'll be right as rain soon enough."

He called her one more time, startled. "Ria?"

She sighed, a bit annoyed now. "What, love?"

"Are you... Did you get hurt?"

She cocked an eyebrow, surprised. "Me? I'm fine, love. Nothing a little sleep won't cure."

"But... there's blood on the back of your shirt." A lot of it. Not enough to be explained away by the mess of combat.

She strained to look over her shoulder, then remembrance came on her. She smiled. "It's not mine, love," she said gently. With that, she turned on her heel and left the room.

"It was brilliant!" Dero crowed enthusiastically. William's other visitors laughed.

It had been a week now since the fight. William had not been allowed to get up, but he had been permitted to sit up in bed and receive some guests.

He'd had a large number. Dero came in all the time. He wasn't out with the other Ëan because of an injury he'd suffered to his arm, so he made himself the bearer of the Ëan's hospitality to William. Also, Tiran had joined him, looking haggard but relieved to see the prince well—or mending, at least. Ekata left him only to tend others. Torhan came once, as had Kerran, Winna, and a few other people he hadn't previously met. He hadn't seen Ovan again, which disappointed him, but Ovan was out with Auria most of the time. He hadn't seen Auria again at all.

Right now, it was Dero, Tiran, Ekata, the ship captain, Wood, and an Ëa named Short (most ironic, as he was the tallest, skinniest man William had ever seen). William's room was fairly large, otherwise it could not have fit so many people, but the wide, white stone walls accommodated his guests easily. They had come to tell their various tales, having finally received permission from Ekata to do so.

Dero was recounting the Ëan's exploits so far. She knew just what to do right away. No doubt of that.

"When you went under, she knew she'd have to get you out, and fast, before they came back. But she couldn't take you too far. So she bound some pilfoweed—"

"What's that?"

Dero seemed surprised by the question, as if everyone should know the answer, but he said, "Stops bleeding—or slows it, on larger wounds. She packed your wound with the herb, then we took you down a burrow. All the while, she's sending birds off with messages, sending the Ëan every which way. Kata came to find us, as did the two sentries closest. Soon as we were underground, the *ona* went off with the sentries, but Kata and I waited until you were able to be moved. Then we took you back to the Nest. With a little help."

"What about you?" William asked Tiran.

"Ooh, yes, tell him, Captain," Dero interjected, bouncing a little. William laughed.

Tiran just smiled. "She did well for us," he conceded, "but

that night was awful nonetheless." He sighed, then told his piece. "She came through the window and told me everything. As fast as possible. Then, before letting me go off to find you, she told me to alert the other guards and have them slip out in twos and threes, by different doors. About half of us got out that way, and the soldiers were getting suspicious.

"Then the alarm went out, and the whole island, seemingly, went into lockdown. There were soldiers everywhere. We had to fight our way outside, and we'd still have been lost without the horses. She'd called them somehow, before she left, and they practically tore down the stables to get to us. Blazer got out, too—first one." William felt a surge of relief. He'd felt guilty that he'd forgotten the horse, but Blazer wasn't quite a priority right now. "We mounted up, still fighting our way out, but a flock of birds attacked the soldiers and so we were able to break free. They pursued, of course. We took the forest road, as the *ona* ordered." William remembered it all too well. "They were hard on our heels, but the Ëan attacked. They fired arrows from a hillside: a good ambush spot. A few volleys was all it took in the dark, and they were finished. The Ëan led us up to the top of the mountain, where they let us enter the Nest."

"What about the embassy?" William asked, already knowing the answer.

"Lord Elber is in prison," Tiran replied, "along with the royal treasurer. The other officials are dead, my lord. I'm sorry. The servants and attendants were thrown in the dungeon. We're still not sure what he'll do with them, but it's unlikely they will live long."

"What about the ship?" he asked Captain Wood. "The *ona* told me it had been burned."

"Yes," the sea captain affirmed sadly. "Most of us sailors were sleeping on board—made the repair work more efficient in the daytime. We woke up to cries of fire from those on watch. The ship was surrounded by rowboats filled with warriors, who fired flaming bolts at the ship. We had no warning, no reason to expect an attack, though I've since heard the truth. We tried to put the fires out, but we could not—they used some strange chemical that did not extinguish with water. A few men got out in the landing boat, but they were swarmed by attackers. They did not escape. The rest of us, myself included, had no choice but to jump for the water. I got clear just in time. The whole ship went up in an explosion. I've sailed the seas my entire life, and I've never seen the like. I've heard that there are pirates that can do such things, but I never credited the tales. I do now.

"Some of my men were lost in the fire; others were cut down as they swam. Then the strangest thing happened—though I'm told this *ona* instrumented it."

"She did," Dero confirmed. "She's a miracle worker."

"It *was* miraculous. We would have been lost, but a pod of dolphins came up under us. Each claimed a sailor, then pulled us underwater and swam away. When we resurfaced, we were out of the reach of the warriors. They pulled us along the coast a long distance, until we reached a break in the southern cliffs—a bay on the east side, one I've not heard of before. The dolphins brought us in to shore, and then some men in masks led us on the underground road. About thirty of us made it—nearly half lost. It's a tragedy, my lord—we failed you. I'm sorry. There's no way off the island now, and the season grows late, anyway."

"The *ona* will find a way," Dero promised. "She always does."

"For my part, I believe you," William agreed. "She's handled it well so far."

"We still have trouble," Short broke in. "The Governor's beating the people and pillaging their homes again. Also, he's scouring the forest. He's started trying to burn us out."

"Will he find us?" William asked, suddenly worried.

The men laughed. "No," Kerran said. "You have not seen the Nest. When you are better, you will see it and then you'll understand. Don't worry; you are perfectly safe here. It is only a trouble to the forest itself."

William relaxed. "What about the people?" he asked quietly.

"The Ëan are returning what he gives them," Short said. "But we can only do so much. We just have to wait it out. You're trapped here. He'd rather kill you, but he'll settle for exiling you if he has to. He'll have to. He won't find you."

Guilt washed over him again. People were suffering because of him. What made him so important that others had to pay the price of his actions?

"It is war," Kerran declared. "We lost a battle, but we'll keep fighting until we win the war. Don't be discouraged. The *ona* leads us well."

A knock sounded at the door. Tiran jumped visibly, instinctively moving closer to the prince.

Kerran answered. Two Ëan in hoods and masks stood flanking a disheveled, dark-haired woman. The instant the door opened, the woman flew into the room.

"Mother!" William exclaimed in surprise.

"Oh, William!" She came to sit by him. "What have they done to you? Are you all right?"

He smiled at her, mixed emotions flaring. He was overjoyed to see her. It made everything feel right, somehow.

The others saw how he reacted, and all except Tiran left the room to give them space. The two Ëan still waited protectively outside the door.

"I'll be all right. It's not so bad as it was. But—what happened to *you*?"

He took in her appearance. Her formerly fine clothes were rumpled and dirty, and her face was scraped and bruised. She looked much more careworn than before.

Lis grimaced. "He wasn't gentle, son. I think he feels I betrayed him. He cast me into his prison with the others. Ria came to rescue me last night. She got everyone out that she could—but most of the ambassador's party is dead. They killed all the servants two days ago, and Lord Elber they executed yesterday. I was to be today..." She trailed off, clearly more shaken then she let on. She was not a physically strong woman, unlike her niece. A week in prison would have used her cruelly.

He extended his arms, and she fell into them. "I'm sorry, Mother," he comforted. "I never would have wanted to get you involved in this mess. He's a devil, but you're safe now."

"He's not a devil," Lis protested softly. "He's my brother."

William disagreed. This man was evil, no getting around it. He wasn't just misunderstood. No. He knew what he was doing, and he was accountable for it.

But at the same time, was he not a man, sinful as any other, but no worse in the end?

William let it go. "You should get some rest," he told her.

She pulled away, soft green eyes resting on him. "I wanted to see you."

"Thanks, Mother." He smiled. "I've been wishing you were here."

She melted, tears forming in the corners of her eyes. She was so different from Ria. Auria's eyes were more beautiful, but they often looked as cold as stone.

"I'm here to stay, William. I'm not leaving you again."

How many times had he wished for *that* in his life?

He touched her hand. "Get some rest—then come back and see me, okay?"

"All right," she agreed, smiling. "I will."

She rose to go, then observed the Ëan still by the door. "Weren't you going to say hello?" she asked them.

"We are only to see you to your rest, ma'am," the first said stiffly. William recognized his voice.

Lis crossed her arms. "Don't be unfriendly, dear. Come, now—Baër, isn't it?"

When he didn't respond, she said to the taller man, "Ovan? What about you?"

Ovan took off his hood and mask. "Hello, sire," he greeted William fondly. "Good to see you awake."

William smiled at this, pleased to see Ovan, at least, if not Baër.

Captain Tiran rose from his seat, drawing William's

attention. Tiran looked suddenly pale, staring wide-eyed at Ovan. Ovan looked at him, a greeting on his lips, then he paled, too. They stood, frozen, staring at each other. The others looked between them, confused. They *were* both Tellorian guards. Did they know each other?

"Tiran?" Ovan asked, at last breaking the silence. "Is it really you? What are you doing here?"

"They said you were killed," Tiran said disbelievingly. William had never seen the captain like this—he was always dutifully businesslike. A chink in his iron demeanor had appeared. He looked stunned.

Ovan smiled sadly. "I know—I'm sorry."

"How?" Tiran demanded.

"I pretended to join the pirates, then I escaped. It was the only way. I had a duty to fulfill." Lis winced at this. She blamed herself for what Ovan had had to do—it was all to protect her. "How did *you* end up here?" Ovan demanded in turn.

"I joined the Guard," Tiran explained, baring the tattoo on his shoulder. "It was better than the army anyway. They made me a captain. I was assigned to protect Lord William."

"Captain?" Ovan repeated appreciatively. "Even *I* was never a captain. You've risen in the world, brother."

Brother?

"I wanted to be like you." Tiran confessed.

Ovan stepped forward, all reserve gone. He tackled Tiran, his equal in height, in a massive hug. "You've done better than me," Ovan said. "Look at you!" he exclaimed, holding him at arm's length. "You're all grown up, now. You were still just a boy when I left. I've missed you, Tiran."

It made perfect sense to William. He could see the similarity in their faces, voices, and personalities. He'd thought them similar before, though Tiran was much younger and still wore the red of a Tellorian guard and not the green-gray of an outlaw.

Lis stepped to the door, touching Ovan on the shoulder. "You stay," she told him.

"Are you sure? I can—"

She nodded. "Baër will see to me."

Ovan bowed to her. "Thank you, my lady," he replied.

Once she was gone, the two men started talking quickly, as if to make up for lost time. Everything that had happened to them was recounted. They mostly ignored William, but he didn't mind. He liked it that they acted normal around him—and that they were so happy.

He was happy just to listen. The conversation answered many questions he'd had. It was the first time he learned how the *Ëan* began.

Chapter 19

"I remember that day clearly," Ovan told Tiran, his voice tinged with sadness. "We fought hard, all of us. I was the second-in-command, not the captain, as you probably remember. But I had to take charge early in the battle when Captain Starm went down. The pirates had three ships and outnumbered us five to one. We had foolishly thought ourselves well-protected when we set out. We didn't have nearly enough, however talented we may have been. We couldn't possibly have won. They slaughtered the Guard and the Imperial soldiers, too. I only got knocked out, by some providence. When I woke up, I was chained to the mast with the Lord Whitefeld, Lady Whitefeld, Lady Elissana, and Lady Karia. I was the only other person left alive, and I'm still not sure why they didn't kill me. It must have been El.

"After they killed the Governor—the *rightful* Governor, that is—they offered me a chance to either join them or face the sword with him. With just the women left with me then, I couldn't leave them all alone, defenseless. Maybe it was wrong, but I did not wish to fail in my duty any more than I already had. I would have gladly taken the sword, had that been my duty. Perhaps I chose wrongly, but I could not have helped them from the grave."

"You were right," Tiran agreed defensively. "It is what I would have done. His Majesty must agree. You did not compromise your oath." He glanced at William, a little abashed at his presumption. "Not that I speak for the King."

"I don't either, but *I* agree with you," William offered. They nodded gratefully and continued talking.

"I joined them. I think Zoc—the second-in-command of the pirate fleet at the time—liked the idea of having a turncoat Tellorian under him. They bought it. Of course, I had to act the part—that was really the worst of it. They were— are—monsters. When we arrived, they made everyone believe the pirate captain—Jeron, his right name is, though I will not disgrace the honor of the Whitefelds by calling him by their name—was Lord Andel. At first, they lauded him as the King's appointed. Then they realized something was wrong. The pirates used the confusion to swiftly conquer the island, appropriating the Belondian garrison to swell their own numbers and changing the government to suit their greed. All Belond's wealth fell under their thumb. The citizens were turned into slaves. Anyone who was strong enough to be a soldier joined the growing army. Everyone else was cowed into submission. The people of Belond were defenseless."

"I had to help them," Ovan said with disgust. He shook his head. "I had to pick my battles. But I tried to be gentle, and I helped when I could. I hope they understood. I don't know. I had no choice. Lady Elissana was my priority." He laughed suddenly. "It was easy to take care of Lady Elissana, but then there was Lady Karia."

"The *ona*, yes?"

"The same. Lady Elissana was content to keep her head down and wait, as I was doing. I looked out for her and made sure she was provided for, and she thanked me for it. Lady Karia was quite different, especially after her mother died. She hated, and still hates, the Governor more than anything. When she was younger, she was very prone to fits of rage. It happens more rarely now. She is still angry inside, but nothing, not even anger can keep her from her duty. She's like her father that way. But as a child, she was always in trouble.

"At first, she was just another servant in the Governor's house. Set an angry six-year-old girl to cleaning floors and see what happens. The housekeeper beat her more than once, and she was given the very worst jobs to do, but her behavior only worsened. She had an uncanny way of getting through the house—the vents, I imagine now—and she'd steal food to share with the servants and play pranks on the Governor, his officers, and anyone else who looked down on her. She was never caught, but everyone knew it had to be her, evidence or no. I couldn't step in, not then. Zoc had always been suspicious of me, and I couldn't expose myself.

"Then she was sent to work in the stables. She was about nine then, I think. She slept out there with the horses. That job didn't go well, either. She put a burr under Zoc's saddle, making his horse throw him—right into the mud, I might add. And she smeared mud onto the Governor's saddle. He mounted without noticing. I'll always remember his expression when he sat down." Ovan laughed at the memory. "She pulled many tricks like that, but she was always clever. Each time, she was conveniently somewhere else.

"But they weren't going to tolerate being undermined even in small ways. She was sent to the mines at ten. Lady Elissana and I were horrified. It is practically a death sentence to send a child into the mines. It is dangerous enough for adults, and accidents are common. I only went in once, and I hope I don't ever have to go in again. The *ona* still goes in sometimes, to help prevent accidents. The Governor has staged several to quell opposition. Even without his interference, the dust is thick, and the equipment is precarious. Used to be, before he came, people were well paid to go in there. Now, their only payment is their lives.

"Somehow, she made it. Cleverness, talent, or just good luck, I don't know. Maybe El was just looking out for her. The supervisors didn't like her any more than her previous bosses had. She had a bad temper, and she actually stood up to them, unlike the other workers. When they tried to force the miners to take unnecessary and near fatal risks, she refused flatly. She paid the price with many punishments, but she saved the others from having to do it.

"Then came the final straw. A miner named Fraidith, a widow with two small children, was accused of stealing pieces of unrefined gold. She didn't, of course. It was probably the guard. But there was no help for her. She was sentenced to hang when she could not produce the gold or the money to pay for it. Public execution is a cruel practice, but that is nothing to them. The whole village was forced to watch. The Governor makes examples of those who oppose him.

"I was in the crowd that day, assigned to keep order. I was near the platform, so I could see everything. They were about to hang her when Ria rushed onto the platform. She was a dirty, small, eleven-year-old girl, but she made short work of half a dozen surprised guards nearly my size, without a weapon. Most of them were too surprised to know what to do, and half the army had never seen a real fight anyway. Ria stole a dagger and cut Fraidith free. The poor woman fled. The soldiers were too busy with Ria to pursue her.

"They caught Ria, of course. She was just a child, and the crowd was too thick for her to escape. I tried to intervene. I promised to take her myself, to restrain her, but she'd gone too far. They could not let her go now. She had successfully defied them in front of the entire village. The Governor ordered her death.

"A child?" Tiran spluttered. "They were going to execute a child? That's against all the laws of Edenia!"

"They'd kill anyone," Ovan replied.

"Only a coward kills a child," Tiran fumed. "It's barbaric."

"They have no conscience. She was becoming a threat. She had Whitefeld blood in her, after all, and the Whitefelds have always been fighters. Most people don't consider children very significant enemies, but they can be very formidable, and children grow into adults. But I agree with you, brother.

"Lady Elissana pleaded with me to help her. I would have tried even without her urging. I couldn't let them kill Lord Whitefeld's daughter, the only heir to the name. I had to choose between her and Lady Elissana. Lady Elissana told me to save Ria, that she could manage on her own. It was the only thing I could do. I told myself I would still see her home one day.

"They were planning to kill her the next day, though she was beaten half dead already. It took a lot to knock the fight from her. I went to the prison that night and I set her free, then we snuck out. When we were seen, I fought my way out with her holding onto my back. They have many guards, but not many skilled fighters. Those endless formations they drill are useless, just for show. They don't help in a real fight. It wasn't hard to escape.

"I ran into the forest. I was still carrying her, so I wasn't moving very fast, and I had no real notion of where to go—just away. I'd have been lost. They were hard on our heels, and I only had a little food and nowhere to hide. I ran to the north, which is how the Djorn found us."

"The barbarians?" Tiran asked. "I have seen several of them. They seem to be good people, if strange."

"They are. They do not normally interact with Edenians, but they are truer servants of *Aiael*, as they call him, than we are. They saved our lives.

"They appeared out of the woods like spirits, three of them. One was Torhan, though he was just a boy at the time. The others were named Melach and Afinaea. They urged us to come with them, or Torhan did. He knew our language, somehow. The Djorn say he has the gift of words. They covered our trail and brought us to their settlement. We saw no more pursuit.

"It was strange for me, but I never felt like I was in danger among them. In any case, I had no better choice than to trust them. What convinced me was how they took care of Ria. They are a gentle people, but I have never seen any healers so careful. Their chief, or *Djor Ona*, named Yewul, tended her himself. He is a wise old man, Yewul, and gentle. Have you met him?"

"I haven't."

"Maybe you will at some point. He is a close friend of the *Ëan*. Greatest healer of this age, and the closest to El. He trained both Ekata and Torhan in their arts, and he taught Ria many things also.

"They accepted us as fellow human beings, and eventually as friends. It was mostly for Ria. They saw something special in her. They knew what she'd done—hence they named her *Vitha Inkosa*, "brave one who stands alone." They wanted to help. Or were called, as Yewul says.

"She wasn't happy just to hide away, though. As soon as she was healed, she wanted to be doing something. She was more determined than ever. She had gotten it into her head that she had to save Belond. Yewul had something to do with that, I think. She had always wanted to bring the Governor down, but the reason now changed a little.

"So she asked me to teach her how to fight. I thought it was foolishness, but I agreed. I taught her the sword. We started off with sticks. In just a week, she managed to hit me with it. I had to stop holding back. She learned everything quickly. I've never seen a more able student, young though she was. We moved on to practice swords, and before I knew it, she was beating me. I was astounded, I'll admit. I am not bragging when I say I'm a good swordsman. I'm a Tellorian guard! But she has the kind of talent that is one in a million. It's in her blood. Her father was the same way. They say Lord Andel was the only man who ever out-fenced the King. I believe it. I saw him fight that day on the ship. It took sheer numbers to take him down.

"I couldn't teach her anymore. I had exhausted all I knew. At twelve, she could have beaten the King's sword-master. That's when Melach took her.

"Melach was the warrior of the Djorn. He was a hunter unlike any I've ever seen, and he could wield any weapon. The Djorn do not go to war, but they train a handful of warriors every generation so that they do not lose the tradition of defense. Melach was the greatest among them. He'd taught Torhan a little, and he was apprenticing Szera while we were staying there. He chose to take on Ria, too.

"Szera didn't like it, at first. The girls fought like cats in the beginning, but they earned one another's respect, and eventually friendship. They have similar minds. They are hardly separable now. I think it was Melach that truly brought that about, though.

"He taught her everything. Bow, spear, staff, hammer, anything he had. Then there were the knives—Melach preferred them, himself, so Ria wanted to learn them. She still uses the knives he gave her.

"He had a unique style of fighting—he wasn't at all Edenian, not regularly trained. He threw anything he had at you. I never knew what he was going to do next. I learned more than a few things just from watching him. He was the best swordsman I've ever sparred, but he didn't fight fair. He was just as good without the sword as with it, so he never stopped when I'd disarmed him—sometimes he'd let me, just to throw me off guard.

"Ria learned everything he knew. She fights more or less like him, but with a little more Edenian thrown into her technique. Sometimes I think she may be better than he was."

"I'd love to be able to see him spar," Tiran said appreciatively. "Or the *ona*, for that matter."

"The *ona* would spar you," Ovan said. He laughed. "She doesn't have many willing partners, though she has little time for practice. But Melach is dead now, I'm afraid."

"Oh," Tiran replied, subdued. "I'm sorry about that."

"It was three years ago," Ovan explained sadly. "The Ëan were on a raid to the storehouses, but the Governor's men showed up, with the Governor at the fore. It turned to pitched battle all too quickly—which we never have the numbers to win. There were ten of us that night, and there were at least thirty of them, with more on the way. And the Governor is a more formidable warrior than most people realize. He's a Whitefeld, too, at least by birth. He learned from Edenian masters and pirate warlords. He doesn't fight often, but he leaves death behind him when he does." Ovan lowered his voice. "Even the *ona* isn't entirely certain of beating him. It's why she always pushes herself to be better. She thinks she may have to face him one day.

"On that night, though, it was Melach who stopped him. It was a hard fight on both sides. None of us could help Melach. They wounded each other, and it was the soldiers' concern about getting the Governor to safety that saved the rest of us. Melach died where he fell, in the *ona*'s arms. He was a brave man, and his loss was a hard blow to all of us, but especially to Ria."

He paused a moment, then Tiran asked, "How did the Ëan even begin?"

"Ah, yes," Ovan continued. "Hard to say, that. It started so gradually, but the vision was there from the beginning. She was always our leader, even when she was still just a girl. She had all the ideas and all the drive. The Djorn called us her followers, and then her flock. When she made friends with Talon, we became the eagles, or the Ëan to the Djorn."

"Who is 'we'?"

"At first, just me, Ria, Szera, and Melach. We went around the Gnomi Road and spent years digging the burrows—Ria's idea, inspired by her journeys in the vents, I think. The Djorn made all those rope ladders for us. We still make new burrows if we need them.

"Then we started stealing from the village grain supply—of which precious little goes to the villagers under the Governor's administration—and giving it to the people. We went a little bigger each time, always striking when it was least convenient. Then we'd spend nights delivering the food. We still do all that.

"Next, we began rescuing people they targeted, and we settled them in what has now become the Nest. It was a better base for us than the Djoran home, anyway, and we needed the room. We have a whole village-worth of people here now. We call them the *Reben*, which means Robins in Djoran. Out of their number emerged most of those who are now Ëan. We trained them to fight, and when they could hold their own they joined—though we developed strict traditions about our members. We are good fighters, all of us—any of the Ëan could be at least a lieutenant in the Guard. There are about fifty of us now. More *Reben* still join the Ëan every once in a while, and the ranks of the *Reben* have swollen significantly this week. There are now nearly five hundred, including the women and children, of course, and every last one of them is loyal to the *ona*."

"The *ona* seems a great leader."

"She is. Times are hard just now with the plan in ruins, but she'll come up with another. She always does. She's inventive."

Tiran nodded in agreement. "I'm sure she will."

They talked for a while longer about the current situation: the *Reben*, supplies, tactics, all the details. William got a bit lost after a while, and he started to doze off. They were still there when he fell asleep, but he didn't mind. They were Tellorian guards, and he trusted them more than ever. They made him feel safe.

Chapter 20

"Easy, now. Don't take it too quickly, my lord," Tiran urged.

"Easy does it—else Kata will have to order you back to bed," Dero agreed.

"And I will do it," Ekata warned with a laugh. "I told you, this is your own responsibility. I do not think it is a very good idea."

William gritted his teeth. She *had* warned him, but he was tired of feeling like an invalid. He wanted to *do* something, to help somehow. When she'd tentatively suggested he could try getting up, he'd jumped at the opportunity.

Well, not exactly jumped. A week in bed, a stomach wound, and blood loss had left him feeling rather weak.

He took a hesitant step. Dero and Tiran grunted as William's full weight settled on them when he faltered. It was a mismatched pair of crutches, for sure—one tall and well-muscled, the other short and slender, but there was no one else he would have wanted helping him.

"There ya go," Dero exulted. "You'll be up and running before you know it! Swinging a sword with the best of them, like as not!" He was always an optimist.

"Mmmf," William grunted. His legs felt like sand, atrophied from disuse. He likely would have received a stinging set of remarks from the *ona*.

"Keep trying, sire," Tiran encouraged. "You're doing well."

He managed a few steps more, and they grew less difficult each time. Still his supporters stifled grunts of effort. "Sorry," he apologized.

Dero waved his apology away. "No need to be. It's good to see you on your feet at all."

They reached the door and stopped for a rest. William caught his breath, then asked Ekata, "Can we go outside?"

"Where?" Ekata asked suspiciously.

He cleared his throat, abashed at her scolding tone. "Um—well, I wanted to see the Nest. And Lis. And Blazer. And the guards, and the sailors, and the *Reben*, and the—"

The men were laughing at him, so he stopped, red-faced.

"Easy, there," Ekata chastised. "You are in no condition to go traipsing—"

"Aw, please, Kata?" Dero pleaded. "We'll go slowly, and if he gets tired, we'll stop. It's only nine. We've got all day."

"I can always carry him back," Tiran offered. "It would be good for him to get out of this room."

The Djor wavered, her pretty face caught in a pensive frown. William looked pleadingly at her. The electric blue eyes darted between the three men, considering.

"Please?" Dero appealed again.

Her eyes lingered on him a moment, then she smiled, and said, "The *ona* will have my head, no doubt, but all right."

"Yay!" Dero exclaimed. "Thanks, Kata."

She blushed. "Go on with you, then," she urged, shooing them. "Have your fun."

"C'mon!" Dero urged. "We'll give you a whole tour! Lots and lots to see!"

They left the room and walked down a hallway, walls made of the same smooth white stone as those of his bedroom. It was a strange building, unlike any he'd ever seen. There were no windows, and not a trace of daylight. Huge, bright, multicolored lamps glowed from the ceiling, providing the only light. It was clearly Gnomi-built; it was exactly like the design of the road. From this he guessed that the Ëan had built their Nest in the abandoned underground city of the Gnomi.

Dero's chatter confirmed his guess. "It's a beautiful city—some say it's better than Ossia." William seriously doubted that. "And it's huge. Even with all the refugees, we don't fill the citadel. This is the healer's quarter—all the healers live here to be near the sick. When you're better, you'll stay in one of the other quarters. *Reben* quarters, of course, though." He coughed in embarrassment. "The *ona* probably wouldn't let you stay with me, otherwise I'd offer. I live in the Ëa quarter, with a few of the others: Kerran, Allain, and Winna and her family. I'll show you, if you like."

"Where do *you* stay?" William asked Tiran.

"They set aside a few houses for the guard, and some for the sailors. We're just below the Ëa quarter. They gave us a whole section, but we hardly need so much room. The place is huge."

"The *ona* wanted you well accomodated," Dero defended. "You're important. It's not every day the Tellorian guard shows up in your city. Besides, she'll want you to be on call to help us, so you need to be close."

Tiran laughed. "You flatter us, but I think the Ëan are quite capable by themselves. You hardly need us."

"You're the best fighters in Edenia," Dero insisted.

"You're the best in Belond," Tiran shot back. They both laughed.

They quieted as they reached a wide courtyard. Wide columns revealed the street at the end.

"Ready?" Dero questioned.

"Yeah," William replied.

"Okay," Dero answered. "Prepare to be astounded!" he exclaimed dramatically.

The sight that greeted his eyes as they stepped into the wide street took his breath away.

It was beautiful. That was the only word that he could think of to describe what he saw.

The ancient city stretched almost as far as his eyes could see, little specks of light glowing in the distance. Glittering with white stone, each building uniquely designed, it must have taken an age to build—and it was not crumbling. It had endured.

They stood within the citadel, which itself could have been a city. It spiraled slowly upward, houses to the inside, streets guarded by a railing to the outside. It overlooked the perfectly flat surrounding city, forming one giant spike in the exact center of the massive cavern. The citadel stretched upward until it melded with the high ceiling of the mountain dome.

The ceiling! Once William looked upward, he could not take his eyes off the ceiling of the cavern. It was dark as the blackest night for the entire space until the roof itself, which was embedded with the most breathtaking lamps he'd ever seen. Unlike the rainbow-colored lights that burned in the city, these were pure, pure white. They were probably huge, but at such a distance they looked like little white stars in a pure black sky.

It was more beautiful than any night sky William had ever seen. It was purer, somehow, without all the haze that obscured the stars. Though these were not real, they shone with a piercing intensity.

"Wow," he breathed. He could have stood here, staring upward, forever.

"The Djorn call it *Ailëandra*," Dero informed him. "'City of Star Lovers.' They say the Gnomi hated the brightness of the sun, but they loved the night sky."

William sighed in appreciation. "Wow," he repeated.

Tiran laughed at his astonishment. "Ovan gave me the grand tour already, my lord, but I admit it's still hard for me to believe. Nobody in Ossia even knows it's here. That city may be the capital of the Empire, but it doesn't even compare."

"No, it doesn't," William agreed. How had he once thought this island backwater? He'd never dreamed of a city as beautiful as this one.

"Would you like to see our settlements?" Dero asked eagerly.

"Absolutely," he answered, tearing his eyes away from the Gnomi stars.

Dero grinned happily. Had he not been acting as a crutch, he would have been bouncing up and down. "Okay. We'll give *you* a grand tour."

They slowly started walking up the gently sloping, curved

street.

There were plenty of people around, but it was not nearly as populous as Belo had been. All the people were common-looking, but they contrasted sharply with the villagers William had recently met. It took him a while to pinpoint the exact difference, but then he realized what it was: they were not living in fear. They laughed and talked openly as they went along, carrying baskets, pushing carts, or driving animals. This place was much happier than Belo. People greeted each other warmly, traded goods, and went about their business. They didn't look like refugees; they looked like citizens, with no cloud of fear hanging over them.

"Where does everything come from?" William asked, referring to the goods they carried and traded.

"We have farms in the northern meadows, and the herdsmen pasture their animals there," Dero answered. "The *Reben* go in shifts to work them—usually following the same occupation they used to do in their old homes. They can't live up there; it's too exposed. The Governor doesn't know those farms are there, but if he went looking for us up there, he could easily find them. They travel in groups at different times of day and come back here to live so they are safe. A few of the *Ëan* stay out there to protect them whenever they work. They do the important job: they feed all the *Reben*, along with themselves. They allot a share for the *Ëan*, and now for the guards, of course, and for anyone who cannot help themselves. Then they take the rest to use or to trade for things they need and also feed the craftsmen who work here in the Nest. We usually have quite a surplus of food; we've been storing it up. We're never short on bread, just hands to make it." He laughed at this joke. "Our trade is simple, but it makes for little conflict. We don't use money here. The *ona* says money is only good when there are lots of people, and they don't have a standard to go by in bartering. We're just a small community."

"It makes sense," William agreed. He was well-versed in the idea of large-scale trade between the provinces due to his high-born position and education, but this concept of community trade intrigued him. It seemed to have worked out well in the Nest, even if it would not have been so wise in a province, or an Empire. Even in the whole of Belond, it might not have worked. But here, things were simpler.

William watched the faces they passed as the three of them walked slowly uphill. They were all polite, and they welcomed him if he spoke to them; however, there were less than welcoming reactions as well. Some eyed him with disdain, scorn for his title and thereby his presumption. Others looked down on his weakened state (not that he'd been impressively strong *before* this incident)—these were mostly those William guessed to be Ëan. Some looked angry, remembering that he had been the one to ruin the *ona*'s plan. A few looked genuinely pleased to see him, but not many. He never had the sense that they were being rude to him, but he knew his being there was not what any of them would have wanted at this juncture. His best welcome had come from Dero, and of course a few of the other Ëan that he had already met.

Dero pointed out many different buildings. Usually he named them as "so-and-so's house," so that William was soon quite confused. He did, however, reflect that he enjoyed this tour much more than he had enjoyed his tour of Belo.

After a brief stop to visit the sailors and Captain Wood, Dero led him to Lis's house. The Ëan had found her a rather small house tucked in among some of the other families of the *Reben*. Tiran had posted two guards outside of it to protect the King's love, now that they could guard her without endangering her.

When the three men dropped in, they found her arranging the few articles of furniture the Ëan had found for her, an apron over her plain dress, a cleaning rag over her shoulder, and her hair a mess.

She fell to making herself presentable. "Sorry," she apologized. "I'm not—uh—" She gave an embarrassed laugh. "I wasn't expecting to see anyone. I was just cleaning." Then she took in who it was. "You're up!" she exclaimed. "Look at you! Much better! But, surely you shouldn't be taxing yourself. Come, sit!" she ordered.

William laughed at her flurried manner. "I'm all right, Mother," he assured.

"Sit," she repeated firmly.

He laughed some more. "All right," he conceded. His helpers lowered him into the indicated chair.

"You shouldn't have let him go out," she said to Tiran and Dero.

"I think it's good for him, ma'am," Dero defended, but he showed her a great deal of respect.

"Not if he gets hurt again," she said protectively.

"Really, Mother, I'm fine. Ekata saw to me."

She huffed a sigh, then conceded. "I *am* glad you're here," she admitted. "I was planning to visit you in a few minutes. How do you like the house?"

"You've fixed it up nicely, my lady," Tiran said admiringly.

"It looks *wonderful*," Dero commented emphatically, enthusiasm making his brown eyes bright.

William smiled at her. "You did an excellent job, Mother," he agreed.

It was not grand, certainly, but she'd built herself a home in a very short time. It felt cozy and warm, but maybe that was just the way Elissana Whitefeld lit up a room.

She beamed with pleasure. "Still more to do," she said, waving away their compliments. "I've been cleaning endlessly. I'm not used to having my own house, though. I've always lived with someone else."

"You're not lonely, are you?" William questioned.

"No, no. There are plenty of people around. The neighbors are lovely people, though I suppose they're just being nice to the *ona*'s aunt. They keep bringing me things, and so does Ovan. And I can always go see you."

There was still something missing. She was happy, yes, but a woman like Lis was not meant to live by herself.

"When I'm better, I'll come stay with you," he decided.

"Like a real family," he added quietly.

Lis melted. "You want to? I mean, I wouldn't force you to…"

"I want to, Mother. If it's okay," he added, glancing at Tiran.

"*I* wouldn't object," Tiran said. "But you should ask the *ona*."

"I'll have Ovan ask her," Lis replied. "She won't mind, I don't think. But… I still don't know what her plans are going to be, and they might involve William, just because of who he is."

William didn't see how. The *ona* had made it clear his only use was if he made it home—which wasn't happening now unless the King came to rescue them all. She'd likely forget all about him. It was a depressing thought. He had just started to feel like she was his friend.

"She's still gone," Dero said. "She hasn't come back in two days. She has eight Ëan with her and another twenty scattered throughout the Road, but things have quieted down some. The panic's dying off. She should be home soon."

They talked some more, but Lis was most pleased by William's idea. It made him even more eager to recover his strength.

After a while, they had to keep going, so he said goodbye to her. She gave him a long, gentle hug before he left. He kissed her on the cheek, and then the men left.

As they kept walking, Dero cleared his throat and asked, "So… maybe it's none of my business, but why do you call her 'Mother'?"

William replied simply. "She isn't really my mother, but she should have been."

Dero looked confused. "But how could you even know her? She and her niece were Lady Seyenne's servants fifteen years ago—though that's too long ago for *me* to really remember."

William glanced at Tiran, who shrugged. The guard knew the story, of course. William had repeated what Lis had told him to Tiran, and Ovan had told the rest. He'd forgotten that few other people knew the truth about who the *ona* was or her real story. They knew the Governor was a fraud, but they had no reason to believe Ria and Lis had been anything but what the Governor said. What did it matter? Surely it only made her stronger.

But it was her affair. If she'd wanted to make it public, she could have. He wasn't about to do it for her. No need to invite her wrath.

"Um," he floundered. He wasn't sure how to answer now without betraying the truth. He looked at Dero. The heartfelt young man wouldn't do anything to hurt anyone. William could tell him, couldn't he? He practically already had.

"She was once a great lady," he said, lowering his voice. "Betrothed to my father, the King."

Dero gasped, so William explained, in short, the whole story as they went along. He told him who she was, and about how things had been in Ossia. Dero couldn't seem to process the information. "But then the *ona* is—that makes the *ona*—"

"Yes, but please—uh—please don't make a fuss about it," William said quickly. "She's a bit touchy about the subject. Pretend I didn't tell you anything. I don't want to make her angry."

Dero nodded. "Of course not," he agreed. "Though I never imagined… You can trust me, though," he added. "I won't spill."

"Thanks." Dero was already a good friend.

They continued up the road until Tiran pointed, saying, "That's where we are staying, my lord."

He indicated three houses joined together into one huge house. It would have provided more than enough room for Tiran's company. The three houses were all surrounded by a low white wall which ran around them until it joined the face of the citadel behind it. They stood before an enormous arched gateway, which was not barred by any kind of door. The Gnomi were clearly not a warrior people, with an eye only for design.

"Not bad," was William's appreciative comment. It was as good as any accommodation they would get at home. "Not quite like barracks, eh? Still, it looks nice. More like a home, I suppose. Who was it for?" he asked Dero.

"The citadel was for the leader—a prefect, or some such title—and his household and staff. They apparently tended to have large families, and so the prefect had an enormous following after a while."

"All this belonged to one family?" William asked incredulously. The citadel alone would have been enough to house several thousand people.

"Clan, more like. But yes."

William whistled. "Well, they were well off, I suppose. These houses are huge!"

"Wait till you see the Sky Palace," Dero enthused. "But let's go see the Guard."

William nodded, and they moved in the direction of the archway.

A single guard stood watching at the entrance. William recognized him as Elix. As soon as he saw William, he gasped and sank to one knee, gaping. "My lord! You're up! We did not expect to see you! It's an honor, my lord—and a pleasure to see you on your feet."

"Thanks," William said genuinely. "Please, get up." He'd tasted the equality of friendship, and he found he enjoyed it more than deference. "No need to kneel."

"As you wish, my lord," Elix complied. He hesitated, unsure what to say next. "I'm sure the others would like to see you," he said tentatively. "Were you going inside?"

"Yes, it's why we came," Tiran answered. "Thank you, Elix."

He saluted. "Yes, captain."

They left him to continue his watch and went inside. Tiran and Dero helped William into a chair to free their shoulders, then they called in the men. A moment later, the whole troop of Tellorian guards flooded the room. They maintained their stoic discipline, never breaking their aura of professionalism, but William could read the pleasure in their faces. To a man, they were utterly devoted to him. The fact that he'd been wounded weighed on them as a failure of their duty, though it had had nothing to do with them. They were pleased to see him recovered, but each was firmly resolved not to let him down again.

He particularly wanted to see the two who had been wounded: Hart and Danick (or Dan, as he was called by his fellows). Hart had suffered only a blow to the arm, which was mostly healed now, but Danick had a broken leg and a number of ugly bruises he'd acquired after he'd fallen. The man was hobbling about, though, and he promised he'd be up and fighting in no time. He had refused to remain in the healing houses, preferring to stay with the Guard. William reminded him to listen to the healers and not rush things, commenting dryly, "Even *I* am subject to their rule." The men laughed at this, and Danick amended his promise to add that he would listen.

William visited with them for a long while. He heard their various stories about their escape, and listened to their opinions on the Nest, the *ona*, the Ëan, everything they had to think about now. He'd lived his whole life under guard, so he'd learned to ignore his armor-clad shadows as a minor nuisance. Now he discovered he'd been missing the fact that those shadows were real people, and some of the best he could ever find.

Eventually, though, they had to continue on. Dero reminded William of the hour and all he still had to see, so William reluctantly left the Guard. They would have gladly accompanied the prince, but Tiran did not think it necessary, nor did he wish to insult the *ona* by making a show of protecting the prince in her place of strength. He ordered them to rest until the *ona* gave him orders.

William's crutches once again took up their burden to help him along. He *was* walking more easily, but he wasn't about to be walking on his own yet. He tried once, and they had to catch him. Dero kept spouting bits of encouragement, unfazed by failure. "You'll be just fine soon enough," he assured cheerfully.

"There!" Dero pointed to a long row of houses just outside a large white gate and a tall wall at the end of the road that wound around the citadel. "The Ëan live in those houses. It's the Ëa quarter."

The houses were no different than the others he'd seen. In fact, they were a little less impressive, probably built for the servants who attended the prefect in his palace (which was clearly beyond that white gate). "Here?" he questioned. "But—"

"I know it's not much to look at, but it's home, and it's far, far better than our old house in the country. This is like paradise compared to that. Besides, the *ona* says we shouldn't take better housing than the people we serve—we shouldn't act superior to them. She'd have us scattered among them, except she needs us together so we can come at call in an emergency. All the Ëan and their families live in the quarter, right beneath the Sky Palace."

"Which one's yours?" William asked.

"That one." Dero pointed to a medium sized house that stretched several floors up. There were flowers in pots on either side of the door, a rare splash of liveliness in the stone city. A large, glittering rainbow lamp was hanging over the entrance.

"Can you show me?" William asked. He was eager to see his friend's home.

But not more eager than Dero. He beamed, grinning from ear to ear. He gave a gleeful chortle. "It would be my pleasure," he beamed.

He and the captain walked William inside the gate. Instead of trying the stairs, Tiran scooped William up like a child and carried him up. Dero opened the door for them.

"Home, sweet home," Dero said jokingly, indicating a well-lit, cozy front hall. He pointed to a chair. "You can have a seat, if you like." Tiran put him down in the chair.

"Aunt Winna!" he shouted. "I'm back, and I've got

company!"

"I didn't know Winna was your aunt," William said to Dero.

"Oh. Well, Winna's my aunt." William cracked up with laughter.

The woman in question appeared. William fought the urge to laugh. She was a rather contradictory sight. She wore the rough clothes of an Ëa: dirty brown tunic, leather breeches. These were covered by a light pink apron. Her hood was awry, revealing her tousled red hair smeared with flour. She balanced a large sword on one hip and a wiggling toddler on the other. She looked thoroughly exasperated.

"Well, good." She nodded to William and Tiran warmly, but distractedly. "You can help me watch the baby. Fred's off with the herd and her mother went down to get some grain." She deftly plucked the round-faced little girl off her hip and into Dero's free arm. "I hope you'll excuse me," she apologized to her guests. "I have to cook." Then she ran back to the kitchen.

William let his laughter out after she left. "Mmmf,"was all Dero said. He displayed the utmost agility in this situation, but to no avail. The little girl nearly wriggled out of his arms, making crying sounds. "El knows I'm no good with kids," Dero grumbled. "I hope Elénne gets back soon. Winna should have sent me to the kitchen instead of having me watch the baby."

William laughed. "You're not holding her right," he said.

"How *do* you hold her right?" Dero asked. "All she does is squirm. She doesn't hold still! Mmmf."

"Runs in the family," William told him. "Here, let me take her." He extended his arms for the little girl.

"Have at it," Dero replied, not hiding his relief.

She was a cute little thing, even if a bit teary. She had a round, not quite chubby face, a button nose, and big brown eyes. Little curls of reddish-brown hair stuck out in all directions. She wore a little dark blue dress that contrasted sharply with her pasty skin.

He set her on his lap, talking softly to reassure her. She

cried a few moments more, then brightened. She cast William a bubbly smile.

"She's beautiful," William declared. "What's her name?"

"Hope."

"Nice name." And it suited her. He bounced her on his knee, receiving delighted giggles for his trouble.

"*You're* good with kids," Dero commented admiringly. "How'd you learn to do that?"

William laughed. "Beats me. I used to play with my cousin's children a few years back when he was still at court, but then they went to live on Rainauldt land." He bounced the girl some more, and she cackled with glee.

Dero took a seat next to him. "She likes you," he said.

"She does indeed," a woman's voice said.

The men all jumped. Tiran's hand moved instinctively to his sword hilt.

"Just me," the woman said, coming out of the doorway.

"Hi, Elénne," Dero sighed. "You scared me, ya did."

The woman laughed, putting down her basket. "May I ask who is visiting?" She glanced at Tiran with a smile, then ran appreciative eyes over William. She tossed her curly hair and a coy smile lit her face.

A shiver ran through William as she examined him. She was bold in her glance, but her confidence was not unwarranted. She was the loveliest woman he'd ever seen, besides the *ona*, of course, but this young lady was different from Ria. Ria possessed feminine beauty but did not choose to flaunt it, preferring instead the virtue of her blades. This girl was womanly in a way that would grab men's attention. She was small, like Dero, and slender. She had reddish brown hair that hung in thick, loose curls down her back, and she had chocolaty brown eyes. She had clearly put thought into bringing out the best of her features. She had a touch of powder and thin lines of paint around her eyes, like the fashionable Edenian women did. She wore a green jewel in her hair. She did not come across as overdone or simpering, like Anjalia; she just seemed secure in her self-image. It was a quality that drew attention like a lodestone.

"Oh," Dero remembered. "Elénne, this is Captain Tiran and this is William."

Elénne gasped, a hand flying to her mouth.

"And this is my cousin, Elénne," Dero finished.

"Pleasure to meet you, ma'am," Tiran said to her. William had trouble finding his tongue.

"William... Tellor?" she asked.

"Yes, ma'am," he managed to answer.

She squeaked. Dero laughed at her. "C'mon, Énne, he's just my friend." Once that would have been a severe demotion; now he liked hearing it. "Don't be so ridiculous."

"Right—um, sorry." She dipped a quick curtsey, but her confidence was undimmed. She still let her gaze linger on his face in a way that made him uncomfortable. Like nearly all women he'd met, she found him attractive. Typical.

She extended her arms to take Hope, who sat tugging on William's shirt. He let her take the little girl, presumably her daughter. "I'd despaired of ever finding a man who's good with children," she told him conspiratorially. William blushed. "Dero's hopeless, and my father is worse."

"Uncle Fred's worse than I am," Dero confided. "It's a miracle Elénne managed to survive at all with him around. Explains some things, eh?" She smacked him on the arm for his comment, but it made William smile.

Elénne fondled the baby. "Is she yours, then?" William asked, just to be sure.

Elénne replied as if the answer was obvious. "Yes, of course."

"Oh," William replied. He wasn't sure if he was relieved or disappointed that she was married.

"Just me, though," Elénne added as if reading his thoughts. "My husband is dead."

"Oh, I'm sorry."

She shrugged, a sad smile on her face. Then she tossed her hair again. "I try not to dwell on it."

"Elénne!" Winna suddenly shouted from the kitchen. "Is

that you?"

"Yes, mother!"

"Come in the kitchen, please! I need your help."

"Coming!" she responded, a little irritation in her voice. "Sorry," she apologized. "Got to go." She gave William one last lingering look, then waved goodbye to all three, taking Hope along with her.

"Would you like to see my room?" Dero asked.

"Sure," William agreed, relieved to be free of complicated young women for a while.

Tiran carried him upstairs, where he saw Dero's room. It was simple: a bed, a washstand, a closet, and some chairs were the only furniture, but he had two sword cases and a bow on its stand as well as a drawer full of various daggers. Also, he had a pile of wood scraps and shavings from his hobby: carving. He'd carved all sorts of beautiful pieces, and he'd poured creativity into patterning all his furniture. William was impressed. He himself didn't possess any such talent. Dero just shrugged off his praise.

When he'd seen the better part of Dero's house, they decided to keep going. They said goodbye to Winna, Elénne, and Hope, as well as Dero's Uncle Fred, who'd returned from tending his herd of cows. (It was clear to William where the relation was. Fred was as small and cheerful as Dero. Fred wasn't an *Ëa*, but he had a good heart, like his family.)

They left the house and walked up to the huge white wall. "Okay," Dero said. "Here we go. Inside the walls is the Sky Palace. It's where the *Ëan* do business." William nodded.

The gate stood wide open. The *Ëan* were perfectly safe here, they feared no attack. The three men walked inside.

The palace loomed up before him. He gasped once again. It was not at all what he had expected. He had seen palaces aplenty. He'd *lived* in one his entire life!

This was less a palace and more a large, wide tower. The King's palace in Ossia was a cluster of buildings put together, all spread out in a large plot of land in the center of the city, like a city into itself. This was all one, clearly, but it could have fit several buildings inside it. It reached upward to span the last of the gap between the city and the mountain roof until its top blended into the ceiling.

Unlike all the other Gnomi creations he'd yet seen, the Palace was not white but rather a deep, glowing blue, like a glacier. Instead of the rainbow lamps, it was lit by pale blue lights. The designs of the walls were made with all blue and white jewels, which sparkled in the light, giving an ethereal air.

"C'mon," Dero urged happily, seeing William's admiration. "Let's go in!"

First was the wide, circular courtyard, bearing statues of small, noble figures named in obscure text. The leaders' portraits, he presumed. Like the Hall of Kings in Ossia.

Then Dero led them through some passages until they arrived at the stables. These were as large as everything else in the city, so despite the number of horses, it wasn't nearly full. The Ëan stocked a much better stable than the Governor, especially after the latest escape. They'd stolen all the horses the Governor kept in his personal stables, leaving only the horses housed in the barracks. Several grooms, both men and women, darted about, along with a few Ëan. They nodded to Dero but only gave William curious looks.

"Where's Blazer?" William asked.

"Over this way," Tiran answered.

Blazer poked his head out of the stall, whinnying when he saw William. "Hey, Blazer," William greeted him. The horse strained to reach to him, nuzzling his master as soon as he was close enough. "I missed you, too," he said to the horse.

Dero whistled. "That's quite a horse. I don't ride much, now that I'm not herding anymore, but my horse—Shala—isn't nearly so grand. May I?" He reached to touch the horse.

"Sure," William answered. The Governor excepted, Blazer was normally very friendly, and he seemed to have affection for the Ëan anyway.

Dero murmured some words in Djoran. Blazer's ears pricked with understanding. He turned intelligent eyes on

Dero. He snorted as if pleased and relaxed under the Ëa's touch.

"Can you talk to animals, too?" William asked. It still seemed strange that the *ona* could.

"No," Dero admitted. "At least, I can't understand *them*. Most of us can't—it's really a Djoran characteristic, though not all of them can even do it. I'm not sure why the *ona* can. I guess she's just special. Some people say she has Djoran blood in her, and maybe she does, and the gift just skipped a few generations. But anyway, the Ëan all speak Djoran, or at least a little, and the animals can understand us. We have certain signals; the *ona*'s animal friends know to alert us if there's danger somewhere that any of us can recognize."

"You know a lot of Djoran?"

He shrugged. "Eh, not much. I'm not the brightest sort, you know... Just a cow-hand who learned to use a sword. Most people give up on teaching me anything like that. I can say 'hello,' at least."

William laughed. "Better than me. It all sounds like gibberish.

"It is a beautiful language, but it defies me. Torhan calls it the music of the earth. Comes in handy, though."

They stayed with Blazer a while, then moved on, though the horse was disappointed. But Dero was eager to show him the rest of the palace.

They looked in on the armory, less a cache for the weapons and more a shop to repair them. It was filled with parts of weapons, whetstones, forges, and a stock of extra arrows. The Ëan kept their weapons with them, and they didn't lose them.

Then Dero showed him the "practice room" as he called it. It had obviously been converted to its current use. Rows and rows of practice weapons stood on shelves that lined the walls, and there were also piles of padded armor to wear while sparring. Rings were marked off in different dimensions to form small arenas, each with a mat on the floor. Targets were set up for a shooting range at the far end of the room, rows of unsharpened arrows standing nearby. Everything bore signs of heavy use, attesting to the rigorous training of the *Ëan*.

"This is where I learned to fight," Dero told them proudly. "Aunt Winna taught me to shoot—though I'm not as good at that. I learned a little hand-fighting from Szera, but I gave up after a while. She's not a gentle teacher."

"Wow," William commented. "How long did it take you to learn?"

"I came to the Nest two years ago. I became an *Ëa* a year ago. I'm still one of the least among them, but I keep training. And they're good to me, all of them. They give me lots of pointers. We're all like family around here."

"So to join the *Ëan*, you just have to be good at fighting?"

"No, not really. It's—um—it's more complicated than that."

A desire formed in the back of William's mind, but he did not pay it much heed. It was a silly idea anyway.

"One last thing to see," Dero pressed on, "and it's by far the best."

"Something even better?" William asked.

"*Oh*, yes," Dero replied. "It's not just called the Sky Palace 'cause it's blue. I'll show you!"

They went up many flights of stairs, past dozens of rooms which were mostly empty. The stairs, however, seemed well-worn by the feet of the *Ëan*. "This is where plans are born," Dero narrated. "The *Ëan* come up here to think and to hold council, to celebrate, to mourn, and to sing."

"Sing?" Dero didn't hear him.

"I just like to sit up here every once in a while. Things are quieter in the summer, and then we have a little more time. That's when I come up here."

One more flight of stairs. A bright light wafted down from the top, clearly no manmade lamp. Daylight? Were they at the top of the mountain, then?

"Here it is," Dero announced. "The Sky Tree Hall."

William blinked as they emerged into full sunlight. His

eyes adjusted, and he stared.

It was a huge, circular room, large enough to fit a few hundred people. Stone chairs stood in a circle around the largest, oldest tree William had ever seen. This tree was completely blue, from its light trunk to its dark leaves. But that was not even the best of it.

The room was made entirely of glass, both ceiling and walls, letting in the sunlight. This room stood on the highest peak of the summit of the mountain. All of Belond lay glittering below them, from the mountainside and the hills to the distant line of the sea. He could look in any direction to see the whole island. Had he been afraid of heights, he might have fainted, but this was exhilarating. He felt like he was in the clouds—in fact, the misty clouds were very near them. He might have been a bird, flying over the island.

"Do you like it?" Dero asked.

"It's—it's—amazing!" William exclaimed. "Beautiful!"

"They say the tree was a gift from the Djorn," Dero informed him. "The Gnomi built this glass room just for it. Look at this, though!" Dero replied. He ran over to the nearest wall and pushed on one of the many glass panels. It swung outward, letting in a blast of warm summery air. William breathed it in. The underground city was not stuffy, but it *was* underground. The outside air felt deliciously fresh.

"It's heavenly," William declared. A thought occurred to him. "Dero why don't you *all* just stay here? I mean, you're safe here and provided for. Just bring everyone here and let the Governor try to stop you. What can he do to you here?"

Dero pursed his lips. "Nothing," he answered. "But it's not that simple. For one thing, not everyone will come."

"Well, why not?" William asked. It seemed utter foolishness to him not to *want* to come.

"Belo is all they know. Even if they're mistreated, they can't leave all they've ever known. They'd rather be slaves." Dero paused sadly. "My own sister is the same. I tried to convince her, but she won't leave our old home."

"I'm sorry," William said. He wanted to ask more about

her, but his normally cheerful friend looked so despondent that he didn't want to upset Dero further. He remembered that Dero had been trying to visit his sister when he'd gotten caught.

Dero sighed. "Besides, even if we're safe here, we're not free, and we believe freedom is worth fighting for. We won't hide away here. We want to reclaim our home. Besides, the *ona* is determined to bring the Governor to justice, so we will see it done. If she fights, we fight, too."

William nodded. He saw that his thought had been a cowardly one, anyway. "You're right," he said. "We must fight." It had become a *we*.

Dero grinned now. "Right you are, brother," he replied. He offered his hand, and William shook it. For some reason, that seemed to seal it for William more than anything.

Chapter 21

A loud commotion began outside. William was sitting in a chair near the kitchen while Lis cooked. Mothers know everything, so he called to her, "What's going on?"

"Don't yell in the house, please!" she hollered back over the noise. "Mind your manners, William Tellor!" She emerged from the kitchen. "How should I know?" she answered.

He laughed. He liked having a mother.

He'd spent another two days in the infirmary, then Ekata had permitted him to move to Lis's house. Two more enjoyable days had gone by, and he was almost feeling normal again. He could walk around by himself without gasping like a galloping horse, and he didn't feel lightheaded all the time. Ekata had pronounced him well-mended.

Now he was just trying to figure out what he should be doing.

"Go ask Pav," Lis suggested, cocking her head. There were downsides to having no windows.

William poked his head out the door. A large number of people were running past in a hurry, all talking. Their neighbors were loudly discussing some subject of interest. Everyone was twittering with excitement.

He turned to the guards posted on each side of the door. There were two more at the back. It seemed Tiran was set on careful security standards, but he supposed they couldn't be blamed for wanting to protect the King's family.

"What's going on?" he asked Pav, one of Tiran's lieutenants.

"I'm not certain, sire," Pav replied. "Doesn't seem like trouble, but those messengers are in a hurry."

William surveyed the crowd moving through the streets, then he picked out a face he recognized. "Fred!" he called to Winna's husband.

Fred came running over, calling a friendly hello as he

came. "Well, now, nice to see ya agin, lad," he chatted. "What cannai do fer ya?"

"Do you know what's going on here?"

He bobbed his head to the guards before speaking. "Well, now, the *ona* is—oh, look! There goes Cherrie off ta tell the news ta her father! A good little lass, Cherrie. Watches tha granddaughter betimes. Cherrie!" he waved to the girl as she ran by.

William cleared his throat. "Um… What news would that be?"

"Oh, right, right. So, now, the *ona* has come back, she has. Last night, it were. So now it's just back to tha regular ways, it seems. Things must o' settled down or she wouldn't be back. But she's called a moot."

"A moot?"

"A council, of sorts, laddie. She musta come up wif a new plan! The messengers are bringin' ever'one to tha meetin'."

He was about to ask something else when a breathless lad of about fifteen ran up to the door. "'Scuse me, sirs," he huffed, "but the *ona* has sent me with a message for William." No one used his title anymore. That was quick.

"I'm William."

The boy bobbed his head like that was obvious. "The *ona* has requested you attend the moot. It convenes in an hour. Don't be late."

"That's not much time," William commented. No wonder now about all the commotion. It was a long walk to the Sky Palace, and there were probably many people to call.

"The *ona* told me to tell you this has nothing to do with your title," the boy intoned coolly. "Just necessity."

"Heh," Fred laughed. William smiled. Trouble hadn't dampened the *ona*'s fiery tongue.

"Madam Lis is requested also," the page added.

William nodded, but his mind was running quickly with questions. He wondered what this was all about, anyway.

"Thank you," William told him.

The page bobbed his head and ran off. *I forgot to ask his*

name, William berated himself. Old habits.

"You'd better be off," Fred advised. "Ya know how the *ona* gets, and this is important. Ah, but who can complain! The *ona* is a genius, she is! She'll have something grand cooked up." He cackled merrily to himself. "I be off now, lad, and you'd best be, too, if ya know what's good fer ya!" With more laughter, he bounded away up the street.

Forty-five minutes later, he sat in one of the stone chairs of the Sky Tree Hall, next to Lis, with Captain Tiran standing behind, along with a dozen or so other guards accompanying them. A handful of sailors stood a short distance away. The *Ëan* ringed the rest of the room, each marked by their battle-hard expressions, the stripes of blue paint on each cheek, and the stockpile of weapons distributed between their persons. Gone were the masks and hoods, however. In the Nest, they did not need such disguises.

Not all were present, of course. The *Ëan* were too careful to withdraw completely from Belo. They were in the center of the island, on the very top of the mountain! They left sentries on the Gnomi Road at all hours, in case of an emergency. If a truly serious problem arose, however, the animals could tell the *ona*, and she could rally the *Ëan* to fly down the mountain at a moment's notice. A very tidy system, it seemed.

Some of the more influential *Reben* were also present, many seated on their side of the circle. Even if someone couldn't fight, that didn't mean their counsel was invaluable. A whole crowd of others stood in the back of the room by the glass walls, not necessarily summoned specifically but too curious to stay away.

"Where's Ria?" William whispered to Lis.

"I don't know," Lis replied a bit nervously. She wasn't used to this sort of thing. She'd lived as a noblewoman for half her life and then a maidservant for the other half. Aside from her niece, she had little experience with dangerous characters. This was a rougher crowd than she was accustomed to.

"Relax," he whispered, trying to reassure her, though he was a little nervous himself. "Nothing to worry about."

They waited a while, the crowd whispering among themselves. Then it hushed abruptly, all eyes going to the stairs. Everyone who was seated rose in unison, so William did the same. He turned to look, knowing all too well what he'd see.

The *ona* stood at the top of the stairs, Szera and Ovan behind her. She looked different than William had ever seen her. Instead of her dingy outlaw's clothes, she wore a chain mail shirt with a green tunic, and she had armor strapped to her forearms and legs. Only the boots were the same. William had the sense that this was less for battle and more to send a message. It was a declaration of war.

Her hair was twisted into an intricate pile of braids, secured at the base of her neck by two long hairpins. It was not quite fashionable, but it suited her well.

Her face, free of its mask, was painted with a column of three dark blue stripes on each cheek, the same paint worn by the rest of the Ëan. The paint, the hair, and the armor all made her look like a cross between a barbarian chieftain and an Edenian general. She was aptly named for the goddess of war.

It was her expression, however, that drew William's attention. To a casual eye, she looked grim, but he saw a glint of mischief, almost arrogance in her eyes. Oh, she had a scheme. William had known her long enough to see that. She was clearly not entirely happy with the situation, but she was determined to have her way, and she took a perverse pleasure in getting it.

She waved to the crowd. "Hello, everyone," she greeted them. "Please, be seated." As one, the people in the room resumed their seats. She cast her eyes over all of them. Her gaze fell on William. He lowered his eyes from hers, flushing. She smiled at him, but he couldn't tell if she mocked him or not. There was something a little too conspiratorial in her air.

"Thank you for your promptness," she said loudly so all

could hear, moving confidently into the room. "Sorry to rush you; however, we have some *deliberating* to do." She said this like "deliberating" gave her a fiendish delight. Her attitude was contagious. It made everyone feel more confident, somehow, instead of desperate. The *ona* made it clear the Governor would not intimidate her.

It was brilliant crowd manipulation. William had to hand it to her.

She moved to take a seat around the circle with the other Ëan. Ovan and Szera sat on either side of her. Ovan cast a reassuring smile at Lis.

"So," the *ona* declared. "Let us begin the council. Torhan?"

The pale-faced Djor rose, somewhere on the other side of the circle. "Let us lift our hearts to our Father in heaven," he said warmly.

All the company bowed their heads, and then he began a sing-song prayer, saying something first in Djoran and then translating it into Edenian. The words were simple, heartfelt, and beautiful, and the deference of the entire crowd seemed sincere. It was very different from the dry, traditional religion back in Ossia. This stirred something in William he'd never felt before. This was a real prayer.

Torhan was an eloquent speaker. He spun words like other men swung swords. Such a gift had to be inspired.

"*Elamar Aiael*—" Torhan concluded, "In the name of El—*hetswan*—let it be so. *Bletar Aiael swa non*—the blessing of El be upon us." He took his seat.

"Thank you, Torhan," the *ona* said to him. She let the music of his prayer linger in their hearts for a moment more, then she said, "Let us begin."

She rose from her seat. "Some of you recall our last council. To that, I called only my Ëan, because it was a matter of war. The King's son was bound for Belond, and we had to decide what to do. Instead of merely protecting him, we decided to use him as an opportunity to send word to the King, a chief aim in our quest to protect the island. To fight an army, we need an army. You all know this, and it was agreed upon."

Here she rose and began to walk slowly back and forth about the circle. All eyes were fixed upon her, hanging on her every word.

"Opportunity for this outcome was snatched from our hands, by the fault of none," she emphasized, "unless it be the Governor's. There is no blame, it just happened." Nods ran around the room. William ducked his head, though on the inside he was grateful for the absolution. A glance at Dero said he felt the same.

"Now, when the usurper's wrath is dimmed, it seems we are back where we started." Her green eyes swept the room, gleaming with conspiratorial delight. "But we are not."

Her eyes fell on William. "The Governor is unsure whether or not our would-be messenger survived. He is here with us, of course, but the Governor thinks it is likely he is dead. We have the advantage now. Sending our message to the King no longer depends on deceiving the Governor."

Whispers flew at this. This was absurd. They were trapped here! Prince or not, there was no ship to carry him back to Ossia.

She held up a hand for silence. "I know, I know. We have no ship, you say. We have no way to get one, you say. And even if we did, we could not sail it because the Governor controls the bay. I am here to tell you that I say different."

She returned to sweeping the chamber with that intense gaze. Her eyes alighted on Captain Wood. "Captain," she invited, "please step forward."

To say the captain was surprised was an understatement. He did as he was asked, but he looked astonished and more than a little nervous. William hoped he wouldn't faint.

"Yes, my lady?" he stammered. He looked like he was about to face execution.

"*Ona*," she corrected lightly. "The *Ëan* need your help."

Before he could respond, she announced, "To those of you who do not know, this is Captain Wood, of His Majesty's own fleet. He has lost his ship, but his knowledge he retains. Captain," she said to him, "you retained three shipwrights on your vessel, did you not?"

He looked taken aback. "How did you know that?"

She grinned, not answering. "And two survived the destruction of the ship, am I correct?"

"Yes, *ona*," again with surprise.

"Excellent." She turned to the crowd again. "The ruin of one plan has led to another. Ladies and gentlemen, I propose we build our own ship!"

Pandemonium ensued. This was as radical a pronouncement as any they'd ever heard from the *ona*. Only the *Ëan* remained unfazed. They'd seen enough to trust the *ona*'s word without question on less basis.

Captain Wood interjected. "*Ona*," he protested. "I cannot build you a ship. I don't have the means or the men, or a place to do it. You cannot set sail from under a mountain."

She smiled breezily at him, which told William she was irritated by his objection. "Hear me out," she responded. "I have given this fair thought, actually. For years I have thought our troubles could be resolved if we could build our own ship. But sailors are scarce and shipbuilders more so. Now we have them, my friends, by the grace of El.

"Means? We'll build them. We have wood aplenty on the north side, and any tools necessary can be made. Men? There are now nearly eight hundred people in the Nest. If the *Reben* agree," the *ona* looked at the crowd of them, "you will have plenty of workers, and the *Ëan* will help also, as we may. A place? Easy enough. Edenia never bothered to explore the eastern half of the island. They settled in the west. The east, however, is as easily accessible to ships as the west. The Gnomi used to have a port there, so we have an easy road to transport any materials."

The people began to see the sense of the plan. It actually might work!

"It will take time, I know—"

"A long time," Captain Wood put in.

"But we can do it," she continued. "When the passage is open again, we will send the King's family home."

Her eyes rested on Lis. She said it gently enough, but there was a tightness in her face for which William could not account. Lis, however, was lit with hope, longing on her face.

"And then may the Empire be just," the *ona* finished. She turned to the people, measuring each face in turn. "Do you agree?"

Only a moment's pause elapsed before the *Ëan* rose as one and shouted, "Aye!" Their voices melded into one cry that echoed with power. One by one, the rest of those present added their voices to the agreement. The Tellorian guard saluted. The sailors agreed eagerly, though Captain Wood still looked dubious. The *Reben* agreed as well, though they would bear most of the burden of this project.

"Good," the *ona* said in satisfaction. "Let's get to work, then. We have a lot of planning to do."

"You were wonderful, Ria," Lis said to the *ona*.

After ages of ironing out details, they'd determined the plans, materials, labor, and time frame to build the ship. If all went well, it would be ready in plenty of time to sail next spring when the voyage could be made again.

Nearly a year.

At least it was hopeful.

The *ona* nodded her acknowledgment of Lis's words. Her face remained stoic. She didn't really respond to flattery. "Glad you liked it," she replied, her voice tinged with sarcasm.

They were walking down the stairs through the Sky Palace, finally getting some personal time with the *Ëa ona*. William had Lis on his arm as they walked.

"This is so different than what I imagined," Lis told her. "You've made a wonderful home here."

"You like your house, I imagine. Raluf is good at managing the space for us."

"Oh, yes, it's lovely! A large space for just two of us, though." She smiled up at William.

Ria cast an eye over William. "I see you've recovered well enough," she said. "Kata tells me you and Dero have already been gallivanting all over the Nest, as well."

"Yes," he admitted. "Dero's been good to me."

She nodded. "He's a good lad. Good swordsman."

They reached the bottom of the stairs. Szera and Torhan were waiting a few paces off, clearly wanting to talk to her. She moved to go. "Excuse me, please. I have to go."

"Wait a second," William called her back. He slipped away from Lis's grasp to catch her.

She turned her head back. "Yes?"

"Um… I wanted to ask… well…"

"Spit it out, love," she told him. "Hurry up."

"What am I supposed to be doing? I mean, I don't want to just sit at home, much as I love Mother. I want to help."

Up until now, he'd been part of the plan. He'd *been* the plan. Now he was waiting while Ria and the *Ëan* did everything. *She* might like that, but he didn't.

She laughed. "Well, love, I don't know. Never had a stray nobleman among the *Reben* before. You can't fight, you can't farm, and you have no trade. I hear you're good with children—you could babysit." She chuckled some more. "Or there's always manual labor. We're building a ship, you know. How good are you at cutting down trees?"

She was making fun of him, but not in a mean-spirited way. She was just teasing.

"I can learn," he offered. "If that's what you want."

She regarded him more closely, with a hint of admiration. "Okay," she agreed. "See Pat tomorrow, then. He'll tell you what to do."

"Thanks," he replied. This was as good as anything he could do, he supposed, but he wasn't quite satisfied. He wanted to know how it felt to actually *fight* for something worthwhile: for justice.

He hesitated, then he plunged ahead. "*Ona*… I know this is foolish, but…" he took a deep breath, steeling himself to voice the question.

"It's only silly if you don't ask," she said.

"How do you become an Ëa?" he said in a rush.

She actually didn't laugh. She raised an eyebrow, then said seriously, "You earn it."

With that, she turned on her heel and went to talk to the others waiting for her.

"Everything okay?" Lis asked William when he came back.

"Yeah. Just fine. I—uh—I need to go talk to someone. Do you mind?"

"Go ahead, dear."

"Thanks." He darted off, feeling purposeful for a rare time in his life.

"Dero?"

"Yeah?"

William cleared his throat, not sure how to ask. "Would you be willing to do me a favor?"

"Sure. What is it?"

"Would you teach me how to fight?"

Chapter 22

William's new ambition taught him only his own insignificance.

Actually, it wasn't *that* he minded. He'd come down far enough from his aristocratic arrogance that he knew he deserved to be ignored. He was no better than anyone else; in fact, he was worse. He was no good at anything. He regretted now all the years he'd wasted in Ossia sitting around doing nothing. He was paying for it now. He had no skills at all.

He was soft, and he had no endurance. He was little use at hard labor. He lacked skills other men considered elementary. He might have been smart, but that was by Ossian standards. What he'd learned in school hardly helped him in this environment. And he couldn't fight. Not really. He knew how to swing a sword as well as any average man, but his talent was pitiful compared to warriors like the Ëan. Dero was encouraging, but even *his* cheerfulness wavered at times.

William was useless.

For the first time in his life, he'd tasted what it felt like to do something worthwhile, to further a cause he could believe in. Then, once again, he'd been left wondering what the point was. He didn't want to go back to drifting. That was the point of all this. It was what motivated him to keep trying. It was too late for it to be comfortable anymore. For the first time in fifteen years, he was choosing to care about something.

Ria wanted him to earn respect? Fine. No problem. His mind was set. He could endure the humiliation of becoming a nobody, if that's what it took. He wasn't going to give up, and he wasn't afraid. He didn't mind being ignored.

But that was just it.

He wouldn't have minded so much if the others had just pretended he didn't exist. But they didn't. No, they watched everything he did, jeering, laughing, and criticizing.

Not *everyone*, of course. Most of his first friends were still welcoming to him. Dero was stuck to him, and no one was driving *him* away. Tiran still watched over him, faithful as a guard-dog. Ovan, Winna, and Kerran were good to him. Lis was, of course, always gentle and supportive, even if she didn't always approve of William's activities (mostly the fighting).

But it was the *Ëan* who were causing the trouble.

They'd never really liked him, ever since they'd first captured him. Baër, for some reason, had taken a particular dislike to him, and a large number of the others followed his leading. They made a point of criticizing everything he did wrong, and loudly so everyone could hear.

He probably deserved it, but it was hard to swallow nonetheless. So he was proud! He couldn't shake his upbringing *that* quickly. No one in Ossia would have dared insult the King's son to his face. It was hard to weather a storm of abuse when he wasn't used to it.

The *Reben* on the worksite were picking it up, too, since at least a few of the *Ëan* were always out working alongside them. The foreman, Pat, had a sour dislike of William that reflected in the way William was treated. William barely kept his temper at times.

And where was the *ona*?

She was everywhere, it seemed. The *Ëan* went out into Belo with regularity, and she always went along with them, but she also found the time to visit the worksite. Sometimes she met with the shipwrights and engineers to discuss plans. Other times, she labored right along with the rest of them. She never seemed to tire, and she was always watching.

William knew she saw the way they treated him and even grew a little irritated at the way her followers behaved, but she didn't step in. She didn't rescue him. He knew she wanted him to handle it himself. If he wanted respect, he couldn't go crying to the *ona* that he was being bullied. He would lose even the little ground he'd gained. Gone was the whiner of the past. He would just have to toughen up.

Oh, but it was hard. He was exhausted from work, and his

temper frayed dangerously thin at times. Why couldn't they leave him alone?

"Let's go, sluggard," said Cob, his typical work partner, in his own gruff manner. "No time fer dawdlin'."

"Sorry," William muttered in reply, barely managing to be civil. He continued clipping off the branches from the pine they'd just felled.

It had been a month since the council. They had been working busily on the construction of the ship this whole time. There were nearly a hundred and fifty workers, including *Ëan*, Tellorian guards, sailors, and *Reben*. They rotated the full-time workers through three days of labor, one day of rest. Each day, the builders left the Nest at dawn, and walked or rode the two hours to the logging site, not returning until dusk.

They had spent three weeks digging a ramp from the surface down to the Gnomi Road so they could transport logs to the construction site, the eastern bay. The forest they were demolishing was in the northeast of the island, just south of and overlooking the *Reben*'s farms, thus avoiding the notice of the Governor and also the home of the Djorn.

It was exhausting work. When Ria had asked if he wanted to do manual labor, he hadn't known what he was getting into. Digging the ramp had proven to be back-breaking work, and the shovel had completely shredded his hands. They still carried blisters, rubbed too raw to heal. Now it was the axe.

They needed several types of wood for the ship. Pine trees were the easiest to cut down. He and Cob were working on those. Only the *Ëan* and the Tellorian guards were tackling the oaks. They worked in pairs, swinging the axes into the trees, half-way on one side, then through on the other side. It had been difficult to master the axe, but once they got going they gained a rhythm. It tore his hands agonizingly and weighed on his tired muscles, but he pushed on.

Once a tree was down, they stripped it of its branches and harnessed it to a team of horses. One was Blazer. William hated to put the proud beast to such labor, but Blazer volunteered, according to the *ona*. In any case, he was one of the strongest horses they had. William decided to just be grateful for the time with him.

"That's all the branches," William called to Cob.

"Mm," he grunted in reply.

Cob was the grumpiest fellow William had ever met. He was old, with gray in his hair and a bit of a hunch in his back. He had stormy black eyes and a scruffy beard. He was entirely unkempt, with dirty clothes, worn shoes, and hair all awry. His manners were far from perfect, as his brusqueness demonstrated. William would have preferred to work beside Dero, but his friend was an *Ëa*. When he was at the site, he was with his fellows.

"Let's go," Cob urged grumpily. William wasn't sure if Cob disliked him in particular, or if he just treated everyone that way. He sighed. It was hard to endure the constant ill temper of this man.

He fastened the rope around the tree trunk, securing it so the horses could pull it down the ramp to the Road. A few women darted around collecting the branches they'd clipped to take back to the Nest for firewood. The *ona* was not wasteful.

William saw Elénne, Hope strapped to her back. He smiled at her, and she grinned back. The women, in any case, weren't affected by the epidemic of dislike for him. He had as many flirts around him as ever, much to his discomfort. But he liked Elénne well enough. She was nicer than most of the other girls, and he knew her better because of the time he'd spent with Dero. She was bold, and not afraid to speak her mind, which was more appealing to him than coyness. She was also pretty. Very pretty.

Hope gurgled at him, and he laughed as he worked.

"Stop yer foolin'," Cob scolded. "Just cause ye got a pair o' pretty eyes gawking don't mean yer less worthless."

"He belongs with the women," the foreman grumbled, coming up behind him. "I've scarce seen a line tied so ill. He undid the rope and retied it himself. "There ye go, ye idiot.

Learn how to tie a knot. Now, move. Ain't no time fer foolin'. Ye'll have to hurry. This'll be yer last trip today."

It took an hour just to haul a tree to the bay. Blazer did the job credibly, but it was still time-consuming.

Elénne waved as she walked away with an armful of wood. He sighed. "Come on, Blazer," he said to the horse. Blazer nickered, then began to strain, slowly moving the log. "That's it," he encouraged. They headed for the ramp.

He and Cob passed several teams of workers. Dero paused to shout a cheerful greeting. William waved back but wished Dero hadn't drawn attention to him.

"Don't waste your time, Dero," a voice jeered. A few others added laughter.

Not again.

Baër paused to laugh at him as he passed. "The noble peasant," he said mockingly. "Haven't you given up yet?"

Baër was shirtless due to the heat, exposing his strong muscles. Baër's dark hair was slicked back with sweat, but it only made him look tougher. He was far more intimidating than William.

William tensed, angry, but held his tongue, difficult as it was.

"Knock it off, Baër," Dero said.

"Why?"

"You're making a fool of yourself."

"*He's* the fool." A few of the Tellorian guards were watching now, hands on their weapons. They didn't take kindly to insults to their master. "Run back to your mommy, boy, like you noblemen do."

William wished he hadn't brought Lis into it. He could hear her voice telling him to stay calm, but his fists were clenched.

"You neglect your duty, Baër," said Winna, his partner for the day, "and you dishonor yourself."

Baër shrugged. The rest of the *Ëan* looked uncomfortable, looking to the *ona* for guidance. She was watching, of course, green eyes blazing with unreadable scrutiny. All the *Ëan*, Baër included, snapped back to work when her eye fell on them.

William paused, wishing once again that she would help. She'd ridiculed him often enough herself, but coming from her, it seemed different. He'd once hated her for her harsh tongue, but now, when she needled him, it didn't grate so much. It was more the teasing of a friend than mocking from an enemy.

He turned away. He heard them still snickering behind his back, and his ears burned. He tried very hard not to hang his head. If he was a prince, he'd have to act like one. That was all there was to it.

It was just hard.

"No, no," Dero sighed, backing away. "You left yourself wide open, William."

William leaned forward, gasping for air. His lessons with Dero in the evenings were depleting. Not only had he worked all day, now he was swinging a wooden practice sword. Every muscle in his body protested. He wanted to just give up, but he couldn't. He knew he couldn't. He had to learn how to fight.

Dero was good. Not as good as some, perhaps, but he was a talented fighter nonetheless. Among the *Ëan*, even being the least was impressive. William could hardly believe he'd been a cowhand most of his life.

"I didn't expect you to do that," William wheezed.

Dero spluttered. "It's a fight!"

Tiran, who'd chosen to spectate tonight and give advice, spoke up. "You *are* fighting dirty, Dero," the captain said. "You throw in all those irregular moves, as if you were fist-fighting *and* sword-fighting. It's not... not..."

"It's how we fight," Dero protested. "You want me to be *predictable?*" He wasn't irritated, just confused. He couldn't understand what Tiran was saying. The *Ëan* didn't fight fair. They didn't think rules applied in combat. One never knew what they would do next.

"No," Tiran pondered, "it's just that you—you're not—I can't quite explain it. I've never seen a style like yours, and all your comrades seem to have their own. It's just not Edenian."

William couldn't even master regular Edenian style back home. Dero pulverized him every time he stepped into the ring, and his friend wasn't even the best. This was hopeless. He had less talent with a sword than he did with a shovel.

And they were laughing at him again, across the room.

Until another voice spoke up.

His heart seemed to sink into his toes, and his face burned with shame. Great. *She* was here to witness his humiliation. Why'd she have to show up *now*? She hadn't approached him in ages.

"Call it Belondian, Captain," the *ona* broke in. She came to stand next to Tiran, accompanied by Ovan.

She knew how to make an entrance. At the first word she spoke, every eye was on her, everyone at attention. She waved away their stares, and they went back to practicing.

She still wore her work clothes, light for the hot June weather. Her green-gray shirt was short-sleeved, exposing her round arm muscles. Her long hair was braided into a knot at the base of her neck. She wore pants that came to her knees. (Leaving her calves exposed would have scandalized an Ossian woman, but it didn't seem out of place for Ria.) She wore leather sandals on her feet. Her skin was well tanned by the sun, which only set off her hair and eyes. She was beautiful. If William hadn't been panting already, she'd have taken his breath away.

Tiran dipped a quick bow to the *ona*. She smiled in return, then continued talking. "We don't believe in traditional swordplay, Captain. It has its uses, of course, but in a real fight, you throw everything you have at your opponent. I wouldn't call it trickery, quite, just cleverness. We are unorthodox, and so we must teach in an unorthodox way. Edenians teach swordplay by learning one move and perfecting it. That only works if you've seen your enemy's attacks before. But if he throws something unexpected at you, you fail. Therefore, you must learn to use your instincts, not your memory."

Tiran nodded as if this made sense. So did Dero. He eyed William as if reconsidering how to teach him.

The *ona* met his eyes. "How about one more, William? Maybe I can help."

He didn't want her to watch him. It was bad enough that the other Ëan did. He was a miserable failure, and he knew it. It would only make it worse for her to see—her of all people. She would laugh at him, too.

He still leaned on his sword. He'd already pushed it hard today. He wasn't even sure he *could* go another round. His muscles burned, and his blistered hands stung.

"C'mon, love," she whispered so only he could hear. Her green eyes held him. "Show me one more."

She wasn't laughing at him.

He took a deep breath. Then he stood to face Dero.

"When you're ready," the *ona* said.

Dero moved first. In these fights, William concentrated mostly on defending. He had enough to think about with just that.

Dero came at him on the high line. He was trying to take it easy, but the wooden sword still whistled through the air with impressive speed. William managed to parry. His shoulders shook with exhaustion.

Several more strokes came one after the other, at his shoulder, chest, and head. Then Dero locked their swords with one hand and shoved William in the chest with the other. As he stumbled back, Dero disarmed him and at the same time, ducked to sweep William's feet from under him.

Maybe thirty seconds that time.

"You okay?" Dero asked, extending a hand.

He didn't take it. Once he was down, it was easier to stay there a minute. "I'm fine," he said, but his pride was wounded. Again.

He closed his eyes, wishing he could disappear. He should just give this up. It wasn't worth the humiliation. They were right.

Then someone stood over him. "Get up, William," the *ona*

said. "Never stay down."

She was deadly serious, not teasing. He opened his eyes, looking up at her. She stood with all the splendor of a war goddess, challenging. She'd stepped into the ring. Her hands were on her hips.

He groaned. It took all the effort he could muster, but he got himself up off the ground. He stood before her, but he couldn't look her in the eye.

She was smiling, a hint of triumph behind her eyes. "There you go," she said. "That's better.

"Now then," she began factually. He waited for her stinging criticism. "You have potential, love, but a lot of work to do."

Wait, what?

His spirits rose, even just a tiny bit.

"Listen, now. I'm not repeating myself." He lifted his eyes to meet hers. She nodded subtly and continued. "Your form isn't bad," she allowed, "though it could be better, and you only know basic maneuvers. Your speed and strength—" she poked a finger at his still-skinny arm, making him wince, "—need work. But you have good instincts. Most people wouldn't have kept up with Dero that long at your level. You could see where he was going as long as he was in your frame of reference. You just need to retrain your instincts so you can see where he's going even when he's outside your frame of reference. You need to see *everything*—all the possibilities there are."

That ended her pronouncement. She turned from him with an encouraging smile. "Your opinion, Captain?"

He nodded agreement. "I think you've hit it just right, *ona*," he answered. Ovan smiled, nodding also.

A sly smile spread over her lips. "Then perhaps a demonstration, Captain? He could learn by watching. Ovan told me you were interested in sparring me."

"Ooooh," Dero said ominously.

Tiran just grinned. "I wouldn't mind a lesson of my own," he admitted. "I think you have much to teach.

She smiled dangerously, then pointed to the rack. "You choose first, Captain," she invited.

They had the others' attention now. William stumbled out of the square with Dero. The other *Ëan* gathered around, nudging each other excitedly, mischievous looks on their faces.

Dero bounced happily like a little kid. "No one spars the *ona*," he said gleefully. "And for a reason. This'll be great. We don't usually get to watch her fight."

Ria heard him, William could tell. She smiled at the two of them. "Then watch closely," she said to Dero. "You might learn something, too."

She removed her sandals, which William thought was odd until he saw the little metal spikes on the undersides of them. She headed for the rack of wooden swords and chose one, almost unthinkingly, but it suited her so well William knew it had just been a habit.

She reentered the ring, facing Tiran. "I hear you're a skilled swordsman," she said to the Captain.

"One can always be better," he shrugged.

"Too true," she agreed. "I say the same myself."

She held the wooden sword with relaxed practice, as if she'd done it a thousand times. "When you're ready," she invited easily.

Tiran moved forward, then feinted quickly to her right.

Two seconds later, he was flat on his back without anyone quite understanding how. He coughed, sputtering. The *ona* held his sword in her left hand.

The *Ëan* gave a cheer. "*Ona*," Ovan interjected merrily, "how can we learn if we can't see anything? Hardly effective teaching."

William was stunned. Tiran was the best swordsman in the King's guard—no mean praise.

"What—how—" Tiran stammered in surprise.

"Sorry," she apologized breezily, not even winded. "Too fast. Again?"

He got to his feet with a groan. She handed him back his

sword. He took it, then paused to catch his breath.

A moment later, they were at it again.

It was still almost too fast to follow, but the *ona* had slowed down enough for the Captain to keep up with her. Slash, parry, stab, the swords whacked together with the cracking of wood against wood. Ria moved fluidly, one instant behind, below, or above Tiran, leaping like a gymnast or rolling under the captain's feet. William could see exactly what she meant. Tiran was a master of the sword, but he'd only ever fought Edenians. Ria was something else entirely.

The fight lasted about thirty seconds this time. Once again, the *ona* sent his sword flying out of his grasp, but she used his momentum in reaching for it to send him sprawling forward. He landed on his stomach with a grunt.

The crowd cheered again, praising their leader.

"Well done," Ria complimented. "You're a rare swordsman. I've seen very few as good as you."

"*You're* amazing," Tiran protested. "I still don't understand how you did that."

"Few can last ten seconds against the *ona*, even if she's going easy," Ovan said proudly. "You did well, Tiran."

"More to learn," the captain said. He got to his feet and then bowed to the *ona*. "I am honored to have sparred you, *ona*. You are truly a legend."

"More to learn," she echoed. "I'm not good enough yet."

This earned a shocked look from Tiran, but she shook his hand. "Thank you for your help, Captain," she said formally. She turned to William, that old smile on her face. "I hope you learned something," she said to him.

"Uh, yes," he replied.

She laughed, then sobered again. "Keep working at it. You have to want it."

"I do," he said.

She lowered her voice, speaking just to him, now. "I'm a woman, and I came from nothing," she whispered with a hint of bitterness. "No one believed in me either. But I earned my way."

She took something from her pocket. "Take those," she said. "Wear them until your blisters heal up and your hands harden." Then she added, very quietly, "There's something I'd like you to see… Your day off—day after tomorrow—I'll come find you in the morning." This brooked no argument.

Without another word, Auria reclaimed her sandals and left the practice room, alone. The small crowd dissipated, going back to their business.

William stared after her, not sure what to think, but his spirits had risen considerably. The *ona* was both human and inhuman at the same time, but she was still his friend. He was certain of that, at least. And for some reason, she'd chosen to believe in him. Something made her see potential, unlike her followers. But it was what the *ona* said that really mattered. What Ria thought of him meant more than what anyone else thought.

He'd do *anything* to make her proud of him.

Chapter 23

His good spirits didn't last long, and it didn't make his day any easier.

William still felt a little depressed, and he couldn't seem to shake it. He'd gone to the worksite again today—and the work was a little easier with Ria's gloves—but it had been the same hostile place as ever.

The *ona* was gone, doing something by herself in Belo. She was supposed to be back by nightfall to organize the *Ëan*'s nightly activities. There were also the usual sentries on the Gnomi Road (now reinforced by William's guards taking shifts for the *Ëan*), including Dero today. The number of workers, therefore, was low, so Pat, the foreman was on edge already, yelling at everyone to make it double quick. The other workers kept ribbing William for his slow pace, including Cob, his partner. William's temper grew thin.

Finally, he snapped, forgetting himself. When Shac, one of the few *Ëan* left, said something particularly nasty, he snarled back a few choice words in response. He should have known better, but he was fed up. Looking back, he wished he hadn't opened his mouth. He'd only made matters worse—and when the *ona* heard, he knew she'd be disappointed in him.

Pat had heard, of course, and naturally it was William's fault. He was punished by having his water ration cut completely for disorderly conduct, on a sweltering June day.

He'd been miserable the rest of the day. He had to skip sword practice, since Dero was gone, but he thought it was probably for the best. He was exhausted anyway.

He'd gone home, feeling lightheaded, and rested a while. Lis was all sympathy. She'd been the only one who kept him going, always encouraging him and boosting his spirits. She fetched him water and rubbed his aching shoulders.

"It'll get better," she promised. "You've come a long way already."

William didn't think so.

"You have," she insisted. "Would you have consented to be a simple workman when you first came? And now you keep at it with a will, son. You've grown up."

She said this with such pride, it was hard not to feel a little better. "I'm not much good, though—I need to improve."

"I think you'll get there," Lis reassured. "You're putting on muscle, at least."

"I am?" he rolled his stiff shoulders, examining his only slightly less skinny arms.

"Not as much as you *could* have," she conceded, "but at least you're getting closer. If you have your father's build—which I think you do, with the height and the frame—you could grow very strong indeed. He had the power of a swordsman, your father." William liked to hear her remember. He tried for years to bury the old times, because it hurt to dwell on them—but now, it was comforting to think of them again.

"I wish he were here," Lis said wistfully. "He would like to see you now. He'd be so proud of you."

Not right now, he wouldn't. William sighed. His glittering home in Ossia was still out there somewhere. Although he'd never felt content there, he wasn't happy *here*, either.

Regardless, Lis could brighten any home. He'd always been closer to his would-be mother as a little boy.

He decided not to contradict her. He didn't want to argue. "Thanks, Mother," he replied.

She smiled playfully. "There is a downside," she teased. "You eat twice as much as you used to. I cook practically nonstop! I'll have to go make dinner soon..." she winked significantly.

He laughed. She *did* know how to make him feel better. They had a running joke about Lis's cooking—not her strong-suit. She fussed over everything, and usually the food was fine, but not exactly amazing. Noblewomen and ladies-in-waiting didn't learn to do much cooking.

Also, she was reading him well.

"You heard," he laughed.

"Elénne and Hope came by today to ask me if I minded. I don't; you can go."

"I didn't want to leave you by yourself."

"Oh, pish. You can go have dinner at Dero's house. Less cooking for me," she teased, "and you might find you like Elénne's food better."

"But Ria wanted to take me somewhere tomorrow, and so you'd be alone again..."

"William," she scolded, "you don't need to babysit me. I love being together, but I also want you to have fun. You can't be hanging around an old lady like me all the time. A young man like you needs his own friends."

"But I like spending time with you," he protested.

"Mm-hm. You're sweet. But you shouldn't keep a lady waiting, William. Elénne was *most* eager for you to come—though I imagine Dero will be pleased, too, if you accept his invitation—assuming he's back by now."

William nodded. "Pav said Dero went by twenty minutes ago."

"So don't keep them waiting," Lis retorted. "Go with our friends. Have a little fun; wipe that frown off your face."

He laughed. "Thanks, Mother—but you're sure you don't—"

"Go!" she exclaimed in mock annoyance, shooing him. "And be sure you mind your manners, William—Elénne's a nice girl; don't let her get away."

He cast her an exasperated look. "Mother!"

She laughed. "Okay, okay," she conceded. "But go on, now."

He gave her a quick hug. "Okay. Goodbye, Mother."

She smiled and shooed him out the door. "Have fun!" she called.

William couldn't seem to concentrate. He missed the bulls-eye again.

"Ooh," winced Dero, laughing.

"Aargh," William laughed. "I give up. Darts are beyond me right now. You and Kerran keep playing." They were both archers. They had well-practiced good aim.

He left them to finish the game and sat down next to Elénne on the couch in the corner. She grinned at him. "They don't have darts in Ossia?" she asked.

They did, but in Ossia it was mostly a tavern-game played by thugs. He didn't say that. "Not really. But I just can't concentrate enough to aim."

Hope, who was sitting on the floor, crawled giggling to William's foot and grabbed hold of it. He laughed, wiggling his shoe, and she cackled with delight. He plucked her off the floor and set her in his lap, teasing her.

She was the prettiest little girl he'd ever seen, having inherited her mother's brown hair and eyes, round face, and cute button nose. She had a smile that would melt anyone's heart. Her two-year-old clumsiness was endearing, and even when she was upset, she was still adorable.

She pulled at his shirt, grabbing fistfuls of fabric and yanking up and down. "She always does that," her mother explained, embarrassed. She reached to take Hope away. "Here, let me—"

"No, it's okay," William assured. He didn't mind Hope at all.

He knew Elénne was blatantly staring at him, a smile on her face, and he tried to keep from blushing, focusing instead on playing with Hope. She had produced a knitted bear stuffed with wool and given it proudly to William. "For me?" he asked. "Thank you." She giggled, then jumped off his lap and ran to the other side of the room. He chased her with the bear, growling, and she shrieked with enjoyment.

By the time the little one tired of the game, Kerran and Dero were finished with darts. They sat across from Elénne, laughing about something. William held Hope in one arm, the toddler clutching the bear. He sat down and set her in his lap, and she curled up against him.

"You've made a friend," Kerran commented.

William had grown to love the little girl, that was certain. He'd seen plenty of her this past month because of Dero. Winna, Fred, Kerran, Allain, Dero, Elénne, and Hope felt like family to him in a lot of ways. They were some of the few people who had always been welcoming to him.

And there was no way anyone could *not* adore Hope. She was easy to love. It was her mother William couldn't figure out.

Elénne was nice, if a bit forward. She'd shown all too clearly that she liked him. He enjoyed spending time with her—she wasn't like the women he'd known in Ossia, empty-headed and flirtatious. But she also wasn't powerful like the *ona* or Szera or Winna. He couldn't figure out *what* she was.

Dero grinned at him from across the room. The circles under the cheerful young man's eyes belied the sparkle they held. Even if he was tired, Dero's spirits didn't flag.

Elénne put in seriously, "You'll make a good father someday, William."

He wasn't sure how to react to that one, so he just smiled.

Fred poked in, breaking the awkward moment. "'Ello, ever'one," he said. "Sorry ta interrupt, but Szera's at tha door, Kerran, wantin' ta talk ta ya 'bout som'tin." Kerran nodded and got up without hesitation. Fred followed him out with a nod to William.

"Orders for tonight, you think?" Elénne asked.

"Probably just telling him where to be. The *ona* always gives the orders," Dero said.

"Did everything go all right today?"

"Fine. It was just sentry duty. Nothing usually happens out there."

"Mm," Elénne said. "Still, I'd be scared silly if I was out there. I *can* fight," she said for William's benefit, "but I'd be terrified to actually do it. It's bad enough when you all go off. I worry all the time." A meaningful glance told William she was referring to the incident that had brought him to the Nest in the first place. "I wish you didn't have to fight."

"It's our duty," Dero insisted.

She nodded. "I suppose. I just wish we could go back to normal, you know? Live in the village again. Go back home."

"Mm-hmm," Dero agreed, but it was a bit surly. He didn't like Elénne's tone.

"Well," she said, clearing her throat, "I should put Hope to bed." William surrendered the little girl, snoring in his lap, reluctantly. Then he stood up, too. "I should get home, anyway. It's getting late, and the *ona* wants to meet me in the morning."

"For what?" Elénne questioned.

"I don't know. She said she wanted to show me something."

Elénne looked oddly skeptical, even annoyed. "Oh. Then I'll see you later, I guess."

"Bye."

"Good-night, William." Then she left the room, and he breathed a sigh of relief.

"She really likes you, you know," Dero confided conspiratorially.

"Yeah, I noticed."

"You're not sure about her, are you?"

"I don't know, Dero. It just isn't comfortable for me."

Dero studied him, and William got the odd sense that his bright-eyed friend could see right through him. "That's okay," he assured. "You don't have to like her, but don't lead her on, either."

"I know; I'm not trying to."

Dero laughed. "I've never been particularly good with women. Why am *I* giving you advice?"

William laughed. "I'm not either."

"Yeah, I figured that out. But who is, anyway? They're confusing."

They shared a laugh over that one.

"I really should go," William remembered. "Thanks for inviting me, Dero."

"It was fun. We'll catch up on your lesson tomorrow, okay? Don't want to lose ground."

"No."

Dero gave him a hug. Not many people in Ossia had done that often. "Bye, William. Good luck with the *ona* tomorrow."

"Thanks. See you later."

With that, William left the house and the *Ëa* quarter and headed home. He turned his thoughts toward Ria, a more comfortable subject, wondering what she wanted to show him.

Chapter 24

William started out of his sleep, thrashing at the figure who clamped a hand over his mouth.

"Shh!" she scolded. "You'll wake Lis up."

He stopped struggling with a groan. She released him, and he struck a light. "Ria? I thought you said *morning*!"

She laughed. "It *is* morning. Just before four, I'd say."

"Uhh," he moaned, his body protesting the awakening. He rubbed his eyes.

"Just like old times, eh? I can sneak around the Nest easily enough. I'll have to talk to Tiran about your guards. I got through the window *way* too easily."

"You broke into our house? Why can't you use the door?"

"*That's* no fun," she protested lightly. "I have to enjoy myself *sometimes*. Believe me, if you could sneak around without anyone noticing, you'd do it for fun, too."

He grunted by way of reply.

She threw him a pile of clothes then turned her back. The tips of his ears burned, but he got out of bed and got dressed.

"Why are you up so early?" he asked.

"I've *been* up. I've been out since last evening. Just got back."

"Don't you ever sleep?"

"The Ëan don't sleep much, no. I'll sleep a little this afternoon, probably. I'm used to it, don't worry."

He made a mental note not to complain about her disturbing his sleep today.

He finished dressing. "Can I grab some food before we go anywhere?"

She laughed. "You've finally developed an appetite. You can, if you make it quick."

"You want something?" he whispered as they went into the kitchen.

She hesitated. He remembered what Ovan had once said,

that she would neglect to eat sometimes. But she clearly didn't want to accept anything from him. He tried to cast it differently. "It's okay, you know. Just making things more efficient. That way, you don't have to go all the way up to the Ëa quarter and back down to get something to eat."

She smiled, seeing right through the tactic, but it worked. "Fine, love," she agreed, pretending to be exasperated.

It was just a little thing, but it made William feel warm inside to have done even something small for her. She didn't like people taking care of her.

He set the lamp on the table and pulled out a loaf of bread, some milk, and some fruit. They ate standing up and wolfed the food—Ria wasn't kidding about being in a hurry.

"Let me leave Mother a note," William said. Before Ria could protest, he found a scrap of paper to write on and scribble an explanation for his absence. Ria looked a bit perplexed as he wrote, studying the movements he made. He left the letter on the table.

"Why are you looking at me funny?" he asked, too curious to keep quiet.

"You write fast," she explained, but it sounded like a hastily invented excuse.

"Oh... okay."

She sighed, then said in a rush, "I'm not very good at writing. My education was a little... abridged." She shot him an embarrassed look as if she was worried he'd think badly of her.

"Probably not your biggest concern at the time," he offered. He was surprised she'd even said anything. He liked that she'd actually admitted a weakness of hers to him.

"Yeah. Doesn't matter," she said quickly. "Well, let's go, then."

They headed toward the door. William opened it, startling his guards, who jumped visibly.

"My lord! What—why—" stammered Elix. Then he saw the *ona*, and his mouth dropped open. "How did *you* get in?" he demanded. "I've been at this post all night and haven't seen a thing!"

She grinned. William tried hard not to laugh. "I'm sneaky," she said simply.

Elix huffed a sigh, sounding irritated. If she'd meant harm, he'd have been in huge trouble.

"We have to go," she excused herself. "Sorry, boys. We'll be back later."

"Can one of us—"

"No," she interrupted, answering his question emphatically before he could even finish it. "I can protect him just fine, should he need any protecting—where we're going, he won't. Stay here."

The pair looked unhappy about it, but they bowed in acquiescence.

"Good. Come on, William." She set off at a quick pace down the street, and William bounded after her.

She led him down the street into the city, the way out of the Nest. Instead of taking the workers' road toward the northwest, though, she headed almost directly north.

"So… can I ask—where are we going?" he ventured.

"I'm taking you to see someone," she answered. "It'll be helpful. *Instructive*."

She was teasing, but she wouldn't put him off his questions.

"Who?"

"His name is Yewul," she answered. "He is the wisest man alive—and yes, I mean that. He will be happy to meet you. He will likely have advice for you. He has advice for everyone, including himself. He hears the voice of *Aiael* more clearly than most."

William remembered the name. "We're going to the Djorn?" he asked.

She nodded. "Yes. Yewul is the *ona* of the Djorn, but he's not to them what I am to the Ëan. They're a tribe; we're just a warrior band. Yewul is entirely peaceful."

William wasn't sure whether to be excited, honored,

nervous, or insulted. He'd never expected to visit the home of the Djorn.

They finally reached the end of the city and entered one of the old roads. Ria plucked a lantern sitting by the entrance and lit it. The city was always brightly lit, but the roads lacked the lamps of the city.

He fully expected a long, dull journey on the underground road, but after only five minutes they came to a ladder and she said, "Let's go up."

"We're going above ground?" he asked, surprised. The *Ëan* were excellent foresters, of course, but it was easier to travel underground, and a lot faster. He hadn't thought the *ona* would choose an overland route.

"Little secret: I hate underground," she told him. "But don't tell anyone I said that. I'd rather walk where there's air. Besides, I have lots of friends in the forest."

"Animal friends?"

She laughed at the nervousness in his tone. "Yes. But they don't bite. Most of them." She poked him in the arm with a laugh. "Gotcha. But c'mon, love," she teased. "Relax. Let's go up."

She started up the ladder, and he followed, trying to keep her sandals out of his face. She'd probably scratch him with those spikes if she kicked him. Even her shoes were a weapon.

They emerged from the burrow under a tall oak tree. Ria shoved aside a bush to get out which then smacked William as he started up. She laughed hysterically at this. "Sorry, love," she apologized. He grimaced and clambered out of the hole.

It was barely dawn, the sun just beginning to cast a pink glow toward the east, but it was still dark under the trees. Birds twittered in the branches above him, and squirrels leapt from tree to tree. It felt very different from the first time he'd been in the forests of Belond, before the ambush. It wasn't threatening; it was peaceful.

"This way," Ria said, waving him forward. He followed carefully, watching his step. After the incident with the bush every single scrap of undergrowth was suspicious.

They didn't go quite so quickly as William's last hike, but he still had a little trouble keeping up. She'd spent years living a rough life; he'd just started. He was fitter than he used to be, but still, the only thing that allowed him to keep up was the fact that she kept pausing to talk to the animals around her. She talked to William, too, telling him about her various "friends" and how she'd met them. He commented occasionally, but he mostly just listened.

Then he heard a growl to his left. He halted, peering nervously into the bushes. Then, out of nowhere, a shape came hurtling out of the trees and knocked him down. He yelped, calling, "Ria!" A full-grown wolf stood on his chest, bared fangs snarling at him just inches from his face.

Ria had the nerve to laugh. "*Nan,* Luna," she called. "*Thringel ai vratha.*"

The wolf stopped snarling, though her bright eyes still looked threatening. She slowly backed off his chest, then she turned to Ria. The *ona* had gone down on one knee, arms outstretched. The wolf ran to her, but not in attack. She acted more like a dog greeting her master, though Luna was far from tame. Even interacting with Ria, she still seemed wild, as if Ria was part of her pack.

"Hey, Luna," Ria murmured to her, smiling and rubbing her gray fur. She said some more in Djoran, and the wolf barked in response.

William got to his feet, and Ria remembered him. "Sorry," she apologized, still laughing. "Luna can be a bit defensive. She's a territorial creature, and a bit suspicious of most people."

William just stared. "That's—that's—a wolf. And you're just—"

"Luna's my friend," Ria explained. "She helps us from time to time, too. She was there when we ambushed you that first time. She usually avoids people, though. She's still a wild creature."

As if to prove the point, Luna growled at William again. He

shivered, taking a step back.

"She won't respect you if you show fear," Ria chided, but she was still amused. "I told her you're my friend. She won't hurt you—probably."

"Oh, thanks," William replied.

"Don't mention it." Her eyes twinkled. "Come on, love, let's go on." Then she said something to Luna, and the wolf fell in behind her, heeling like a dog and nuzzling her calf. They walked on.

They kept on going for four hours until the sun was well up. They met a host of different animals. She introduced him to a panther, a snake, a hawk, several squirrels, and a large number of other creatures. William couldn't help wondering how she'd managed to acquire so many "friends," but he didn't ask. Somehow, she knew all these creatures and had given them all names. She'd clearly spent a lot of time in the forest.

Finally, she slowed to a halt, Luna stopping behind her. She turned back to look at William. "We're here," she told him.

He looked around, confused. He saw no village. The woods looked exactly the same as before. They hadn't been using a trail, so this part of the woods was no clearer than anywhere they'd been. They stood just before a large mound of rock—which would be difficult to climb. A sheer cliff dropped to the right. Dense undergrowth blocked the left. The best way to go would have been back the way they'd come. This was *not* a good place for a settlement.

"Here?" he asked uncomprehendingly.

She laughed at his expression and pointed. "Up there," she said, indicating the rocks.

He looked again at the rock pile, dubious. It was less a pile, he realized, than a shelf. It jutted above them, perhaps thirty feet high, the top invisible. He didn't think it was climbable.

She grinned. "Just wait," she told him. "The guardian's

not sure of you yet. He's reasonably cautious. It's his duty."

She stepped forward and called up in Djoran. She paused, cocking her head as if listening, then she said something else. Then she turned back to William.

"He will let you come up," she told him. "Look."

As he craned his neck upward, he saw a huge snake slither to the top of the cliff. It examined him with slitted eyes, then pulled with its coils at something above them. A moment later, a rope ladder (not unlike those in the burrows) descended.

She said something to Luna, probably, "You'll have to stay here." The wolf whimpered but sat down as if to wait. Ria patted her head then began to climb. When she was high enough, William followed.

They got to the top. The giant snake had disappeared, which made William nervous. He looked around him for any sign of it, but it was gone. He took in his surroundings. They stood on a sort of tableland, covered with widely spaced trees. Each tree was huge, towering to impossible heights and possessing a massive circumference. They looked ancient; the largest trees he'd ever seen—even more so than the tree in the Sky Tree Hall. This place felt almost like a garden, but much more wild and strange than any Edenian garden. Everything was very green and very alive, but also very empty.

He saw no one, no sign of a settlement. He looked at Ria in confusion, but she seemed unperturbed. She called out a short greeting in Djoran, probably something clever like, "Hello."

As he watched, the still grove began to stir. First it was just a slight movement in the leaves, then sounds of life. Then the trees opened, and the people emerged. William's jaw dropped.

They literally lived *in* the trees. Those huge trunks were hollow, and entire families lived inside, probably with multiple floors in those towering trees. It was amazing. It must have taken decades, even centuries, to create these homes. It was also quite possibly the strangest thing he'd ever seen.

Then he looked at the people themselves.

He wasn't sure what he'd been expecting. Part of him thought they'd be wild savages, without an ounce of refinement. Part of him thought they'd be like the Djorn he'd met, who spoke Edenian, wore Edenian clothes, and acted almost normal (or what he considered normal).

They were neither.

Unlike the ethereal quality of the Gnomi constructions, these people seemed very grounded with reality—they were one with it. He might have thought them part of the landscape if he hadn't been looking for them. Their clothes, light and well-fitting, were woven of threads that looked like cotton but were bright green. Some of them wore paint on their faces, arms, and legs, but they wore no other adornment. They moved gracefully, with furtive motions—they must have taught the *ona*. What struck him most was how very peaceful they looked—like children, but not naïve. They did not show any fear or any emotion besides serene acceptance. He might have called them carefree except for the ageless wisdom in the eyes of even the young ones, which showed both sorrow and joy.

They reminded him of Torhan—more specifically, the spirit of Torhan's prayer before the council. It pervaded this place, filling and enriching everyone it touched.

The Djorn came forward, electric blue eyes wide with curiosity. Ria smiled, greeting many by name. Then she gestured to William, and understanding passed through the people. They smiled and nodded.

The Djorn appeared welcoming to him, but he had the sense they were more pleased to see Ria. They clearly adored her from the way they spoke to and embraced her. She seemed happy, too, as if the atmosphere of this place made her relax. She continued to talk to them.

"What—" he started to ask.

"I told them we wish to see Yewul," she answered. "They will take us to him."

A tall woman, white-blond hair tied simply but elegantly

atop her head, stepped forward. She and Ria exchanged words. Not for the first time, William wished he could speak Djoran. The woman crooked a finger, indicating that they should follow. Ria turned to him and explained, "This is Yewul's attendant, Hlein. She is his niece. She takes care of him and his home."

The crowd melted away as they passed through, the Djorn disappearing as if they had never been there at all. Their guide remained ahead of them, gliding through the trees. They continued into the grove for several minutes, until they were deep into the heart of the plateau.

One tree, larger than all the rest, loomed in the center. It was clear their guide led them straight to it. It drew William's gaze like a lodestone. Its leaves were so dense that it cast the ground into shadow, but it did not feel dark. A sound emanated from it which took William a moment to place.

Laughter. Children's laughter.

The Djor woman opened a cleverly hidden door at the base of the tree. They had to stoop to get inside, then the door closed behind them.

They were instantly swarmed by children, all rushing forward to greet them. Most looked no older than five or six, but they all cried eagerly, "*Vitha! Vitha!*" and fawned on Ria. She seemed genuinely excited to see them, and she bent down to hug them. *She* was good with children, too. She knew just what to say to each one to make him or her beam with pleasure.

The tall woman said something firmly, and the children backed away reluctantly. She beckoned them to a rope ladder and began to climb up.

Ria waved goodbye to the children. She explained briefly to William, "The children love Yewul. They spend most of their time in his house—if Hlein lets them."

They climbed several ladders, leading through holes in the ceiling. The inside of the house was wholly unremarkable-it looked like a tree. It was not a house in the Edenian sense, but it felt cozy nonetheless.

At last, when William figured they had to have climbed a mile, they emerged into the highest room. He stopped and looked around.

It was small, barely bigger than a closet in William's home at the Nest. It had windows, fashioned like natural holes in the tree trunk, which let in sunlight. It was bare except for a woven rug on the floor and a single wooden chair with a hunched figure in it.

It was Yewul—it must be.

He was very old, but not feeble. He had snowy white hair, bushy eyebrows, and smile lines that wrinkled his face. He wore an odd necklace made of woven grass, and he clenched a staff in his hands.

And he was sound asleep.

Hlein nudged him gently, rousing him with a word. He stirred, lifting his head and opening his eyes. He had the brightest blue eyes of any Djor William had yet seen, not at all dimmed by age. They twinkled with interest as he regarded his guests.

Ria moved forward and gave the old man a hug. "*Eshwel, ona Yewul,*" she said warmly to him.

"It has been... long time, my child," Yewul answered in Edenian. William's eyebrows lifted in surprise. The chief hesitated with the words, but he spoke well and clearly.

"I have brought someone to see you," she told Yewul. "This is William, *ona.*"

Yewul turned his gaze on William. "Ah," he said knowingly. "The prince of Edenia. *Aiael* told me you would come someday."

William wasn't sure what to say, so he said probably the least relevant comment he could have thought of. "You speak Edenian?" he asked stupidly.

Ria rolled her eyes, but Yewul laughed merrily. "Yes, my son. I know your... language. Many of us learned it when *Vitha* and Ovan came to us, if it was our gift. *Aiael* has long... blessed me with the gift of words." He paused, examining William closely. "What is your gift, my son?" he asked seriously.

William looked blankly at him. "Gift?"

Yewul turned to Ria. "This is why you brought him, is it?"

"You are keen as ever, Yewul. He could use your clarity of thinking."

"Cannot you explain it to him?"

"Your people are closer to it than us. Perhaps I could have asked your grandson, but Torhan has not your experience."

"I see," Yewul agreed. "Yes, you are wise." He turned back to William. "Sit, my son," he invited, "and let me tell you a story."

Yewul's treatment of him was completely natural, as if he'd always known him. He put William at ease. He sat on the floor at the old man's feet. Ria sat on the other side of the chair. Hlein left the room, climbing down, leaving them to talk. Yewul began to speak.

"In the beginning of our world, *Aiael* created us—mankind, his children. He created a people to fill the land and rule over it, to live at one with it. He made us to display his glory in the world, each in his own unique way. We were patterned after his nature, designed to be creative as *Aiael* is. To this end, each child of *Aiael* is granted a gift—which he or she may use to fulfill his calling. Do you understand what I am saying?"

Yewul's *Aiael* seemed far more tangible than William's conception of El, though they were one and the same. Yewul referred to him like a real person as if he'd just been casually chatting with the creator of the universe. But his sincerity compelled William. His conviction drew him to want to agree.

"Yes," he answered. It was actually true.

Yewul continued. "There are many gifts. Do not mistake me—not all are..." he paused, clarifying a word with Ria.

"Dramatic," she put in.

"Yes," Yewul agreed. "Some seem insignificant, but all are important. *Aiael* does not always work by storms, sometimes it is just a drop at a time. He moves in ways both large and small, but he always knows what he's doing. He is wiser than any man. He can show his glory in anyone.

"There are many gifts. *Vitha* was given a gift for combat and leadership. I was given a power over words, like Torhan. Ekata has the gift of healing. But some are more ordinary, though not less important—like loyalty, respect for authority, or the ability to listen. To each, *Aiael* gives a calling, a particular way a gift can be used for his glory. Have you been seeking yours?"

William hesitated, glancing at Ria. Her expression told him exactly why she'd brought him here.

He considered his distant dream of being one of her *Ëan*, fighting for something worthwhile. Desire still burned in him, but it seemed foolish in the light of his circumstances.

"Yes—that is, I'm trying," he replied. He was very conscious of Ria listening, but he could not help but be honest with Yewul. "But I don't know what my gift is. I'm not really good at *anything*."

Yewul smiled at him reassuringly. "*Aiael* delights in using those who seemed least qualified. Don't fret. Seek *Aiael's* will—do you pray?"

He shrugged, not sure how to answer.

"Start. Ask him what he wants you to do, and then he will empower you to do it. He is the giver of gifts; he will give you the strength to fulfill his calling. Trust *Aiael*, William. He will not disappoint you."

William sighed. Trust. Yewul was asking him to do things he hadn't dared to do for most of his life. He wanted to, but he wasn't sure how.

"What if it's just a crazy dream?" William asked.

Yewul smiled. "*Aiael* is very interested in your dreams, my son. He is the one that gave them to you." He paused, considering. Then he added. "I will pray for you, my friend. I sense you will bring *Aiael* much glory in your life—though perhaps not quite how you imagined."

"Thank you," William said, but it came out as more of a question.

Yewul laughed. "Don't worry, William. You have no need

to be afraid."

Yewul nodded as if this was a decided point. Then he leaned back, quiet. A moment later, William realized he had fallen asleep again.

"Come," Ria whispered, rising. "Let us leave him."

Chapter 25

William retreated behind Blazer so the others wouldn't see him, but that didn't block out their laughter. He had tripped and dropped a pile of branches, his third or fourth clumsy moment of the day, and he'd had to collect the branches over again, his face red and his head down.

He couldn't help his clumsiness. He was preoccupied.

His visit to Yewul last week had only made him more depressed. No matter what anyone said, it seemed as hopeless as ever. No matter how much he wanted to succeed, no matter how much he "believed," nothing changed.

Cob applauded him sarcastically. "Well done, lad," he said gruffly. William turned away, forcing himself not to respond.

He piled the branches with the rest, stacking them where they could be taken for firewood, then he moved to take Blazer's halter.

"Wait a moment," a voice interrupted.

He turned. It was Pat, the foreman. He approached with Kerran behind him. He looked annoyed, as if he resented what he was having to do.

"The *ona* wants you," he said brusquely. "Kerran is to help Cob with his load." Kerran cast him an encouraging smile, but Pat and Cob both looked stormy. William understood why, with a twinge of anxiety.

Kerran was Ria's partner today.

What was the *ona* up to? The *Ëan* didn't work with the *Reben* for a reason—mismatched strengths. They wouldn't like this, and he wasn't sure he'd be up to whatever she wanted him to do.

Her orders couldn't be disobeyed. He breathed a sigh, but he followed the foreman reluctantly.

He found her securing the ropes to pull down an oak tree.

But not just any oak tree. This was a strong tree, clearly, with a circumference wider around than his arm-span. Its bark looked tough as iron.

She was preparing to chop it down? She was ambitious, but he would have believed she could do anything. Him, on the other hand...

"William," she called, all business. "You're with me." She regarded the tree. "Ten strokes, alternating. I'll go first. The rope's all ready. When it gets close, one of us will start the pulley."

The Ëan all stared, even his friends.

She wanted him to do *what*?

"Um," he stammered. "*Ona, I—*"

"Let's go," she cut him off. "Kerran left you his axe. Use that one." Kerran's axe was twice the size of William's. He wasn't sure he could even swing it. She leaned close. "Just trust me," she said quietly. Then she pulled away again. She wasn't throwing him any pity in front of the Ëan.

He wanted to run away right there. They would laugh at him. He would be a miserable failure. *Forget all this*, he thought. *It's just a stupid dream. Not worth getting humiliated again.* He almost walked away.

But he made the mistake of actually meeting those fierce green eyes.

He picked up the axe.

A ghost of a smile formed on her lips, yet her eyes betrayed nothing but challenge. She glared away the gawking stares of the other workers, who immediately returned to their tasks.

She picked up her own axe and made the initial cut into the tree. He watched, unable to keep from staring. Her lithe, strong body was already covered in sweat from her day's labor. Every time she swung, her bare shoulders rippled as her muscles contracted. She was so strong! How could a woman be so strong?

"Your turn," she prompted impatiently. He moved forward, flustered.

He tried to do as he was taught. Chop down, then straight, then down again. His strokes were too timid. He barely made a dent. "Harder," the *ona* commanded. Her voice was steely. "You call that hard? Move it!"

He couldn't find a rhythm. It was too hard. His ears burned with shame.

It was Ria's turn.

She cast him a challenging glance, daring him to do better. His pride rose, but his reason told him he was a fool. This was the *ona*. He was just William.

"Harder; faster; put your back into it!"

Ria grunted with each swing.

William's blisters began to reopen, despite the gloves Ria had given him. His shoulders burned from using the heavier axe.

She started to sing, timing her strokes with the song. It was a simple tune, and the words were common, like a blacksmith's song. She kept singing while he worked.

He lost himself. The crowd felt distant. His strokes fell in time to the song, even. He groaned with effort each time.

On, off.

One, two. Three, four. Five, six. Seven, eight. Nine, ten.

Down, straight. Down.

"Other side," Ria said.

She began a new song. This one was faster, and it spoke of smiting and striking.

"Harder," she urged. Harder.

One, two.

One, two.

Ria. William. Ria.

His muscles burned. He paused to wipe the sweat from his eyes.

"Don't stop. Harder. Is that the best that you can do?"

Down. Straight. Down.

More, William. Move.

The song went on. He started to sing with her under his breath.

On, off.

Once more. And again.

Again.
Again.
Push harder.
One more time.
One more time.
"Hold it," the *ona* said.

He paused mid-swing, not sure why they'd stopped.

She released the pulley system to put tension on the tree. A loud crack sounded. A moment later, the tree was down, falling with a crash.

Wait, what?

The other workers stood still, mouths gaping. William felt dumbfounded.

The *ona* favored him with a triumphant smile. She spoke very quietly to him. "Who says you can't do anything? You just have to believe you can."

The workers stopped staring. Some looked impressed, some gratified, some shocked, and some angry. Baër fixed him with a venomous glare.

But Auria, who'd once said he wasn't good for anything, had just proven him to the others. None of the Ëan were chopping down trees that size. Only them. He didn't know how to feel.

"Now," she said, "We move this monster." One of those devilish grins appeared. "Then we find another one." She smacked him playfully on the arm.

Just in case he was getting an ego.

He heaved a sigh. He wasn't sure he could even move, let alone repeat the performance. But at the same time, he felt excited. He had accomplished something.

William walked tiredly up the streets with Dero. He'd refused to forgo his lesson, though he definitely didn't feel like swinging a sword. He was paying for his determination now.

"You know," Dero told him, "I think they're warming up to you."

William laughed. "That's a little hard to believe."

"No, really," he insisted. "They've only been hard on you because you're a nobleman—no offense, it's not personal. They just think noblemen believe they're entitled to having everything handed to them. But you're proving you can do things. *I've* never chopped down a tree that big. You've gotten strong."

That much was true. He weighed far more than he had a few months ago, and it wasn't from over-eating (though his appetite had certainly increased). The sword master in Ossia had deemed him "scrawny," but weeks of hard labor had made him the opposite.

"It was mostly the *ona*," he protested.

"No, it wasn't," Dero argued. "She was with Ovan two days ago, and they chopped down one that size—but it took them almost twice the time it took you today. The *Ëan* noticed, William, let me tell you. You remember Shac?"

William did. He'd given William an insult that still made his blood burn a bit. "Mm-hmm."

"Well, he told Baër that maybe they'd been wrong about you, and we ought to give you a chance."

"He did?"

"Yup. Considering Shac blames a nobleman for the death of his family, you shouldn't be too hard on him, but even he's come around. Torhan always tells us we should treat everyone with kindness, and the *ona* has always said a person should be judged based on character, not race, birth, or gender. The *Ëan* aren't bad people; they just forget themselves sometimes. We're all followers of the same El, after all. Most of them don't mean to be hard on you, they just didn't know what to think of you. And at first, you weren't all that impressive, if you remember—no offense. But when I last had sentry duty, Ceth told me he thought you weren't so bad. And Rosie said—" he blushed and broke off. "Well, maybe I won't tell you what Rosie said."

William laughed, but he still had trouble believing what Dero was telling him.

"The only one who still doesn't like you is Baër—and I'm not sure you *can* win *him* over."

"Why does Baër hate me so much, anyway? I never did anything to him."

"He feels threatened by you," Dero confided. He blushed.

"What? Why?"

Dero reddened more. "Um, I'd rather not say. Not really my business. It was a long time ago, anyway, and Baër ought to just let it go."

"What are you talking about?"

"Never mind." Dero changed the subject hastily. "Let's talk about your lesson. I've been thinking. You want to be an Ëa, right?"

Dero said it so casually, like it was normal to be an elite fighter in an underground movement to overthrow a usurper and restore the rightful government, throwing yourself from danger to danger to protect the people of Belond. He said it like it was an easy thing, when to William it had always seemed more remote than the stars in the sky. Dero easily pronounced the dream William had held inside for such a long time.

"Yes," he admitted, and somehow the audible admission made it seem more real to him. He remembered Yewul, who told him that it was *Aiael* who gave him his dreams. He supposed if *Aiael* wanted him to believe in something, he would be the one to make it possible. And it seemed to be, now. It wasn't so crazy after all. At last he could do it.

"Good," Dero said happily. "I knew you could have no other real reason for wanting to learn sword-fighting. At least, none that would make you work so hard at it. But I was thinking—you'll need more than that."

"What do you mean?"

"Well, with fighting, you need to know how to use more than one weapon. What if you're caught without a sword? Ëan have to be prepared for anything. You should probably learn hand-fighting at least, to start with. Then if you're disarmed you're not helpless. And then the bow, for another thing.

Kerran taught me to shoot after Aunt Winna taught me the sword. It's enough for me, but you may wish to learn more: spear, axe, staff—and knives, of course. The *ona*'s favorite. In any case, we'll have to get you your own sword.

"Also, you should learn a thing or two about healing. You don't have to be an expert, just enough to go on in an emergency, you know. Most of us could give you pointers about that. But being an *Ëa* goes beyond war. You should try to talk to us, and don't let us intimidate you. If you join us, we'll be your family. The *Ëan* can refuse to allow someone—though I've not seen it happen.

"And you should try to learn some Djoran. It's a beautiful language, though a bit tricky—I've not mastered it yet. You'll probably catch on quick—you've got a real *education*, so you're used to studying. The language comes in handy; we send a lot of messages through the animals. All of us know at least a little.

"You should probably get some trail-craft, too. We have to be able to manage the woods and also cover our tracks when we go out."

"And, of course, we all follow El. That is most important to us." This last was said very sincerely, which made William smile.

"I see," he replied. "Well, I will try." For some reason, he heard Ria's voice goading him. *More. Harder. Is that all you've got?* "I'll do it," he amended, speaking more decisively. "How do I learn all this, though? Can you teach me?"

Dero shook his head. "No. I may be a decent swordsman, but I'm only a mediocre bowman." William highly doubted that. "And with the rest I have little skill at all. You need someone who specializes in the weapon you're learning."

"Who?"

Dero considered. "The *ona*'s the best at everything," he said, "but I doubt she'd have the time. She's already everywhere at once. Besides, she'd knock you flat in two seconds. No offense to you—she's better than all of us."

"None taken."

Dero thought some more. "For hand-fighting, you'd best ask Szera. She uses an axe most of the time, but she was taught by *Melach*." Dero said the name with reverence. "He was the best hand-fighter ever, they say. Szera'd teach you well."

William was a bit intimidated to ask the Djor for help. She made him more nervous than most of the Ëan. He'd seen her with an axe. She was incredibly strong, with muscles like a man's. Her no-nonsense demeanor and harsh temper frightened him. But she was Ria's best friend, from what he could tell. She could in no way be a bad woman.

"For archery, you could ask Kerran. Or Rosie. Or Lagan. He might be best. He's been here longest, and he's more experienced. He deserted from the army after the Governor came.

"You can probably start with that, but you may want to learn other weapons, too."

"A little at a time, please," William laughed. "What about the language? Who taught you?"

Dero reddened significantly, making William look at him more closely. "Well, I—uh—I'm not—I mean," he stuttered. "I'm still learning, uh, sort of, I guess."

William looked at him curiously. His friend was oddly flustered for such a simple question—and he still hadn't answered.

"But who's teaching you?" he repeated.

Dero coughed. "Um—Ekata." This he said quickly, ducking his head.

"Oh," William said, understanding. He tried not to laugh.

"But you'd probably ask Torhan," Dero said quickly. "He teaches most of us that want to learn. He could teach you a lot, Torhan could. And he's an easy fellow to talk to. He's good with words."

"Mm-hmm." Yewul's grandson, he remembered. He might be good with more than just words.

"I think that should do," Dero decided. "Any of us could teach you trail-craft—if you want, and anything else you want to learn."

"Will I have time for it all?" William asked.

"I would think so. We're all in and out with our duties, of course, but you can learn something from whoever's around. Even while we work, I imagine. I think Pat'll place you with us after today."

It seemed daunting, but also exciting somehow. He could do it.

They reached the practice room. "Enough talking," Dero declared. "You'll have time enough to worry about everything else later. Let's practice." He bounded inside with his irrepressible energy.

William grinned and followed him eagerly.

Chapter 26

The summer began to fly by. Slowly but surely, he felt things really changing. He began to make progress.

The work crew stopped harvesting trees only a few days after he cut down the oak with the *ona*. They now traveled each day to the eastern bay, where they began to turn the immense pile of logs into the frame of a ship, all under the observation of the King's builders. The work was scarcely less difficult, but William enjoyed it more. The other workers were less hostile to him, and he no longer felt so unskilled. He was able to be of use. He worked side by side with the Ëan, and he found many friends among them. Once he began to know them, it was just as Dero said—they were good people. They started to include him—all except Baër. He remained the only one who was unfriendly to William, and William tried to avoid Baër as much as he could. He did not wish to create unnecessary conflict.

The Ëan were soon only too happy to teach him. Lagan taught him to shoot. The bowman was one of the oldest Ëan. His whitening hair contrasted his very dark skin. He had twinkling eyes and a deep laugh, but he was unyielding as a teacher. William had used a bow before, but with little more skill than he had possessed with a sword. He built up enough courage to ask Szera's help, though he quailed at her scowl. In the end, she enjoyed the prospect. She gave him regular beatings, not sparing him at all. He eventually learned to ignore her fiery temper and forgive her disdain of him. She was a hero, if ever he'd met one. She was not feminine in her manners, but she possessed the kind of fierce protectiveness one would see in a mother among wild animals. Despite her savage nature and sharp tongue, he began to admire her.

He also spent time with Torhan. The calm, peaceful Djor was just the opposite of Szera. He had an air of confidence that was compelling. When William asked to learn Djoran,

Torhan was only too willing to help. He had an odd way of teaching. Instead of words or grammar, Torhan would tell William stories, intermingling the languages. He told fabulous tales, stories few Edenians would ever hear. Sometimes folktales of his people, or ancient histories, sometimes tales of the Ëan and their exploits, sometimes just words of wisdom about *Aiael* or the ways of men and nature. They spent hours talking, often while they worked on the ship, and William learned far more than just a language. But he learned Djoran, too. Eventually, Torhan was speaking mostly Djoran to William and little Edenian, and when William tried to talk to Blazer, it seemed like the horse actually understood him.

But William wasn't always working. He spent a lot of time with Dero and his family. He played with Hope every time he came, and he couldn't help feeling proud when one day she learned his name and thereafter squeaked "Wee-yum!" every time she saw him. He spent a lot of time with Elénne, too, but mostly with other people around. He liked her very much: she was fun to talk to, smart, pretty, and caring; however, he saw her only as a friend. He knew *she* didn't know what to do about it. She was a bold girl, and not at all shy about pursuing him. He never encouraged her, but that seemed only to make things worse. All William's friends would joke to him about her, except Dero. Even Lis teased him about Elénne. He usually passed it off. He just didn't feel anything special for her.

He enjoyed most the times he went with his friends into the hills. They would go swimming in the cold mountain lakes, or hiking, or talking to the animals, if a Djor was with them. It was these times William could forget the troubles of Belond and remember just how beautiful the island was, shining in the full summer sun. He saw woods, rivers, and meadows, and he learned to treasure them like the Djorn did. Still, the land would have meant little without his companions. It seemed brightest when the *ona* went along, though it was rare that she allowed herself leisure. Her laughter could have set the Empire smiling. She could be playful, despite her serious nature. He learned not to underestimate her in the water, certainly. She swam like a dolphin—more of her "friends." The Ëan all laughed like children when she was there, like a huge family. But the *ona* had no time for pleasure, and the Ëan had little more. Still, some of William's best memories came from those times with them.

Lis began to complain that he was never home. She was not serious, but he still felt the reproach and tried to spend more time with her. She *was* his mother. And while he had almost too much to do, she had only to cook and keep house. She claimed perfect contentment with her role, but William knew she must be lonely. A few times he brought a couple of his friends over to meet her, and Elénne came several times. Tiran was still around most of the time, and Ovan was constantly looking in on her, but Ria never came. Lis hadn't seen her niece since the night the *ona* had announced her plan to build a ship.

William mentioned this to Ria, and he'd been a bit surprised by her reaction. She'd sighed and said, "I know. I'll see her soon." But William got the sense that Ria was avoiding Lis, for reasons he didn't understand. He remembered the vague sense of conflict between the two, but he knew either would do anything for the other. But she still didn't come.

William began to become truly good at what he was learning. He'd never in his life been a natural student, but he actually showed real improvement.

He would never forget the first time he beat Dero at swordplay. He'd had the song the workmen sang stuck in his head all that day, and he'd been fighting to its rhythm. He let his instincts guide him without losing touch with his concentration. He even pulled a few of the tricks he'd learned by watching the Ëan.

To his everlasting surprise, he'd found an opening, and seizing it he twisted Dero's sword out of his grasp. He was so shocked Dero ducked under his guard and knocked him over.

They came up with Dero beaming. "That was fantastic!" he exulted. "You had me there! Look at you!" He bumped William playfully with his shoulder. "Let's do that again."

It wasn't long before he was even with Dero, then he began to beat him. Soon it was William dealing out the bruises. "I think you need a new teacher," Dero declared. So William began to spar with Tiran and Ovan, and he was back to *getting* bruises. He never stopped practicing with Dero, but they sparred together less often.

He could more or less put an arrow in a target, if he wasn't the best shot. He could at least hold his own against Szera. He could speak enough Djoran to be understood. He could bind a cut serviceably. He wouldn't be helpless in a wood, though he might still get lost by himself. He could cover his tracks well enough not to be followed.

He knew the *ona* was watching, trying to measure him. She often tested him, subtly, but he knew she was weighing his abilities—and his character. He never let up. He felt a strange sort of energy he'd never felt before, as if he could toil endlessly and face anything. He knew it had to be El—he couldn't have lasted on his own. He felt happy for the first time in fifteen years.

As the summer dwindled into fall, he only grew stronger. He knew he would be ready, and soon.

Chapter 27

Then one night the *ona* showed up at his door.
William had been practicing with Tiran, and the two were walking back to his house. They were talking and laughing when they came up the steps and Corran, the guard on duty, cleared his throat. "Um—sir?" he ventured. "You have a visitor."

William had looked at him in surprise. He'd planned to spend the evening with just Lis. None of his friends was supposed to be here. "Who?" he'd asked in bewilderment.

"The *ona*," Corran answered. "You'd better go in, my lord."

"The *ona*?" he asked incredulously. "How long has she been here?"

"About twenty minutes. I daresay her ladyship—" they always referred to Lis that way, "—was surprised to see her."

She'd promised to come soon, but that had been a month ago.

"I'm sure," William muttered.

"You shouldn't keep her waiting," Tiran advised. "I'll just head back to the barracks." (That was what they called the Guard's quarters.)

"Okay." William wished Tiran was staying, but he understood the captain's reluctance to interfere. He wasn't sure what had made Ria come, but he didn't think it was a pleasure call. At least she made an effort to see Lis. She'd come at a normal time of day, and she'd even walked through the front door instead of breaking into their house.

"Good night, Tiran," William called as the captain walked away. Tiran waved his hand in response.

William walked inside. He found Ria in their sitting room, clearly placed there for her greatest comfort and Lis's hospitality. In fact, she looked *uncomfortable* and very out of place in the fine setting of Lis's well-kept house with her ragged, dirty clothes, but she smiled when she saw him come in.

"Hello," he said brightly. He actually was pleased to see her, even if her visit was strange.

"Hello," she echoed.

He paused, not sure what to say. It wouldn't be polite to come right out and say "what are you doing here?" though doubtlessly she would have in his place.

"Um... have you seen Mother?"

She nodded. "She's in the kitchen making dinner. She's persuaded me to stay."

William cocked an eyebrow. "Really? Well, um, good."

She laughed. "I don't bite, love. Honestly."

He smiled at her use of his old nickname, which she used less often now. It used to annoy him, but now it was endearing.

"I know," he responded. He put his bag in the corner. "Hold on a minute, okay? I'm going to check on Mother. I'll be right back."

"Sure," she allowed. She sat back down. From the tight line of her mouth, he surmised she was a little disappointed, but he couldn't think what else to do. He ducked out of the room and headed for the kitchen.

"Hi," he said to Lis as he walked in.

"Oh, good, you're here," she said breathlessly, without pausing in stirring the stew she was making.

He peered playfully into the pot. "So what have you concocted for us tonight? I hope it's especially good," he teased.

"Stop it," she scolded. "This isn't the time for joking. Ria's here! Didn't you see her?"

"Yeah. Why—"

"Is she here? I don't know, but I think she wants to talk to you."

William wasn't sure whether to feel scared or honored that the *ona* had come to pay him a personal visit, but he said, "Well, she certainly made an effort to see you, too, Mother," he put in. "She could have talked to *me* just about anywhere, but she came to our house. And she's playing along with your hosting, too."

Lis looked miffed. "What is that supposed to mean?"

"C'mon, Mother. She's not really into formalities, you know."

"I'm just being hospitable! She's—"

"All I meant was that she's trying," he explained. "She's making an effort to connect with you. Why has she been avoiding you, anyway?"

"I'm not quite sure," Lis admitted, "but I can guess."

"What, then?"

Lis sighed, not meeting his eyes. "Old disagreement. I'd rather not talk about it."

He backed off, but he was still curious. "Okay, Mother." He stole a piece of the carrot she was chopping and popped it into his mouth before she could smack his hand away. "Well," he said, "I guess I'll go back to Ria."

"Mm-hmm," was her only response.

He laughed and left the kitchen. When he got back to the sitting room, Ria was polishing her knife. She didn't look up as he came in. He got the feeling she knew everything he'd said to Lis.

"You still don't have a weapon," she commented bluntly without preamble.

Technically not true. He still had his dagger he'd used to save Dero. They'd retrieved it for him while he was unconscious. But a dagger wasn't going to do him much good. He needed a sword, but he had no idea where he would get one. Even Dero wasn't sure on that point. Dero had guessed he'd have to ask a smith to make one for him. The Ëan had only enough to get by, and they kept all their weapons close.

"I need a sword," he agreed. "But I don't know where—"

"I brought you something," she interrupted. She reached for a bundle on the couch beside her that he hadn't noticed before. He felt a surge of excitement.

She took out a long sword in a leather sheath. It was a simple blade, yet elegant, somehow. She handed it to him, and he took it hesitantly. "This is for *me*?" he asked disbelievingly.

"Mm-hmm. If you plan on defending yourself, you'll need a weapon. You're still no good at hand-fighting, you know." He laughed, but he couldn't deny it.

He pulled it from its sheath. It was made of a white metal, the same as Ria's knives. He got the feeling he wouldn't need to sharpen it often or worry about it breaking. "Where did you get this?" he asked incredulously. It was the finest sword he'd ever held, if less showy than others he'd seen.

"The Djorn. They still have a number of Gnomi weapons acquired a long time ago and still pass down. Mel—my teacher gave me my weapons from the same cache. Yewul sent that for you."

"Thank you," he said earnestly. He was quite aware that it was a generous gift—it was not as if everyone in the Nest had one of these. He'd only seen Ria and the Djorn carry them. "It's beautiful." Honestly, he was surprised by the sword's age. It was over a thousand years old, but looked like it had been made last week. He felt awed to be holding something so ancient.

She smiled. "I picked it for you. Had to guess on hilt size and weight, but I'm pretty good at that. I know weapons."

The *ona* was prone to understatement, but she was right. It fit his hand perfectly and felt like a part of his arm. He had to resist the urge to swing it around because he knew Lis wouldn't appreciate him slicing up the furniture.

"It's amazing," he declared. He put it reverently back in its sheath.

"Glad you like it," she said dryly. Then she added, "Make sure you take care of it. Keep it clean and sharp. It could mean your life someday."

He nodded. "I'll remember that."

Next she brought out a bow and quiver, but no arrows. "You'll have to learn to make arrows," she informed him.

The bow was clearly newly made. She read his curious glance and said, "Lagan made them for you, so you can thank him later."

He laughed. "Okay." He set the bow and sword down. "Thank you, *ona*."

"You're welcome," she said. "But like I said, if you plan on fighting, you'll need weapons."

If you plan on fighting. She might as well have said, *If you plan on being an Ëa.*

She went back to polishing her knife. He sat down across from her, watching. She obviously knew what he wanted. Did the weapons mean he was ready? He'd surely proven himself by now! He'd trained endlessly. He was not the helpless, naïve nobleman he'd been that spring. But she did not broach the subject. She never did.

He wrestled with his desire to ask, but before he could, Lis called, "Dinner's ready!"

He set aside his new weapons and stood up. He smiled at Ria, saying, "Let's go in, then." He had to restrain himself from the irrational urge to offer her his arm. Playing the host put him in mind of old Ossian etiquette, but this was *Ona* Auria. She'd scorn such a gesture.

She followed him to the table. Lis had set out as fine a table as she possessed, though William wasn't sure Ria would necessarily enjoy the finery. He could picture her more easily beside a campfire eating roasted meat off a stick.

Lis took the head of the small table, leaving William and Ria across from each other. Once they'd taken their seats, Lis asked William to bless the meal, which he did. It no longer seemed like a routine tradition, but an actual prayer. Even if he didn't feel like El was listening, he knew he was. When he looked up, he found Ria was smiling at him.

"Eat all you like," Lis invited. "I made plenty. I'm sure you two are hungry."

She'd made stew and rolls. The stew wasn't exactly bad, but far from delicious. Ria took her first bite and had to feign appreciation. She kept on eating it, but she paid more attention to the rolls.

"Do you get enough food, Ria? I imagine you're too busy to cook," Lis asked in a motherly fashion.

She clearly chafed at the question, but she answered, "A woman among the *Reben* named Fraidith sees to my food, Lis. Her children leave it in my room for me."

"Room?" William asked. He'd never given any thought to where the *ona* stayed. He'd always supposed she lived in the *Ëa* quarter.

"Mm-hm. I live in the basement of the Sky Palace."

It struck him as odd, for reasons he couldn't explain. It just seemed strange she would live apart from the others.

"Do you live by yourself?" Lis asked.

"Yes," she answered, clearly wanting to change the subject. She didn't like talking about her personal life. "It's closer to the top of the mountain so I can get out quicker in an emergency."

"Makes sense," William put in, trying to be helpful.

Ria busied herself with the food. They were quiet for a minute or two. William tried to work up the courage to ask the question he'd been wanting to ask. Finally, he couldn't stand waiting anymore. "*Ona*," he began carefully. The use of her title in this setting got her attention. "I wanted to ask you..." He just forced it out, speaking quickly. "Do you think I'm ready to be an *Ëa*?"

Lis looked sharply from him to Ria, almost alarmed, but William had eyes only for the *ona*. Her green eyes bored steadily into his. Her meal was temporarily forgotten.

She answered him after a moment's standoff. "You've become strong, William," she said seriously. "You've learned to fight, and that you've done well. Your progress is impressive for such a short time."

He flushed at the praise, which he knew the *ona* would not have given idly. But he sensed there was a "but" coming.

"But—" (there it was), "—you still lack something."

"What?" he asked crestfallen.

"It takes more to be an *Ëa* than being able to fight. You've earned respect and even affection from the Ëan. You've lived among them. But I still do not see the character you need.

"So far, this has all been about you, William. How you can improve. How you can get what you want. An *Ëa* must think of himself last, William. And you have grown, but not enough. We need to see that you'd give anything, without thought for yourself, for someone else. That is our cause—we fight, we die for Belond. When you embrace that, then you will be ready, William. I will keep watching."

He nodded, accepting her decision. She went back to her stew.

"I wish you wouldn't fight," Lis put in. This was said more to William than to Ria, but Ria turned angrily to Lis, pausing with the spoon half raised to her mouth.

"What do you want us to do?" Auria demanded. "Nothing?"

"No," Lis countered mildly, surprised by the vehement reaction. "I just wish you weren't always in danger. I worry about you, that's all, dear."

"You always *criticize*," Ria muttered. William heard her, but Lis did not.

"If only the King would come with his armies," Lis continued wistfully. "It would have saved you having to fight, Ria."

"There *was* no one but me!" Ria exclaimed angrily. "None of us would be here if not for me!"

"I know, dear, I know," she placated.

"I don't have to wait on someone else to save me," Ria continued. All her anger had suddenly burst forth. Her spoon clattered into her bowl, unheeded. "Unlike you. 'The King will come, the King will save us.' So you've always tried to tell me. Then one day, I realized that the King wasn't coming. Not unless I brought him. El put *me* here, Lis, not the King, and for a reason. I'm not going to waste my life waiting, praying, for someone else to do what *I'm* supposed to do. It's *my* fight, Lis. It always will be. And if I'm in danger—if I die—so what? At least my life will mean something."

Tears sprung to Lis's eyes, but behind her sweet nature Lis had a mind to match the *ona*'s. "It shouldn't have been," she argued. "You were born to be a lady, Ria, though you've forgotten it. You were born to be a Whitefeld. This should never have happened."

"But it did! You're so stuck in the past you can't see anything else!"

"I've tried, Ria."

"Oh, have you? You did nothing! A lady, you say? Did you ever think that maybe El meant for women to do more than keep the house while men protected them? What kind of life is that?"

"It is the way of things! Women *should* follow their husbands!"

"I don't need to find a husband to protect me! I can protect *myself*! If I ever married, I'd marry someone who was my equal, someone that I love—not for my own security!"

"You'd never let any man get close to you. You don't let *anyone* get close to you!"

"I don't need someone to take care of me! I learned a long time ago that no one would!"

That hurt Lis more than anything she'd yet said. She stopped, tears running down her cheeks.

"I failed you," Lis said softly. "I know I did. I'm sorry, Ria. I truly am."

Ria lowered her voice, but she only sounded more angry. "Of course you are. That's all you ever are. *Sorry*. You've never really fought for anything, have you? You want to show me you're sorry?" She stood up, pushing her chair back. "Prove it. Do something for someone else. Prove you have a will of your own, and you're not just another helpless noblewoman."

With that she turned and stormed angrily away. Lis burst into tears, no longer angry. William blinked. He could scarcely believe what he'd just seen. For a moment, he just sat there, feeling a bit shocked, debating what to do. Then he got up, saying to Lis, "Be right back," and ran after Ria.

"Wait!" he called. He caught her in the hallway.

"Don't make excuses for her, William," Ria snapped at him. "I don't want to hear it. I'm leaving."

"Wait, no," he put a hand on her arm. "I'm not making excuses." He didn't know what to say. All he wanted to do was put his arms around her, but she wouldn't have let him. It tore his heart to think about what she'd been through. Despite all her anger, all he saw was a wounded little six-year-old girl, grieving for her father and wondering why her mother and aunt weren't helping her. And despite her fierce glare, so different from Lis's sobs, he got the sense she was close to tears, though she would never have cried in front of him.

"I'm sorry," was all he could manage.

Her glare softened, just a little. She bit her lip. "It's not your fault," she said heavily.

"Are you all right?" he asked.

The barest trace of a smile formed on her lips. "Yes." She hesitated, as if she wanted to say something more. "Thank you," she said, then she turned away. She never let anyone get close to her, Lis had said. "I have to go."

"I know," he said, releasing her arm. "Thank you for coming."

"It was a mistake," she answered, keeping her face averted. "I won't be back." She moved to the door. "I'll see you later, William."

She let herself out, bidding a surprised Corran good-night. William watched her go, until the street was empty. Then he went back to Lis.

She was still crying. William felt caught in the middle. He cared about both of them, and both were hurt. He didn't know which was right, if either really was. He wanted to do something, anything, to make things right between them, but he didn't know what he *could* do.

He put his arms around Lis. He didn't say anything, he just held her. He couldn't find anything to say.

After a while, she stopped crying. "She was right," she

said softly. She sounded awful. William pulled her tighter.

"You did your best," William consoled.

Lis shook her head. "No, I didn't. I was too busy grieving for myself. I didn't do anything for her. She was right."

"Then do something now."

"What? I can't fight—and I wouldn't even if I could. My place is in the home."

"And you've made us a beautiful home," William told her. "Yewul told me that not all gifts are earth-shattering, but they're all important. You don't have to be Auria to make a difference."

She snuffled. "Is that why you want to be an *Ëa*?"

"I don't know. I think so. It just feels right—like I'm meant to do it."

"I'm not sure I *can* fight for something," she said. "I'm not a brave woman, William."

"Just think about it. You're brave in your own way, you know."

"You think so?" He nodded. "But it wouldn't change anything for her. I can't change the past—it's too late. Ria will never forgive me, and I don't blame her."

"She loves you," William assured. "You're her only family. You may argue sometimes, but that won't change."

"The *Ëan* are her family. She loves them more than anything, and they'd do anything for her. Why would she need me?"

"You're her aunt. And she *does* need you."

Lis sighed. She didn't say any more. She stayed there a minute more, then she got up. "I'd best clean up," she said. Lis was as devoted to her duty as any *Ëa*. She dried her face with a napkin, then stood.

"I'll help," William offered.

She smiled, and then they cleared away the dishes.

Chapter 28

The days continued to pass by, as fall deepened into cooler weather. The work on the ship advanced steadily, with more urgency in the hope of completing as much work as possible before the winter weather set in. The foremen pushed the workers to their limits, whether *Ëa*, guard, or *Rebe*, but the King's builders seemed well-pleased. They had already finished the frame of the ship, supported by a massive network of scaffolding and machines to lift the pieces of wood. Work would go slower when the weather worsened, of course, but their progress was admirable so far.

More often now, the *Ëan* were gone. Harvest time was passing, and it was harder than ever for the people on the island to get food. The Governor's men appropriated all their crops and put them in massive barns, to be "distributed later." It was the *ona* who did the distributing. She raided the storehouses with regularity.

William remained diligent with the workers. As much as he disliked neglecting his weapon training, he didn't take days off any more. He still sparred after coming home, but it was less often than he used to. Much as he would rather be improving himself, he knew the *ona* would want him to be serving a cause other than his own.

Today, a gray October day, was one of the rare times when a whole crowd of *Ëan* was going to be working among them. William walked the underground road to the building site beside Dero and a few other *Ëan*, listening to them laughingly tell stories of how they had weaseled the guards of the storehouses. More than ever, William wished he could be with them.

They emerged into the open. As ever, it was a shock to come up suddenly into the daylight, but today less than some. The sun was hidden behind dense, angry-looking cloud-cover. It was raining lightly, but could be worse. The sea before them looked as gray as the sky, but the wind had whipped it into a frenzy.

"Looks like short work today, boys," the *ona* called. "Make it count!" She was perhaps the most eager to see this boat finished, and understandably so.

Pat began assigning work groups. These were always different, probably by the *ona*'s orders. Doubtlessly she wanted to force everyone to work with different people to keep her fifty Ëan from splitting into factions and also to include outsiders (like William). She was not arranging specific assignments herself, William guessed, she just left it to the foreman to change things up.

"Elix, Dero, Rosie," Pat called. "Szera, the *ona*, Tiran. Baër, William, Ovan." He continued on, but William stopped listening.

He heard the murmuring. Everyone knew Baër hated William. His heart sank. He'd tried to avoid the angry young man. He didn't want to start unnecessary conflict. Now he would have to spend the whole day with him. He suspected *this* partnership was made on purpose. He saw the *ona* looking at him. He steeled himself and forced a smile.

Ovan walked to meet him. "Just like old times, eh?" He smiled.

William nodded agreement. "Yeah," he agreed. He remembered his first hike in Belond all too well. Things had been so different then.

Baër approached, too. "Morning," he said to Ovan. He said nothing to William.

"Hello, Baër," William ventured, trying to smile, but Baër completely ignored him. He didn't understand why Baër hated him so much, and no one would explain it, so he supposed he must have done something to offend him. He hated having this conflict hanging over him.

"Let's go," he said to Ovan. Then he turned on his heel and stalked away toward the construction.

Just like old times, indeed.

William looked to Ovan, hoping for some advice, but Ovan

just sighed heavily and followed Baër. He clearly disliked this assignment as much as any of them. William felt badly for him. Ovan was stuck in the middle.

They got to work. Fastening ropes, lifting boards on the pulleys, waiting for the groups on the scaffolds to hammer the boards into the frame. William soon almost welcomed the cold rain in his face, but it made his hands more slippery. They worked together in silence, not wanting to further Baër's foul mood.

The hours wore on. The weather got worse, but the *ona* pushed them anyway. They were soaked to the skin, and William could barely see because of the rain pouring on him, but there was no thunder yet. For a while, the *Ëan* began to sing in strong rhythm, with the hammers falling in time to the song. William, Ovan, and even Baër sang along. William never felt so inspired than when the *Ëan* were singing together. They drowned out even the rain. The *ona*'s voice rose above the rest, strong but beautiful.

They stopped to eat a soggy lunch. William and Ovan ate together, but Baër ate by himself. William decided to ask Ovan's opinion, if he would give it. He whispered, "Why does he hate me so much?"

Ovan sighed, clearly as uncomfortable as Dero had been at the question, but it was just as clear he knew the answer. "It's complicated, William. I'm not sure I ought to tell you. If you don't know already, I don't think it's my place to explain. But don't be too hard on him. He's a good man, but he's lost a lot, and he's had many disappointments."

William sighed. No one would explain Baër's behavior to him beyond "figure it out yourself." He gave up trying. He just wished he could make it up to Baër somehow.

They got back to work, lifting plank after plank, each as heavy as the last. The *ona* decided they would continue go one more hour before it began to thunder. (She was good at predicting the weather, among other things.)

Baër began to grow moodier (if that were possible) and more easily frustrated. Several times, he'd jerk the rope too hard and unbalance the plank. Pat came by and admonished him (he didn't dare yell at any *Ëa*) several times, but that only made it worse.

They were fastening a plank to the lifting mechanism and were about to hoist it when William pointed out, "Baër, your side is loose." It was the first time anyone had spoken since lunchtime.

Baër fixed him with a glare, one eyebrow raised. "It's fine," he growled, the first time he had spoken to William all day.

William wanted to fix it, but Baër wasn't accepting help or criticism from William. He sighed and they went on, though he didn't like it.

The plank only made it halfway up.

As they were lifting it, Baër's side came loose from the rope, leaving the weight suddenly all on William's rope. The pulley broke in the sudden shift, leaving all the ropes slack. The plank came hurtling back down.

"Baër!" William shouted. William had only a second to dodge, but Baër seemed frozen in place. William lunged for him and grabbed his arm, pulling him forward an instant before the plank would have fallen on his head.

The crash drew the attention of the whole site. Everyone was shouting and running toward them.

"Baër!" William and Ovan both called, down on their knees beside him. William had saved him from being killed, but the plank had landed on his legs, and he was trapped. He was barely conscious and moaning in pain. A blow like that had certainly broken both his legs, if not worse.

The *ona* was beside them in an instant. She was deadly calm, but William could see the distress in her eyes. She checked Baër carefully, her hands gentle. Then she gave sharp, quiet, urgent orders to the onlookers. "All of you, on my mark, lift that plank off of him." The workers, William included, found a grip on the huge board. The *ona* stayed with Baër one hand on his shoulder, the other gripping his hand.

"Slowly, and don't shift the weight. Keep it flat. One, two, three, now!"

They lifted the board, slowly. Baër cried out as the weight lifted. They rasied it clear and set it down again.

"Dero, with me," the *ona* ordered. "The rest of you, back away. Ovan, Szera, Kerran, make a stretcher."

William withdrew with the crowd, who still watched in numb shock. Dero began examining Baër carefully, like a healer. Then William realized that was why the *ona* had picked him. He must have learned more than Djoran from Ekata. He was probably the best healer in this crowd.

"Orben! Short!" the *ona* called. She chose a Tellorian guard and an *Ëa*, two of their fastest runners. "Start running back and get Ekata. There are horses at the third branching. Go, and hurry! Have her meet us on the road."

The two ran off. Ovan, Szera, and Kerran ran up with their makeshift stretcher. "Lift him onto it," the *ona* told them. "Gently. But we have to get him out of the rain."

Dero force-fed him some herbs, most likely meant to lessen his pain. Then they lifted him slowly onto the stretcher. He groaned with pain and fell unconscious. They bore him up and walked slowly away, Dero beside them. The *ona* let them go, walking back to the crowd.

"Dero thinks he'll be all right, but we'll let Ekata examine him," she announced. "Enough for today. Make everything fast and let's go home."

The walk back was very different than the walk there. They went slowly, keeping well away from the stretcher so as not to overwhelm them. No one talked, except in soft whispers.

William felt horrible. As much as he didn't get along with Baër, he wouldn't have wanted something like this to happen to him.

He found Ria at his shoulder. "You okay?" she asked him.

William couldn't meet her eyes. "I should have made him fix it. I saw it was loose."

"I know what happened. And I know Baër. He's a

stubborn fool. I am hoping this will teach him a lesson. It's not your fault. It might just as easily be you on that stretcher. But you saved his life. Don't take blame on yourself. He'll recover, though it may take a while. He ought to be thanking you."

"He won't, though," William muttered, mostly to himself.

She grimaced. "No, I don't think he will. But we'll see what I can do with him." She patted his shoulder. Then her voice brightened considerably. "But we'll need someone to fill in for him while he gets better."

His mouth dropped. "You mean—"

She winked. "Have a chat with Dero, when we're all done here. He'll help you. But I think you're ready."

She threw him a smile when she saw his stunned expression. "You've earned it," she stated. Then she walked on ahead, leaving him alone.

Chapter 29

William waited for Dero outside the healers' house. It was late when he finally came out, and his normally energetic friend looked tired.

"Hi, William," he said, brightening only a little.

"How's he doing?" William asked.

Dero sighed. "He'll heal. Both legs are broken, and he won't be walking around for a long time. Kata set the bones and says they weren't damaged as much as they could be. He's awake now, and none too happy. The *ona* had a long talk with him an hour ago. I hate to think what she said. She's not one to tolerate neglect of duty for any reason, especially emotion." He sighed. "Baër'll catch it now, if that's any consolation."

William was taken aback. "Not really. I didn't want him to get in trouble, let alone hurt."

"Sorry," Dero apologized. "That was mean."

"It's okay," William replied. "You've had a long day, I guess. You holding up okay?"

"Yeah, I'm fine. Ekata did most of the work. She's an amazing healer." He was too tired even to blush.

"Did you get any dinner?"

"No."

William dug some cheese and bread out of his bag. "Got this at my house, so it isn't wet. Mother's cooking, though."

Dero laughed. "Can't be worse than Winna's. That woman wasn't meant to be a cook. Elénne's okay, but Winna doesn't understand the difference between a brick and bread." They shared a laugh. Dero took the food, saying, "Thanks."

"Sure."

Dero munched the bread. "Did you practice with Tiran?" he asked through the bite in his mouth.

"No, I didn't go down. I was waiting for you."

"Oh? Why's that? Not sick of me yet?"

"No. The *ona* said I should talk to you."

"The *ona*?" Dero looked at him curiously. "Why?"

"She said I'm ready," he replied slowly, trying to keep his excitement from spilling over.

Dero had no such reservations. Effusiveness was in his nature. "What!" he exclaimed. He forgot his exhaustion and tackled William with a hug, cheese still in hand. "That's fantastic!" he crowed in excitement. "Oh, this is great!" he continued, half to himself. "We'll have to moot it, and then we'll switch you to the *Ëa* quarter—"

"Wait, slow down," William laughed. "I still don't even know what I have to do!"

"Oh. I guess I should explain *that*. It's not a terribly easy process. No, don't get me wrong!" Dero interjected, reading William's expression. "No fighting involved. No challenges. Heh! That'd be awful! You could just challenge me, though." He bumped William with his shoulder. "Then you'd make it in easy. But there *is* a process.

"See, the *ona* is the leader of the *Ëan*. *Ona*—first. She's not a dictator, and she doesn't make all the decisions by herself. She's the commander and battle chief, of course, and we obey her without hesitation. But she doesn't decide who joins. Not by herself.

"She took a special interest in you, for some reason. Normally joining is an *Ëa*-initiated thing. We've kind of developed our own traditions over the years until they've become standards. There is a certain process we always observe now before someone new joins.

"This is what happens. First, the potential candidate asks an *Ëa* to stand for him. (That'll be me, if you don't mind.)"

"Of course I don't mind! You're my best friend."

Dero blushed and grinned. "Well good, then. So if I'm going to stand for you, I have to moot the *Ëan* to a sort of council—a bit like the one time you attended, but with only the *Ëan* present and none of the *Reben* or anyone else. Not everyone can come, of course—we can't leave Belo unwatched. So their votes are collected in advance before the candidacy is mooted."

"Votes?" This system was democratic to a degree even Elber, rest his ridiculous soul, could not have failed to disapprove of. The *Ëan* were still Edenian, after all.

"Oh, sorry. Let me go back. So I ask all the *Ëan* available to attend the moot. Then I introduce you and explain why I think you should join. Then the *ona* opens the floor for anyone to speak for or against you, then you have an opportunity to answer for yourself. That was the scary part, when I did it—but you'll be fine."

"Who stood for *you*?"

"Aunt Winna. Kerran would have done it, but Aunt Winna's more forceful—which was good, 'cause I was scared silly. It seems odd I was ever afraid of the *Ëan*, but I was. Though the *ona* still scares me sometimes, much as I love her."

William laughed. "She is a frightening woman, all right."

"First time I saw her I wasn't sure whether I should fall in love or run in terror," Dero confided with a laugh. "Most of us felt the same at some point."

William nodded. He knew *exactly* what Dero meant.

"But she's not usually involved much in the moot," Dero continued. "She just listens and watches. Until the end."

"What happens at the end?"

"Hold on, I haven't gotten to that yet," Dero said, enjoying William's curiosity. "After all the arguments, the *ona* calls for a vote. You'll leave the room (so there's no hard feelings if you see someone vote against you) and they'll each decide whether or not to vote for you. The *ona* can change any verdict, of course, but I've never seen it done. She wouldn't force anyone on us. It's a very fair system. Anyway. A 'no' vote counts one and a half times—the *ona* doesn't want to harbor dissent. If a large enough minority is against someone, it will cause trouble later. Someone who's voted down can always try again sometime, though they have to wait two months. It hasn't happened since I've been here."

"Do you think I'll make it?" William asked anxiously. If no's weighed more heavily, it would be more difficult.

"Oh, of course!" Dero exclaimed. "Everyone likes you! Or just about everyone."

"They do?"

Dero bobbed his head enthusiastically. "Yup. You've made a good impression."

That reassured him. "Thanks."

"So when—" (Dero stressed the "when"), "you get approved, you come back in and are told the verdict (though not the exact tally). Then the *ona* swears you in and you pledge your loyalty to us. Torhan will pray, then we all accept you, one by one. Some may shake your hand, give you a hug—that sort of thing. They have to do it, even if they voted against you.

"After that, the *ona* reminds us of our calling, and we remember both the fallen and the living we protect. Then there is the *song*."

Dero said this with grave emphasis. "What song?" William asked.

"Our call to war," he replied. "Our battle song. When you hear it, you'll understand. When it's over, the moot is done."

"Seems awfully complex."

"It's failsafe. We're a family; we can't include just anyone, or it would destroy who we are."

"I guess you're right."

Dero bounced up and down rather than nodding. "I'll have to make the arrangements. After you're an *Ëa*, you'll have to move to the *Ëa*-quarter. We'll find a place for you. Or you *could* stay with me, if you wanted."

A pang of guilt stabbed through William. He'd be leaving their house! Lis's only pride was in making a home for the two of them. This would upset her as much as the idea of him being in a war.

"Will my mother come, too?" he asked quickly. He would have forgotten the whole idea if it meant leaving his Mother alone. He couldn't be that cruel to her, or that hard on himself.

To his relief, Dero assured, "Oh, of course! All the families of the Ëan live in the quarter. The *ona*'s not so harsh as to split families. It would be wrong."

"Good—I wouldn't want to."

"The two of you could join us," Dero offered again. "We still have room, and then your Mother wouldn't be too lonely. She'd have Fred and Elénne for company—and Hope, of course, though that little girl screams something terrible."

"She does?"

"Maybe you'll be a good influence on her," Dero joked. "She's *always* good for you."

William laughed, but he was thinking more about Elénne than Hope. It would be a bit awkward to live in the same house as the girl who had a crush on him, and he could only imagine the gossip. But Lis would probably be happy.

"So will you come?" Dero asked. "I know it's a bit awkward for you—" (Dero was one of the only people who understood William's disinterest in Elénne and sympathized with his situation), "but I'll always be around, and Kerran, and Allain, and—"

"I'd love to," William interrupted, laughing. "But let me talk to Lis, Tiran, and Ri—I mean the *ona*—about it first." He flushed at his accidental near use of her nickname. Dero pretended to ignore it, but William knew his friend was more perceptive than that. "I'm sure they'll have opinions.

"Okay. But tell me what they say, all right?" he demanded excitedly.

"Okay," William promised.

Dero laughed, almost a giggle, as they reached William's door. "Ooh, this is great," he enthused. "I'll start on the moot tomorrow."

"Thanks," William replied. "Are you working tomorrow?"

"No, I have sentry duty tomorrow. I'll see you in the practice room, though, okay?"

"Okay, Good night! And get some good rest after today!"

"I will! Bye!"

With that, Dero skipped off, a smile on his face.

William had waited to tell Lis the news until he'd talked to Dero first. Now he knew he had to talk to her about it. She was knitting in her bedroom (a pair of socks for him to wear when the weather got cold). She was dressed in her nightgown and lying in bed, but the lamp indicated that she had been waiting for him.

He knocked, even though the door was open. She looked up. "There you are," she said. "I'd nearly given up believing you'd come home at all tonight."

"Sorry," he apologized. "I had to wait a long time."

"Did you find Dero?"

"Yes."

"Was he all right? Hard day for him. It's awful."

"Tired, but fine otherwise."

"How's Baër? Did he say?"

"He'll mend, but it might take a while."

"Oh, good." Lis knew how much Baër mistreated her son, and she instinctively disliked him because of it, but she was too sweet-natured to wish harm on anyone.

"Mother?" he ventured, unsure how to start. He didn't want to hurt her feelings, especially in light of how distant Ria was behaving toward her.

"What?" she asked, putting aside her knitting. Concern showed in her face. He was easy to read; everyone told him that. His father said he wore his heart on his sleeve.

"Can—can I talk to you?" he said hesitantly.

She smiled, patting the bed beside her. "Sure, sweetheart. Come sit down."

He sat on the edge of her bed. "I'm going to try to become an Ëa, Mother.

"I know, dear. You're working so very hard and you're doing well," she encouraged.

He smiled at her words but kept talking. "No, Mother—I mean soon. Like, now."

Her brows furrowed. "Oh," was all she said.

She looked so upset, he felt terrible. "Look," he said

quickly, "do you really not want me to do it? I'll give up the whole idea if you ask me to. I'd rather be with you than anybody else."

She made a sound that was part laugh and part sigh. "Oh, William," she replied. "You are as much my son as any young man who ever belonged to his mother. I love you. But I can't keep you forever, and I wouldn't want to hold you back. I may not like it, but it's your life. I'm not going to tell you no. If it's what you really want, then do it—put your very best into it, and never let yourself down. You've grown into a fine man, William. You can do whatever you set your mind to."

"Thank you," was all he could say. He gave her a hug. The enormity of her surrendering was clear, but she did it with grace.

"I have just one question, though," she added. "Why are you so set on this?"

"I told you," he replied, surprised. "It feels like the right thing to do. This place has become as much my home as Ossia, and defending it is a cause I can believe in. It's the first time in my life I've been able to stand up for something."

"I know," she said. "And I'm proud of you. But is that the only reason?"

He arched an eyebrow, confused. "What do you mean?"

"I mean Ria," she said gently.

He pursed his lips, not sure how to respond.

"I'm a woman, William. I'm not blind. And I know you. I've seen the way you look at her, how you talk about her. You're partial to her, aren't you?"

He sighed, uncomfortable. Dero said all the men in the Nest were half in love with her, and he was no different, but he wasn't about to admit it. He'd buried any idea of pursuing Ria deep inside him. He valued her friendship too much to dare any further attachment, much as he would have liked to... No. It wasn't possible.

"I've noticed for a long time," Lis continued, "but I'd hoped you'd forget the feeling. And there was Elénne for you to take an interest in. She's a nice girl, easy to please and quick to love. You'd do better courting a woman like that."

"What do you have against Ria?" he asked defensively, a bit sullen. He didn't like this whole conversation. It bothered him to have her discuss his feelings so openly, when he would not even acknowledge them to himself.

"She's too independent. She's willful and proud, and her standards are impossibly high. She's not an affectionate girl, which I think you need. She keeps all her emotions bottled up inside her so she doesn't get hurt. You can't romance a girl of her disposition. Only a rare few could even befriend her—though I think you are among the few. But I fear if you tried to pursue her, you'd only get hurt, sweetheart. I don't want you to live life unhappy, but that's better than living it brokenhearted."

He knew she was speaking wisdom, but his heart wouldn't hear it. His mind told his heart to be quiet, and it was his mind that spoke. "I'm not going after Ria, Mother. That's not what this is about."

"Are you sure?" she questioned.

"Yes," he said firmly. "Now can we not talk about this?"

Lis looked unconvinced, but she didn't push him. "Okay," she conceded.

"Good. There's one more thing I need to ask you," he said, feeling a bit more relieved, but this wasn't a comfortable subject either.

"Yes?" she asked, a bit wary.

"If I become an Ëa, I have to live in the Ëa quarter so I can come easily at call."

She looked down. "I see," she said heavily.

"But you can come, too," he added. "We just can't stay in this house together. Dero says we can stay with them. It won't be all your own house, but you'd have lots of company—and I think their home could use a hand like yours on it. Would you mind? I know it's not ideal..."

"Ideal? It's lovely!" she declared, brightening. "I thought you'd have to go off alone. Tell Dero we'll be happy to stay with him. Just think—you'll have a best friend (or brother, if you like), and I'll have women to be with. Perfect! Thank you, dear."

"I'm going to ask Tiran and Ria first," he cautioned. "But I'm glad you like the idea."

"Mm-hmm," she agreed. "Was that all you wanted to ask, sweetheart?"

"Yes," he answered.

"Good," she said. "It's settled. Now go off to bed—you look exhausted, and it's late. We can talk more in the morning, if you like."

"Okay, thanks, Mother. Good night."

"Good night, dear. I love you."

"I love you, too, Mother."

He left the room, and she blew out her light.

Chapter 30

The moot was arranged to be held in a week, a date given by the *ona*. Then Dero had to run around telling everyone about it and figuring out who could and couldn't be there and who would have to vote in advance. Those who had sentry duty reported to Ovan, and he wrote down their votes to be read after all the others voted.

In all, forty-five *Ëan* were able to attend, since the outposts were supplemented by Tiran's men at times. The *ona* leaned heavily on them on this occasion so as to allow most members to be present. Dero told him there had never been so many at a moot before, but William wasn't sure whether this made him more or less nervous.

The day finally came. The work on the ship dragged on endlessly, a miserable business in the cool and rainy weather. William spent all day going back and forth between excitement and anxiety.

He was going to be an *Ëa*!

It wasn't guaranteed, of course. He had to pass the moot. But Dero seemed confident he would.

Dero was more excited than *he* was. He fidgeted all day, willing the time to pass more quickly. Pat reprimanded him for sluggishness, but Dero never neglected to pay attention. The memory of Baër's accident was still too near for negligence to occur again.

The foreman called the signal for home, since the *ona* had been absent all day. William had no idea where she had gone, but he assumed she was spying on Belo as she so often did. She still made her "expeditions" to the Felds with regularity, and it hardly mattered whether she went during the day or at night. They never even knew she was there. She had promised to be back by the time of the moot, and no one doubted she would be.

The workers began the long trudge home on the Gnomi

Road. Dero came running to catch up to him.

"At last!" he said breathlessly. "I thought this day would never be over! I'm so excited I can hardly stand it! Aren't you?"

William nodded, but he still wasn't sure what to feel. After all this time and effort, it didn't seem quite real.

Dero talked the whole walk back, babbling on in his enthusiastic manner. William laughed, glad for the distraction from his worries.

Dero had invited him to eat dinner at their house, and Lis had let him go gladly. "Go have fun," she had told him. "You'll be just fine!"

Hope was thrilled to see him. "Wee-yum!" she screamed. He tickled her and chased her, which made her giggle and scream with delight. Besides Dero, at least one other person would be excited if he moved into the house.

No, more than one. Over dinner, everyone was discussing the moot with anticipation. Winna, Kerran, and Allain were all going to attend. They were trying not to say *too* much before the moot, but William could easily feel their encouragement. This house held some of his best friends among the Ëan. He knew they would support him.

Fred and Elénne had no such reservations, and neither did Dero, of course. Fred, who was nothing of a fighter, could express only admiration for his progress. Elénne fixed shining eyes on him all throughout the meal, showering him with compliments and encouragement. *That* didn't help him much, though he appreciated her intention.

In the end, he hardly touched his food, between talking and nerves. Before he knew it, it was time to go.

"Come on," Dero urged, hurrying them all out the door. "Bye, Énne! Bye, Uncle Fred! Bye Hope! We'll be back soon!"

"Good luck!" Elénne called after them.

"El go with you!" Fred called. "And enjoy yourself, William!"

The Sky Tree Hall awed William anew. He hadn't been

there since the *ona* had called together nearly the whole populace of the Nest to announce and organize the building of the ship. It seemed like years ago, though it was only a few short months. The clear walls and sheer height of the huge room, looking down over all of Belond, lent gravity to what they did. They could see clearly what they were fighting to protect.

All the Ëan had arrived except the *ona* and Szera, and all were seated around the ring of stone chairs, with the exception of Baër, who had been given special accommodation for his injury. (The *ona* had thought it unwise to exclude him, or he might cause trouble about it later.) The gathering did not even fill half the circle, so wide was the hall. Each Ëa wore his choice weapon, as William did himself. There was a wide variety among them, as much as there was among the Ëan themselves. They were old and young, tall and short, light and dark, man and woman. The only consistent feature among them was the stripe of blue paint smeared on each cheek as the *ona* had worn the last time she had been here.

William stood before the tree beside Dero, waiting uncomfortably. He faced the circle, which was very quiet, on the side where the stairs led up into the room. He tried not to fidget. It would not do to look nervous. He put his hand on his sword, glad for the resting place. Even in Ossia he'd hated appearing before crowds, and experience had never increased his confidence.

He wasn't sure whether he was relieved or more nervous when the *ona* entered, followed by Szera. She looked like a barbarian queen, with her bright golden hair, leather armor, and blue war paint. Szera stood behind her, still wearing her usual clothes and her short hair gathered in a headband.

The Ëan rose as one, raising their hands in a salute. William did the same.

"*Éle, Ëan Galant,*" she cried aloud.

"*Éle!*" they shouted in unison. William knew enough Djoran to know that she had said, "Hail, gathering of Eagles!"

"We have come at the word of Dero, our brother, to

measure the merit of William Tellor to join the Eagle Flight. May all listen and judge wisely."

"*Aya*," they answered. *Yes.* Then they sat down together. The *ona* took her seat on the edge of the circle, not at all like the leader of an Edenian council, but she still drew the eye like a lodestone, and no one could have questioned who was in charge of this gathering.

"Speak, Dero," the *ona* invited. "You may speak freely."

"Thank you, *ona*. I have called this moot," Dero began, "though I am the least among us." His strong, confident voice belied his words. William was amazed to hear his friend, normally so humble, speak with such assurance. "I wish to speak on behalf of my friend, William."

Dero talked a long time, presenting his case. It was difficult for William not to blush at the sincerity and simplicity of his praise, mentioning things William didn't even remember or didn't know Dero had noticed. He talked about William's determination to succeed and long efforts toward his goal. He talked about William's character, and growth therein. He talked about William's treatment of others. He talked about William's progress as a warrior and his increased strength. He cited many specific instances to support every statement he made, leaving no claim undefended. Had he been a lawyer in a high Ossian court standing before the King himself as a judge, he could not have stated his case better or more eloquently. William marveled at his friend. Dero had once been a simple cow-hand, but this man had more nobility and honor than most of the whole bickering crowd of men who called themselves lords in Ossia combined. William wondered how he could ever have been blind to the value of these people.

Dero at last finished his speech, all his praise only leaving William feeling more humble. "That is all I have to say," he concluded. He stepped back to stand next to William.

"Thank you," William whispered fervently.

Dero bobbed his head almost imperceptibly, grinning from ear to ear. "That was good," he whispered back, clearly trying not to giggle with glee.

"Let us now hear from the *Ëan*," the *ona* said. "Anyone may speak."

The room remained silent for a moment or two, then Ovan stood up to speak. "I would commend him," he said simply. "I have trained him and labored beside him, and I see his potential. I would be honored to fight beside him."

William smiled gratefully at him, and the tall man sat back down.

One by one, others stood up. Many of his friends supported him: Winna, Kerran, Lagan, Allain, Rosie, Ekata. Even Szera said something. None said much, just a short statement of affirmation, but William felt grateful to all of them.

Then Baër spoke. He could not rise, but he still offered his opinion. "William is a nobleman," he stated, his words clipped short, but his tone was restrained in the presence of his fellows. "No nobleman has ever been an *Ëa*. They are a superior, entitled breed, and so far have only been our enemies. Why should that be any different now?"

Ovan jumped up as soon as he finished. "All respect to you, Baër, but that is ridiculous. You're generalizing the way most noblemen do about peasants. It is impossible to measure all people by their social class. It is not our way. The *Ëan* take men for their individual worth, not their station." There were appreciative nods at this, but Ovan wasn't finished yet. "And besides, what you say is not strictly true. There is more noble blood in this body than you think. I come from a noble Ossian family, remember, though not as influential or wealthy as some. You may not realize, but I am not the only one with a tie to the nobility."

Curious murmurs. They all looked at each other in confusion. They did not know their own *ona* had been born within the highest realm of society, in as honorable a family as ever one existed—until the Governor had sullied the name. William doubted Baër would have dared use that argument if he had known. William's eyes slid automatically to her to see her reaction. Her eyes were narrowed, and she did not seem pleased at Ovan's hint to her bloodline, but she did not comment.

"And remember: we are all loyal to our lord and King, His Majesty King Eduar Tellor—a nobleman. We are Edenian subjects all, and we will be again, El willing. I took an oath to serve the King until I die. No nobleman will ever receive condemnation from me because of his birth." With that, Ovan sat down.

Baër's argument had fallen far short. He'd have done better never to raise the point.

Then a small, dark man rose. Grayem, William remembered, normally called Gray. William had spoken to him a little, but never for long. He was an older man, who had been part of the Belondian army in the days of his youth, before the Governor came. He was perhaps the best staff-bearer among the *Ëan* (the *ona* excepted of course). He leaned upon it as he spoke.

"Forgive me if I misunderstand," he said slowly. "I do not doubt the arguments the *Ëan* have presented on William's behalf. But it seems to me it does not matter. The *Ëan* are a permanent brotherhood, until we die. Belond is not William's home. He must go back to Ossia in a few months, where he will stay after the Governor is overthrown. He will be gone and he will forget us. Why should we accept someone into our family only temporarily? It cannot be done."

William's heart sank. He'd scarcely given thought to more than the immediate future. It was a good point.

Gray sat down. No one rose to counter him, making William more nervous. The *Ëan* looked less sure now, trying to work through Gray's argument.

Then Torhan stood. "I have one question," he said. "Apart from what Gray said." His peaceful demeanor made him as unreadable as ever, even though William had gotten to know him fairly well. His pleasant voice, odd accent, and eloquence made him compelling to listen to. "I have known William as long as any of us," he said. "When I first met him, he had little conception of *Aiael* except vague, cold traditions and stale phrases. I have seen him grow immensely, but I would still wish to hear from his own lips: does he follow *Aiael*? It is too crucial an aspect of who the *Ëan* are to be ignored." Torhan sat down, finished.

When there seemed to be no one else who wished to speak, the *ona* stood. "Is there anyone else?" she asked, holding the eyes of each of the *Ëan* for a brief moment. She nodded, satisfied. "Then let William speak for himself. Anyone who would be an *Ëa* must have a voice of his own. What have you to say for yourself?" Dero left his side and took a seat, leaving him alone to face the circle.

William swallowed. This was the real test.

He felt more nervous than ever. He knew he had to answer these arguments, and well, before he could win them. And he *had* to win them.

It took him a moment to find his voice. Then he remembered everything he had been through to get here. He remembered how clearly he'd felt this was his calling. Even if he couldn't hear the voice of El audibly, he knew this was what he wanted him to do.

If you want me to do this, he thought, *you make it happen.*

"I don't know how I should speak to you," he began quietly. "I did not come here assuming you would accept me—though I have hoped and prayed you would. I have strived to be worthy of you, though perhaps I can never match what you all have done. But I believe in what you do, and I want nothing more than to join you.

"But perhaps this isn't about me," he said, looking straight at the *ona*. "It is less what I want than what *you* want. It is your choice. I can only try to convince you.

"I will attempt to answer the questions Grayem and Torhan have brought up. I will speak first to what Grayem asked.

"I don't know what will happen when that ship at last sails. It may be I will indeed never come back. If that happened, I must admit that I will leave half of my heart behind. Belond has become as much my home as Ossia, and I cannot pretend they will not conflict. But it seems to me that family is forever, no matter how far apart it may go. If the Ëan are a family, then an Ëa is an Ëa forever—no matter how far away he or she may go. That is the best answer I can give.

"As for Torhan's question..." he paused. He'd never been comfortable with speaking publicly about his religious stance. Now they were asking him to bare his soul in front of all of them.

"I have come to understand more than I used to. I have learned to trust El as best I can, and I have learned to follow his calling. I am not perfect, and I never will be, but I will keep believing. That is all I can offer." He paused, glancing around the circle. He saw looks of approval, doubt, thoughtfulness, and encouragement. He couldn't tell whether his words would be enough, but he could do no better. "I am finished," he said to the *ona*.

She stood. "Then let us make our decision," she said to the room at large. "William, leave us while we vote. Dero, take him downstairs and then rejoin us."

Dero rose to go down with him, and they left the Sky Tree Hall wordlessly. His audience was over, for good or ill.

He waited downstairs for what seemed like an eternity. He paced, he sat down. He prayed, he was quiet. How could voting possibly take so long? He could hardly bear waiting anymore.

Then Torhan came down for him. William jumped up immediately, searching his face for any sign. There was none. Torhan's face was entirely flat, unreadable, doubtless on purpose for the sake of the integrity of the moot. Had it been Dero, he probably would already know.

"You may rejoin us," Torhan said calmly. William followed him back upstairs.

When he came up, all the Ëan were standing and had turned to look at him. Every last one of them was straight-faced. Even Dero was forcing a neutral expression, and William couldn't tell whether he was suppressing a smile or a frown. His heart hammered. Had he failed?

The *ona* stood alone by the tree, behind all of the *Ëan*. "The moot has spoken," she intoned. "And we have an answer."

A dreadful moment passed, the longest moment of this time so far. William could feel his pulse roaring in his ears.

"What say you, *Ëan*?" she cried loudly.

As one, they saluted him. "*Aya!*"

William felt as if a physical weight had been removed. He sighed with relief, an irrepressible smile coming over his face. Dero, too, was openly grinning now.

"Come forward, William Tellor," the *ona* commanded.

He entered the circle as the *Ëan* took their seats. She beckoned him on until he stood face to face with her.

"You will now take the oath of the *Ëan*," she said. "Kneel."

He did so, looking up at her as if in a dream.

"Place your sword at my feet," she told him. He unbuckled it and laid it on the floor before her.

She paused, ceremoniously, before she began.

"Is it your wish to join the *Ëan*—yours alone and no other's?"

"It is," he answered.

"Do you swear to uphold your brothers and sisters as your own family, for good or ill, never forsaking them?"

"I do"

"Do you swear to serve the poor, the sick, and the weak, to protect and aid them without bitterness?"

"I do."

"Do you swear to use this sword only for the defense of justice and protection of others?"

"I do."

"Do you swear to obey me in any command I give to you, or those of any *Ëa* I appoint to lead you?"

"I do."

"Do you swear to serve first El, then Belond, then the Empire, as long as you live?"

"I do."

"The *Ëan* have heard and are witnesses," the *ona* declared, concluding. "Do you accept his pledge?"

"*Aya!*" They cried again.

"As I do also," the *ona* said. "Take your sword and stand before me." He did so. She reached into her belt and took out a small jar. When she opened it, he saw it contained paint like all the *Ëan* wore. She smeared it onto her finger, then drew a line across each of his cheeks. She closed the jar and put it away, rubbing her hand on a cloth. Then she took him by the shoulders, smiling at last. "You are one of us, now." She turned him to face the *Ëan*, and in unison, they cried. "*Elé!*"

What William felt then, he could never have put into words.

Torhan rose, coming to stand beside them. "Let us remember our Creator, *Aiael*," he said, and he began to pray in Djoran. He thanked El for his blessings, asked for protection and success, and asked that all the *Ëan* and William would be blessed through what had taken place that night. It was not a long prayer, but it was beautiful and stirring nonetheless. The words Torhan used to pray often came back to William in later times.

When Torhan concluded, he took his seat. Then the *ona* said, "Let us accept William as our brother."

She remained behind him as one by one, each *Ëa* came up to William. Some pressed his shoulder, some shook his hand, and a few gave him a hug. Each had a word of welcome or congratulations to give him. All his friends went by. Dero tackled him with a huge hug, unabashed, and said, "I knew you could do it." Even Baër was brought up on his stretcher. He shook William's hand and said welcome, but from his expression William could tell the rift was wider than ever.

Then the *Ëan* had all passed, and it was the *ona*'s turn. She came like all the others, shaking his hand. "You are welcome among us, William," she said with a warm smile. That smile meant more to him than a whole roomful of greetings from the rest of them. Then she surprised him by reaching up and planting a quick kiss on his cheek. She did it calmly, as if it was not unusual, but he heard the *Ëan* murmur and felt his face burn.

Then she said, "Take your seat, William." Awe came on him afresh. He was now an equal of the *Ëan* that he could sit among them. He moved to the edge of the ring, taking the empty seat next to Dero. Dero beamed enthusiastically at him.

The *ona* spoke again. "*Ëan*! You have been reminded today of your obligations. Let today serve as a reminder to you to go about your duties with honor. We will always fight. We will always remember those who have fallen. We will always remember those who remain. We will fight to our last breath to see justice rule once more in this land. We will break the power of the usurper and see this island a land of freedom once more!"

The *Ëan* cheered loudly at this. The *ona* could stir men's hearts in a way even Torhan could not. She made William want to jump up and take on all the soldiers of the Governor.

"Let us sing the battle song," the *ona* said, "and let us go to victory!"

Then she turned away toward the tree. She began the first verse of the song alone. Her strong voice filled the room. When the first verse was sung, half the *Ëan* joined, then the other half joined a line later to sing the words at the same time. The tune was compelling, and with all the *Ëan* singing, the very room seemed to vibrate. He later learned that the sound carried down to the citadel, and the *Reben* each paused and took up the song. And with all those voices, traces of the song whispered through the empty Gnomi caverns and reached every corner of Belond, so that the armies trembled with a nameless fear.

This was what they sang:

> *Hear, hear the call*
> *Hear, hear the cry*
> *We will never fall, and*
> *We will never die*

SONG OF THE ËAN

Hear, hear the call
Hear, hear the cry
We won't let them fall
Into battle we will fly
Hear, hear the call
Hear, hear the cry
Soft the eagle calls, and
Swift the eagle flies
Hear, hear the call
Hear, hear the cry
See the warrior tall, how
Blood his freedom buys
Hear, hear the call
Hear, hear the cry
Some things never fall, and
Some things never die
Hear, hear the call
Hear, hear the cry
We will never fall, and
We will never die

It was the song of the Ëan. It filled them with their purpose. William did not sing with them that first time, but he always remembered the song. It was who he had become.

Chapter 31

Winning isn't the end of the game.

It is the funny thing about dreams, especially the craziest ones: when you finally reach your goal, you realize it wasn't the end, after all. Beforehand, all you can think about is achieving your dream. You pour everything you have into earning it, pushing yourself, even when it seems too far out of reach. Then you finally win. There comes a once-in-a-lifetime thrill, a joyous excitement that cannot be matched by any other feeling: you know you earned success, and now you have it. But then there follows disbelief, an almost surreal quality to your circumstances. You remember just how impossible it ought to be for you to be standing here. You've cherished this dream for so long, you can scarcely believe it can be accomplished now. It is difficult to move on; you want it to last. Then you realize you must find a new dream, take your last goal to a new level and fight for it just as hard as you did the first one—but with more confidence this time, because you have already seen yourself succeed and you believe in yourself this time.

Becoming an *Ëa* could not be an end in itself. It was, rather, the beginning of something even more intense than anything William had yet experienced.

He was thrown almost immediately into a new lifestyle. The day after the moot, he was free from duty in order to move himself and Lis into the *Ëa* quarter. The *ona* gave her blessing to Dero's offer, and Tiran agreed as well, though he still posted two guards to watch over Lady Elissana. The Guard helped him and Lis take everything they needed from their old house and move it into Dero's. Elénne and Fred helped, too, as pleased as Dero had been at them being there. William was placed in Dero's room upstairs, next to Kerran and Allain, and Lis was given her own room another floor up, across from Winna and Fred and next to Elénne and Hope.

Elénne was especially happy to have "another woman in the house," and William knew they would get along well, since they'd liked each other to begin with.

William was in the clouds that entire day. The *Reben* showed him a new-found respect, besides their growing welcome of him. Many congratulated him when they saw him in the street. Many who used to be cold to him were friendlier now. William could hardly keep from smiling at every turn.

But he did not have long to enjoy his new status. The life of an *Ëa* was not one of leisure. In Belond, the leaders slaved away more than the followers did.

He was called to be sentry with Ennor, a tall, dark spearman, that very night. That was probably the most difficult adjustment. The *Ëan* hardly seemed to sleep, and when they did, it was always at strange times. It was the same with meals. William had grown used to Dero's irregular schedule (he was often just waking up when William got home from work on the ship) but it was difficult to adjust himself to it. He had always depended heavily on sleep, but now he had to do without. He began to understand the *ona* better, whose long hours no one could rival.

Ennor was to show him what to do, since he had no experience at all. Sentry duty was not hard. There were two men stationed at five different points on the Gnomi Road under the settled countryside at all times. The animals, the *ona*'s "friends," spied on the movements of Zoc's men. If the people appeared to be in danger, they would send a message to the sentries and then on to the *Ëan*—but since it was a long journey to the Nest for all except the *ona*, flying with Talon, any immediate action would be taken by the sentries.

Still, they were rarely needed. For one thing, it was unusual for the Governor to mount an attack against the people at random, and if he did, the *ona* usually had enough warning to get a larger band of the *Ëan* to the scene in time. So the sentries were only an emergency failsafe to watch over the people. They were rarely active, Ennor said, but their presence had averted slaughter several times, so the *Ëan* performed this duty gladly. They took it in six hour shifts, so with Tiran's fifty men to help they were not called on often.

No, the *Ëan* spent most of their time on more important work. In the winter, once a week, the *ona* led a raid on the Governor's grain barns. He allotted only a pitiful amount to the people, so the *ona* brought them a better share. The *Ëan* went in twos and threes each night, delivering bundles of food to all the houses. They would care for the sick, visit their families, and bring any supplies the people needed. In truth, the people of Belond were as well looked after as the *Reben*, though they were in considerably more danger.

The Governor's anger often raged unexpectedly, and he might strike at the people. Zoc was his chief instrument, and he was as brutal a captain as ever oppressed a people. He slaughtered anyone who defied their rule, so the people were wholly cowed, living in fear. From miner to farmer to craftsman, all the thousands living on the island knew they might die at any moment. The *Ëan* were their only protection. The name of Auria, the name they had given her, they whispered with faint, tentative hope and awe. They did not dare speak aloud, for merely speaking her name was enough to enrage their masters.

It made William angry, as it did all the *Ëan*. They were Edenians, free people by rights. That his countrymen should be made little better than slaves enraged him. Even the *Reben*, hiding away, were not wholly free, even if they were safe. The island lived in constant fear of the Governor's wrath.

For now, William had only to wait. He was an *Ëa*, but he was new. The *ona* left him to sentry duty, nothing more. He watched on the road, sitting in the dim torchlight each night, fighting off sleep. In the morning, after a few precious hours of rest, he joined the workers at the construction site. He still practiced the sword and bow each night. He spent a lot of time with the *Ëan*, and they became dear to him. They were truer hearts than any other men and women he'd ever known. Once loyal, they were loyal forever. They welcomed him into their number as a brother, and he began to forget he had ever been anything but an Ëa. Dero, however, would always be his best friend. They had little free time, but they spent most of it together. His enthusiasm never dimmed, no matter how tired he was. Nothing could make him unhappy.

In truth, perhaps the only ones who *were* unhappy were the women. Elénne found that having the young man she favored under her roof did not mean she saw more of him. William actively avoided her, preferring instead to play with Hope. As for Lis, she had more than her share of homemaking to do, to her pleasure, but she also saw little of William. William felt guilty, and he tried to make every moment count, but he was always off doing something, never at home where she was. She'd said she didn't want to hold him back, but he knew it upset her nonetheless. He just didn't know what to do about it.

This became his life for the next month. He guarded Belo, built the ship, practiced with the sword, and spent time with the Ëan. If felt almost like a trial, an introduction to see if he could handle more. He had not yet been forced to feel any danger, or yet surfaced from the Gnomi Road. He longed to do more. Some of his best memories were the faces of the people he'd met before coming to the Nest, travelling at night with Ria. He wished he could see them again. He still felt guilty that he'd caused the failure of the *ona*'s plan. He wanted to make it up to them.

Then, one day, he got his wish.

He was polishing his sword in their room when Dero rushed in. "Guess what!" he yelled excitedly, bouncing on the balls of his feet. He didn't wait for an answer. "Ovan says that the *ona* says that you're supposed to come with me and Kerran to deliver packages tonight!"

So William was to go on his first real expedition.

Chapter 32

Dero shoved them out of the house, saying, "C'mon, we don't want to be *late!*"

Kerran and William just laughed. Dero was overly concerned. They'd left more than enough time to meet the Ëan.

"Good luck, and don't get hurt!" Lis called after them.

"We'll be fine, Mother—this isn't even all that dangerous," William replied.

"Still," Lis said. "Goodbye, boys!"

William ducked his head and kept walking.

"Your mother's nice," Dero said.

William smiled. It was silly of him to be embarrassed by her care. He might have been forever without it. "Yeah, she is," William agreed.

They kept walking up the citadel until they entered the tall white gate. They headed to the stables, the designated meeting point for the Ëan's delivery parties.

The *ona* was already there, but they were the first of the twelve going out that night. "Hi," she said to them.

"Hello, *ona*," Dero said.

"You're all very prompt," the *ona* said. "I suppose you're ready to go?"

"Yes!" Dero replied, bouncing on his toes a few times. William stifled a laugh. Dero didn't go on many deliveries at this point either, so he was as eager to demonstrate his capabilities as William was.

"Well, good," she replied to Dero, but she was looking at William. "I guess I'll give you your assignments, then. You're doing five houses tonight, farms above the south road." She listed five names which William didn't recognize, but he carefully committed them to memory. "Mercan's daughter is ill, so you'll need to ask the healers for a bundle to give them. And I think Quimph's wife finally finished making those socks and the cloak for her brother (Hervy), and he'll be bringing them in with him. You can take whichever horses you want to the cache. Kerran, you're in charge—you know what to do. Try to be back by one; I'd like you boys at the bay tomorrow morning."

William groaned inwardly, but he didn't dare complain. Still! *Maybe* four hours of sleep for a day of hard labor? But the three men said, "Yes, *ona*," in unison.

"Go saddle up," she said, a smile dancing on her face.

"Yes, *ona!*" they all said again, with more enthusiasm this time. "Thank you," William added as his friends ran off.

Ria's eyebrows rose. "For what?" she asked.

William didn't quite know how to explain. "Uh—" he fumbled. "For your time, I guess. And for, uh—giving me a chance."

She laughed. "You earned a chance, love. Now go do a good job." She gave him a light slap on the shoulder. "Saddle that giant horse of yours," she teased. "If you still know how to ride, that is."

"How could I forget?"

"Well, he's missed you. So I suggest you say hello, too."

It seemed a rather odd idea to say "hello" to a horse, but this *was* Blazer. William bobbed his head and ran off. Ria laughed after him. "I think Dero's rubbing off on you!" she called teasingly.

"Good!" he shouted over his shoulder. "No one better."

Her laughter wafted after him. He walked to Blazer's stall. The big black horse stamped and whinnied. "Hi," he said to the horse. The he laughed. "*Velá*," he added in Djoran. Blazer whinnied in response, and William stroked his nose. William wished he had Ria's gift to understand the language of the animals, but that was a Djoran gift, and apparently not even given to every Djor. Ria was fortunate in her ancestry.

He saddled his horse. He'd had to learn to do that. For most of his life, Blazer had appeared magically saddled already. Then William discovered that there weren't always servants around to saddle his horse for him.

He really hadn't ridden much. He'd brought Blazer to the bay as a work horse, but he hadn't actually ridden him. Unfortunately, he wouldn't be riding long, and then Blazer was going to be a work horse again. They were bringing the horses just to move the grain bundles.

He led Blazer out of his stall to stand by the entrance, where the *ona* was organizing the *Ëan* and giving them assignments. She was going, too, of course—with Baër and Torhan. They would probably bring food to about sixty homes, tonight—not a tithe of the people. They brought enough food for a family for nearly two weeks, but still it was hard to reach everyone. In the winter, it was especially important that they feed the people. If they didn't steal this food, no one would eat. But they had to be careful. If the Governor's men caught anyone with "stolen food," they would suffer for it. So the peasants carefully hid the gifts so that they could survive.

William drew up next to Kerran and Dero. Kerran had found Quimph and retrieved the bundle of new clothes, which Kerran had tied to the back of his saddle. They were all ready, so the *ona* cleared them to go. So the three men rode out.

They made a quick stop at the healers' house. Dero dismounted and ran inside, since he would know best what was needed. He came back with a small bundle of herbs, which he tucked into his belt. He remounted Shala and they kept riding.

They rode at a trot, since it was a long journey, and they would need to hurry to get back by one in the morning. It was a long way just to get out of the Nest. The reason they lived at the top was because the very fastest way to get to Belo was flying with the eagles, so they had to be by the palace near the windows of the Sky Tree Hall in case of an emergency. But the rest of the time, if felt like it took forever to just get to the road.

They talked as they went. William was glad to be on a mission with these two. Dero was, of course, his best friend, but William had grown close to Kerran also. The tall young archer was not as effusive as Dero, but he was unfailingly cheerful, he was a good listener, and he was unerringly loyal. William figured that when he'd joined the Ëan, Kerran would have stood for him if Dero hadn't.

They reached the cache (the name for the spot on the Gnomi Road where the Ëan piled all the grain they stole from the Governor's warehouses). "You know," Dero informed William, "Just another five minutes down the road, and there's a burrow that goes up right under the grain warehouse. The soldiers don't even know we're in there half the time and they don't notice the grain is gone, sometimes. They have *so* much in there. Most of it goes to the army. And they get *meat*, too, every day. Heh. I'll warrant we eat almost as well as them. We have plenty to go around." It was true. They didn't have meat all the time at the Nest, but they had it often enough.

They dismounted from their horses and began taking sacks of grain from the enormous mound and piling it onto the horses' backs. They tied the bags to the saddles, two for each of the families they were visiting. They put a little more on Blazer than they did on the other horses since he was the biggest.

Once they finished loading, they started the long walk to the south side of Belo. They were under the town on the east side of the island, but they had to go all the way to the southern countryside just above the road that ran along the coast. They had a fairly innocuous task, actually. It was far, far more dangerous to deliver goods in the town itself, where there might be soldiers about. The *ona* would be handling that kind of work, along with the more experienced Ëan. They always went in threes—never alone—just in case of an emergency.

They made their first stop. They paused by a burrow, then lugged three bags of grain up. They left these hidden in the bushes, then went back for another three and pulled those up, too. It was rather precarious work on the sometimes unsteady rope ladder. If it had not been Djoran-made, William might have worried that it would snap with the strain of their weight.

They could reach three of their five homes from that burrow. They were very careful—one never knew when soldiers might appear. They went across the fields, never on the road. There was a fierce winter wind blowing, so William was glad for his mask, thick cloak, and the socks Lis had knitted for him. He also still wore the gloves Ria had given him all those months ago.

They stopped at each house and knocked softly. It usually took a while to get an answer, but then the father of the house, still in his nightclothes, would usher them in. At each house it was the same: the family would take the grain and hide it quickly, showering them with thickly accented phrases of praise and gratitude. "Bless ye," the first farmwife said. "Ye be too good fer the likes of us," the second man said.

To this, Kerran replied, "You are our brother. We are happy to help you."

They did not recognize William as the prince of Edenia. To them, he was just another Ëa—which was enough praise for them.

Their third house was Quimph's brother-in-law, Hervy. Hervy was eager for word of his sister, and the three did their best to oblige, but none of them knew much beyond the good health of her and her two children. Hervy begged them to greet her for him, his wife, and five little children. The whole family clung to them desperately, not wanting them to leave. The littlest boy, probably about three, flung both arms around William's boot and wouldn't let go. But the Ëan had to hurry, so they escaped as soon as they could. They high-tailed it back to the burrow and climbed down.

Once they were back on the road and moving again, William asked, "Do all the Ëan have family still outside the Nest?"

"Probably about half," Kerran answered. Dero grew uncharacteristically quiet.

"Isn't that dangerous?" William queried. "The Governor

could use them against you."

Kerran grimaced. "He does. But unless we bring *everyone* to the Nest, we can't destroy our roots. We're too interconnected to cut all ties. But when we take in refugees, we try to do it subtly enough that it doesn't draw undue attention to those left behind. Still, we've had to rescue more than one."

"Do you have family out here?"

Kerran colored. "Um, no—" he floundered. "Not exactly."

A girl, William guessed, but he didn't press the matter. He turned to Dero. "You do, right? A sister?"

Dero sighed, deflating. Kerran looked away.

"Sorry," William apologized, "should I not ask?"

"No, it's okay," Dero sighed. "Yeah. I have a sister."

"What's her name?"

"Betta." Dero spoke heavily. It hardly even sounded like him. "Her name's Betta."

William wasn't sure what to say. Dero had never talked about his life before coming to the Nest, besides a brief mention of his former occupation as a cow herder. William hadn't really thought about it much. Now, he wondered what had happened that made Dero so reluctant to talk about it.

"Why didn't she come to the Nest?" he asked gently.

Dero sighed. "It's complicated. But—I guess I should tell you. You're my best friend. You ought to know, I suppose."

"You don't have to talk about it if you don't want to," William told him.

"No I will," Dero said, squaring his shoulders and lifting his head.

"My father was a cow herder, you know—his name was Darrin; my mother's was Beth. We were pretty well off when I was little—we had a house, stables, and a huge herd. When I was three and Betta was six, there was an accident. My mother fell off a horse and injured her head. She lived, but she couldn't talk or understand anyone. She was hardly even a person anymore. The healers said her mind was damaged permanently. We couldn't do anything for her, so we just took the best care of her that we could. The only thing she recognized was the house—she knew the rooms and everything. Sometimes she'd sort of recognize us, but not for long."

"That's awful!" William said, aghast. He couldn't imagine growing up with something like that.

"My father was always good to her," Dero explained. "He helped us get through it. It was El's will."

Dero's acceptance humbled William. Dero had clearly loved his mother, but he was not bitter about what had happened to her. William had lived for fifteen years resenting the loss of his own mother.

"She died when I was ten," Dero explained. "Betta never got over it. She decided she'd never leave our house—it had been so valuable to our mother."

"Oh, I see," William said.

"Well," Dero continued, "it wasn't that easy. The Governor had been taking a lot of our herd. One day, my father protested when they came to steal our cows. That sort of thing isn't allowed," Dero said sarcastically. He laughed dryly. "My father laughed in their faces when he came back. He said they were fools for taking earthly wealth, and they'd be paying for it later. He gave them a sermon, he did—that was my dad." Dero smiled, but the smile faded. "They killed him for it."

"I'm sorry," William said quietly.

Dero nodded. "I was fifteen. It was only four years ago. I still miss him. But he always told me never to let sadness get the best of me, so I haven't. He said living with grief was as bad as living in prison. He told me El wanted me singing."

He paused, then went on. "But the Governor didn't care about my father. Since I wasn't old enough to inherit, he took all our property—to steward it, he said. Ha. We lost everything. I was for leaving. I'd heard about the Ëan and the Nest. But Betta wouldn't leave. So we stayed, becoming little better than servants in our own house. Another man took my father's place. Betta became the housekeeper and I became a cowhand. I lived in the stables.

"Then when I was seventeen, I was out with the herd—there were some other boys, too. I started singing—my dad and I, we always sang. The overseer got mad and tried to get me to stop. (He was always suspicious of me 'cause Winna and Fred had left for the Nest the year before.) I stopped for a while, then I'd start again. He got so mad!" Dero was laughing now. "He ordered the soldiers to teach me a lesson. I got scared, so I ran away on Shala. I galloped all the way to Belo, with them hot after me. I went straight through the town and up into the woods, singing the whole way. The Ëan found me and brought me to the Nest. But Betta wouldn't come." His face fell again. "I came back and tried to convince her, but she wouldn't leave."

"You should have made her come," Kerran said angrily. "You know what they did to her." William suddenly remembered the conversation he'd overheard all those months ago in the stables. Betta was the girl they'd beaten to try to find out where the Ëan were.

"I couldn't force her," Dero protested. "They left her alone until this spring. Vurlen stopped protecting her. The overseer was partial to her, though she never encouraged him," Dero explained for William, disgust tinging his voice. "But what could I do, Kerran?"

William understood that his guess earlier had been correct, but he'd never have guessed that the object of Kerran's affection was Dero's sister! It explained why the two were so close. But William had never seen Kerran snap at Dero that way.

Kerran softened. "I'm sorry. Forgive me, brother—I shouldn't have spoken that way."

"I know you miss her as much as I do," Dero consoled.

"Please don't," Kerran interrupted. "It only makes it worse."

"You were trying to visit her," William remembered. "That night the *ona* rescued you."

Dero grimaced. "Mmmf," he said in disgust. "I was being an idiot. I'd asked the *ona* if I could go visit her that night. She said yes, but she assumed I'd take others with me—that's the rule for all missions. I wasn't thinking. I didn't follow it. I went by myself. I got caught.

"If this were the army, the *ona* wouldn't have come for me. I didn't follow the rules, I deserved what I got. She could have left me to my fate, but the *ona* isn't like that. She scolded me something fierce later, but she wasn't about to let them capture me. Honestly, I've never been so scared in my entire life. You always think you'll be strong under pressure, but you never know how much you can take. I was worried I might end up betraying them," Dero confessed. An *Ëa*'s worst nightmare. "I'm glad I didn't have to be tested."

"You'd have made it—you're not a traitor," Kerran defended. William agreed fervently.

"Not willingly, no."

They were quiet for a moment. Then William asked, "Is your sister all right now?"

Dero sighed. "I haven't seen her."

"At all?"

"Not for a year. After my last attempt, the *ona* didn't think I should try again. She doesn't want to draw any more attention to Betta than there has already been. Smart, I guess."

"Oh. Sorry."

Dero shrugged. "It's probably better that way."

"Thank you for telling me," William said to him. "I appreciate it." Listening to the *Ëan*'s stories always made him feel lucky in comparison. Still, none had yet moved him the way Ria's story had.

"You're my friend," Dero said simply. They grew quiet and walked in silence to the next burrow.

Chapter 33

In the beginning of January, the Nest began to buzz with activity. The *Reben* began to make decorations and food, and William noticed them carting things up to the citadel.

"What's going on?" he asked Dero one day on the way to the practice room.

Dero grinned, loosing a gleeful giggle. "It's the party!" he exclaimed. "Haven't you heard about it yet?"

"No," William replied, confused. There weren't any major Edenian festivals in January. It seemed odd to host a party at this time of year. "What's it for?"

"The *ona*'s birthday party!" Dero proclaimed as if it was obvious. "The *Reben* host it every year. She doesn't like it, but it's great fun! Music, dancing, food, everything! And since she won't let us give her presents, we throw her a party!"

Now it made more sense. William grew strangely excited. The way Dero described the event incited anticipation.

"When is it?" William asked.

"Next week—Monday."

"Right. I knew that." He should have remembered Karia Whitefeld's birthday. It was exactly one week before his own.

"It'll be in the Sky Tree Hall. That's the only place everyone fits—'cause just about everyone comes. It's a great party! Just you wait. They'll be putting up all the decorations and lights this week. I can't wait till the party..." he said enthusiastically.

"You *do* hate waiting," William laughed.

Dero made a face at him. "Well, aren't *you* excited? Last year I danced all night—and you probably will, too. All the girls will be after you, now that you've actually got some muscle. Girls always go for the tall ones anyway," he teased.

"Ha! Don't even talk! You've got your own pair of blue eyes after you."

Dero blushed crimson.

"You know it's true," William teased, elbowing him in the ribs. "You're done for, Dero."

"Am not," he protested.

"Are too," William shot back. "Ekata, Ekata, Ekata! Who'd you dance all night with last year?"

Dero shoved him away, his face afire. He mumbled something in response, but William couldn't understand him. He had a sneaking suspicion of what Dero said, but he wasn't sure.

"Didn't catch that. What'd you say?" he asked playfully.

"Nothing," Dero said quickly. "C'mon we'll be late to meet Tiran and Ovan. You know they'll be disappointed to miss their daily thrashing. You *enjoy* beating people up."

"I do not! And I don't 'thrash' them. They beat me up, too."

"C'mon, William—everyone knows you can beat either of them. Behind Baër and the *ona*, you're probably the best swordsman in the *Ëan* now."

"No, I'm not," William protested. "You're just biased."

"Nope. I heard Nat tell Baër you've caught up to him. *Boy* was he mad. It took him a while to get back up to speed after the accident. He's been kinda touchy since then. (Well, more than usual.) So it's not just me. You really do have a talent for sword-fighting."

"Maybe," William conceded, his face red. He didn't like being compared to Baër. *That* certainly wouldn't help lessen their animosity. He tried to put the compliment aside. "I'm still a klutz at everything else. Szera kills me at hand-fighting, and I'll never outshoot Lagan."

"Mm-mm," Dero corrected with a bouncy shake of his head. "Szera told the *ona* that you've gotten better. And you've floored her more than once."

"She can still beat me."

"*Nobody* beats Szera but the *ona*," said Dero. "You've gotten that good."

William countered, "It hardly matters. It's just practice. I've never been in a *real* fight."

"What about the night you saved my life?" Dero asked.

"That doesn't count. I wasn't really *in* the fight. Who knows how I'd do out there?"

"You'd do fine," Dero insisted.

"Maybe," William responded. He laughed. "Wow. I sound gloomy. Let's just go practice."

"Distract us till the party," Dero agreed. "*Ooh, I can't wait!*"

William laughed at him. "Back to that, eh? Silly. Come on. I'll race you!"

"Uh-uh," Dero said. "You may throttle me with a sword, but I'm still quicker than you!"

William laughed and ran up the hill, Dero hard on his heels.

Dero complained the whole week about having to wait. William could hardly blame him. It was hard to see all the preparations and not be excited. Thirty-five of the *Ëan* would be there, half of the guards, and a few hundred *Reben*. It would be a party like none other in the Nest. Oddly enough, the only person who wasn't looking forward to the party was the one for whom they were hosting it. William had asked her at one point if she was excited. She'd sighed, frowning. "Eh," she replied. "I go along with it. I don't really like parties."

"But it'll be fun!" William told her, surprised.

"I guess. I'd rather be delivering the grain."

"The *Reben* need this," William told her. "The *Ëan*, too."

"I know," she said. "That's why I go along with it." She hesitated, then she said, "Don't tell anyone what I said, okay? I don't want to offend them."

It was odd, then, that she would choose to say it to William at all. "Okay," he answered. "I won't."

"Thanks," she said, and then she promptly changed the subject.

Despite the *ona*'s reticence, the day of the party finally came. It was to start around six in the evening, but the women started getting ready at three. Elénne consigned

Hope to William's care. William thought they had the better end of the deal. He and Dero chased the little girl around the floor while the women put on their best dresses, arranged their hair, and put on cosmetics. The men got dressed just about fifteen minutes before they were supposed to leave. They didn't have many options for clothing, so they didn't look much different than usual.

The ladies, on the other hand, looked stunning. William saw Winna in a dress for the first time—though the dagger ruined the image. She'd let her voluminous curly red hair down, so she slightly resembled a lioness, but she looked fiercely beautiful at the same time. It was clear where Elénne got her good looks.

Ah, Elénne! When she came downstairs, William could hardly breathe. She was *so* beautiful. Her hair was half braided back and had a flower in it. She wore a brilliant green dress, which showed her figure to a good advantage. She'd carefully accented her brown eyes so that they flashed in the lamplight.

She sauntered up toward the men who stood waiting. She smiled politely at the whole group, but she had eyes only for William. "How do I look?" she asked.

He had trouble finding his tongue. Dero gave him a subtle kick to help him. "Beautiful," he managed. "You look beautiful."

She inclined her head, clearly pleased. She gave a half laugh, half sigh. Then she extended her arms for Hope. (The toddler would be coming along, since the whole house was going. Likely, she'd get passed around all night, since her mother would be too busy having a good time to watch her.) William handed the child over. Elénne appeared even prettier, he thought, with Hope in her arms. He couldn't seem to tear his eyes away from her.

Then his mother came downstairs.

He didn't have words to describe Elissana Whitefeld. This woman had been the toast of high society in Ossia fifteen years ago. She had not lost a bit of her beauty. She was probably more at home dressed up than she was in peasant's clothes, even if what she wore now didn't even compare to what she had once worn at court. But she could've made any dress look beautiful.

She wore an embroidered white blouse and a blue-green skirt, which set off her eyes. She'd let her hair loose, so it hung down her back in waves. She had on a necklace of silver, with a white stone set in it.

"Mother," he breathed, Elénne forgotten. Fred whistled appreciatively, earning a scolding whack from Winna.

Lis blushed and laughed girlishly. William kissed her quickly on the cheek.

"Where did *that* come from?" he asked, touching her necklace.

"I hid it," she explained. "I've always kept it with me. Your father gave it to me."

William smiled. "You look beautiful in it, Mother." He offered her his arm, as a gentleman in Ossia might do. "Since my father's not here, may I have the honor?"

A smile rose on her face. "You may, my lord," she said playfully, taking his arm.

"Aw," Winna said. "What a good son."

"Oh, he is," Lis agreed, beaming up at William.

"Mmm," Dero said, his face red. "Very sweet. Can we go now?"

Everyone laughed. "Okay," William answered. "Let's go."

William had been to feasts, balls, and parties aplenty. He had never seen one like this. It was not as grand as anything they might have had in Ossia. Indeed, it was rather provincial—these people *were* peasants. But that was just it. When they threw a party, they put it on for pleasure—not for politics or obligation—and they actually had fun! There was nothing stiff or formal about this gathering, no etiquette or careful behavior. No, no one cared a whit about that.

When they entered the room, the force of the revelry hit him like a physical blow. Already there was quite an assembly.

There were a dozen men playing instruments in the corner, and practically everyone was dancing in a huge ring outside the circle of stone chairs, and all of them were singing along. There was laughter everywhere, practically drowned out by the noise of the dance. These were not the rigid, careful dances the nobility favored—no, they were the wild, carefree dances of the common folk. To his surprise, William found he actually knew them, different as the setting might be. It was a part of the Tellorian heritage that had not been forgotten. The first Tellor had been a man like these people.

A few people saw them come in and waved hello: Torhan, Ovan, Tiran, Rosie, Lagan, and others. Dero brushed past William waving and calling, "Ekata!" She turned to look, and a smile rose on her face. A moment later, Dero had joined the dance. It was the kind of party that swept everyone into it.

"I'll take the baby," Lis offered to Elénne, letting go of William's arm. Elénne thrust Hope unhesitatingly into Lis's arms and grabbed William's hand before he could react. "C'mon!" she laughed, pulling him into the dance.

(In Ossia, the nobleman always asked the lady. Elénne's behavior would have shocked his old acquaintants at court. But apparently, women here had no such reservations. She didn't even *ask*.)

He had to admit, Dero hadn't exaggerated. He'd never enjoyed dancing more. And Elénne! She looked stunning. She had to be the loveliest young woman in the room, which was now full to its limit.

Then the dancing stopped abruptly, the song drowned out by a massive cheer. William stopped, his hand still in Elénne's, and craned his neck. He knew immediately what had caused the fuss.

He saw her. It was just a glimpse, but it made him feel a little dizzy. He'd never seen her that way. She looked beautiful, for once not hiding behind dirty clothes and a mask. It was her hair that was most striking. She always kept it pinned up in braids—tonight it was loose, its rare color given full voice. She was not wearing a dress, but she'd put on a nicer tunic that *almost* looked new—at least it was not so drab as her typical clothes—and its dark green color set off her eyes. She still wore her knives tucked into her belt, and she'd donned the *Ëa* paint stripes on her cheeks. But it was the loveliest William had yet seen her, and he could tell the rest of the room agreed. Whether she liked it or not, her Whitefeld blood was telling. With her in the room, no other woman could compare.

Torhan stepped up onto a stone chair, raising his voice to call for attention. "The *ona* is here!" he called, receiving a resounding cheer. "Let us wish her a happy birthday!" The crowd responded, William shouting the phrase with them. He couldn't see the *ona*. He strained to look past the people in front of him, Elénne forgotten.

"Thank you," he heard the *ona* reply. Her cheerful tone sounded a bit forced to William, but no one else noticed. They cheered and applauded as before.

"Let us bless this gathering!" Torhan said. The room quieted instantly. Torhan led a prayer to thank El for the *ona*, her work, and her family—the *Ëan*. He asked for blessings on their efforts and on their celebration. Finally, he blessed the meal, and ended the prayer in El's name.

"Let it be so," the crowd answered.

"You may eat now!" he declared with a laugh.

The dancing halted for a while so everyone could eat. William stood trapped in the line with Elénne clinging to his arm and talking. He looked for Ria, but she'd disappeared. He saw Dero, holding hands with Ekata. He gave Dero a wink and a wave. Dero noticed William's predicament in turn and grimaced, but it was hard for Dero to keep the grin off his face for long.

They finished the meal, and before long the company was dancing again. They danced for hours, the whole room singing. They never seemed to get tired.

William, on the other hand, grew tired rather quickly. He could not seem to rid himself of Elénne. A few other men asked her to dance—she breezily turned them all down and stayed with William. He didn't mind her company, but honestly, it wasn't much fun to be stuck with just one person at a party like this. And fond as he was of Elénne, he didn't have the same level of affection for her as she did for him, which made things awkward.

To his surprise, it was Lis who saved him. She came up still holding Hope, and said to Elénne. "Sorry, dear—mind if I cut in? You can't keep the handsomest man in the room to yourself *all* night."

Elénne blushed. "Yes, ma'am," she answered. She took Hope and walked off.

"*Thank* you," William whispered to her.

"You didn't seem to be having much fun," Lis commented with a laugh. "But do be nice to Énne, dear. She really likes you, and you could do a lot worse, you know."

William remembered their little heart-to-heart and knew what she was implying. "Mm-hmm," he said noncommittally. Almost automatically, he looked again for Ria. He still couldn't see her.

"Come on, dear—dance a round with your mother, eh?"

"Okay," he answered with a chuckle.

They finished their dance. Then, when they stopped, William saw Elénne headed back over, Hope passed off to someone else.

"Argh," he whispered under his breath. "Stall her for me, okay?" he said to his mother.

"Why? Where are *you* going?"

"Nowhere." He scanned the crowd some more.

Lis frowned, pursing her lips. Then she sighed and said, pointing, "She's over there. I'll go stall Elénne for you."

He smiled. "Thanks, Mother," he said sincerely. If she was helping, she wasn't stopping him.

He ran through the crowd to where Lis had pointed. Sure enough, he found her.

She was in the furthest corner of the Hall, sitting in a chair half behind one of the tables. He'd have been hard-pressed to find her back there. She'd chosen a good hiding spot.

He walked up to her. "Hi."

She looked up at him. Her frown faded just a little. "Oh, it's you. Hi."

He plopped down on the floor beside her chair. "What are you doing?"

"Hiding," she answered.

He laughed. "I see that. Why?"

"I told you. I don't like parties."

"But it's *your* party. I'm sure any man here would ask you to dance. C'mon! You should be having fun."

"This isn't my idea of fun."

"And sitting miserably by yourself is?"

She glared at him. "Why did you come over here?"

"To ask you to dance."

She shook her head. "I don't dance."

"Why not?"

"I just *don't*. Why don't you just go ask someone else? You could have your pick of girls—they've all been staring at you. I'm sure Elénne would make a much better partner."

What?

"Look," he said, a bit impatiently, "I don't want to dance with the other girls, or Elénne. I want to dance with *you*. Why do you think I came over here?"

"No." She crossed her arms and looked away.

"Okay, fine," William shot back. "I'll just sit here miserably with you."

She hid a smile, but she kept up her angry attitude. "Just go away. You and Dero have been looking forward to this party for days, so you may as well enjoy yourself."

"No," he said, imitating her clipped voice.

She laughed despite herself. "Oh, you are *annoying*," she said, but this time she couldn't hide the smile.

"Mm-hmm. That's what friends are for."

"I'm still not going to dance."

"No?"

"No."

"Scared?" he asked playfully.

"No!"

"Do you know *how* to dance?" he bantered.

"Sure I do."

"*Really?*" he drew out the word. "Have you done it before?"

"No. But I've watched plenty."

The idea of Ria not participating over so many years saddened William. "Why do you hate parties so much, anyway?"

She sighed. "I don't know. It's just—not me. Out there, with the Ëan—that's me. I'm a fighter, not a dancer. That's all I know. This is just crowds and noise. I've never liked it. They're trying to be nice to me, poor souls. What do I say to them?"

"They should have staged a sparring tournament," he joked. She didn't laugh. "Ah, I'm sorry," he said, more seriously. "But you can do both, you know. You don't have to be just one thing."

"I've spent years becoming who I am. I can't change it now."

"Honestly, Ria, what you've got is an image. Now, don't get mad! Just listen. You want everyone to think you're invincible, and in some ways you are. But you never let your walls down, Ria, 'cause you don't want to get hurt. That just means you miss out. It's okay—you can do different things, and who cares what people think of you? People love you. No one's going to think less of you if you have a little fun. Quite the contrary, in fact. They're your people, Ria. Aren't you the one who told me that a leader has to be a part of the followers' lives?"

She glared at him, but he could sense her indecision. "And how, William the wise, would you suggest I do that?" she asked at last.

He tried and failed to keep from grinning. "Get up out of that chair and dance with me."

She huffed a sigh.

"Just one time," he promised, "and if you don't like it, I

will personally escort you back to your chair so you may continue being miserable."

"You, sir, are manipulative."

"Am I? Oh, good."

"Your politician's upbringing is showing its colors."

"Only if I convince you."

She frowned.

"Please?" he pleaded, looking pleadingly at her.

"Oh, fine," she said. "But only once."

"Deal," he said, springing to his feet.

He took her hand and walked out to the dancing ring. The *ona* forced a happy expression, because they soon found themselves the object of everyone's stares. People whispered as they walked by, but if the *ona* looked at them, they'd greet her with a warm "Happy birthday!" and stop gawking at them. William did, however, note Ovan's surprised stare and Baër's dark frown (but then, Baër was always frowning). Elénne looked a bit displeased, but she was off dancing with someone else. He couldn't read Lis's expression: it was somewhere between satisfaction and disappointment.

He danced with her, oddly enough, to a song with the same tune as the one she'd sung when they'd chopped down that tree. He sang the words, which were quite silly, along with the crowd, and he made all the appropriate faces to match. He soon had Ria laughing her head off, so they could barely keep the dance going. She was not the best dancer—certainly Elénne was better—but she was light on her feet and could keep up easily enough.

The dance was over quickly enough, but he knew she'd had a good time, which brought him far more satisfaction. "You want to go again?" he asked, breathless with laughter.

She smiled, but she shook her head. "Thank you, but no."

"You're going back to your corner?"

"Mm-hmm." She shot him a challenging glance.

"Okay," he conceded. "A deal's a deal."

She grinned.

He walked with her back to her chair. On the way, several

other people asked her to dance: Ovan, Torhan, Baër. She declined each of them as patiently as she could. "See what happens when I dance *one* time?" she grumbled to William.

"It's good for you," he retorted.

She smacked him lightly on the arm. He just laughed.

He left her back in her hiding place. He would have been happy enough to stay, but she told him, quite adamantly, "Now go *away*! You're not getting anything more from me tonight!"

He managed to find Rosie before Elénne could come after him again. She looked lovely, wearing red and her black hair done up in ribbons. He danced twice with her, laughing the whole time. Then Elénne got him back, and he spent the rest of the night with her—but he didn't mind so much, now.

Eventually, of course, the party was over. The *ona* had left early, so the rest of them just went home when it got late (or early). William found the rest of their group, and the nine of them went home.

Dero, once he'd said goodbye to Ekata, ran straight up to William. "That was *so fun!*" he enthused, not at all tired.

William yawned. "Yeah," he agreed.

"But you danced with the *ona*! We were all shocked! She never dances with anybody! How'd you get her to do *that*?"

"Convincing. Hasn't anyone else tried?"

"Sure—lots of times. (I haven't; I'm not that brave.) But nobody ever got her to stand up with them. *And* you got Elénne all night. Everybody was jealous."

"Mm-hmm."

"Oh, it was great fun! Kata and I were together the whole time. Except she danced with her brother once, and I—"

"Ekata has a brother?"

"Yeah, Torhan. You didn't know that?"

"No."

"Anyway," Dero continued. He launched into a lengthy, enthusiastic spiel about the party. He was still talking when William tumbled tiredly into bed, then at last they turned off the lamp and went to sleep.

Chapter 34

Only a week after the party, there was another celebration. The ship was finally finished.

A whole crowd of *Reben* assembled for the last day of work on the ship. The crew labored for hours to finish getting the completed ship into the bay. At last, it was in the sea. It was rowed out into the ocean, then the sailors dropped the anchor. A massive cheer arose on the shore.

Honestly, though it was selfish to think it, William was just relieved it was done. He'd poured blood, sweat, and tears into building that ship. But at the same time, it was brought home to him that he would be leaving this place as soon as spring came. That was the plan. It would fix all their problems. He should be happy about it, for every imaginable reason, but it was depressing nonetheless.

The sailors rowed back into shore in small boats, and then the whole crowd turned for home. William found himself walking alone. Dero had gotten sentry duty this morning, so he'd missed the completion of the ship.

All of a sudden, he found Ria beside him. So suddenly, he nearly jumped out of his skin.

"Good heavens!" he exclaimed. "Don't *do* that! You scared me!"

"I *excel* at sneaking around," she told him with a laugh. Then she said, "Happy birthday, by the way."

He smiled. He'd practically forgotten it was his birthday. Lis had wished him happy birthday that morning, but he hadn't really made a big deal out of it.

"You remembered," he stated.

"Mm-hm. I think I can be forgiven for remembering your birthday is *one week after mine*." She poked him as she said each word, grinning the whole time. He just laughed. "And since the *Reben* aren't making *you* endure a party, I have a better present for you." She reached for her belt and pulled out a wrapped package, thin and long.

"Wow," William said, surprised. "Thanks." He was quite flattered by her giving him a birthday present.

"You don't even know what it is," she scoffed. "Don't thank me yet."

He opened the package with a laugh. Inside, as he guessed, were knives. They were simple, unadorned blades, designed to be functional. They were similar in length to the *ona*'s knives, but the hilts fit his hands perfectly. He pulled one from its sheath. It was newly polished and sharpened, the steel shining in the torchlight.

"They're beautiful," he said appreciatively. "Thank you."

She grinned. "You're welcome."

"*These* aren't Gnomi," he reflected, turning the blade. "Where did you get them?"

"I made them."

"*You* did?"

She looked insulted. "I know how to forge a blade, love. No one better."

"I guess *so*," he agreed. He gave the knife an experimental swing. "I'll have to learn how to use these."

"Mm-hmm, and not like that." She chuckled. "I can give you a few pointers, if you like."

"You mean beat me up."

She shrugged.

"So this was all just a convenient excuse to get me to spar you?"

"Maaybe," she joked. He elbowed her, mouth open in mock indignation. "All right, no," she amended. "It's just a present."

"Well, thank you," he repeated. "I really appreciate it."

She nodded. "So I'll see you later, okay? Don't be late."

"Dero wouldn't let us be late."

The *ona* laughed. "Well tell him to take a nap when he gets home, would you? He can't keep up that energy forever."

"Oh, I think maybe he can. But I'll tell him."

"Okay. See you tonight." With a small wave, she ran ahead just to catch up to Szera.

William just smiled and tied the knives to his belt.

William walked up the citadel road to meet for another night of deliveries. He was by himself again, since Dero had been asked to fetch a parcel from the healers' house. Dero didn't mind at all, of course. He'd left early so he could take his sweet time.

William entered the Sky Palace and headed for the stables. Yet another night of deliveries lay before him, but the fact that he'd been paired with Ovan and Lagan implied that this trip would be a little more dangerous than most.

He paused as he passed by a group of empty rooms in the hallway. There was no one in the hall but him. (There were so many ways to get anywhere in the palace, practically any hallway could get a person where they needed to go, and not many people used this way.) But he thought he heard voices.

He stopped by a door that was partly ajar, certain now. Two people were talking privately together. He recognized the voices immediately: Tiran and Ria. He felt a sudden curiosity, only heightened when he heard his name. He felt like a child at school being talked about by his schoolmasters. He couldn't help himself. He knew it was wrong to eavesdrop, but he could not seem to cure himself of the habit.

"I have a favor to ask you," Tiran said.

"Ask, then. *You* requested this meeting. Make it quick, please, captain. I don't want to be late." She didn't sound irritated, just businesslike.

"Yes, *ona*. Now, please, don't be offended. I would like to ask to accompany the prince."

"Why do you want to go? He's an Ëa. He can take care of himself. He doesn't need protecting at all hours of the day."

"Yes, *ona*. I do not doubt your or his own ability to keep him safe. But Ovan told me tonight might be dangerous. It is for myself I ask this, *ona*. I am uneasy in my mind because of all this. I was charged with protecting the King's son. That is my duty. Whether he needs me or no, I must protect him. But I have done little but stand by these past months."

"You've taught him to protect himself. That *is* protecting him. He's not helpless anymore."

"I know that, but even so, I cannot in good conscience neglect my duty. The King gave me orders."

She sighed. "I understand what you mean." She paused. "I will allow it."

"Thank you, *ona*. I—"

"I wasn't finished. You can go *tonight*. Watch carefully, and if you still feel uneasy, we will talk again. However, I cannot have one of my Ëan under constant guard. It would not only encumber him, but it would also differentiate him from the others. Considering the contention his rank has caused already, I do not want to risk it. Do you agree?"

"I understand, *ona*. But you see him as just another Ëa. I still see Lord William Tellor."

"He is both," she said. "So let *him* decide who he wants to be."

"Yes, *ona*."

"Let's go, then."

William darted away before they could come out and see him.

About twenty Ëan assembled together for the *ona* to map out assignments. Tiran stood off to one side, next to Ovan. The two brothers were whispering together.

"Szera, Grayem, and I will take the houses along the square." She listed the names, mostly craftsmen. "Baër, Quimph, and Joff will go along the northeast side." Names again. "Ovan, Lagan, and William will go on the southwest side. Captain Tiran will be accompanying them. " She listed seven houses they were to visit. "Also, one more stop: Vurlen's house, a mile from the last house I listed. Raekel, one of his servants, is ill. Dero picked up a package from the healers for her. You'll deliver them to Betta, the other woman in the house. Straight in, straight out. No delays." She lowered her voice, speaking to Lagan. "Don't endanger Betta. It's risky to involve her again at all, but I have no better alternative."

William looked to Dero. He clearly hadn't known about this before. His face was a flurry of emotions: jealousy, worry, surprise, hurt. William felt bad for him. *He* should be going on this mission. It was his *sister*. He hadn't seen her in months. He cast a pleading look at the *ona*, casting his eyes from her to Dero and back. She met his eyes and gave a slight shake of her head. Her face tightened, but she kept talking.

William made his way to Dero. "Look," he said, "it should be you. I'm sorry. I'd give up my place for you if I could."

"I know. But the *ona* wouldn't let you, and she's right." He sighed. "You'd be less dangerous. I'm a klutz. I'm liable to mess everything up again. It's too risky."

"Dero," William protested.

"I know, I know." Then he brightened. "But you'll say hello to her for me, won't you?"

"Of course I will."

"And tell her I miss her."

"Okay. Anything else?"

Dero considered then decided, "No. Better keep it short."

"Okay."

"Tell me how she is, okay? Honestly."

"I will. I promise."

Then Dero had to attend to the *ona* as she listed his group's assignment. William moved off to saddle his horse.

Interestingly enough, Tiran had virtually no trouble fitting in with the Ëan. Perhaps it helped that he knew William well and that Ovan was his brother, but he was easy even with Lagan. Lagan had been an archer in the Edenian garrison at Belond, so they had lots in common, and they had ample opportunity to talk while they assembled the grain.

"So you were in the army?" Lagan said to Tiran.

"Yes—years ago."

"What part?"

"Ossian garrison. I joined up when I was seventeen, two years after my brother left."

"The two of you are far apart in years, then."

"He's ten years younger," Ovan admitted. "My mother died young and my father remarried."

"Ah," Lagan replied.

"Are they still alive? Your parents?" William asked.

Ovan sighed. Tiran answered, "No. They both died years ago."

"Oh. I'm sorry."

Tiran smiled, his head dipping with a slight nod.

"Do you have any other family?"

"No," Tiran answered. "It's just us. I mean, everyone with an old name will have some distant cousins, but not close family."

"What *is* your surname?" William asked curiously.

"We don't use surnames in the Guard," Tiran reminded.

"Or really in the Ëan, very often," Ovan added.

"But what *was* it, then?"

Ovan answered a bit reluctantly. "Arnaugh."

"Arnaugh!" William exclaimed. "But then you're Ria's cousin!" Seyenne Arnaugh Whitefeld was the name of Ria's mother.

Ovan winced.

"Who's Ria?" Lagan asked.

William remembered himself. "Oh, uh—" he stammered. "Someone I know." He wasn't supposed to call her that. Or talk about who she really was. Oops.

"Hardly a close relation, anyway," Tiran rescued him. "We're descendants of younger sons, without inheritance. A noble title isn't worth much without an estate. All the men in our family ended up in the army."

"A noble profession which few privileged noblemen bother to enter," Lagan said. "No offense," he added to William.

"None taken. It's quite true." They laughed at that.

William was still burning with curiosity, but he didn't want to make another blunder about the Arnaughs. Besides, this wasn't the time. They finished loading the bundles onto the horses and headed to the west side of Belo.

The town missions were a lot different from the country ones. Even on the edge of Belo, there were guards patrolling the streets at all hours, and even a few posted on the corners. It was probably some of the most dangerous work the Ëan did. No one, so far, had gotten captured, but no one was under any illusion that it was impossible. If they were caught in town, it was unlikely there would be time for a rescue.

The burrow they used on the west side came up in the cellar of a smithy, which reeked of mold. They could risk no light, so they hauled the sacks up the ladder in the dark.

They didn't wake the craftsman, but they left him his bundle of grain. The rest they left in a pile to be moved bit by bit to the other houses, with painstaking care.

Tiran and Lagan stayed in the cellar to hand the grain up. William and Ovan carried the sacks to the neighboring houses. William stood watch while Ovan climbed down into each basement, and then William handed the bags down. Then up again and back to Tiran and Lagan.

More than once, a guard passed by, and they had to hide in an instant. The whole time, William's heart hammered so loudly that he was afraid it would give them away. They had to be perfectly silent, and every move had to blend with the shadows (not an easy feat while carrying sacks of grain). It was nerve-wracking work.

He wouldn't have wanted to be anywhere else.

Five. Only one more in the town, then they would move a few miles outside.

William and Ovan gathered their last load. Lagan made a hand signal, barely visible, that told them that Lagan and Tiran would be waiting in the burrow. Ovan jerked a nod.

They slid slowly along the wall of an alley. William peered carefully around a corner. He caught a glimmer of torchlight, so he recoiled, motioning for Ovan to move back. The torches came closer. The two men pressed close to the wall and held perfectly still. There was no time to run. It would give them away.

"I don't see anything, Captain," a voice hissed close by. William tried not to breathe. His heart thudded. *Benjen.* The torches halted just around the corner. They couldn't move or their shadows would betray them.

"Our intelligence says they're on the west side tonight." Zoc's voice chilled William. He'd forgotten how grim the captain was. It had been months.

"Maybe he was lying," the lieutenant responded.

Ovan tensed. William's eyes widened. *He?*

"Perhaps. Or perhaps your incompetence has warned them off again. I grow tired of this, Benjen. *You're* the one who found this source—is he truthful or not?"

"I know no more about it than you—and we shouldn't be discussing it. Not out here."

Zoc slapped him across the face. William winced at the sound. A blow like that would have certainly drawn blood. But Benjen just grunted. He was, after all, a pirate.

"You presume too much," Zoc retorted. He turned away. "This is useless." He raised his voice. "Company, turn about!"

The soldiers wheeled around and marched away. Only when the torches were no longer visible did they relax.

William released his pent up breath, leaning his head back against the wall. He ran a hand over his masked face, then he looked to Ovan.

"Ovan?" he breathed, barely a whisper.

"Later. Finish. Go," Ovan signed, his face tight. He looked more disturbed than William had ever seen him.

They delivered their last round, then bolted back to the burrow. Just as they closed the cellar door, they saw the torches again. But they just replaced the pile of scraps covering the burrow entrance and climbed back onto the road.

As soon as it was safe, William exploded, "Ovan!"

"Peace, William," he rebuked. William knew he did not

mean to be harsh, he was just upset.

"But there's a tr—"

"Enough!" Ovan interrupted, indicating Lagan and Tiran. He stopped William before he could say what they were both thinking: traitor. There was a traitor. But Ovan did not want to spread the idea. That much was clear in his face.

"What?" Tiran asked, looking concernedly at both of them.

"We leave it for the *ona*," Ovan said. "It is best that way. Come."

Tiran nodded. Lagan accepted this without question, but he asked, "Are you both all right? You were gone a long time."

"Ran into some guards, or nearly did," William explained.

"Thank El you're all right!" Tiran exclaimed.

"He did well, brother," Ovan put in quietly. It took William a moment to realize they were talking about him.

Tiran just nodded.

They paused a moment, then Lagan reminded, "We have one more stop; let's keep going."

"Right," William remembered. He'd forgotten Betta.

They headed off.

The four of them emerged from a burrow half a mile away from Vurlen's cattle ranch. They stood on a hilltop covered by a clump of trees looking down on the pastures below.

This was yet another difficult mission. There were many farmsteads in the countryside where one of the Governor's men had stolen the ownership of the land, and the farmers lived in ramshackle cottages dotting the property. These were the houses the Ëan normally delivered to. The main houses were generally avoided. They were loyal to the Governor. They were well supplied with food, for the most part.

"All right," Lagan said. "Ovan and I will go up to the house. You two stay here."

"No," William protested. "I promised Dero I'd check on Betta."

"William," Lagan chided.

"I promised! I *have* to go."

"I don't think it's—"

"Oh, let him go, Lagan," Ovan spoke up. "Look at his face."

Lagan frowned, thinking it over.

"I'll stay with Tiran," Ovan offered.

"Are you sure it's a good idea?" Tiran questioned.

Ovan cast William a smile. "Yes," he answered. William gave him a grateful look.

Lagan agreed with a sigh. "All right. Let's go."

The two headed off across the fields, slick with frost underfoot. They saw no sign of activity anywhere. It was easy work to get to the house. They crept along the back wall, stopping at a dark corner.

"I'll stand watch," Lagan whispered. "Listen for my signal. You climb up and open that window (the kitchen one). Go out the far door and turn right. Down the hall in the servants' quarters, last room on the left. Don't make a sound."

William nodded. "I won't."

Lagan looked doubtful, but he handed William a small bundle of herbs. "Be quick."

William followed his instructions. It was hard work getting the window open (he had to pry it with one of his new knives), but he managed it at last and climbed inside. Then across the room, and out the door. He had to open it very, very slowly or else it would creak. No one woke up. He crept down the hallway. There were only three doorways. He eased open the last one on the left and slipped inside, shutting it behind him.

There was a small bed, a chest of clothes, and a nightstand with an unlit candle. That was all. Very poor conditions. William never got over the shock of how impoverished these people were.

A girl lay shivering under a thin blanket. He could see her feet sticking out from beneath it. She was tiny, small like Dero. She was painfully thin, and there were circles under her eyes. He marveled that she could have survived a beating, but despite her appearance of weakness, she must have a strong will. It took courage to not leave her home, foolish though it might seem.

He moved quietly to her bedside. He felt awkward invading a girl's room like this, but he reminded himself why he was there. He reached out a hand to cover her mouth, giving her a gentle shake.

She awoke a little fuzzily. "I'm up, I'm up," she murmured behind his hand. "I'm coming. I'll get breakfast ready."

"Betta. Betta. I'm an Ëa."

Her eyes cleared, and she looked a little frightened, shrinking away from him. He released her. "I've never seen you before," she said nervously, looking around the room.

"I'm a friend of Dero."

Her dark eyes widened.

He pulled off his mask and pulled back the hood so as not to appear too threatening to her. "He says to tell you hello. And that he misses you."

She smiled as if this was the best thing anyone had ever said to her. "Oh, Dero," she murmured happily. She looked at William. "Who are you?" she asked.

"My name's William."

Her eyebrows rose. "Tellor? But you're supposed to be dead!"

It shouldn't have surprised him, but it did. He'd never really thought about the fact that everyone here thought he was dead, though he'd known it before.

"I'm not." He paused, then remembered his package. "Here, the *ona* sent this for Raekel."

"Oh. Thank you," she said gratefully. "I've been worried. She's very bad. The cold weather doesn't help."

"I'm sorry." He hesitated, then unslung his cloak. "Here," he said. "Take this—just to help." He couldn't just leave her like this. She was Dero's sister!

"No, I can't! They'll think I stole it."

"Hide it. Just use it at night."

She considered this, then she took it. "Thank you."

He dipped a nod, then replaced his mask. "I should go."

"Wait!" She grabbed his arm. "Tell... Tell Dero I love him. And I'm not angry. Okay? And tell Kerran..." she paused. "Tell Kerran I haven't forgotten. Tell him to keep fighting—for me. Will you do that?"

"I will."

"Thank you, William."

He smiled at her, then snuck back out into the night.

Chapter 35

"No, listen to me, *ona*," William protested, trying to keep his voice lowered.

It was early in the morning after the delivery. He'd been practicing with Tiran, but he'd seen the *ona* come into the room and rushed to talk to her. He'd been trying to explain to her what they'd overheard.

"Ovan already talked to me," she said.

"I know. He said he would. But then a few minutes ago, he said—"

"That I didn't give the notion any credence."

"But *ona*—"

"No, I'm serious, William. Think about it. If we had an informant, one, the animals would know. Two, the Governor would know far, far more about us: the Nest, the burrows, the ship—and he doesn't. It's far more likely that he coerced a villager into giving information, and he made something up on the spot that just happened to be right."

"But it was too good. They were close, *ona*—too close. Someone had to have spilled. I just think it's strange that it was us, not you."

"You think someone's targeting you?"

That was exactly what he thought, but he couldn't say it to her.

"William, I don't want you pointing fingers. It will create distrust among us, which is as divisive an enemy as any. Let it go. Put it out of your mind. I'll look into this, though I doubt it's as catastrophic as you think. Okay?"

He sighed. He couldn't set his suspicions aside so easily. His instincts told him he knew exactly who to blame, but he couldn't believe it. If it was true, it would shatter the *Ëan*. And his personal feelings weren't enough to justify accusations, especially of such an extreme nature.

"Okay," he agreed reluctantly.

"Good. I don't want to argue with you, anyway. I came in here looking for you, actually."

"Oh?" He felt a little flattered.

"Mm-hm. Ovan said you did well last night."

He smiled. "I was terrified the whole time," he confessed. "But we did it."

She smiled back. "Little secret, love: we're all scared when we do this. It's dangerous."

"Even you?"

"No, of course not. I'm not scared of anything," she said sarcastically.

He chuckled. "Mm-hm."

"No, I'm afraid. But I can't cave to fear when I have a job to do." She paused, then continued, "Anyway—what I wanted to talk to you about was this: I want you to come on the raid tonight."

"Me?"

"No, I'm talking to that stone in the wall."

"But—I don't have enough experience, do I?"

"No, but how exactly do you think you get it?"

"But I haven't been in a real fight. How do I know I can—"

"I've watched you. You have talent, William. You've learned to tap your instincts and you still keep your head. Look at you—you were giving Tiran a thrashing when I came in here. You can do it."

He nodded reluctantly. "If you think so."

She nodded back, smiling. "Good. I'm glad you agree. Now why don't you go back to practicing? Your audience is missing you."

Dero, Rosie, Winna, Kerran, Shac, and Lagan still stood by his ring waiting for him to come back. Tiran stood hunched over, resting.

"Okay," he agreed.

"One of these days, you'll have to agree to spar *me*," she said with a smile.

"I could never equal you!"

"We'll see."

Parry. Duck. Slash. Roll.

Over and over and over again.

Somehow, it always worked. He always got where he needed to be, every time. Tiran couldn't touch him, but William hit Tiran more than once. It was a wooden sword and he pulled the blows, but they'd still leave some nasty bruises.

His crowd cheered every time he scored a hit. It had grown some. Szera, Ovan, Baër, and Short were watching now. Even the *ona* had stayed to observe.

He floored Tiran and confiscated his sword. The crowd cheered, and Tiran groaned. "Sorry, Captain," he apologized.

"Sorry? Don't be sorry. That was wonderful! Where'd you learn to do that?"

"Uh... watching." He didn't say he'd copied it from something the *ona* had done once. That sounded creepy.

William helped Tiran up, both breathing hard. "I'm not much help to you anymore," Tiran admitted.

"Do you believe me now, Tiran?" the *ona* asked with a grin.

"I guess I have to," he responded. "He's handled himself well." William got the feeling he was talking about the conversation he'd overheard last night, not this bout. Tiran continued. "A deal is a deal. I am satisfied."

"Good, but you've handled *yourself* well, too. We could use your help more often, if you're willing." The Ëan voiced their approval.

Tiran glanced at William. The prince was his final authority in the King's absence. William gave him a nod of encouragement. Tiran smiled at the *ona*. "At your service," he said.

She grinned. "Good."

Then the crowd started talking again. Someone asked William who he was going to spar now. He glanced at the *ona*, but he replied, "I don't know."

"Baër, you should spar him," Shac said. The room lapsed into an awkward silence. William's face reddened, but Baër's darkened.

"I'm not sparring *him*," Baër said disdainfully. He turned to stalk away, as he always did. A word from the *ona* stopped him.

"Baër," she said calmly. He halted, turning back to face her.

"I've had enough of this," she said, speaking evenly. "You're making a fool of yourself and of us. Is this how you honor El? There is no place for pettiness among us. Stop this childish behavior and act like a man, or you'll suffer the consequences."

William watched his face. She'd confronted him in front of all the *Ëan*. He could not gainsay her authority—not here, not now. But William could tell he wanted to.

"Yes, *ona*," he said sullenly.

"Apologize, please," she said. Her voice grew tinged with a hint of anger. Her eyes were hardened by his reaction.

"But—"

"Now."

Baër looked at William—in the eyes, for a rare change. William knew nothing would check his hatred. This would only make things even worse. He could see it in Baër's eyes.

Baër put out his hand stiffly. "I apologize," he snarled.

"Apology accepted," William said coolly, but he could not make his heart feel it. They were both struggling right now. William just couldn't trust him.

They held each other's grips a moment, squeezing hard. Baër pulled his hand away. He looked at the *ona*, sighed, and asked William through his teeth, "Do you want to spar?"

The idea of fighting a very angry Baër, who might or might not be better than him, was a scary prospect. Baër probably saw in the fight a way to reclaim his dignity.

"Uh—you don't have to if you don't want to."

"I'm *happy* to be of service," he said affectedly. A dark glint shone in his eye.

There was no good way to get out of it, so William agreed.

William waited while Baër stalked to the shelf of practice

swords and chose one. Tiran exited the ring and Baër stepped inside. They faced each other. William felt a thrill of fear. Baër wouldn't really hurt him, would he?

Everyone watched carefully, but it might as well have been just the *ona*, testing them. That was the real contest. He could feel the intensity of her gaze on them.

"Are you ready?" William asked.

Baër answered with a sword thrust. William barely had time to backpedal before Baër's sword hit him, and while he was off balance, Baër kicked him in the stomach. William gasped, winded, but Baër was still after him. His opponent knocked him down, and he was left parrying from the floor. Baër swept his sword out of his reach and across the mat. He stopped, looking down triumphantly.

But hand-fighting with Szera had taught him that a fight wasn't over because you were disarmed. William kicked Baër's legs from under him and pushed him as he went down, so he fell hard. William retrieved his sword and stood to face him. Baër got to his feet with a growl and came flying at him again.

They sparred a long time. William had to use every ounce of his abilities, but Baër could still catch him off guard. He was punched in the face and hit with the wooden sword on the arms, legs, and chest, and Baër wasn't pulling the blows. William hit him, too, but nothing that would really hurt. He certainly didn't draw blood, though he could feel the warmth of it on his own skin. He could sense Baër mocking him every time he held back, but he didn't have it in him to fight the way Baër did. Despite what his opponent thought, this wasn't a real fight, and they were on the same side.

Baër had no such reservations. He fought like a madman, heedless of anything but the path of his sword. He *was* good, the kind of fighter enemies run from. He'd fight relentlessly, until his last breath. He had more than enough determination to be an Ëa.

But it was also his weakness. He was so focused on his fury, he couldn't think straight. He abandoned his mind for emotion.

He threw a maniacal set of blows at William. They came so fast William could hardly avoid them, but they were just wild. Quick as he could, William intercepted a desperate lunge and pulled Baër's sword away. He shoved Baër back and then knocked him to the ground. Baër landed on his stomach, groaning. William stepped a foot on his back to keep him down and placed his sword by Baër's neck, declaring that he'd won.

Dero clapped and cheered enthusiastically, but he was the only one. Everyone else looked to the *ona*, not wanting to worsen the rivalry. Baër would not take this well. He hadn't expected William to be able to beat him.

"It seems William is the winner," she said dryly. "Help him up."

Baër refused the extended hand. He stood up himself.

"You can both improve. William, a little more work on anticipation, and a little more speed. You didn't take every opening you could have. And Baër..." Her voice grew quiet. "Never let your emotions cloud your judgment. They have no place in any real fight. It's not about anger."

She dismissed them. "Go clean up," she said to William. Her gaze played over his bloodied face, then met his eyes. A ghost of a smile rose to her lips, and she nodded almost imperceptibly. Then she turned to the *Ëan*. "All of you rest up if you're going out tonight. Baër, come with me, please."

"Yes, *ona*," they all said, and the crowd dispersed.

Dero whooped with excitement. He was always cheerful, but he'd been in an especially good mood ever since he'd gotten word from his sister. He'd been so happy to know she was all right it had made William feel badly about his not going all over again. Dero knew she wasn't as well off as he would like, but she was safe, at least. And her message had put an irremovable grin on her brother's face.

"Oh, man," he chattered. "You *destroyed* him. Ha! Take that!"

William was too busy trying to stop his lip from bleeding to say much more than "Mm-hmm." He'd torn a strip of cloth from his tunic and was pressing it against his face.

"Who'd've thought? Baër's always been our best swordsman—behind the *ona*. And boy did she like *that*! You should've seen her!" Technically, William had been there to see her, but this fact seemed to have slipped Dero's mind. "She's been paying a lot of attention to you—and she should. You're one of the best, now. What were you talking to her about earlier?"

"Um... She wants me to go on the raid tonight."

Dero's face lit up. "Ooh, *yes!*" he shouted. He practically danced with glee. "You can come with *me!* Yes, yes, yes!"

"You're going, too?"

"Yes! And I don't get asked often. You're lucky. I've only gone twice in all the time I've been here, and I've been here a while. But then, you're the *best*, now."

"Am not!"

"The *ona* will always be *the* best, but you know what I mean," Dero allowed. "Woo-hoo!" he burst out. "This is so *great!*"

William laughed and followed his capering friend into the house, calling after him, "You know, we'll have to settle down to rest up for tonight."

Dero waved this away, bounding off to the kitchen. William followed him a little more slowly.

"You boys are going out again tonight?" William heard Lis ask Dero, a bit unhappily. She always worried.

"Yup!" Dero answered, snatching up a biscuit and talking with his mouth half full.

"Is it a—" Lis stopped when she saw William come in. "Good gracious! What *happened*? You were fine an hour ago!" She rushed over and tilted his head back to look at his split lip.

"I'm fine, Mother," he assured.

Elénne came to look. "Fine, indeed," she scoffed. "What'd you do? You look like you ran through a hailstorm."

"It was a fight! It was *great!*" Dero enthused. "He won!"

"*William!*" Lis scolded, looking sternly at him. "Honestly! You don't need to go looking for opportunities to get beaten up."

"I sparred Baër," William stated by way of explanation.

Lis clucked her tongue, giving him a disapproving look. "I can't let you two out of my sight," she chided. "Énne, could you get me a cold cloth, please, dear?"

"Yes, ma'am." A moment later, "Here you are."

Lis handed it firmly to William. "Press that on it. Much better than that sweaty shirt. I'll go get you some salve. Oh, you're all bruised! You might have a black eye in the morning. Ugh. I'll be back." Elénne followed her out.

When they came back, William wasn't holding the cloth to his face. He'd joined Dero at the table, stuffing his face with biscuits. They'd probably eaten four or five each when the women came back.

"William!" Lis scolded. He put the cloth back on hurriedly, still chewing.

"Those were supposed to be for lunch!" Elénne complained.

William and Dero laughed. "We were hungry."

Elénne rolled her eyes. "Men." She repositioned Hope, whom she'd fetched from upstairs, on her hip. The toddler cooed at Dero, who made a goofy face at her.

"So," Lis said as she smeared salve on William's face, "where are you two going tonight?"

"It's raid night. We get to go!" Dero explained.

Lis frowned. "You're already bruised like this, and you're going to fight some more?"

"Really, Mother, I'm fine."

"He'll look so ugly, anyone we bump into will run away!" Dero reasoned. William smacked him playfully on the arm.

"Or just intimidating," Elénne offered, fixing him with a smile that made him feel awkward.

Dero cleared his throat. "Yeah, right. Anyway, the *ona* told us to take a nap. Call us for lunch, okay?" He pulled William out of his chair. His bruised arms protested.

"You ate it already," Elénne reminded.

"More will magically reappear by the time we get up," Dero teased, winking at her. "C'mon, William."

It was infinitely more fun going anywhere with Dero.

They went on foot, this time, jogging. The *Ëan* working deliveries would have more need of the horses. There were still about a dozen out tonight besides them. The *ona* took five with her: Szera, Ovan, William, Dero, and Winna. Dero had confided that Baër was originally going tonight, but the *ona* had decided to take Winna instead—a little piece of discipline. And Baër was flaming mad. William hated to think how things would be between them *now*.

Normally, he felt a bit awed going on missions with the elite among the *Ëan*. They were the best for a reason, and they took their duty seriously. But tonight, Dero lightened all of their moods. Throughout the journey (which took several hours), William and Dero ran at the back, laughing like crazy. Dero cracked jokes and told funny stories, delighting his best friend.

Szera gave them disapproving looks, but William could tell even she was struggling not to laugh. Ovan and Winna chuckled from time to time. The *ona* tried to maintain a businesslike demeanor, but she laughed right along with them.

Dero was relating a story about his old neighbor's cat falling into a well when he was little, making sound effects and gestures to accompany the tale. William could hardly breathe he was laughing so hard, the way Dero told it.

"That cat *never* went near the well again," Dero concluded. "Not that I blame him. I hate water, too."

"Wait, really?"

"Oh, yeah. I never really learned to swim."

"We'll have to work on that, Dero," the *ona* called back.

"But not in January, okay? That's *way* too cold to swim." They all laughed.

Dero turned on William. "What are *you* scared of?"

William considered. There were lots of things he could have said, but in keeping with the tone, he answered, "Spiders."

Dero chuckled, but it was Ria who exploded with laughter. "Ah, I'd forgotten about that!" she said. "Your *face* when I dropped that spider on you! Oh, that was *hilarious!*"

"What?" Dero asked incredulously.

"Oh, yeah," William said. "She thought it would be a good idea to wake me up in the Felds by dropping a spider on my face."

She was still laughing. "It was *beautiful*," she said. "C'mon, you know you thought it was funny. Even *Legs* thought it was funny, and you threw him across the room."

Everyone was laughing, now, even Szera. The Djor was less severe than she made herself out to be.

"What scares *you*, *ona*?" William challenged.

"*Nothing*," she said teasingly.

"Oh, come on, *Vitha*," Szera urged. "Tell them."

"Ooh, what?" Dero asked curiously.

She grinned sheepishly. "All right, fine. It's not a fear, exactly, but I really hate chickens."

"*Chickens?*"

"*They* hate *me*! I can talk to just about any animal, but chickens are the worst! They *never* listen to me. And those birds are *nasty*, believe me."

"We'll have to work on that," William said in a dry imitation of her voice. She laughed hysterically. Even Szera liked that one, though she was normally defensive of the *ona*.

Dero kept them all laughing for hours, but at last the *ona* said, "All right, now, boys. Simmer down. We're nearly there. Time to get serious."

They quieted instantly. In just another moment, they were passing their stash of grain, nearly empty at the moment. Then they came to a halt under the nearest burrow.

"Wait," the *ona* whispered. They were right under the huge grain storehouse William remembered seeing in Belo.

She gave a soft whistle into the tunnel above them. They

waited, then a tiny brown mouse came crawling down the side of the ladder. It squeaked in agitation as it came. The *ona* picked it up in her hand, saying, "Slow down," in Djoran.

The mouse kept chattering. Szera's jaw dropped. The *ona* just narrowed her eyes. "*Dän*," she said to the mouse. "Thank you."

The mouse scurried back up.

"There are guards—*inside*," the *ona* said angrily.

"What?" gasped Winna. "How did they know?"

"I don't know," the *ona* replied testily. She wasn't meeting William's eyes. "It doesn't matter. They're there."

"Wait until tomorrow," Ovan advised.

"No. We need the grain now."

"We can tap the *Reben* stores for now."

"There isn't enough. They need it. I can't take it from the Nest. There won't be enough for anyone."

"It's too risky," Ovan argued. "The last time we had a skirmish here was when Mel—" he broke off under the fierce glares of Melach's students.

"We'll do it, *ona*," Szera declared.

"We'll just have to keep it quiet," the *ona* reasoned. "There are twelve—facing the door, inside (as if we use the door!). Another twelve outside. If they hear us, they'll call for reinforcements. If we can kill the ones inside without alerting those outside, we can just get the grain and carry on as usual."

"It's too dangerous," Winna said.

"We have to try. We all sneak up there, get behind them, and it's two to one. Don't let them draw swords."

Dero nodded. "We can do it," he encouraged.

"All right," she agreed, her voice tight. "Not a sound."

They crept up the ladder one by one. The *ona* went first, climbing soundlessly. William tried to keep his breathing quiet.

They reached the top. The *Ëan* had cut away some of the floorboards to make a sort of lid for the burrow, which could be replaced with none the wiser.

The *ona* left the burrow, darting silently into hiding. Ovan followed, then William. When his head came up, he got a brief look at the room. The warehouse was enormous, both in height and dimensions. There were four or five massive stacks of grain sacks, stretching almost to the ceiling. The burrow came up behind the rearmost of these, so they could hide quite easily behind the grain pile, as long as they did not make a noise. Ordinarily, it would have been quite dark in here, but each of the twelve guards held a torch, bathing the front of the warehouse in an eerie glow. They were standing right by the door.

The torches would complicate things. One, the shadows would make it harder to sneak up. Two, they would have to catch them when the soldiers were killed, along with the men themselves, to avoid making noise—and all this without setting anything on fire.

They were all up now, hiding behind the grain. It was the last chance for the *ona* to back out.

She gave them the signal to wait. Then she darted forward, running from behind one pile to the next she probably wanted a look at their formation. She was always a shrewd planner.

Ovan peered around the pile to watch her progress, tense. A few long moments passed for the *Ëan* as they waited blindly. Then Ovan waved them all forward, presumably on the *ona*'s signal, also signing for them to fan out. They glided forward, each moving to a different part of the warehouse, spreading out until they drew level with the *ona*.

William saw the guards. They stood as one group, facing the door. The trick would be killing those in the middle, not giving them time to react to those on the outside. They would have to be lighting quick.

The *ona* watched for one moment more. All their eyes were on her, waiting, agonizing. She drew her knives without a sound. The *Ëan* drew their weapons likewise. William gripped the Gnomi sword, his palms sweaty inside his gloves.

He could hear the blood roaring in his ears.

Then the *ona* gave the forward signal.

Instantly, the Ëan flew from their hiding places and fell upon the soldiers.

It would not have been hard, except that they had to be utterly silent. They took the guards completely by surprise. William took one in the throat, the other through the chest. Then he caught them and their torches, lowering them carefully to the ground and avoiding clinking the armor. He switched the torches to his left hand, still holding his sword. All the Ëan had done their work, Ria and Szera taking the middle. The guards all lay dead.

They listened for a full thirty seconds for any sign of alarm from outside.

There was none.

They breathed a sigh of relief. As he did so, William looked down.

Seeing the dead bodies of the men he had killed—killed!—unnerved him. He'd killed before, but that was to save Dero. And it was not up close like this. He felt like he might be sick.

He found the *ona* looking at him, a sort of pride in her eyes. She nodded at him, and he steeled himself. They were doing this for a reason—for Belond, for the people, for freedom. *El forgive me.*

The *ona* then sent them back to the rear to steal the grain. She stood watch while the others carted the sacks up and down the burrow. After half an hour, the *ona* halted them, and they climbed back down. Safe, this time.

William and Ovan fell back behind the others to talk to the *ona*.

"So what do you think now?" William asked.

"Don't rub it in," she snapped angrily. "This is serious. I still doubt there's a traitor—there's too much they don't know. But something's going on. I'll tighten surveillance and get to the bottom of this. If someone's talking, I'll find out."

"Thank you, *ona*," Ovan said.

She gave a tight nod. "Go catch up, now. I have work to do."

Ovan opened his mouth to protest, but she turned and ran back toward Belo. Before they could stop her, she was gone.

Chapter 36

William whistled as he walked up the street.

It was about two in the afternoon. Kerran and Allain had sentry duty today; Fred was looking after his herd in the north, and Dero had run off somewhere (probably to the Healers'). Winna was still sleeping off last night's raid, and Lis and Elénne had gone to the market to pick up their food. William had been left all to himself to look after Hope. Elénne had handed her daughter off to him and rushed out before he could protest.

Not that he minded. He loved Hope. The little girl, now three, was as adorable as ever. He walked slowly enough for her to keep up, holding onto her hand. His other hand held a basket that contained the fruit of his time alone today.

He walked into the practice room. He waved hello to the few people who were there—a couple *Reben* and Rosie and Szera, who were sparring. He walked over to watch. Szera was making mincemeat out of Rosie, but Rosie didn't seem to mind.

They stopped for a break. "Hi, William," Rosie greeted him cheerfully. "And 'ello, cutie," she said to Hope.

"What's going on?" Szera asked, warm enough, but matter-of-fact.

"I was looking for the *ona*," he answered. "Do you know where she is?"

Szera frowned. "Why?"

"I wanted to talk to her. And I have something to give her." He indicated the basket.

Szera pursed her lips. "Well," she said hesitantly, "She got back early this morning. She's probably awake by now, but I haven't seen her yet."

"Oh. Well, can I go find out?"

Szera cleared her throat.

"You don' usually bother the *ona* in 'er room 'less it's an emergency," Rosie told him meaningfully. "She don' rest near enough, so we don' disturb 'er when she does."

"Oh," he said, disappointed.

Rosie looked at Szera. Szera sighed, then she said, "She probably won't get mad at *you*. I guess you can try. Go back through that hallway, then down the stairs on your left, down the second staircase on your right, then all the way to the end of the hallway. Okay?"

He mentally repeated her instructions. "Okay. Thanks, Szera."

"Mm-hmm." She didn't smile, more just glared. He felt like she was challenging him, weighing whether he was worthy to see the *ona*. From her expression, she was doubtful. She was sentimental that way.

"See you later," he said to Szera. "Bye, Rosie."

"Bye, William. Bye, Hope."

He left them to resume their practice. "Wee-yum," Hope said, tugging on his cloak (which he'd borrowed from Kerran until his new one was made).

"What, sweetie?"

"Where go?"

"*We* are *going* to *see* the *ona*," he said dramatically, taking a step to emphasize each word.

"*Ona!*" Hope exclaimed excitedly.

William smiled. Hope had only met Ria once or twice, but she loved her. She jumped down the hallway now instead of walking. He laughed and copied her, to her delight.

He endeavored not to get lost. The Sky Palace was huge, and he'd never gone down into this part before. It was certainly off the beaten path. He would never have thought there would be a part of this city he would call run down, but this place came close. Why did she live down here, all by herself? It seemed strange.

He found the room, at last—or hoped he had. He knocked on the door, softly, in case she was asleep.

"Szera?" came Ria's voice. "It's open."

"It's William," he responded.

A moment later, she opened the door. "William?"

Before she could say anything else, Hope squealed. "*Ona!*" she exclaimed.

"Hope!" Ria said in surprise. "Hello!" She swept up the little girl in her arms. "I wasn't expecting to see you!"

Hope giggled.

"To what do I owe the pleasure?" she asked William dryly.

"I just wanted to talk to you," he said. "Am I intruding? Szera thought you might still be resting."

She shook her head. "No, I've been awake for a while." She brushed the loose hair out of her face. She looked like she'd tumbled into bed in whatever she was wearing on the raid, minus the boots and mask. Her hair was a braided rat's nest, and she had circles under her eyes. She'd probably slept about four hours in twenty-four, from the look of her.

"You okay?" he asked.

"Yeah, I'm fine. Why'd you come down?"

Always right to the point. "Well—uh—I wanted to apologize."

She arched an eyebrow. "For what?"

He grimaced. "I think I came off wrong last night. I didn't mean to sound the way I did."

She smiled. "I know that."

He shrugged. "Well, I brought you a present, anyway." He proffered the basket.

She shied away. "You don't have to do that."

"No, I want to," he insisted. "Please?"

She sighed. "What is it?" she asked warily, peering at the basket.

William took the cloth off the top. "Bread."

"I have food already," she told him. "You don't have to bring me anything."

"Aw, c'mon," he argued.

She wavered. "Is this from Lis?"

"Would I make you eat that?" he teased. "Nah, I'm kidding. I made it this morning."

"*You* did? Now I really *am* scared."

"Hey, I can bake," he protested.

"*Really*? And where'd you learn to do that?"

"When I got bored as a kid, I'd go down to the kitchen and watch the cooks, and sometimes they gave me things. And the head cook taught me some things—said everyone should know how to cook. So that's genuine Ossian sweetbread, thank you very much."

She laughed, and he could tell she'd given in. "Is that so? Well, I guess I can't criticize. I can't cook at all, you know…"

He laughed lightly.

She took the basket from him. "Thanks."

"You're welcome."

She hesitated. "You can come in, I guess," she offered.

"I don't want to bother you. I can go if you'd rather I not—"

"No, it's okay." She set Hope down and moved out of the doorway. He followed her inside.

He wished he could compliment her on her room, but he couldn't find words.

She had nothing. A pallet on the floor, a small clothes chest, a case full of weapons, a cupboard for food. Nothing else. It looked like a poor man's hovel, not a leader's home. There was no reason for her to live like this, either. The least of the *Reben* lived better.

"Don't say anything," she said preemptively. She glanced at Hope who was building a blanket fortress on her bed. "I'm just… more comfortable this way."

"Oh." He suddenly realized that, to her, wealth and comfort represented the life she'd once had—which it was easier not to think about. He felt sorry for her.

He changed the subject. "So what did you find out last night?" he asked.

Not a good tack. She glowered. "Nothing. If we have an informant, he's covering his tracks well and being careful. I'm just not sure what the point is—if he wanted to ruin us, he'd just expose the Gnomi infrastructure. But he hasn't. I just don't understand."

"What are we going to do?"

"I don't know what we *can* do. I've got a tighter watch on things now, and I'm going to keep my plans closer, changing them up and not giving them out so early. Spoil the scent. Keep them guessing."

"Good idea."

She sighed. "For over five years, I've been one step ahead of them. Now they're catching up." She forced a smile. "But I can't do anything more. It'll have to do."

"Right."

Now *she* changed the subject. "So, you're watching Hope, eh?" she asked.

"Yeah. I don't mind though. I love her."

Ria favored the little girl with a smile. Hope beamed back, then continued making a blanket mountain. "She's wonderful," she agreed. "I imagine you're close to her mother, then."

Now where was this coming from?

"Yeah. I mean, I guess so." What was he supposed to say? "But Elénne and I aren't, you know—" Ria looked infuriatingly matter-of-fact, "—like that," he finished uncertainly.

"Well, maybe you should be," she replied calmly, an unreadable undertone coloring her voice.

William was taken aback. "What?"

"You heard me."

"I just don't feel anything special toward Elénne," he protested. Why were they talking about this?

"I'm not thinking about Elénne," she said, lowering her voice so Hope wouldn't hear. "I'm talking about Hope."

"What does she have to do with me and Elénne?"

"Everything! Do you know what it's like for a little girl to grow up without a father?"

That hit him hard. He had nothing to say. Her eyes stared accusingly back at him. The eyes of a little girl, not the *ona*. "It's not my fault," he wanted to say. He wanted to hug her, make all this go away. He couldn't.

"Of course you don't," she said.

"I grew up without a mother," he offered.

"So did I. And so will Hope, if Elénne won't grow up. The girl's irresponsible. She doesn't take her child seriously."

He couldn't deny that either. "But I don't love Elénne," he protested. "I can't marry a woman I don't love just for Hope. It wouldn't be right."

She shrugged. "I guess you'll have to think about it."

He sighed. "Yeah. If you say so, *ona*."

He turned to leave. How had things turned sour so fast? His chest felt tight. "I guess Hope and I should go," he said. "My mother will be getting back soon."

"Okay," Ria answered. She looked a bit remorseful that she'd spoken so strongly, but she didn't apologize. "See you later, then."

"Okay. Bye, Ria. C'mon, Hope."

She smiled. "Bye, Hope."

"Try some of the bread for me, okay?"

She laughed. "I will."

William walked back up through the Sky Palace, Hope on his shoulders. As he passed an open entrance a blur of movement caught his eye. He looked in.

It was a wide courtyard with a fountain in the middle. Under the water, a blue lamp was set, making the water sparkle. It was a lovely place.

Two people sat by the fountain, facing away from him. He recognized them immediately: Dero and Ekata. He suppressed a grin, watching for a moment. Dero would be embarassed if he knew, but William couldn't help it.

Dero held in his hands a necklace he'd made, the pendant carved from wood. William had seen him working on it for hours and guessed who it was for. Ekata turned her head and moved her pale hair out of the way for him to fasten it for her. They smiled at each other.

William moved quietly away before he could watch them kiss.

He had trouble keeping a grin off his face the whole rest

of the way home.

He walked inside, trying to be quiet as Hope had fallen asleep in his arms. The sound of voices in the kitchen told him that Lis and Elénne were home. He moved to the stairs to take Hope up to Elénne's room, but he paused when he heard them talking.

"If you'd just settle down, dear," Lis said. "You'll have a house of your own, one day. You'll have to take care of these things."

"You sound like my mother," Elénne said crossly. That surprised William. Normally the two women got along well. "I already *had* a house of my own, and look where I am now."

Lis sighed. "I know, sweetheart. But—"

"It lasted all of two months. Then I was back with my parents again, but with a child to raise."

"What happened?" Lis asked gently.

"Mining accident. Killed instantly."

"I'm sorry."

"It was stupid of me to marry a miner. I should have known better."

"If you loved him, it shouldn't have mattered what he did for a living, Elénne."

"I only said yes because he was the first person to ask me."

"You *didn't* love him?"

"I hardly knew him. My father was a rancher. He was a miner. He lived in town. We met at some dance. I hadn't really met *anybody*, living in the middle of nowhere. He was the first man ever interested in me."

"I see," Lis said, sounding a bit disappointed.

"I just... don't want to be alone," Elénne confessed.

"You're not alone, child! You have wonderful people all around you that love you."

"That's not what I mean."

"But you shouldn't pass it over. It's worth more than you'll ever know."

"But I don't want to be unmarried my whole life. And now I have a child to raise by myself. I can't do it!"

"I know it's hard, Elénne. But you shouldn't focus so much on what you don't have. El has you right where he wants you. Do you need to be married to serve El?"

Elénne sighed.

"Can you serve El without a husband?" she asked again.

"I'd be happier with one."

"Would you? Elénne, you have innumerable opportunities right where you are. You have a beautiful child to love and care for, and a family around you. Learn to appreciate that before you go searching for more."

Elénne huffed a sigh.

"Look, sweetheart," Lis said. "I've been wanting to ask you something for a while. Just between women, you know?"

"Okay."

"I've seen you and William together. I know you like him. Do you love him?"

No answer.

"Elénne. Do you really love my son?"

Another sigh. "He's the nicest man I've met in a long time. He's sweet, he's loyal—he's everything I'd want a husband to be. And he loves Hope already."

"But do you love him?"

"I don't know. I'm not sure I even know what that means."

Lis laughed lightly. "It's easy, dear. Not easy to do, of course. It just means you come second to the person you love. You're willing to do anything for them. You're not selfish. You give them all your loyalty, support, and care. Now what do you think?"

She sighed. "I still don't know, Lis. Do—do you think he loves me?"

Now *Lis* sighed. "Sweetheart, I don't know everything he's thinking, but... I don't think he does. He likes you, and he would never hurt your feelings. But think... I don't think he feels that way for you. His affections lie in another direction,

I'd say."

"You know... I think I already knew that."

"Then why have you still been pursuing him?"

"What other choice do I have? *I don't want to be alone.* I'd practically given up when William came along."

"Elénne! There are *plenty* of nice young men around here, and some have already shown interest in you. Think about that party. There were lots of boys staring at you, if you'd been paying attention."

"You think?"

"I'm quite sure. I think you should talk to William—get this sorted out once and for all."

Elénne sighed.

"He just doesn't want to upset you. He's very sensitive to others' feelings."

"I know."

"Just talk to him."

"Maybe I will."

"Okay."

He heard a chair scrape across the floor. He hurried over to the stairs as they came out, so they wouldn't know he'd been listening.

They came into the hallway.

"Oh, hi, William," Elénne said, coloring a little. "Did you just get back?"

He was halfway up. "Uh—uh, yeah."

Lis looked suspicious of his answer, but she asked, "Where were you?"

"Sky Palace."

"With Hope?"

"Yeah."

Elénne extended her arms for Hope, and William handed her over, gently so as not to wake her. "I'll go put her in bed."

"Okay." She walked upstairs as William walked back down.

Lis cleared her throat. "Were you eavesdropping?"

William reddened.

"Yes, you were. That's extremely rude, William."

"I know; I'm sorry."

She frowned, but she relented. She never stayed mad long. "Well, I *do* want you to talk to her. She deserves honesty from you—and I think she's ready to hear it."

He grimaced, but he said, "Okay, I will."

When Elénne came back down, Lis had disappeared. William was waiting awkwardly in the hallway for her.

"Hope's asleep," she told him. "You wore her out wonderfully."

He nodded, trying to smile.

She looked carefully at him. "Lis told you to wait here for me, didn't she?"

"Uh, yeah. Yeah, she did."

Elénne laughed. "You needn't look so happy about it."

"Sorry," he laughed. After a deep breath, he said, "Look, I've thought a lot about this. This really isn't easy for me to say... Sorry." He started over. "I just don't think we're right for each other, Elénne." It felt relieving to say it, hard as it was.

She sighed. "I know, William. And thank you."

"I'll always be your friend," William offered. "And..." he thought about what Ria had said. "I'll be anything you're willing to let me be to Hope. She's a wonderful girl, and she deserves all the love she can get."

Elénne smiled. "Thank you," she replied. "I really appreciate that."

They were silent a moment, then Elénne said, "I should go help in the kitchen."

"Right. Okay."

She smiled briefly, then she walked away. And that was that.

Chapter 37

William stood by the sword-fighting ring, watching Dero spar Allain. Dero had improved quite a bit since he first started teaching William, and now he was about as good as Allain. Every time either one managed a hit, William cheered them on.

It was the morning after he'd talked to the *ona*. Oddly enough, she'd sent him on sentry duty last night instead of helping with the deliveries like he usually did. He hadn't received an explanation for this, but he hoped the *ona* wasn't mad at him. Word traveled quickly in the Nest, so just about everyone knew that there was no more possibility of William and Elénne being romantically involved. Nobody was teasing him about her anymore, at least.

He was surprised, then, to suddenly find Ria at his shoulder. She hadn't said hello; she was watching the fight.

"Hi," he ventured.

"Hi," she replied, not taking her eyes off the match. He loved the way her eyes looked when she was watching something: fixed, focused, and noticing everything. She had an uncanny ability to immediately analyze what she saw.

"So..." he started, not sure what to say. She turned to look inquiringly at him with that same gaze. "You're not mad at me, are you?"

"Mad at you? No, of course not. *Should* I be? What'd you do?"

"Uh... I meant about Elénne."

"Oh." She looked away. "Actually, I meant to apologize about what I said yesterday."

She was *apologizing*? He wondered for a brief moment if she was feeling all right. "You did?"

"Yeah. Don't look at me like that! I just think I came off a little sterner than I meant. I tend to be overly... practical... in my views. And it was really none of my business anyway."

"Oh. Well, don't worry about it. It's fine."

She smiled. "And your bread was actually quite good."

"Oh, good!" He grinned.

They went back to watching the match. Both men were working hard, but neither could pull out a win. "Did you spar today?" Ria asked.

"Yeah, with Szera and Ovan."

"I should've realized. You're still all sweaty."

He laughed. "Sorry."

Another quiet moment followed. "Ooh, good one!" William called to Dero. Dero, despite his exertion, was grinning from ear to ear.

Ria just smiled. "He's certainly gotten better," she decided.

"He's worked hard."

"I know."

She paused again. Then she cleared her throat. "William, I've been wanting to talk to you about something." She'd put her *ona* voice on, so he knew she was talking business.

"Does this have to do with assignments?"

"Yes. I'd like to take you out of the picture for a while. I didn't have time to talk to you about it last night before I assigned you. I'm taking Ovan out, too—just to rule out that factor."

"You mean the spy?" He lowered his voice.

"Yes. I still don't quite believe we have one, but if someone's been trying to get either of you killed for some reason, then this might help us figure it out. Does that sound all right to you?"

He *was* disappointed, but he wasn't about to argue. "It's for the best."

"I'm still trying to get information. No one's heard *anything*." She sounded frustrated, which was unusual for her.

"Is that where you went last night?" She hadn't gone on a delivery, but she also hadn't told the Ëan where she was.

"Yeah."

An idea occurred to him. "Can I come with you? I want to help."

She balked at the idea. "That's not putting you out of the picture, William."

"I can sneak out. Not tell anyone where I'm going."

She pursed her lips, considering.

"Still too risky?" he asked.

She just gave him a pensive look.

"I wouldn't get in your way," he promised. "And isn't it better for you not to go alone?"

She sighed.

"Please?"

She relented with a smile. "All right, love," she teased. "For heaven's sake, relax."

"Thanks."

She lowered her voice still further. "I'm organizing deliveries at six tonight, so you'll have to meet me at six-thirty. Don't tell anyone, and don't let anyone see you."

"Where?"

She gave a mischievous smile. "Sky Tree Hall. Fortunately, it's not snowed under."

"But... oh."

She grinned. "Don't worry; it'll be fun! Besides, it's a lot quicker."

"Okay," he agreed, but he still felt a little nervous. He'd never been entirely comfortable with the eagles.

"I guess I have some work to do," she said with a wink. "See you later, William."

He almost blew it.

First there was that cat he startled in the alleyway. Then, there was that group of kids playing behind one of the houses. Then, he almost ran smack into Dero's delivery group as they came down the citadel.

Once he made it to the Palace, however, things were easy. There were plenty of ways to sneak upstairs without using the beaten path. Fortunately, William made it up there without getting lost, and even before the *ona*.

She came right on time. "Hello," she said, startling him. He'd been sitting in one of the chairs, looking at the tree.

He jumped right up. "Oh, hi," he said quickly.

"Nobody saw you, right?"

"I don't think so. No," he amended when she glared at him.

"Okay. Let's go then."

"*Where* are we going, exactly?" he asked. She'd never really said.

"You'll find out." She had that devious grin on her face again.

"Fine," he sighed, but he wasn't surprised. She'd always been hard to crack, all the more now that she'd decided to keep information closer.

She pulled her mask on, and he did likewise. She opened one of the glass panels, letting in a cold January blast of thin mountain air. He shivered despite his thick cloak.

"*Ara!*" she called loudly into the air, leaning way out over the mountainside. He worried for a moment that she might fall. Then a loud eagle cry answered. And another. And another. Soaring up from below, three eagles alighted on the floor of the room. Talon gave a croak and moved up to the *ona*'s shoulder. The other eagles, smaller than Talon, examined William with keen eyes.

"William, meet Pearl and Dragon. They very courteously agreed to meet us here and give you a ride."

He said hello in Djoran, trying not to sound timid.

She threw him a pair of plain leather bracers. "Here. Put those on or you'll get sliced to ribbons." She wore a similar pair. "And I'd suggest wearing them all the time, too. Never know when you'll need them."

He did as she said.

"You go first," she told him.

"Me?"

She nodded. "Then Talon and I can close the panel."

"Oh. Got it." He stood there, watching the birds. They

didn't move. He looked to Ria.

She laughed, rolling her eyes. "It's not that hard." She moved over to him. She grabbed both his wrists and moved them. "Extend your arms. There. Now move to the edge."

He felt very silly, standing there with his arms out, right next to a rather sheer drop. But Ria was right at his shoulder. She wouldn't make him do anything foolish.

She backed away. "Now. You call to them, and then jump."

"Jump?"

"Yeah. They'll catch you."

He had no choice but to trust her, frightening though it was. "*Ara!*" he called. "Come!" His voice lacked the boldness of the *ona*'s. Reluctantly, he jumped out of the window.

The eagles responded. They rushed after him, talons extended. He closed his eyes, feeling the rush of air. Then he was jerked upward by the wrists, and he found himself floating over the mountainside. Pearl and Dragon waited until the *ona* and Talon followed. The *ona* had closed the panel, and William realized for the first time that the glass did not look clear from outside. If he hadn't known he was looking at the Sky Tree Hall, he'd have thought the mountain continued smoothly to its peak.

They took off down the mountain. William knew he should be afraid, but he couldn't be. The moment they started to fly, all he could think of was how amazing it was. The wind rushed past his face, and Belond flashed by in the dusk below him. It was by far the most incredible experience he'd had so far.

"This is *fantastic!*" he called over to Ria. She only laughed.

They flew for a while, but William could not tell how long. Sooner than he would have expected, he saw the distant lights of Belo up ahead.

"*Daethol!*" Ria called. At her command, the eagles sank to the ground. William's boots crunched in the snow and they released his wrists. Ria landed right beside him.

She thanked the eagles, taking a bit of dried fish out of a

pouch at her belt and giving some to each of them. They cawed one more time then flew away.

"Thanks for letting me come," William said breathlessly. "That was amazing."

She grinned. "Good thing they like you. I think Szera's the only other one who's flown with me."

"Wait, you mean they might not have—"

"Relax," she told him. "They did."

He reminded himself not to trust the *ona* so quickly the next time she told him to jump off a cliff.

"Now, let's go," she said, grinning mischievously. "This is where the real work begins."

He looked around. Despite the snow cover, this place seemed familiar. Memory clicked. "Hey! This is where Ovan and Baër left me! I went down there to Tiran by myself, and they disappeared."

She smiled. "That's because this is the west Felds burrow," she said. "The aboveground entrance closest to the Felds. Gets me to the cellar, but I can get in the stables, the gardens, and the servants' hall, too."

"So... Are we going to the Felds?"

She nodded. "Zoc has to report to the Governor tonight. I'm hoping they'll say something about their new source of information."

"Okay."

She smiled. "They're still bad at keeping their councils secret," she said exultingly. "Come on, let's go."

The eagles had saved them several hours of walking, but they still had two miles to walk underground to the house. But, of course, the *ona* didn't walk. She ran.

They at last reached the burrow that led up into the cellar. A moment later, Ria was quietly taking the cover off the vent.

"It's been a while," William whispered jokingly.

She gave him a grudging smile, but she was all business at the moment. "It'll be hot, since it's winter. Take off your warm clothes."

He complied, removing his cloak, jacket, and woolen socks. He was about to take off the mask, but Ria said, "Leave it." They put all their things down the burrow hole, draped over the ladder.

It was strange seeing the *ona* with a mask but no hood. The whole top half of her face was hidden behind brown leather, but her golden hair was visible.

"Come on," Ria urged, and she began to climb up. He followed.

Oddly enough, he still remembered a lot about this maze of vents. He recognized a lot of the turns they made. He probably could have navigated back to his old bedroom without any trouble. But soon they were in parts of the house he hadn't visited with Ria.

They were both completely silent, moving slowly and not making a sound, so they could hear snippets of conversations coming from the rooms they passed. Servants, mostly, snapping orders at their subordinates. It was probably right after dinner for the Governor, so they were busy cleaning up.

Then it was quiet for a while, and it got even darker inside the vents. William had a feeling they were in that hallway where he'd once overheard the Governor and Zoc discussing *him*. Clearly, they still believed they could talk here in private.

Up ahead of him, Ria stopped, listening. He inched forward to hear, until her feet were practically in his face.

He didn't hear anything. It was completely quiet in this room they were next to.

Perhaps they were too early? Ria showed no signs of moving on. He stifled a sigh of disappointment.

They waited. He was glad they'd removed their winter clothes. It was suffocatingly hot in here. His shirt stuck to his chest and sweat dripped in his eyes. He longed for the outside cold again, unpleasant as it had seemed before. He was roasting.

After what felt like an eternity, he heard noise outside the vent. A door opening. A chair scraping across the floor. The light of a candle flickered across the cramped walls where they waited. But no voices.

Ria flashed some quick hand signals back at him. *Wait. One.*

Only one was here.

They waited some more. William focused on keeping his breathing quiet, though he wanted to pant with the heat. They could not make a sound or it would echo in the vents, and anyone in the room might hear it.

Then there was a light knock on the door. "Come," the Governor's voice sounded.

A slight chill ran through William's gut when he heard that voice. He'd learned to loathe this man over the past few months, but he hadn't seen him since coming to the Nest. Time had not changed anything.

"You're late," the Governor scolded.

"My apologies," Zoc answered sarcastically.

The Governor let it go. "So?"

"Nothing. No more word."

The Governor growled. "This is *your* fault! The first good lead in *years*, and you've let it go dry!"

"You know what the last message said. He fears discovery!"

"I don't care! I *want information*. I want Auria dead—which you've failed to accomplish."

"This source, whoever he is, wasn't reliable anyway. We found nothing."

"Except those guards dead in the storehouse. Good work, that. An *accurate* tip, Zoc."

Zoc growled. "That wasn't my fault. Those men were purely incompetent."

"They waltzed right in!"

Zoc didn't answer.

The Governor heaved an angry sigh. "It doesn't matter now. Just go get that source back, understand. I don't care how high the bribe is."

"He wasn't taking bribes, my lord."

"Then give him one, idiot! Men work for money."

"Yes, sir."

They heard both men leave. From above him, Ria signaled down. They crawled away, nothing more to hear.

Ria was in a bad mood on the walk home. "That didn't do *any* good," she grumbled.

William tried to put a better spin on it. "At least your efforts worked—I mean, tightening things up. They said he was afraid of being discovered."

"Which so far he's avoided. I want to know *who* he is. I want to know how he's getting messages out without me knowing."

"Well, he can't anymore, so that's good at least…"

"And I want to know why!" she continued to fume. "What's the motive? Why give the information he did? He doesn't want money. So what *does* he want?"

"Relax," he told her. "We'll figure it out."

"You're right," she admitted with a sigh.

"I am?"

She still wasn't really listening. "We'll have to reconstruct the past few days. Figure out who's been where and where Zoc and Benjen could have gone to collect a message. Then we'll know who *else* has been there, then…"

"Slow down," he told her.

"We've got to plan," she snapped.

"Okay," he placated. "But just calm down, all right? How can you think straight when you're all riled up like this?"

"You're right," she said again. "I should keep my temper cool. I'm just angry. I can't *believe* someone would betray us."

"I know," he soothed. "I can't either. But we'll catch him, okay?"

She crossed her arms, nodding grimly.

They walked along in silence for a while. Then they began to talk about other, more casual things: the raids, different deliveries, practice. It took some work, but he started to iron out her foul temper. He even managed to make her laugh once or twice.

He'd thought he knew just about everything about the *Ëan*'s doings and motivations by now, but talking to the *ona* opened a new perspective for him. She had so many ideas and plans. Her mind was always, always working. It was what made her such a good captain.

A thought occurred to him. "Why do we only ever raid the grain storehouses? I mean, there's all that gold they mine, too."

She looked perplexed. "Why should we? We only raid the grain because we need it to feed the people. Otherwise I wouldn't bother. We don't need gold. Besides, it would be dangerous to give it out. They'd get in trouble for stealing."

"That's not what I meant. No, really, listen. I was taught all about warfare and politics in Ossia. And this is both. War isn't always about improving your own position. Sometimes, you have to worsen your opponent's."

She looked almost impressed. "How would stealing their gold help me?"

"Well, we don't need money—but *they* do. Take their gold, and they can't pay their soldiers. They can't buy all their Ossian luxuries. They can't pay the tribute."

A savage light grew in her eyes, but she still looked a little skeptical.

"We've never tried to get in there. It would be *very* dangerous. The only place more heavily guarded than that on this island is the barracks."

"Do you have a burrow going up there?"

"Sort of. It's dug, but we've never used it—so the cover hasn't been taken off."

"I see."

She gave him a considering look. "The idea has merit, though. Not bad."

"You think we could do it?"

"Maybe. I'll think about it. We'd have to get this spy business worked out before we could try something like that."

He promptly changed the subject again.

Chapter 38

They spent a week trying to track down the source of Zoc and Benjen's message. They talked to practically every insect, animal, or person who might have heard something, but both men had been so many places Ria and William could not get any leads. No one had seen or heard anything.

Ria grew increasingly frustrated. She hardly spent any time at the Nest—brief visits to the Sky Palace to relay orders, a few hours of sleep—she was always out searching. William didn't always come along. He couldn't maintain the kind of tirelessness she did. Besides that, after a few days, he was put back on duty. He went on the next grain raid, led by Szera and himself (oddly enough) with no incidents.

He still ventured out with Ria sometimes. Most of his help comprised calming her down. There was little he could do to improve the situation. He wasn't even sure why she brought him along (although he could make a strong case for it if she was deliberating, he just couldn't remember afterward what he'd argued).

One morning, Ria decided to go out to meet a couple of mice who lived in the barracks, hoping for information about Benjen. It was a fairly innocuous task, since she wouldn't even be going aboveground. The mice were going to climb down to them. He gladly skipped his practice session with Ovan and went along.

She seemed especially tired today. They were fairly quiet as they walked along, since Ria didn't feel like talking. He figured she'd been up all night, with maybe an hour of sleep this morning. When she had proposed the trip, he'd wanted to question whether she should go—but *that* certainly wouldn't have gone over well.

They were about an hour's walk from the Nest when William really started to feel concerned. Ria was coughing but trying to keep it quiet—obviously wanting to avoid his notice.

Finally, he couldn't stand it anymore.

"Are you okay?" he asked.

"I'm fine," she insisted with a frown. But her voice lacked the force it usually did, and it sounded raspy.

"Mm-hmm. Right. You were out all night, weren't you?"

"What does that have to do with anything?"

"Ria, you *do* need sleep, you know."

"I'm *fine*," she repeated. She turned away, stalking a little way ahead.

"Hey, hold on," he said, catching hold of her wrist.

"Let go," she snapped.

He didn't. "You're really warm," he said with concern.

"I'm wearing winter clothes, William, and it's not that cold in here."

Before she could protest, he put a hand on her forehead. "You've got a fever," he said in amazement.

"I do *not*," she shot back, smacking his hand away. "I don't get sick."

"Yes, you do. You *are* human, you know. Now, come on. I'm taking you home."

"No! I have to go find out about—"

"Ria, it's not that big of a deal. You've been chasing this for days and haven't found anything. You're way too important to be risking your health over something as trivial as talking to some mice."

She glowered, but he could tell she wanted to listen. She just had to put up a fight first.

"We're going home," he said firmly, "if I have to drag you kicking and screaming."

She gave a weak laugh. "I'd like to see you try."

He smiled. "So cooperate."

She sighed. "Oh, fine," she conceded. "But in a couple of hours, I'm coming back out here."

He took her by the hand and pulled her back along the road, gently. "Oh, no, you're not," he scolded.

"You don't tell me what to do. I have to—"

"The only thing you have to do is go to the Healers'."

"Absolutely not. What will people think? I've *never* had to go to the Healers', and I'm not about to go for some little fever. For El's sake, this isn't that big of a deal."

An hour later, he brought her inside the Healers' House. She was feeling even worse at this point, and she could barely keep her eyes open. William was half carrying her she was so tired. He found Ekata.

"The *ona*'s not feeling well," he told the healer.

"That is an understatement," Ekata muttered, her face worried. "Come, bring her this way."

She led them to an empty room. "Here, *Vitha*," she said gently.

"I'm fine," she protested weakly. She still didn't want to go in.

Wordlessly, William picked her up and put her on the bed. Ekata nodded her thanks.

"You can go, William. And thank you."

He hesitated, looking to Ria. "Are you sure?" Ria didn't say anything.

"I will take care of her now," Ekata promised. "Go on. Let her rest."

William agreed, reluctantly. "See you later," he said to Ria, but the *ona* was already asleep.

"No," said Ekata firmly. "Leave us to work, please."

"But..." He wanted to see her.

It was about four in the afternoon. He had come back after catching a little sleep, but Ekata wasn't letting him in.

"William," she chided. "She needs rest, not visitors. I only let Szera in, and *Vitha* was asleep then." She tried to keep her voice down, since they were right outside her door.

"Is she still asleep?"

"I think so."

"Can't I just see her quickly?"

"No, William. Many people have come by. I just cannot flood her with visitors. She is really very ill."

Dero looked like he wanted to help, but there was little he

could do. "I'll tell you how she is when I get back tonight, okay?" he offered.

"Okay," he conceded. His face fell. It wasn't as if he had any more right to see her than anyone else. Szera was her best friend. He was just a friend.

As he turned to go, he heard Ria's voice from behind the door. "Ekata, let him in, please," she said hoarsely.

Dero stifled a laugh, beaming and bouncing on his heels. "She's *not* asleep," he commented mirthfully.

Ekata looked at William with a sigh. "A few minutes," she allowed.

"Thank you," he said with a nod.

"Go on, then."

He stepped inside.

She was lying on her side, face to the door. She was well covered in blankets and had a wet cloth on her forehead. Her eyes were still glazed with fever, but she looked a little better than when he'd left her.

"Hi," he greeted her. "How are you feeling?" he asked.

"A little better." Her voice was thick.

"That's good," he replied.

She patted the bed. He sat down on the edge.

"I want you to take the assignments to the Ëan for me," she said abruptly. "I haven't told anyone what they are yet."

He didn't know how to respond. "Uh... Me?"

"Yes, you."

"Why me?" He was flattered, but he would have thought she would want Szera or Ovan to do it.

"Because I think you will do it well. They'll listen to you better than anybody."

"Except you."

"I'm imprisoned in this room by Ekata, thanks to you," she said. He laughed. "Will you do it?"

He hesitated only a moment. "I will. If you're sure you want me to."

"Do you think you can remember it all?"

"Uh..." he considered the length of her recitations. "Can I

write it down?"

She considered this. "If you do, hide it until you speak it. Then burn the paper. Understand?"

"Yes."

He got up and poked his head out the door. Dero was waiting outside with Ekata. "Dero? Could you please find me some paper and a pen?"

"Sure."

"I hope you are not taxing her," Ekata said meaningfully.

"Her fault."

"She is not supposed to be thinking of the Ëan; she should be resting."

"I think it's okay. We'll be quick."

Dero came back with the paper. "Thanks," William told him. Before Ekata could stop him, he retreated back into the room.

He sat on the floor so he'd have something to write on. Ria dictated her list with specific instructions.

"I don't know how you remember all this," he commented.

"Practice," she answered. "I have a map of Belond in my head."

"Yes, you do," he agreed. He kept scribbling.

"Is that everything?" he asked at last.

"Yes, I think so."

He rolled up the paper. "Okay. I'll call the Ëan to meet at six."

"That's good."

"All right. Now you get some rest, okay? I'll try to come back and see you in the morning."

"Tell Ekata I said to let you in," she told him. "You can tell me how things went."

"I will," he promised. He stood to go.

At the door, she stopped him. "William, wait." He turned back. "Thank you," she added.

He smiled. "You're welcome." With that, he left her.

Chapter 39

William waited between rounds for Allain to catch his breath. He was easily beating his opponent, but there wasn't anyone else around this morning to practice with.

"C'mon, Allain," Dero goaded from the sideline. "Let's go!"

"*You* get in here," Allain challenged, "and see how *you* do against him!"

"Nope, not me," Dero laughed.

He turned as someone walked past behind him. "Oh, hi, *ona*," he said. "How ya feelin'?"

It had been four days since she'd gotten sick, and she'd left the healers yesterday. She looked much better; she probably hadn't gotten that much rest in years.

"Just fine, Dero," she responded. Her voice still sounded a bit scratchy, but it was more cheerful.

William didn't say anything, but he cast her a smile. She smiled back.

"So, *ona*," Dero continued, "A bunch of us are going over to our house for lunch today. Do you want to come?"

William winced. Even if it was just the Ëan, the *ona* didn't like crowds, unless they were conducting business. Getting together for fun wasn't her idea of a good time, and it was rare she did so.

"Thanks, but I think I'll pass," she said. "I've got a bit of work to do."

"It had better not be too stressful. You should be taking it easy, you know."

"I know, I know. I'm not even going aboveground. Relax."

"And *walk*, all right? Or even better, ride. No running."

"All right, already," she grumbled to him. "Fine." She turned and kept walking. "See you later," she said to the three men, but she was looking at William. "Practice hard."

"Bye," they all said.

When she'd gone, Dero commented, "I hoped she would come. It would be more fun." He shot a quick glance at William, but his eyes darted away again.

"Ah, let her be," William said. "She needs to settle back in."

"I guess so. Now let's go! Spar!"

A fairly large party assembled at their house. There was no particular occasion; Dero just wanted to have some company. Most of the younger Ëan were present: Allain, Kerran, William, and Dero, of course, then Rosie, Ceth, Shac, Aeric, and Ekata. They didn't eat a formal meal; they just sat around snacking and talking. Dero did quite a large percentage of the talking, of course.

Of the rest of the residents of the house, only Lis and Elénne were there. Winna had helped make the food this morning, but had sentry duty now. Fred had taken his granddaughter off with him today, freeing Elénne to socialize to her heart's content. Lis busied herself serving food and cleaning up, but she popped in to talk every once in a while.

While the men started a game of darts, the ladies sat and watched. (They challenged Rosie to play, as one of their best archers, but she declined.) Lis came in to bring some bread and cheese, and Rosie said to her, "Oh, now quit runnin' around! Sit, relax. Come join us!"

Lis looked reluctant. "I don't want to intrude," she said.

"No, no. Come on."

"Yes, come, Lis," Elénne agreed, smiling.

William was pleased when she sat with them, but then it was his turn at darts. He'd gotten pretty good at this game.

When he started paying attention to their conversation again, they had clearly been talking for a while.

"No one special for you, then, Rosie?"

Rosie laughed. "No, ma'am. I've hardly got tha' time."

"Not even when you're with all the Ëan?"

She laughed again. "It ud be odd to court one o' them," she commented. "They're all like ma brothers—if I'd had any brothers. It ud seem strange, for me at least."

"You don't have any family?" said Lis to Rosie.

"Nah, not me, ma'am. I's always an orphan, ya know? I watch out for me old friend's kiddos, though: Melia and Rej. She's gone now, so they got no one but me. Other than that, no 'un."

"Well, that's awfully good of you. How old are the children?"

"Seven and eight."

"So young?"

"Yes, ma'am. They well behaved, though."

"What do they do when you're gone?"

"Ah, I hardly know. They're good at lookin' after themselves. Play, mostly, wi' the other kids."

"I suppose they're independent, but it seems a shame there's nothing else for them."

"If they were out in Belo, they'd be workin' already, ya know. Probably in the mines, like me an' their mama."

"That would be awful!" Lis exclaimed.

Rosie nodded agreement. "Here, the kids don' work—at least, not like that. Give 'em a childhood, I say."

"I am glad of it. But still, I wish there was something else to do for them. In Ossia, the children would be in school, learning, and then they could choose what to do in their adulthood."

"No one's got much need to learn beyond cows, dirt, gold, and swords 'round here," Rosie replied with a laugh. "We're not much educated, ma'am."

"Perhaps not," Lis argued, "but a good education is invaluable. It would give them more opportunities in the future."

"I suppose you'd know more'n me," Rosie admitted. "If I'da learned somethin' maybe I wouldn'a been in the mines."

"Someone should start a school," said Elénne.

"Start a school? Here? Who'd do that?" Lis asked.

"You could, Lis," said Elénne. "You'd do it better than anyone else."

"Me? No, no. I couldn't do something like that."

"But you've got a real Ossian education," Elénne argued. "You could teach them. You could do something really great. I'll help you, and we can still get the housework done."

Lis looked thoughtful. She glanced at William, and he could tell she was thinking of Ria. "Well, I *would* like to help..."

William smiled, but it was his turn again. A moment later, he heard the women discussing details, and the dart players were paying attention, now, too, and giving input. Everyone seemed to think it was a good idea.

"We'll have to ask the *ona*, though," said Kerran.

William suddenly found everyone looking at him.

"Uh," he said, not sure why they were looking at him.

"Well?" Rosie said.

"You want *me* to ask her?" he surmised.

Everyone nodded.

"Oh." He wasn't sure he wanted to know why they thought that. It felt strange that they went to him almost as a leader.

"I just don't understand," Ria said angrily. "*Why* does she want to do this?"

William had been surprised by the reaction he'd received from Ria. She hadn't been against the idea—that wasn't the problem. It had just brought out in full force her old conflicts with Lis.

"She just wants to help."

"Why?"

"I think she's trying to connect to you. You told her before to *do* something; this is a way she knows how: ideas, not swords."

Ria frowned.

"Just give her a chance," William urged.

"Why should I?" she muttered, crossing her arms.

She was trying to pick a fight, but he couldn't be mad at her. He actually felt sorry for her.

"Look," he said quietly, "I know you feel like she gave up on you. But she really does love you. I know she does."

Ria didn't respond.

"For heaven's sake," he said in exasperation. "I love you both too much to watch you fight. Just let it go, Ria."

"I can't! We've never gotten along," she argued. "She's always *criticizing*. Surely you've noticed, too."

"I know what you mean," he admitted, "but that's only because she cares about us. She doesn't mean to be harsh."

"She's never understood me. It's always, 'I wish you didn't have to fight,' or 'I wish you weren't in danger all the time,' or 'I wish the King would come.'"

"Well, maybe *you* should try to understand *her*," he shot back.

She frowned, clearly wanting to retort but unable to come up with anything.

"You know," he said more gently, "I don't get it. You're mad at her for doing nothing, then when she tries to do something worthwhile, you get mad."

"That is *not* true."

"Yes it is. Come on, Ria, just forgive her and be done with it."

Ria sighed, still frowning.

"You can't hold something against her for the rest of your life. It will only make you more unhappy. You have to let it go."

"And how, wise one, would I do that?" she asked dryly.

"Go talk to her."

She sighed.

"Please? I'll go with you if you want."

"No." She sighed, considering. "Fine, I'll try."

"Thank you."

Ria went to see her that evening. William never knew what she'd said to Lis, but he could tell by Lis's expression that they'd at least started to air things out between them. Lis beamed for several days straight, setting up her school with

Elénne. They'd been given a small building in the *Reben* quarter to use, and people had donated supplies. Lis had even found a few old, tattered books to use. And lots of people liked the idea. About two dozen children were coming to learn, with a large range of ages. Lis was more than pleased. That smile stayed on her face for a long time.

Dero woke him up in the afternoon. "William."

"What?" he asked sleepily.

"The *ona*'s here. She wants to see you."

He was down in a minute. Dero didn't follow him, leaving them alone.

"Is something wrong?" he asked. The *ona* rarely made house calls.

"I wanted to talk to you," she said calmly, but a devilish smile lit her face.

"About what?"

"I'd like your help."

She certainly was making him drag it out of her. "With what?"

The smile grew. "Your idea—we're going to steal the Governor's gold."

Chapter 40

"On my mark," was the *ona*'s order. Her three followers would never have dared disobey her, especially not now.

They were really doing it.

It had taken nearly a week of preparations. William and Ria had spent endless afternoons scoping out this mission. How many guards, placed where? Doors? Room layout? Lights? She needed to know every detail before she could effectively plan a mission.

Yesterday they'd finished the long uncompleted burrow. It had required careful precision and absolute quiet, but they could get in now.

Ria was still concerned about the risks involved. There was a strong possibility the Governor would retaliate with drastic measures.

"Then there's always Plan B," William had said.

"And what's that?"

"We come up with drastic measures of our own."

"Like what, for example?"

William told her his idea. It took a little time to sell her on it. At first, she wasn't convinced it would do any good, and it was also more extreme than anything she had ever attempted. But in the end, she decided, "I think it'll work."

So they were going ahead with the raid.

Surprisingly, the gold was actually less guarded than the grain. Perhaps it was because they thought no one in their right mind would attempt to steal gold. The Ëan had never attempted it, and any peasant found with unsanctioned precious metals would be killed without hesitation. No, it was much more likely that thieves would try for the grain, if anything.

There were certainly security measures, however, no doubt of that. Two dozen guards ringed the perimeter of the outside walls, a rather large area. Two guards stood inside each of the two doors, watching over the locked strongboxes, illuminated by torches along all the walls. These boxes stood on shelves arranged in rows and columns, organized by substance and degree of refinement. The more valuable goods, which the craftsmen had already purified, were what they were after.

It shouldn't be too much trouble to get the gold. It was just a matter of keeping it.

The *ona*'s plan seemed flawless. She'd brought only her very best: William, Ovan, and Szera. No one even knew they were here. Everyone thought they were making a delivery. That was what the *ona* had announced to the others. They'd made sure they weren't followed. No spy could betray them this time.

The *ona* gave the signal to climb, leading the way herself. William followed her, then Szera, then Ovan. The burrow came up in the back corner of the warehouse behind one of the shelves. William and Ria would sneak along the wall to the front door, while Szera and Ovan covered the back. On signal, they would rush the guards all at once.

Ria eased up the lid of the burrow (a couple of floorboards they'd pried up earlier). Then she glided up and into the room, sliding along the nearest shelf very slowly. They had to be careful not to create shadows, or the guards might see them and call the alarm. Then they'd be dealing with the two dozen guards outside and the rest of the soldiers just a shout away.

William came up, imitating the *ona*'s movements. He focused on keeping his breathing slow and silent.

As they passed between shelves, he caught brief glimpses of the sentries. They were staring listlessly into the center of the room, clearly bored with their duty. All the better. One even appeared to be nodding off, and his partner would poke him as his head lolled over. William almost felt sorry for them. Almost. He couldn't truly pity any of the cutthroats that served the Governor's schemes.

"Hey," said one at the front to his partner, shattering the silence. William and Ria froze. "Did you see something move—over there?"

So they *did* have eyes in their heads.

"Probably just a rat. This infernal town is crawling with vermin."

"Yeah, you're right. Forget it."

William could breathe again.

They crept along until they reached the front end of the room. They waited one tense moment, then the *ona* made eye contact with the rest of her followers. Then a very subtle movement of her hand started the attack.

The guards didn't even have time to go for their swords. With only one to one, they had no chance.

They lowered the guards carefully to the floor, not clinking the armor. Ria pressed an ear to the door, listening for any sound of alert.

She tensed as they heard one sentry say, "Did you hear something?"

"Probably just a rat," one of his comrades answered.

Ria pulled away, hiding a grin. William didn't bother hiding his.

They met up in the middle of the warehouse. Now came the actual work.

Ria lifted a label on one of the boxes. She studied it a moment, then she sighed and looked to William. She couldn't read.

It was a box of diamonds, still in raw form. He shook his head. He moved through the boxes, reading the labels. Ovan helped, too. The women waited, not particularly patiently.

Finally, they found a section that was more valuable. William gave Ria a nod. She and Szera moved to lift the boxes, and they set them beside the burrow entrance. Gold, silver, jewels. They picked up eight boxes.

When they had enough to do some damage, the *ona* called a halt. Now they just had to lower the boxes down. But of course Ria had a plan for that, too.

As arranged, William and Szera climbed back down the ladder. Once they reached the floor, the *ona* and Ovan lowered the first box by rope. When it was down, they untied it and the two at the top pulled the rope back up. They did this for each strongbox, every moment under pressure. Even underground, they could not make any sound.

At last, Ria and Ovan came down with the rope, floorboards replaced with no one the wiser.

When she touched the floor, she burst into soft laughter. The others looked at her like she'd gone crazy, but William laughed with her.

"Well," she whispered, "I think we've learned an important lesson today."

"What's that?" asked Ovan, confused.

"We misnamed ourselves Eagles. We should have been called 'Rats'!"

William lost it. Even Szera and Ovan began to smile.

Ria shook her head with another laugh. "Come on. Let's smuggle this back into the Nest."

They didn't tell anyone about the gold. They hid the boxes in an empty storeroom in the Sky Palace and locked the door. Ria didn't want to attract attention.

But even if the Nest didn't know about the theft, the Governor did.

Ria, Szera, and William stayed in the area to gauge his reaction. It wasn't good.

The soldiers discovered the theft three hours later when the guard was supposed to change. They went immediately in outrage to Zoc, who reported the matter to the Governor. They tried to keep the matter quiet at first, but it did little good. Half their wealth was gone. The soldiers were incensed, as William had expected they would be. They were mercenaries, working only for money. This would end up coming out of their wages, and they knew it.

They nearly rioted. Only an emergency speech from the ever charismatic and assuring Governor stopped them.

Unfortunately, it was just what Ria had feared.

He decreed to all of Belo that until the value of the stolen goods were recovered, the taxes on the people of Belo would be increased. The citizens would be paying for the army, replacing what was lost. If they could not pay, they would be duly punished. They could not pay. They had nothing.

It was enough to satisfy the pirates. They did not mind the idea of pressing the peasants for money. It was an appealing prospect for them, a way of revenge.

To the Ëan, it only meant more work to do.

"What are we going to do?" asked Szera worriedly.

"Plan B," the *ona* answered with a smile at William.

And that was how William found himself crawling through the vents in the Felds, Szera on his heels.

The *ona* had stayed in the area to keep watch, though for the time, there was nothing she could do. She sent word back to the Nest for the Ëan to be ready in case things went sour. William and Szera had been assigned to Plan B.

"Have you got the letter?" Ria asked.

"Yes."

"Good. Harry volunteered to show you the way through the vents, and the eagles are waiting in the trees outside. I'll meet them at the rendezvous point and you meet me there. Got it?" At his nod, she added, "Go on then. And good luck."

He squeezed through the vents, following the little mouse. It was his first time without the *ona*, but he wasn't really nervous. This mission wasn't that difficult. It was Szera who was having trouble. The Djor was as tall as he was and *not* enjoying the enclosed space.

Harry halted by one vent cover with a candle glowing behind it. He squeaked at William. William hadn't been to this room before, but he trusted the mouse.

He eased off the vent cover. It wasn't as easy as Ria made it look. He slipped into the room soundlessly and Szera followed.

It was a very, very large bedchamber, filled with opulent

furniture. A lush carpet lay under their feet, and large windows stood at the east side, curtains drawn over them. A huge bed with curtains drawn back stood opposite a large closet from which a sample of many dresses poked out. A figure lay sprawled in the bed, and another was curled up in a blanket on the floor at the end of it.

William nodded to Szera, and they both sprang into action. Szera moved toward the mistress while William moved toward the maidservant.

He put a hand gently over the girl's mouth and shook her awake. She started and would have cried out, eyes wide. "Shh," he whispered. "It's okay. I'm a friend."

Szera was not so gentle. He heard well-muffled shrieks from the bed, then Szera hissed, "Quiet, *princess*, or I'll gut you." Then there was quiet as Szera hauled Anjalia out of her bed, whimpering.

"Are you an *Ëa*?" the little servant asked William tremulously.

"Yes."

"Oh..." she breathed. "What're ya doin' here?" She looked in fear at Szera, holding Anjalia and waiting for William.

"We're kidnapping your mistress. Unfortunate, but necessary."

"Oh, yah," she agreed with a nod. She almost looked excited about it.

"Now—your name is Aggy, yes?" He remembered her.

She nodded, eyes huge in the candlelight.

"I need your help, Aggy." He handed her a folded piece of paper. "The minute we're gone, I want you to run down and give this to the Governor. Tell him exactly what you saw. All right?"

She trembled. "Won' I get in trouble?" she asked.

"No," he promised. She'd only get in trouble if they found her here with no mistress and no explanation for it. "Tell him the truth. Will you do that for me?"

She nodded, looking up at him. "You're... you're Lord

William, aren' ya?" she asked incredulously.

What good were masks, anyway? Smart kid.

"I am," he admitted.

"You're s'posed to be dead."

"I'm not. But don't worry about that. I'm just another Ëa, okay? Don't tell anyone you saw me."

Aggy nodded.

"Good girl. Auria thanks you."

He turned to Szera, who looked ready to explode with disgust. Anjalia was whimpering, staring at William in confused terror.

"Are you *sure* this is necessary?" Szera complained. "She's just a spoiled little brat."

"Exactly. He loves her. He'll do whatever we want."

Szera rolled her eyes.

William looked to Anjalia. The fifteen-year-old still wore eye-paint and powder even in bed, but her dirty-blond hair was a mess. Her night-dress was made of costly silk, adorned with lace. Useless frippery. He rolled his eyes, too.

"You hold her, I'll tie her up," he whispered. Anjalia's eyes bugged.

Szera kept a hand clamped over the girl's mouth. William tied her feet and gagged her, but left her hands free. He also placed a blindfold around her eyes. Despite how pathetic she was, he couldn't bring himself to be hard on her. All the bonds were loose.

He took off his bracers and bound them to her forearms. Then he opened the window.

"What are ya doin'?" Aggy asked, perplexed.

"You'll see," answered Szera matter-of-factly.

Szera lifted her onto the windowsill. Anjalia shivered in the cold. Szera moved to call the eagles. "Hold on," William stopped her. He went into Anjalia's closet, coughing at the ghastly smell of dozens of Ossian perfumes, and returned with a cloak and socks.

"*Really?*" Szera protested. "Let her suffer. She'll be fine."

"She'll freeze."

"It's not that far. She won't be out long. She's fine."

William gave her a chastening look. "Just because she's a spoiled noble doesn't mean we should be unkind to her. I was one once, you know."

"And we saved your sorry hide. You weren't happy about it, either."

He laughed. "Yeah. See?"

"Oh, fine," she conceded. "Have it your way."

He did.

Once they were ready, Szera gave a soft bird-call. The quiet call of an eagle answered.

"Have a nice ride," joked Szera.

As she was picked up, she would have screamed, but from the way her head lolled to one side, it was clear she'd fainted.

"Go on, now, Aggy," William said to the little girl. "And thank you."

When Aggy had run off, William said to Szera, "Back to the vents."

"Great," the Djor groaned.

"Shouldn't you go talk to her?" William asked Ria.

They didn't have a prison, so they'd locked Anjalia in a spare storeroom. Szera had been happy to have the girl off her hands.

"What good would that do?" Ria questioned. "We'll just leave her until we find out what the Governor answers. Might take a while. He'll try to find her himself. We needn't bother with her for a while."

Strange as it seemed, Anjalia was Ria's half-sister. "I just feel like you should talk to her."

She sighed. "That sounds like a road to frustration. If she's anything like *you* used to be," she teased.

"Hey," he protested. "I wasn't *that* bad. And you got something out of our first conversation, didn't you?"

"Took some serious effort," she shot back. She sighed, growing serious again. "Fine. I can try, I guess, even if it's completely useless. Will you come with me? She already knows you."

He grimaced. Anjalia might still have a crush on him. "If you want. Sure."

"Okay. Let's make this short."

"Deal."

They went in. Anjalia was sitting in a chair. Someone had brought her a warmer cotton dress to wear. The make-up was gone. Without all the showiness, she was actually better-looking—almost pretty. But she had nothing on her sister.

Oddly enough, though, he could see the resemblance. The hair and eyes were different, and the attitude and air pitifully so. But her nose, the lines of her face, and the shape of her mouth all recalled Ria's. Or rather, a Whitefeld's.

She shrank from them, cowering in fear. "Please," she squeaked, "don't hurt me."

Ria rolled her eyes. She looked at William in exasperation. He shrugged.

"Lord William," she pleaded, "surely you're not one of those traitors. Help me!"

"No one's hurting you, child," Ria broke in.

Anjalia's pride snapped back, "That's 'my lady' to you, peasant. I'll not be demeaned by a vagabond like you."

The *ona* smiled winningly, which meant she was quite annoyed. "Do you know who I am?" she asked breezily.

"*My lady*," Anjalia reminded.

"Just answer her," William growled.

She wilted. "No. How should I know?"

"I am Auria," the *ona* answered quietly.

This was too much for Anjalia. Her title was forgotten. "Whatever you want," she said hysterically, "My father will give you. Please!"

"Oh, that's the point, sweetheart," Ria informed her. She turned to William. "This is pointless. Let's go. We have better things to do."

"Okay," William conceded.

Before they shut her in again, the *ona* called back, "I'll tell Lis you're here. Maybe a *real* lady will deign to visit you. Not that you deserve it."

That she made the promise at all told William that she had more sympathy for that puffed up little girl than she let on. He smiled.

As they walked away, Ria sighed. "Come on. Let's go see how angry we made her darling father."

Very angry, in fact. He abandoned his money-making scheme and set his grumbling minions to work scouring the island. They ranged all over, even up north. The Ëan, now fully aware of everything that had happened, had to send out several sorties to keep the farms from being discovered. He burned a few sections of the forest (leading to a sudden and inexplicable attack by wolves). He overturned every stone in Belond, but he did not find his precious daughter.

After three days, he gave in, angry as it made him. He announced publicly that no retaliation would be made for the stolen money, and it would just be taken as a loss, following the orders of the letter.

Some of the soldiers accepted this, but others did not. Fighting broke out in the barracks. The revolt was put down by Zoc, but one hundred soldiers lay dead by the end of it.

After it was over, Anjalia reappeared, wandering the woods above the Felds. The Governor now spent all his attention on guarding her, while Zoc spent all his efforts cleaning up the mess the revolt had made.

And in the Nest, the Ëan celebrated. They'd won the stand-off and a huge blow had been dealt to their enemies. Everyone, including the *ona*, credited William with their success.

But at the same time, the fight was at a new level now. The Governor would not forget this, nor would he forgive them. This was war.

Chapter 41

"Aw, come on, Dero," William pleaded. "I need someone to practice with."

"Nope. I'm not letting you beat me up."

"You beat *me* up *lots* of times!" he reminded.

Dero grinned. "That was before you were any good. Nope. Not happening."

He'd asked a whole crowd of Ëan, and no one would spar him—refusing even his offers of two or three on one. Things had slowed down a bit the past few days, so there was a large group in the practice room today. But they'd been treating him differently lately. Not even Tiran was willing to spar him. William had made mincemeat of him yesterday, and the captain wasn't keen to repeat the experience. Tiran was practicing with Ovan today.

He sighed. "Okay, fine," he conceded. He retreated into a corner by himself and just worked on form. He didn't like doing it this way, as it wasn't very challenging—or interesting, for that matter. He just tried to work on his speed. No matter how fast he moved, he pushed his muscles to go faster.

He spent a long time by himself. First sword, then knives, then fists, then sword again.

He spun, bringing his sword down.

To his enormous surprise, it landed with a clang on a short blade.

Ria's face smiled up at him. "I see you lack a partner," she commented. There was a hint of mischief in her eyes.

He felt the sweat turn cold on the back of his neck. He'd never sparred the *ona*. Nobody did unless they were *asking* for a beating. The room suddenly went silent, and William felt everyone's eyes on them.

He lowered his sword. She lowered her knife.

"Uh," was all that came to him.

"Come on," she invited. "I can practice with you."

Excited whispers ran around the room. Last time the *ona* had sparred someone, the Ëan had acted like it was a great joke. This time, there was less mirth and more curiosity.

Her eyes issued her challenge all too clearly. He met her gaze firmly, not letting her intimidate him.

"All right," he agreed, forcing confidence into his voice.

A half-smile sprang onto her lips, a look of satisfaction. "Good. Knives? I think you've learned them well enough."

He shook his head. "Too much advantage on your side. Swords?"

"That's *your* strength," she countered.

So? he wanted to complain. But he held his tongue. "Something else, then. Hand-fighting?"

The lop-sided smile grew. "Perfect," she agreed.

They looked for an open ring, but they were all open. Every match had stopped. Some two dozen Ëan stood staring. The *ona* moved easily into their midst, William following her. The crowd parted silently for them to pass.

He studied their faces as he walked by. These were his friends. Dero, grinning, of course. Kerran. Ovan. Tiran. Szera. Ekata. Torhan. Lagan. Allain. Winna. Baër. Grayem. They all looked at him with a certain sense of awe, of expectation. When had he become so different from them?

The *ona* chose a place and entered the ring. William followed her. Their audience pressed around the circle, eager for a good look. The *ona* doffed her cloak and outer tunic. William had already taken his off.

She shot a smile at the crowd. She was enjoying this. He wasn't. He didn't really want to fight her, especially not with an audience, but he could hardly back down at this point. He took a deep breath.

"Ready when you are," he said.

He tensed, waiting for her to fly at him. They circled each other for a few steps. William stared into her eyes, looking for some sign, any sign.

They narrowed just a fraction.

He ducked, correctly judging and dodging her strike. He

flew up at her and they engaged, arms and legs moving with incredible speed. Their arms locked. He started to push, forcing her backward. Was he stronger?

He didn't have time to find out. She stopped resisting, intending to unbalance him, but he anticipated the trick. They disengaged and went back to circling.

This became the pattern. Fight. Stalemate. Disengage. He attacked, he defended. They both landed a few hits, but neither could dominate the other.

Duck. Swipe. Kick. Block.

He went all out. He forgot it was Ria he was fighting. He forgot this was the unequaled *ona*. He *was* her equal. He could see all her attacks and keep up. Perhaps he could even beat her.

The crowd cheered at everything. They could not choose a favorite because they could not tell who was winning.

The fight dragged on. Minutes, hours, he didn't know. He actually began to grow tired, unusual when sparring these days. Even stranger, so did the *ona*. He'd never seen her out of breath before. Now she was. A hint of question flickered in her eyes. Was the *ona* wavering?

He forced her back. He landed a blow to her arm, and she winced. A moment later, he had her pinned to the ropes lining the ring. Their hands were locked, one above their heads and one below. He pushed as hard as he could. She began to waver. The crowd gasped, all eyes fixed on them.

His eyes were locked with hers. He felt determination surge through him. He pushed harder. Then he saw something flare in her eyes. He tensed, expecting her to try to throw him.

She didn't. She did the last thing he expected.

She yielded to his force, bringing them close together. Then before he knew what was happening, she darted forward and kissed him.

He heard the crowd gasp. Then he forgot everything.

He'd dreamed what this might feel like, but he'd never imagined he'd ever experience it. He'd never dared believe

Ria might feel for him anything beyond friendship.

It lasted a few moments, but it seemed like forever. He wished it had been.

She pulled away. She kept her hands linked with his a moment longer. "Draw," she whispered.

She'd never looked so proud. A mass of emotions flew through him. Blood rushed to his face. He felt rather dazed. The only thing he could recognize was elation.

"No," he managed to respond. "I think you won."

That old devilish smile lit her face again.

She withdrew from him, turning to look at the crowd. Instantly, a cheer went up. Some looked excited, even triumphant. Some looked shocked. Some, or rather, one, looked irate.

She held up a hand for silence, waiting to address the crowd.

She took his hand and lofted it, laced with her fingers. "Ëan—William!" she presented.

They cheered, loudly. Of course they did. She had them rapt from the moment she opened her mouth whenever she spoke.

"Has he proven himself well?" she asked.

Another cheer. He felt pride stir in him, but also suspicion. This was just a bout, even if she had kissed him for it. No need for a speech like this.

"And not only in this fight, but in many. Do any deny he has earned your respect?"

They cheered him again. William watched only the *ona*. What was she up to?

"William is a leader among us!" she declared. She raised her voice still more. "As such, I name him *Ëa kosatona*. What say you?"

The crowd roared.

Wait, what?

He opened his mouth to protest, but no one was listening.

She dropped his hand and turned to face him. The crowd quieted. In a normal voice, she added, looking him in the eye,

"And my *ailë*."

The crowd reacted with a mix of gasps, cheers, and whistles. William didn't know what she was talking about. He knew Djoran, but not the words she had used. *What was going on?*

She favored him with a smile then turned away. "Back to practicing," she suggested, to the others. "We have work to do tonight."

The crowded cheered one last time, then dispersed. Ria said to William, "I'll talk to you later, okay, William?"

"Uh... okay."

Another of those smiles.

She stepped out of the ring, reclaiming her belongings. As she passed Ekata, she said to her, "Would you mind getting him cleaned up for me, please? Thank you." Then she just left, leaving William to stare after her in a wild mix of bewilderment and exhilaration.

Chapter 42

Dero was more excited than anybody.

"Man! You were at it for forty-five minutes!" he exclaimed. "Forty-five—count 'em! Nobody else could even last *one* against the *ona*! And you almost beat her! Oh—that one move you made when you went like—uh—" he imitated the motion, "that was seriously awesome!"

William didn't respond. This was all feeling like a strange dream. He kept seeing her eyes, the way they'd looked right before she kissed him.

Ekata's healing fingers brought him sharply back to reality. "Ow!" he said as she touched a bruise a little too hard.

"Sorry," she apologized, "but it would help if you would hold still."

"Mmf," he responded. Ria had left him thoroughly bruised. Ekata rubbed some more salve on.

"And you're *kosatona* now," Dero said gleefully.

"What does that even mean?" William interrupted. "*Kosa*—'alone,' *ta*—'not,' *ona*—'captain.' 'Not alone captain'?"

"It's like a second-in-command," Dero explained.

"Not quite," Ekata corrected. "In practical terms, yes, but it is more like a right arm, an extension—a part of her. Without the *ona*, you are not in authority, but her authority is yours. She has made you her partner."

William's mouth dropped. He hadn't thought that she'd done anything *that* serious.

"It's a *huge* honor," Dero told him enthusiastically.

"It also means," Ekata continued, "that you would be *ona* if something happened to Vitha."

The mood dropped significantly, but William only felt more shocked. She'd trust him to lead the *Ëan*? They were everything to her. It had been her whole life's work.

"Well," he said, "nothing's going to happen to her."

"Right," Dero agreed. He opened his mouth to say something else, but William interrupted again.

"And what does *ailë* mean?" he asked.

Dero reddened, clearing his throat. "Haven't you heard *that* word before?"

It sounded familiar.

"Ailëandra," Dero prompted. "The name of this city."

Realization kicked in, but he could hardly believe it. The name of the city meant "city of star-lovers."

"It means 'love'?" he asked incredulously, his face heating.

"Translated literally," Ekata corrected. "It implies more the idea of 'other half,' like something that completes you. She has made you her partner in more ways than one."

"I always knew it," Dero declared. "You've been crazy about her since I met you."

"I have not," he protested. "We've only ever been friends. We're *still* friends."

"No, she likes you, too. Aside from the fact that she just said so in front of everyone, she's been partial to you for ages."

He didn't enjoy all this attention, but he liked what Dero was saying nonetheless. Still, he had to deny it—he'd grown so used to suppressing even the idea of feelings between them, he hardly knew how to do otherwise. "No she hasn't," he protested. "She's treated me like everybody else."

"She paid attention to you. She didn't do that for any of the other *Reben* trying to be *Ëan*. Not me, at least. And now you're always cooking up schemes together. You're one of the commanders now. You've been *kosatona* for a long time before now, in reality. And she opens up more to you than anyone. Most of us don't even really know her, but *you* do."

"He is right," Ekata agreed. "I have known *Vitha* as long as anyone. I know what she is like. She took an interest in you from the beginning. She is not like most girls—or most people. She does not like to show any emotion. But she did— for you. *And* you almost beat her in combat, which I cannot recall ever happening since she was a mere learner."

"She won," he countered.

"She did," Ekata agreed.

He took a deep breath. He felt a little dizzy. Ria actually loved him. In his heart, he'd always known it, but he'd never been able to believe it.

The sound of footsteps jarred him from his thoughts. Ovan and Lis were coming upstairs to find them. "He's in his room," Lis was saying.

Lis had been a bit shocked by the way they'd chosen to announce their affection. ("Brawling in public! Honestly!") Furthermore, she was shocked Ria *had* any affection, much less admitted it. But though she was scandalized, she couldn't help being happy for him. She still had her misgivings, but he was so happy she couldn't be angry.

She knocked. "William—Ovan's here. He'd like to talk to you."

William greeted him with a smile. "Hello, Ovan."

Ovan responded with a tight nod. He didn't look particularly happy.

"Is something wrong?" William asked.

"Ekata, are you nearly done?" Ovan asked.

"Certainly, Ovan," she answered. She gathered her things and stood up. "Come along, Dero," she said and pulled him out of the room. Lis closed the door.

William imagined he was in for a lecture. Ovan was the closest thing Ria had to a father.

"What is it?" he asked.

Ovan sat down. "I'm not here to lecture you. Ria's needed someone like you for years. I couldn't be more pleased. You understand her well enough to treat her well, in any case."

William grew confused. "Then what did you want to say?" he asked.

The big man sighed. "I'm here to give you some advice," he said. "As your friend."

"Oh. Thanks." He appreciated it. Ovan was one of the first

people in Belond to be kind to him. He was really grateful for Ovan's friendship, which wasn't just because of his birth. Ovan would have helped him whether he was a Tellor or not.

Ovan nodded, smiling, but it still looked a little strained. "I want to talk to you about Baër," he said.

William's eyebrows rose. "Baër?" He felt his spirits drop a little. He'd practically forgotten his old rival. Baër hadn't seemed important lately.

Ovan nodded. "You've gotten yourself into a dangerous place with him. I think the *ona* could have been a bit more tactful, but she doesn't see him as a problem. I do. He worries me." Ovan sighed. "I didn't think I should tell you before, but now I think you ought to know why he hates you so much."

William listened carefully. He knew from Ovan's manner that his was serious.

"He loves Ria—the *ona*—doesn't he?" William asked. He'd thought a long time about it, but it seemed quite clear now.

Ovan nodded. "You have good intuition. I'm not sure it's quite love—not the way you love her. Baër was one of the first to become an Ëa, and he was infatuated with her from the beginning. She never liked the way all the young men admired her. Until you came along, she had no interest in romance. Things didn't go well."

William could imagine.

Ovan sighed. "I don't think the *ona* would object to me telling you. There are others that know, anyway."

"Does Dero? It seemed like he did."

Ovan looked a bit surprised. "Not firsthand. Maybe Ekata told him. He wasn't in the Nest at the time. But he's got more intuition than one would think to look at him. He can pick up on just about anything. Smart lad." He smiled wryly.

"Let me tell you about Baër," Ovan continued. "It's a story like most of the *Ëan*. His past is less than glorious. He had a sad childhood—born to an unmarried mother with a," he cleared his throat, "*reputation*. Probably the son of a soldier, but we don't really know. He fended for himself, mostly. Kind of a low character. I remember him as a boy. He got in all sorts of trouble for stealing, and for fighting. Temper like Ria's. It wasn't his fault—not entirely. Life used him badly.

"He was sent to the mines. We picked him up there, later. He landed in some sort of trouble, and we fished him out. One of the first. He remembered Ria and had always idolized her. She was only about seventeen, but he was constantly pursuing her. She put him off for a long time, but it only encouraged him. He was madly infatuated with her, and he was convinced she loved him back. I tried to warn him off—I knew she was disinterested—but he didn't listen to me.

"He pushed her too hard. He revealed his feelings to her all at once. I think she hadn't really taken him seriously until then, and the extent of his obsession took her by surprise. She got angry at him. I don't know exactly what she said, but it wasn't gentle. She told him flatly that she didn't return his feelings. She also said she had no intention of involving herself with *anyone*," Ovan added.

Salt in the wound. William understood now why Ovan was warning him.

"So now he hates me," William concluded.

Ovan shook his head. "No, I don't think so. *He* thinks so, but it's not as simple as that."

William didn't understand what he meant, but he didn't have time to ask.

"Anyway," Ovan continued, "the *ona* made up with him more professionally later. He was still angry, but he took it well. She considered their friendship mended, the incident forgotten. She moved on. He didn't. He pretended to, but he couldn't get over her. I think he was biding his time to try again, but he has only grown bitter. I felt sorry for him, but there was nothing to be done.

"Then you came along. The first and only young man ever to successfully win over the *ona*. You have no idea how many have tried, William," Ovan said with a smile. William smiled back. "But I'm afraid he's going to cause trouble over it. He had a black scowl on his face when he left the practice room. He wanted to be you. He won't get over this easily."

"What should I do? Should I go talk to him?"

"No," Ovan said emphatically.

"But I have to make peace with him. I can't just—"

"No," Ovan repeated. "He'll take it as a threat. It'll only make things worse."

"Then what do I do?"

"Watch him. Don't trust him. I can't believe I'm saying this. He's an *Ëa*! Saved my skin a thousand times. The *ona* trusts him unreservedly, so I really shouldn't say this. But I think she's wrong. He's trouble."

William looked seriously at him. "You don't think...he wouldn't betray us, would he?"

"I don't know, William. I'd like to say he wouldn't, but I don't know. The *ona* won't hear it, as I imagine you've found out. But you're helping her track down the spy—so keep your eyes open. And watch your back. And the *ona*'s."

"I will," he promised.

"Good," Ovan said. He stood. "Then that's all I have to say—except, of course, congratulations, *kosatona*."

William smiled, but then he asked, "You're not upset about that, are you? I mean, you've always been with her, and you've been sort of her second-in-command all this time, so—"

Ovan cut him off with a laugh. "You top me, William. Believe me, I really don't mind. Szera might, a little, but she's just defensive of Ria. I think she's accepted you, anyway. Don't worry about putting us out."

"Thanks," he said with a smile.

Ovan moved to leave. "See you in a while. Oh—maybe not. The *ona* told me to tell you to meet her in the Sky Tree Hall. Special spying, I imagine." He winked.

William's ears burned. "Okay. Thanks, Ovan."

"Not at all. Bye, now. And good luck."

He was glad not to be meeting up with the other *Ëan* for tonight. He didn't like all the fuss this was causing, excited as he was himself. But he was getting *way* more ribbing for the *ona* than he had for Elénne. Maybe just because it was taboo to tease the *ona*, so he had to take it all. Fair enough.

He waited for Ria. He'd gotten very efficient at sneaking around. Doubtless they'd notice he wasn't downstairs, but they also wouldn't know where he *was*, though they might be able to guess. But no spy could have pinned down his movements.

He turned as Ria entered, more materializing than walking, she was so quiet. "Hi," he said.

"Hi." She smiled at him. They were quiet a moment, not sure what to say.

"You're not angry at me, are you?" she said in a rush.

"Angry? Good heavens, why would I be angry?"

"I kissed you in a fight, and I didn't really ask before I made you *kosatona*."

"Do you ever ask?" he laughed. "No I'm not mad. I know what an honor it is, and I'd like to thank you. As for kissing me..." He moved closer, then he kissed her lightly. "Why would I mind that?"

She smiled, saying, "Good." Then she added. "Look—I don't want things to be different, okay? That's not what I meant to do. I don't want us to change. Lots of people forget to be friends as soon as they fall in love. Let's be friends before anything else, okay?"

"Okay," he agreed. He knew exactly what she meant.

She laughed, a bit nervously. "I'm not a sentimental person. I don't really *do* romance. I can stretch for affection, if I must—but don't get all sentimental on me, okay? No ridiculous promises or airheaded flattery."

"Okay," he laughed. "I figure you'd smack me if I tried, anyway."

She grinned. "Yes, I would. And don't try holding my hand either, unless you turn into a toddler. And keep the kissing to a minimum for now."

"*You* started that," he protested.

"Mm-hmm, but *you* might get carried away."

"Okay," he conceded with a laugh. He liked that she

wasn't beating around the bush. She said exactly what she wanted to say. "Ground rules set. I surrender."

She grinned. "Good. Now let's go jump out a window, eh, love?"

"*Kosatona*," he corrected in a pompous imitation of her voice. She feigned indignation. "Just kidding. You can call me whatever you want."

"*Whatever* I want?"

"No. Well, within reason."

She laughed. "That's right. Have to stay *reasonable*. Now let's go."

Chapter 43

William, Ria, and Szera led their laden horses down the road, delivering food to the east side of Belo.

After two weeks, things had started to sink back into place. Being *kosatona* wasn't really all that different than what he'd been doing before, and being with Ria hadn't changed much either. They were a little more than friends—he could feel the difference—but for all intents and purposes, they acted the same, especially in front of the Ëan.

They passed a pair of sentries—Lagan and Elix. "Hi," they all said. Another five minutes and they reached the burrow. They began to unload the horses.

Ria moved to start up the ladder, but a bird suddenly flew twittering down the tunnel, and she halted. She and Szera both listened carefully.

Sometimes William really hated not speaking animal. He was always the last to know what was going on. But this was serious. He could see that from their grim expressions.

The bird flew away.

"What is it?" he asked quietly.

Ria and Szera were already starting to mount their horses. "Fire. Vurlen's."

Betta.

He sprang on Blazer. Ria was all efficiency. "Szera, go for the sentries, then call anyone in the area. William, come with me."

"Yes, *ona*," they said together.

They galloped down the Gnomi Road. Blazer sensed the urgency and ran hard, nearly leaving Ria's mount behind. It was only a few miles to the burrow, but a fire in a farmhouse could take only minutes to leave the building in ashes.

He saw a ladder and cried for Blazer to stop. He threw himself from the saddle and began to climb, Ria on his heels. All his thoughts were on Dero. This was his home.

They surfaced and sprinted across the frosty grass. A short distance away, they stopped, looking on in horror.

The whole building was aflame. The nearby stables were so far untouched, but not for long if the wind changed. The cows were frightened, though, and the farmhands were struggling to calm them.

Lanterns dotted the dark yard, and shouts rang out. One or two people ran in with water buckets, but it was far too late for that.

Ria rushed down the slope. "Get away from the house!" she shouted.

The dozen or so dim faces looked up in surprise. "Auria!" one or two voices cried.

Vurlen (or so William assumed), sat coughing on the ground. He looked up at the call of the *ona*, and his five guards pressed closer to him, shouting alarm.

"To Belo, you idiots!" Vurlen cried. "Send the alarm! It's Auria!"

Two men set off at a run.

"*Honestly,*" Ria grumbled. William might have laughed.

She ran past the soldiers to find a friendly face. William watched her back as she grabbed a man by the shoulder. "Is everyone out?" she demanded.

"No," the man wailed, stopping to cough. "The girls. Couldn't get to 'em!"

Ria let him go. She tore off a strip of her tunic and tied it around her mouth and nose. "William—keep watch for me! We're going to have company!"

"Wait, no! You'll be killed!" he screamed. "Ria!" Before he could stop her, she was gone. Terror seized him. She couldn't go into that inferno!

He had to tear his eyes away. With the *ona* gone, Vurlen's men now dared to attack him, thinking him an easier target. They all came at him at once, swords drawn. The displaced servants screamed in the yard, backing away. He shoved his feelings aside, turning to face them.

A moment later, they were all dead. He hadn't even had

time to draw his sword.

He drew one soldier's sword from his chest and advanced on Vurlen. The man cowered, his twisted face contorted into fear. "Please," he whined.

William didn't even hesitate.

He knocked him on the head with the sword pommel, and Vurlen toppled, unconscious. He wouldn't kill a defenseless man. Let the Governor deal with him.

He turned back to the house. "Get back!" he shouted to the peasants. They were staring in awe at him. He had to literally drag them away from the fire.

A loud crash sounded as a roof beam collapsed. "*Ria!*" William shouted. He felt nearly hysterical. She couldn't get out of there. He ran closer, wincing at the heat.

Shouts rang behind him. Szera, Lagan, Elix. "*Kosatona!* Soldiers are coming!" Lagan cried. "*Squads!*"

William called over his shoulder, "Get the people back behind the stables! Out of danger! Then get out of here! Back to the burrow!"

"We can't leave you!" Elix cried in protest.

"*Go!* Take care of them—get them out of the way!"

He ran into the house, near collapsing. He had only a minute. "*Ria!*" he screamed, his voice raw.

Panic filled him. For one tense moment, he believed he'd lost her.

Then he heard a cough, and a response came weakly back. "Here! Over here!" He crawled, coughing, toward her voice.

He found her. "We have to get out! It's about to collapse!" He moved to put an arm around her, but then he realized she had a limp form on her back. Betta.

He took the slender girl from her. "Come on, *ailë*," he said gently to Ria. "Almost there."

She couldn't breathe.

"I'll carry you," he told her. He eyed the roof. They were out of time.

She knew it, too. "Just go," she said. "Take her."

"No! Hold on to me."

She had no more breath to protest.

He crawled out, half-carrying, half-dragging the two women. The roof started to give. He grunted with effort. A cascade of sparks flew in his face, making him moan with pain.

He wasn't going to make it.

Then he found a pair of hands pulling him along. "Come on, *kosatona*," Szera urged. She took Betta.

William made a final effort. He could see the door now. Ria was starting to go limp. All her weight was on him now.

A loud crack told him it was all over. One more lunge. He strained. A moment later, the roof crashed down.

They made it. Just barely.

Szera pulled him and Ria further away. He coughed, arms still around her. She wheezed, choking. "We have to get out of here!" Szera cried. "They're coming!"

William took a quick sip of water from his pouch and then forced some down Ria's throat. He got to his feet, slowly, pulling her up. He lifted her, arms shaking. Szera held Betta. "Go," he said hoarsely to the tall Djor woman.

They stumbled away, just before the reinforcements rode up. They found nothing more than a burned-out wreck, some dead soldiers, and a few frightened servants. The *Ëan* had disappeared without a trace.

An hour later, they sat on the Gnomi Road, exhausted.

All the *Ëan* nearby, about a dozen, had come at call. If it had come to a real fight, the firefighters would not have been without reinforcements.

William sat with his back to the wall, shoulder to shoulder with Ria. They both felt tired from smoke inhalation, but though they certainly looked like they'd been walking through fire, they'd been fortunate enough to escape serious burns. Ria sat with her head leaning back against the wall, eyes closed. Her face was covered in soot, and the end of her braid was singed. Despite the grime, William couldn't help reflecting that she was still beautiful. What if he'd lost her? He'd never thought much about it before. What would he do?

"Lucky," William sighed.

"No such thing," Ria chided, though her voice was a bit scratchy. "El was watching over us."

"You had me scared to death," William told her. "I thought I'd lost you. Don't *ever* do that to me again."

"I'm fine, William, thanks to you."

"That's not the point. I'm your *kosatona*. We're a team. We have to *work together*. You can't just run off and be the hero all the time. I don't want you getting hurt. I'm here to help you, like it or not."

"I know. I'm sorry. I'm not used to that, you know."

"I know."

"And I had to move fast, William. Betta would have died if I didn't get her out of there. And both of us nearly died anyway. There's still a chance she will, you know."

Betta hadn't been so fortunate as them. She'd been badly burned on her back and her left arm was both burned and broken where a beam had fallen on her. She was still unconscious.

Dero had found them first. He'd been surprisingly calm, though William could see in his eyes how upset he was. He'd tended her as best he could, but they'd called for Ekata and wouldn't move her until they had her expertise. Dero just sat beside his sister now, blank-faced. William wished he knew how to help.

"I wish we'd been in time for Raekel," the *ona* said mournfully. The other servant girl was burned in her bed, never even waking up.

"I know," William commiserated. She'd take this hard, he knew. She considered the welfare of everyone on this island her personal responsibility. "It was an accident. We did our best."

She shook her head. "It wasn't an accident," she said angrily.

He stared. "What?"

"The bird said that one of Vurlen's soldiers was drunk and dropped a torch near the wall. Cost him his life, and Raekel's. And all those people's livelihood. Where will they go now?"

"We can bring them to the Nest."

"If they'll come."

"Surely now they will." He looked at Betta. She'd be devastated when she woke up. Her home had been all she'd been holding onto.

She followed his gaze. "I think she'll agree," she said. "We have to take her back to heal her, anyway."

"Do you think she'll be all right?"

She nodded. "If those burns heal. It'll take time."

They looked up when they heard hooves' clattering echo down the Road. Ovan and Szera, standing watch, held up torches.

"That'll be Ekata," Ria said with relief.

Four horses slid to a stop. Ekata was among them, to everyone's immediate relief, along with Torhan, Winna, and Kerran, coming from the Nest.

Kerran came up first, throwing himself from the saddle and rushing to Betta's side. "Is she all right?" he demanded frantically.

Dero looked calmly at him. "She'll heal. Give her space, brother. Let Ekata help."

Kerran didn't back away. He took Betta's hand in his and kissed it, tears in his eyes. She didn't stir at all.

"Why *you*?" he murmured, distraught. "If only they'd been a little faster!"

Ria tensed beside William, angry. William put a hand on her arm. "He's just upset," he whispered. "Let it be." He knew how Kerran felt.

Dero looked aghast. "Kerran! The *ona* and William nearly *died* saving her. How can you criticize? She'll be *all right*."

"All we can do is pray," Torhan added.

Ekata knelt beside Betta. She put a hand gently on Dero's shoulder and whispered something to him. He gave her a half-hug and moved away. "C'mon, Kerran," he said stiffly. Kerran glared at him. "*Come on,*" he repeated. Kerran stood aside at last, but he hovered close by. William smiled faintly. He could see himself in Kerran's behavior.

Dero came to sit beside William. William wordlessly put an arm around him.

"You all right, Dero?" the *ona* asked gently.

He nodded. "I—" His calm broke down. "I'm just afraid," he sighed. Tears sprang in his eyes. "I want to make her better. She's my *sister.*"

"It'll be all right, Dero," William told him. "You've done well. Ekata will take care of her; you know that. She'll be fine."

Dero sniffed. "I know." He paused, then said to both of them, "Thank you for rescuing her. I know it wasn't easy. I... I owe you everything."

Ria smiled. "Wouldn't have done otherwise, Dero," she told him.

A ghost of a smile appeared on his face. "I know," he replied. "You're the *ona.*" He looked carefully at both of them. "Are you sure you're both okay?" he asked.

William nodded. His few burns hurt but not unbearably so. Ria nodded, too.

Dero was unconvinced. He *was* a healer. "I have some salve," he said, and before they could protest, he had it out and began to utilize it.

"There you go," he said a few minutes later. Clearly, the action had made him feel better.

"Thanks," Ria said.

"Yes, thank you," William added with a smile.

Ekata interrupted, saying to those around her, "All right, I think we can move her. Get the stretcher. Dero, come, please."

He sprang away.

Ria got to her feet with a groan. "C'mon," she said. "Let's go home."

William couldn't agree more.

Betta woke up along the way. Kerran, right beside her, cried to the stretcher bearers to stop.

They set her down. Kerran took her hand again. "Can you hear me, Betta?"

The rest of them, even Ekata and Dero, moved away to give them space. William gave Dero a hug to encourage him.

"Kerran?" she whispered.

"It's me, Betta," he promised.

"Is it you?" she questioned.

"Yes, darling, it's really me."

She sighed, a weak smile on her face. "I missed you," she said.

He kissed her forehead. "I missed you, too," he said tearfully. "It's been a long time."

"Where am I?" she asked. Her face went from confused to panicked. "Why am I here?"

Kerran opened his mouth to answer, but Ekata interjected. "Don't upset her," she said urgently, moving forward. "She needs to stay still."

Betta's eyes were wild. She was in shock and pain, but it was still hard to see Dero's beautiful sister so desperate. Dero turned his face away. "It's gone, isn't it? There was a fire. I was burned. It hurt... it hurts. Kerran!" She clutched at him. "It's gone!" She started to cry. "What do I do? Mama's house—gone!"

Kerran held her, as much to keep her still as comfort her. "You'll come with me," he said. "And Dero. We'll take care of you."

"Dero?" she sniffled.

"Dero's here," Kerran told her. Dero moved forward and knelt next to her. Betta calmed down, just a little.

"Dero," she said in amazement.

A smile sprang on his face. "It's okay, Betta," he told her. "Don't worry; you're gonna be fine," he promised. "We're taking you somewhere more comfortable."

She nodded weakly. "But Dero... our home..."

"Let it go, Betta," he said. "It wasn't a home anymore. It's just stuff, Betta. It doesn't matter in the end. Come on, now. We have to take care of *you*."

She nodded feebly.

Dero waved the stretcher bearers forward again. "Just hang on," he told Betta.

She spent a week in the Healers' House, recovering. Kerran and Dero scarcely left her the whole time. By the end of the week, William knew she must be better, because Dero had recovered his cheerful energy.

He burst into the house one afternoon calling, "Lis! Elénne!"

"Hello," William said to him.

"Hi, William," he said breathlessly. "Where's Lis?"

"Hasn't gotten back from the school yet. What's going on?"

"Kata says we can move Betta to our house today. She's feeling great! Not quite herself yet, but she's up today."

"That's great, Dero!" William exclaimed, excited for him.

"We need to make room in Elénne's room. She'll stay there."

William repositioned Hope, whom he was babysitting, on his hip. The toddler had been nearly asleep, but she looked at Dero now with bleary eyes.

"They should be back any minute. Where's Kerran?"

"Still down there. I forgot how much they liked each other. Talk about sentimental," he complained.

"You're one to talk," William teased.

"I'm not *that* bad," Dero argued.

"Mm-hmm."

"I could turn that back on *you, kosatona.*"

He laughed. "Nope. The *ona* and I don't do *sentimentality.*" He said the last word in a tone like Ria's.

"You mean *she* doesn't. *You* do."

"You got me." They both laughed.

Lis and Elénne came in. Dero whirled on them. "Elénne! We have to make space for Betta to move into your room!"

"Oh, good!" Lis exclaimed. "Dero, you're a miracle-worker." Lis had actually spent a lot of time at the Healers', visiting not only Betta, but the other patients. Dero said she worked wonders. She'd taken a special interest in Betta, though, talking to her for long periods of time. According to her brother, Lis had helped Betta finally start to accept what had happened to her and her home. Now, she just had to readjust to a new life.

An hour later, they brought her up to the house. Kerran and Dero supported her carefully as she walked, then Kerran carried her up the stairs.

"Welcome home," Kerran told her, eyes shining.

Betta certainly looked improved. She wore bandages, and her arm was in a sling, but her eyes were bright again. She was smiling.

"Elénne!" she exclaimed happily.

"Hello, Betta," her cousin said, smiling.

"Aunt Winna, Uncle Fred. Hi, Lis." She turned eyes on William. She recognized him, clearly. Her mouth dropped a little and she seemed to lose her tongue.

"Betta, this is William, the *kosatona*," Dero said. "My best friend. I think you met him once."

"Hello," she said shyly. "*Kosatona*. You were with Auria that night, weren't you?"

"Yes," he answered.

She paused, then said sincerely, "Thank you." He only smiled in reply. Then Kerran and Dero escorted her upstairs.

Chapter 44

"Hey, William?" Dero began.

They were both lying in their beds, the time somewhere around noon. William had just woken, but he wasn't quite ready to get up. He'd had a long night, and he still felt tired.

"Mm," was his response.

"You know, Kerran's going to ask Betta to marry him," Dero stated.

That woke William up. "He is? That's wonderful!" It had only been two days since Betta moved into the house. "How do you know that?"

"He asked me. My permission—you know?"

"Oh, right." It seemed a little sudden, but then, they'd known each other a very long time. "Wow."

Dero was quiet a minute. William thought maybe he'd fall back asleep, but then he said abruptly, "Would you do me a favor?"

"Sure, Dero. Anything."

He could see Dero grin. "Thanks." Then he said, "I've been thinking... and, well—I was wondering... " He finally said in a rush, "I need to talk to Yewul."

That was hardly what William expected. "The Djor *ona*? Why?"

He coughed. "Um..."

It clicked. "Oh. I get it. Ekata's grandfather."

"Yeah," Dero said, blushing.

"Hey, you should," William said admiringly. "I know how much you love Ekata. She's a lucky girl."

"Thanks," Dero said gratefully.

Still, William couldn't help but feel like he was losing his friend. Maybe it was wrong to feel that way. He shoved the emotion aside.

"What did you want me to do?" William asked.

"Huh?"

"The favor."

"Oh! I was wondering if you'd... come along."

William laughed. "Moral support, eh? Yewul's not that scary, you know."

"I've never met him."

"No?"

"No. We don't really go over there much. The *ona* goes sometimes, and Szera and Torhan. Kata has too much to do here, she says. And there's only her grandfather and her brother, anyway."

"She doesn't have parents?"

He shook his head. "Died of a fever, both. Yewul's the greatest healer in the world, but he couldn't help, Kata says. Her older sister died, too. Kata doesn't remember them."

"That's sad," William said.

Dero nodded. "That's why she wanted to be a healer. And she had the gift, and a great teacher." He paused. "So I have to visit Yewul," he continued. "I was hoping to go today, but I'll have to ask the *ona*."

"We'll have to ride if we go today," William said, getting out of bed. "I have to go out tonight."

"Do I?" Dero asked quietly, conspiracy in his voice.

"Can't tell you," William said firmly.

"Aw... You and the *ona* are thick as thieves."

"Technically, we *are* thieves," William put in. He pulled his shirt on.

"True," Dero agreed. He jumped out of bed, already dressed. "Let's go down. I'm hungry."

William followed him with a laugh.

William halted Blazer with a word before the jumble of rocks that led to the Djor village. They'd gotten here quickly, even riding overland. William was lucky Pearl and Dragon had showed up to say hello to him, or else he might not have found it. But the eagles led him by the straightest path possible.

"Thanks," he told them in Djoran. They cawed and wheeled away.

Dero caught up to him. "Is this it?" he asked breathlessly. His horse had been hard-pressed to keep up with Blazer.

"Have you never been here?"

"No," Dero said. "I met a few Djorn in the forest, and I've talked plenty to Ekata, so I know what it's like. The snake'll let us in, right?"

"Your guess is as good as mine. I've only been here once."

A moment later, a rope ladder bounced down the rocks. They caught a flash of the snake at the top.

"Oh," they both said at the same time.

"Wait for us," William told the horses in Djoran. They both tossed their heads. There was no need to tether them. They would listen.

"Okay," William said. He began to climb the ladder.

Fortunately, Ria hadn't minded him going at all. Honestly, he was excited to see the old *ona* again. He'd come a long way these past months.

Dero, on the other hand, was a nervous wreck. William didn't blame him. This was hard for every young man courting a girl: talking to her father. But this was especially exceptional. The only Djoran woman to marry an Edenian (that they knew of) was the young woman who started the Whitefeld family. It was no small thing for Dero to ask for Ekata. When the island was restored, she would remain with the Edenians, not go back to her old home. As an Ëa, she might have, anyway, but marrying Dero would seal it. Yewul might very well say no.

William didn't really believe that, but he knew it was on Dero's mind.

Dero hadn't told Ekata he was doing this. He was waiting to see what Yewul said before he tried asking Ekata.

They reached the top. William pulled Dero up the last few feet. "Thanks," he said.

They looked up. A few Djoran had come out to see them, curious.

"Hello," he said to them in Djoran. He tried to sound confident. "We've come to see Yewul, if we may."

"You speak well," a man said admiringly, "Ëa kosatona."

William's eyebrow arched.

"Torhan told us you are *kosatona*," a woman explained. "And we remember you, anyway, Edenian."

"Oh." He gestured to Dero. "This is one of the Ëan, my friend, Dero."

The Djorn greeted him. He smiled nervously. "Hello," he said. They laughed lightly.

"I will call Hlein," one of them said. He moved off among the massive tree-homes. A minute or two later, he returned with the tall woman in tow.

"Dero, this is Yewul's niece, Hlein," William said quietly in Edenian.

"Ekata's cousin?"

"Yes, I suppose—different generations, though."

"Mm-hmm."

William raised his voice and returned to Djoran. "Hello, Hlein. It is good to see you again."

She nodded lightly. "Greetings, *kosatona*. Hello, Dero. At last you come to meet us. Yewul has been waiting a long time for you. He will want to see you."

Dero didn't think that boded well.

William and Dero followed Hlein to the tree-house of Yewul. As soon as they walked in, they saw that the big room was full of children surrounding a snowy-haired old man. He was quite awake this time, crawling on the floor with the young ones. William and Dero grinned at each other in the doorway, trying not to laugh.

Hlein clapped her hands. The children all stopped, Yewul responding like one of them. "Enough, now," Hlein said. "The *ona* has visitors."

The children looked with wide-eyed, unafraid excitement at them. "Ëa kosatona," they whispered enthusiastically to each other.

"How come *you're* famous?" Dero complained in a

whisper. William just laughed. He found it as strange as his friend.

The children were shooed out by Hlein, who left with them. She closed the door, and they were left with just Yewul.

"Ah, Edenians!" he said merrily in their language. He remained plopped on the floor, making no move to get up. He looked a rather comic sight, and from the way his eyes twinkled, he knew it. "Even better, Ëan! Welcome, my children."

"Hello, *ona*," they said at once in Djoran.

"Ah, speakers of the earth-music," he said, still in Edenian. "You've learned well. Come, sit," he invited pointing to the floor.

They felt a little silly, but they obeyed.

"So, my son," Yewul said to William. "Has El shown you your gift yet?"

The question caught William off-guard. He paused, unsure how to answer.

"You have changed," Yewul mused. "You have your dream, I think, and your calling. But you are not finished yet. Have you been seeking *Aiael*, my son?"

"Not as much as I should," he admitted.

"Of course not. None do. That is why we admit to him our faults and weakness and ask his help. You will need his help, William, before your task is done. Don't forget that."

Then Yewul added, "I hear you've stolen the heart of my *Vitha*," he said wryly.

William laughed sheepishly. "I suppose so," he said.

"Yes, you have. I am glad. See you look after her. She is a leader, but in the end, you must lead her. She will need you."

He nodded, absorbing all the words.

"And speaking of stealing hearts," Yewul continued. "It is good to meet you, my son," he told Dero. "I have heard good things about you, healer."

"You have?"

"You sound... surprised. Are they not true?"

"No, I mean—uh..."

Yewul laughed. "Be easy, friend. I know why you came, and I am pleased you thought to do so. But there are things we must speak of." He stopped and looked at William. "I know you came for your friend," he said, "but will you leave us alone, *kosatona*?"

William looked at Dero. He looked terrified but also resigned. In the end, this was his task.

"Yes, *ona*," he agreed. He walked out and closed the door behind him.

He waited nearly an hour, or so he guessed, though it felt like a long time. He started to worry whether they'd make it back on time, and even considered calling the eagles to fly back. Then Dero finally came out of the tree.

William rushed over to him. "Finally!" he exploded. "What did he say?"

Dero's expression was blank. He looked vaguely dazed. Then his eyes focused.

He laughed. "He said yes," he giggled. "I can ask her."

"Yes!" William shouted.

Dero jumped in the air. "Woo!" he yelled, ecstatic. He was giddy with excitement. The Djorn stared curiously, but Dero didn't care about that at all.

William gave him a hug. "C'mon, weirdo," he said. "Let's go home."

"I have to find Kata," Dero exclaimed, bouncing on his heels.

"Then let's go!"

"Yes!" Dero raced away. "Woo!" he screamed again. William just laughed, shaking his head, and followed.

Chapter 45

"No, no, no," Ria scolded. She confiscated his practice knives and showed him a movement. "*This* way. If you do it *that* way any swordsman could get through you."

They were sparring again, just for practice, not challenge, this time. As Ria put it, "It's been a long time since I've had someone to train with. Just 'cause we sparred once doesn't mean we're done. No getting out of it, love."

So after sparring with knives for a while, Ria decided to teach him about fighting knives with a sword or vice versa, since it would be rare he'd fight knives on knives in the real world. Right now *he* had the knives. She was a lot better than him with knives, but he could *almost* out-fence her with a sword. But she preferred teaching.

"Okay," he agreed. He practiced the motion himself. "Like this?"

"Better."

They went at it again. Ria managed more hits than he did, but he made a good account of himself.

She made a tiny mistake—too small and too fast for most people to react to, but he exploited it. A moment later, he had one knife on her throat, the other behind her, her arms pinned, and her sword on the ground.

From across the room, there was some scattered clapping. The *ona* had forbidden that the *Ëan* crowd around their ring, but they still watched.

"Mmf," Ria grunted. William moved away, a bit reluctantly. She retrieved her sword with frustration. "Stupid," she berated herself. "That was stupid."

"What does it matter?" he said. "Most people wouldn't even *see* that. Besides, nobody's perfect. You expect too much of yourself."

"I have to be better," she insisted.

"You're the best there is," he contested in amazement.

She glowered. "If you can beat me, someone else can. I learned a long time ago that no matter how good you are, someone can always be better."

"So don't worry about it. Just focus on yourself," he advised.

"I have to be better," she repeated. "I have to be able to beat the Governor." This she said more quietly.

His eyebrows shot up. "Is that why you work so hard?" he asked.

She clipped a nod.

He felt amazed. "Is he that good?"

Another short nod. "He killed Melach."

He'd heard the story from Ovan, but it was the first time he'd heard her talk about it.

"I know," he said. "But anything can happen on a battlefield. You could be the very best and still fall."

She shook her head. "No. It was a fair fight between them. He was better." She sighed. "I'm going to have to fight him one day," she declared.

"Maybe you won't—I mean, if we bring the army like we plan, he'll just be captured."

She shook her head again. "No. He's not going down without a fight. And army or no, I'm taking him down."

The anger in her voice surprised him. He'd forgotten the extent of her hatred for the Governor. His first act in the sack of Belond was to kill a little girl's father in front of her. It had defined her life.

"Let's go again," she said.

"Are you sure? Maybe we should take a break."

"No. I want to keep going."

"Okay..." he said hesitantly.

"Go," she said.

When they were done, William walked over to get some water. Ria went to put the weapons back in their places. He dipped a cup into the water barrel they kept in the back corner for anyone practicing to use. He took one sip and then paused to swallow.

Someone walking past bumped into him—too hard to be an accident. William fell forward, his chest hitting the rim of the water barrel, and the barrel nearly overturned. He steadied himself and caught it, but water sloshed all over him and onto the floor. He was dripping wet.

Baër laughed. "Ooh, sorry," he said sarcastically. He'd backed up, managing to stay quite dry.

William looked him in the eye, forcing down his annoyance. He would not let Baër get the better of him. Ever.

"That's okay," he said with exaggerated cheerfulness, but his eyes were cold as ice. "Needed to cool off anyway."

People were looking, now. Ria was half-way to them, her face filled with thunderclouds.

Baër glowered. He lowered his voice. "Don't parade your idiocy, *kosatona*." He spat the word mockingly. "You're nothing. You wouldn't even be an *Ëa* if you weren't the *ona*'s pet. I'm not going to kowtow to the likes of you."

"That's your decision," William replied. "As an *Ëa*, I expect you'll consider it well."

Baër sniffed disdainfully and stormed away, just escaping the *ona*.

"Honestly," Ria grumbled. "He's acting like a two-year-old."

"Mm-hmm."

She sighed angrily. "Take your wet shirt off. Follow me to my room; you can get dried off."

He toweled the water off of himself while Ria wrung out his shirt over a basin. "What am I going to do about him?" William asked Ria.

She sighed. "He's an *Ëa*. Stubborn as he is, he's a good lad. You're just going to have to work with him. You did well enough today."

"But he doesn't listen! He never changes. He'll always hate me."

"I'll talk to him again," she promised. "He can't let this

interrupt his duties, character flaws aside. You just keep trying. Do the right thing. Maybe he'll come around."

"Ria, do you honestly think he'll forgive me for being with you?"

She frowned.

"Ovan told me about it," William confessed.

"Mm-hmm. I'm not surprised. He's been worried about it for a long time. I'm not. That issue was dropped a long time ago."

"You really think that?"

"Yes. Baër's an adult and an honorable man. If he had *any* respect for me, he'd leave me be. And he has."

"I'm not so sure about that."

"It's dropped, William! That's all there is to it. He sees you as a rival in combat."

"He hated me long before I was any good with a sword."

"But you had potential. Anyone could see that."

"No, not anyone. Only you."

She smiled. "I'd practically forgotten how pathetic you used to be," she joked.

"Gee, thanks."

She laughed. "Well, now look at you!" she continued. She poked his round shoulder muscles. "You used to be so skinny. How much food do you eat, anyway?"

"Speaking of which—do you have any?"

She laughed. "Men," she grumbled playfully.

"Hey, you work hard—you must eat plenty yourself."

"I know. Come to think of it..." She found a small basket. "Fraidith's kids brought me these this morning. Biscuits. I don't think I could possibly eat them all."

"I can help with that."

"Mm-hmm." She gave him the basket.

He stuffed his mouth full of biscuit. "Mm, these are really good." He went for another one. She took one, too.

"But, Ria," he said, going back to their original conversation, "are you sure you can trust Baër?"

She glared at him. "Please tell me you're not talking about

that spy again."

"What if I am? We never traced him. It could be anyone."

"William, if I can't trust the Ëan, I can't trust anyone. We can't have accusations flying around. Whatever Baër's weaknesses, he's been a faithful Ëa. Yes, I trust him."

It wasn't enough for William. He remembered Ovan's warning all too clearly.

"Okay," he conceded, but he was thinking the opposite.

"Good," she said. She spread his shirt out to dry on the lid of her clothes chest. She reached to get another biscuit. "Good gracious! How many of these did you eat?"

"Um, I lost count."

She snatched away the basket. "When you said help, I had no idea how much that entailed! You'll make yourself sick!"

"Aw, c'mon. I'm hungry."

"No!" She held the basket away from him but took another for herself. She set the biscuits back down. "Don't they feed you at home?'

"I'm always hungry," he joked.

"I guess so!"

She sat on the floor and patted the ground beside her. "Come on. Let's talk about the organization for tonight."

He sat beside her. For a moment, he was unable to focus. It hit him once again how lucky he was: this beautiful, strong woman next to him actually loved him. He enjoyed the knowledge for a moment, savoring everything around him.

"Pay attention, love," she scolded, but her eyes were smiling. She felt it, too.

Then it was back to business. "They changed the guard pattern on the east side. I think we should use the blacksmith burrow tonight and trace the alleyway along the south..."

Chapter 46

Kerran married Betta only two weeks after she moved into the *Ëa* quarter.

It was a beautiful wedding, held in the Sky Tree Hall. All the *Ëan* that could be spared were there, along with a huge crowd of the *Reben*. The *Ëan* formed an honor guard for Kerran, and Dero gave his sister away. There was a feast for the whole day, the Nest celebrating for them.

Oddly enough, William's heart was not in it. Perhaps the *ona*'s dislike of parties was rubbing off on him. But in truth, he was growing ever more conscious of the fact that he was going to have to leave. It was only about five weeks now until the ship could sail. He wasn't sure he could bear to sail with it.

He hadn't talked to Ria about it. He sensed it was on her mind, too. But he knew what she'd say: it was his duty—especially as *kosatona*.

He tried to put it out of his mind. If he had his way, he would put in at Ossia and sail right back. It wasn't permanent.

But it felt that way. He'd have to be gone a month if he left the same day he arrived, and he could only return if his father consented—which he might not. It weighed on his mind, and he couldn't shake his dread.

It was back to business. The night after the wedding, the *ona* organized the delivery schedule.

They were working together. He and Ria had already discussed the assignments, so she grouped them off and they went to William for their route.

"William, Torhan, Dero," she said. "The *kosatona* will lead." Dero grinned and shot him a thumbs up. "Szera, Ovan, Lagan. Szera will lead."

William shot her a questioning look. That wasn't what they'd decided. Ovan was supposed to go with the *ona*.

She ignored him. "Myself, Baër, and Ceth. I will lead."

He frowned. She'd traded Ovan and Baër, and he didn't like it. She glared at him, clearly telling him to keep his mouth shut in front of the Ëan. He did, but he didn't fail to catch the smug smirk on Baër's face.

They finished up briefing the Ëan. The moment they were done, he ran to catch Ria. He found her saddling her horse.

"Ria!"

"Now, don't even get started on me, love. Baër asked to go with me tonight. I switched it."

"He *asked* you? And you said *yes*?"

"Yes, I did."

"Why?"

"Look, William, I know—"

"No, no, no, I don't like this," he said. "Did he say why he asked?"

"He wants to visit his mother. She lives on the north side, but it's hard to get to her. He can't go without me."

It sounded fishy to William, and he said so.

"I'm for the north side, anyway," she argued.

"Exactly! How did he know that?"

"He didn't. He asked next time I was going to the north side and if he could come when I do. Honestly, William, enough. It's *fine*."

"*I* don't think it is."

"*You* don't tell me what to do," she said angrily. "Don't start getting jealous, love."

"*Jealous*? You think I'm *jealous*? I'm worried about *you*!" She glared. "I can take care of myself."

He felt like they'd just lost all the ground they'd ever gained. She was shutting him out. It stung him, but more than that, it made him sad.

"Fine," he replied, and he turned away.

"Wait, William," she called to him. All the anger was gone. Her face was all apology. "I'm sorry, I didn't mean to snap."

He smiled half-heartedly at her. "It's okay," he said, but she failed to make him feel better. The damage was already done.

"I appreciate your—"

"I get it," he interrupted. "It's fine."

She sighed. "Okay," she said dejectedly. "I'd better go."

"Yeah. Yeah, you should."

"See you later, okay?"

"Yeah."

"All right." She looked like she wanted to say more, but she didn't. She reached up and kissed him lightly on the cheek. Then he moved out of the way so she could lead her horse out of its stall.

Even Dero failed to cheer him. Dero was in the clouds; he had everything set with *his* girl. They'd get married when William came back to Belond (Dero had no doubt he would), when everything was set to rights. He was abundantly cheerful. He joked and laughed and bounced around, drawing even the stoic Torhan in. Torhan was excited for his sister, of course. He couldn't help but be happy tonight, either. William just couldn't match their spirits.

"Hey, what's with you?" Dero asked him at one point. "You okay?"

How could he begin to explain? A knot of worry formed the core of a mix of emotions. He couldn't put a label on it. "Sorry," he said. "Don't mind me."

Dero gave him a searching look but didn't question him anymore.

They made their first two deliveries, no trouble. They were in the middle of the town. Szera had the south side and some outlying houses. Ria was on the north side. Each group had eight houses to visit tonight.

They led their horses along the Road to reach another burrow. Dero prattled on with Torhan, but William wasn't listening. For some reason, everything seemed ominous to him. His gut told him something was wrong.

Blazer rumbled, pausing in his step. "What is it, boy?" he asked in Djoran. Blazer shook his mane, brown eyes fixed keenly on him. He wished he could understand the horse.

"Torhan?" he prompted.

Torhan clearly thought he was overreacting, his calm demeanor unshaken. He said a few words to his horse. Blazer rumbled back. Torhan's forehead wrinkled.

"I can't understand him," Torhan said in confusion. "He seems to be nervous about something; I can't think what." William didn't need Torhan to tell him that, he could see it for himself. And he didn't like it.

The knot tightened. He frowned, uneasy.

"Let's go on," Torhan said.

They came to the next ladder and stopped, unloading the bags of grain. William put a hand on it to begin climbing, but he was interrupted by the sound of squeaking. He looked up. Several dozen mice were descending the rope ladder, screeching with what could only be described as panic.

William's heart dropped. He couldn't breathe.

"One at a time," a perplexed Torhan told the mice in Djoran. One emerged to speak, squeaking madly.

Dero and William watched Torhan's face. He listened carefully, a long time.

William had never seen an ounce of fear in the serene Djor's face. He did now. Torhan's face whitened with shock and fear.

"What is it?" William demanded urgently. "What's happened?"

Torhan gaped, unable to speak.

"Is it the *ona*?" William demanded.

"I scarcely know how to tell you," he breathed. A tear formed in his eye. "It is too terrible."

"Is she dead?" William demanded. "Tell me, Torhan!" William grabbed Torhan by the shoulders, shaking him as if he would wrest the words from Torhan by force.

"No," Torhan answered.

William could breathe again. He let go of Torhan, but he did not back away. "*What happened?*" he asked urgently. "Tell me!"

Torhan shook his head disbelievingly. "She is not dead—

but she will be. They caught her."

He felt his legs grow weak. If not for Dero, he might have collapsed. "How?" he asked weakly, all the force gone from him.

Torhan still found it hard to answer. "The soldiers knew they were coming. Zoc set an ambush, cleverly planned. They had no warning. She fought, protecting the others. She might have made it out, but..."

He knew it.

"Baër turned on her. She did not expect him to strike at her. He killed Ceth then attacked her. He would have killed her, but she deflected the blow. It hit her leg—they say it is bad. She could not stand. They took her alive up to the prison."

"How long ago?"

"Half an hour."

"Why so long? We should have had word ages ago!"

"I do not know, *kosatona*. I am sorry."

He stifled a sob. He felt like his heart had been ripped out. Dero had his arms around his shoulders, close and calm. Oddly enough, he was the brave one—though William knew he was as scared as them.

"What do we do?" Dero asked quietly. "We have to rescue her."

Dero's words jolted William's emotions. He wiped his eyes and took a deep breath. All his energy grew channeled to one feeling: cold anger. He set his jaw.

"Yes," he agreed.

He forced himself to be businesslike. "Torhan—I want you to put everyone on alert. Get *every Ëa* down here—now. Rally the animals. I want eyes everywhere."

"What about the sentries?"

"Leave one at each of the outer posts. Everyone else— Belo. *Immediately*. Wait for my signal."

"Yes, *kosatona*." He threw the grain sacks off his horse and galloped away.

William turned to Dero. "Do you know your way through

the prison?"

"I've been there," he offered hesitantly.

"Can you get me to her?"

"Shouldn't we wait for the others? She'll be heavily guarded, and—"

"I have to get to her, with one or a hundred—I don't care. If we can't free her ourselves, then we'll try something else."

Dero argued no more. "Then I'll go with you."

William smiled at him, heartened by his loyalty. "You're my best friend, Dero," he said.

"I know."

William nodded. "Let's go, then."

Raiding the prison was far more dangerous than anything William had ever done. Not only was it heavily guarded (in the basement of the barracks!) they also weren't very familiar with the building structure, and they couldn't ask the animals for help.

They crept along a dimly lit corridor, past empty cell after empty cell. There was one sentry at each corner, but they were easy to sneak past.

They couldn't find her. This prison was empty.

Panic welled up in William again.

Dero touched his arm. He made a few quick signals. *That way.*

William crept in the direction he'd pointed. At last, at the end of one hallway, they saw one patch more brightly lit than the others.

It had to be Ria.

They actually hadn't set a heavy guard, only four men. They probably figured no one could get into the barracks unnoticed. One would have thought they'd learned by now.

He met Dero's eyes. Dero nodded ever so slightly. A moment later, they were racing down the passage to the torchbearers. Without even bothering to draw a sword, William downed both the men and lowered them silently to the ground. Dero did the same.

They listened for a few tense moments for any sign of an alarm. There was none.

William rushed to the door of the cell, looking through the bars.

She was there.

He felt part relief, part horror.

She looked worse than he'd ever seen her. Her skin had gone pale. She had bruises all over her face, arms, and legs, along with angry welts. They'd taken all her warm clothes, so she was shivering. She lay in the back corner, eyes closed, curled against the wall. But that was not the worst of it. Her left pant-leg had a long, ragged hole torn in it, exposing a deep gash in the middle of her thigh. She'd tied a strip of her already torn tunic around it, but that had hardly helped. A puddle of blood lay on the floor.

"Ria," he called to her. "Ria!"

She looked up. Her face was gray, and her eyes were dull with pain. This was not the Ria he knew. She looked desolate, hopeless.

"William?" she whispered.

"Yes, it's me," he assured. He struggled to hold back tears.

She crawled to the edge of the cell, groaning with pain. He took her hand through the bars. "You shouldn't be here," she said. "It's too dangerous. They'll catch you. Go, get out of here."

"No! We're going to rescue you."

"You can't," she murmured.

"What? No, we're getting you out of here."

"I'll go find the jailor," Dero said. He gave William a grave nod. William eyed him with a silent thank you.

"I'm so sorry, Ria."

She shook her head. "No. I should've listened to you. I'm sorry." He thought he saw a tear slip from her eye, but the *ona* never, ever cried. "I guess you were right."

"It wasn't your fault."

"Yes, it was. I should've seen it. I was an idiot. I walked

right into that trap."

"You couldn't have known."

"It's my job to know! You warned me—you were right."

What could he say?

"It's all right. It doesn't matter. We'll get you out. It'll be fine."

"I told you—you can't. There's no key."

Dero was just coming back. He held a ring of keys.

"Dero has them," William told her.

She shook her head as Dero tried various keys. "The Governor took it. He has it in his pocket right now."

He didn't want to believe it. Despair threatened him.

Dero tried every key. "I can't get it!" he growled.

William pulled at the door, ready to tear it down with brute strength. He had his sword halfway out of its sheath to try that, but Ria exclaimed, "Don't! They'll hear you!"

He put it back with all the force of his frustration. They couldn't get through those bars.

"We'll get the key," he said.

"No! That would be a suicide mission! Do you know how well-guarded he is? You'll be killed."

"We'll dig in here," he said.

She shook her head. "It would take weeks—the Road doesn't run under here."

He slammed his fist on the ground. "Let me think," he said.

"It's simple, William. You have to leave me here."

"No! They'll kill you!"

She nodded. "Tomorrow. In front of everyone. Like he tried to do over ten years ago."

"And you want me to just *leave* you here?"

She nodded again. A little of the old fire came back into her eyes. "Yes."

"No!"

"Yes! Listen to me. No, just listen. If you try to rescue me, it'll be pitched battle at some point—you can't get around it. And you'll lose. You don't have the numbers. The Ëan will die, and the Governor will win. But if you let me go, you can finish the plan. Go get the King. Free Belond. Make everything right."

"No! Do you think everything could be right without you?"

"I don't matter! I never did! It was only Belond."

"You *are* Belond, *ona*. You are the heart and soul of us. You. Not me, not the *Ëan*, not the *Reben*, not the people. You. If you die, it doesn't even matter anymore what happens to us."

"I think you're biased."

"No, I'm not! Do you think the *Ëan* can go on without you?" He couldn't believe this!

"Yes! William, if I die, don't make me die knowing my entire *life* was a failure. I don't mind dying if you carry on for me. Then it means something."

"Any one of the *Ëan* would die for you. We'll fight."

"I won't let you! The price is too high! I'm not worth more than the rest of you."How many lives for my life, William? And it can't succeed!

"You'd do it for any one of us."

"That's different."

"How? You'll sacrifice yourself for everyone else but no one can sacrifice for you? Do you think the *Ëan* can keep fighting knowing we let our *ona* die? It goes against the oaths we took, against everything we are!"

"Yet I'm asking it of you," she said firmly. "You also swore to follow my lead, *kosatona*."

His jaw tightened.

"Please, William—I don't want to argue with you. This may be the last time we ever see each other."

That was the single most frightening thing anyone had ever said to him.

"Please, just promise me—you'll let me go." She was really crying. She held out her arms through the bars.

He couldn't be angry at her, not now. He hugged her, crying himself now.

She winced.

"I'm sorry—you're hurt, I forgot!" He pulled quickly away. "Dero, can you help?"

Dero gave a quick nod. He'd stayed back to give them space, but he moved close now. "Move a little closer, *ona*," he said gently. He examined the wound, which was still bleeding. He poured a little water, smelling of herbs, onto it. She flinched, stifling a cry.

Dero didn't look pleased with his work. His face was tense. "Sorry, *ona*. Little more." She nodded.

He tried to clean it, removing the cloth she'd put there. He had her slide up her pants so he could get a better look at it. It was hard, painful work for her, but she did.

"I don't like it," he said. "No herb's going to stop this for long. It needs to be stitched, but if I do it here, it'll get infected for sure. It may be too late for that already. But if I don't, you may bleed to death."

"Stitch it," she said unhesitatingly.

Dero looked her in the eye. "Are you sure, *ona*? I don't have anything to give you—it'll hurt."

"Doesn't matter. I can handle it. Stitch it."

He sighed. "All right." He pulled a small bundle out of his belt, which contained healers' necessities. He threaded a needle. "Give her some water, William," he said. That done, Dero sprinkled some herbs on the wound. She moaned.

"You have to stay still *ona*," Dero warned.

She nodded.

"William—hold her hand, hold her down with the other."

He nodded. His gut wrenched as he watched Dero begin.

She was brave. She never screamed, though her face contorted with pain and she squeezed his hand so hard he thought it might break. Once or twice, he thought she was close to fainting.

Then it was done. "Sorry," Dero apologized. He was sweating. It had been hard for him through the bars of a jail cell.

She breathed hard, nodding. "I'm okay," she mumbled. She let go of William's hand.

Dero rubbed some salve on her bruises. That done, he packed up his things, wiping the blood off his hands onto his shirt.

Ria regained her composure. "You should go," she said with a sniff. She was trying hard to be brave, like the *ona* was supposed to be. "They'll change the guard soon."

He just looked at her. He couldn't leave her here.

"I love you," she offered.

He hugged her again. "I love you, too."

"It's okay, William. Don't let this ruin you. Trust El."

If El was just, she would not be here now. How could she say that?

"Lead the Ëan for me. Tell them I love them. They will not understand. Do you promise?"

He nodded.

"Then go, William. And forgive me."

He pulled her close and kissed her through the bars. "You know I do," he said.

She smiled sadly at him. "Then go."

She pushed him away.

He gave her one last long look and sprinted away, feeling hollow.

In the tunnel a few minutes later, he broke down.

He sank against the wall and sobbed, unable to hold back. Dero put his arms around him and sat with him, but what could he say? There *was* nothing to say.

Chapter 47

William picked his head up. He felt his mind stiffening into an iron-hard resolve. He'd already decided what to do, but now he needed to figure out how to do it.

Please, El, he pleaded silently, *if you're there, if you care at all, help me. Please. I need help right now.*

He felt nothing tangible. No words, no lightning sensations, but somehow, he managed to get to his feet.

"What are we going to do?" Dero asked quietly.

He grimaced. He felt strangely calm now, almost detached. His emotion had run its course. He had nothing left but reason.

"We have to find the Ëan," he said wearily. He moved to the horses. Blazer nuzzled him sympathetically. He mounted. "Let's ride."

"I'll follow you," Dero promised, but he meant more than just that moment.

William nodded his thanks, then they started off.

They met Szera and Ovan on the road. They'd sent Lagan to help Torhan.

"Where is she?" Szera demanded angrily. "Did you see her?"

"Yes," answered Dero.

"Why didn't you get her out?" she asked incredulously.

"We couldn't get the key. The Governor has it."

Szera looked ready to explode. "Then let's get it! They've never caught any of us before! We can't leave her there! They'll torture her terribly and then kill her!"

"They *are* going to kill her." William said dully. "Tomorrow morning. Public execution."

"We have to get her out!" Ovan exclaimed. "William!"

"We can't. It's impossible."

Szera's jaw dropped.

"She's asked us not to rescue her," he added.

"*What?* She did *what?*"

"You're just giving up on her?" Ovan spluttered. "We can't do that!"

"I'm *not*," he countered fiercely. "I have a plan. Not a great one, not even a good one. But it's the only option there is for me—for us."

"What is it?" Szera demanded. They were all looking at him.

William summarized it briefly for them. When he was finished, they all looked as grim as he did.

"You're right," Ovan agreed. "It's the only way."

Szera nodded.

"We have to talk to the *Ëan*," William said. "I'll have no one follow me who does not do so of his own free will."

Szera gave him an *Ëa*'s salute. Ovan did the same, then Dero.

"We will," Szera said firmly.

He knew how much they were honoring him. He was the only leader they had right now, and they would be loyal to him.

"Thank you. Now let's go."

A short while later, a huge crowd was gathered on the Gnomi Road. Every single *Ëa* was there—a first time occurrence. It made them feel the *ona*'s loss more keenly. Also, Tiran and a large number of his men were present, one or two sailors, and a few of the more influential *Reben*. They were all clamoring in distress, if not panic.

William called above the noise. "Listen to me!" he cried. He stood on Blazer's back (a precarious position, but Blazer held very still for him).

They quieted remarkably quickly, all eyes fixing on him.

He prayed for the words. These were his friends, but this was not an easy thing he was asking. They might die if they followed him, a chance the *ona* never took for anyone but herself.

"You all know what's happened, and what it means. Whatever we do, it is the end of the *Ëan* as we know it." Murmurs.

"The *ona* has asked us not to rescue her," he said.

Outcry. "No!" everyone said.

"Listen! She told me to tell you that she loves you—all of you. She is not willing to risk open battle for her own sake. The *Ëan* have never dared it because of our numbers. She believes we cannot fight without being destroyed—which is the end for Belond."

There was much truth in this. Which was right? It was not a clear choice.

"But I say that the death of the *ona is* the end of Belond," he declared.

The *Ëan* cheered this. They loved the *ona* more than anything in the world. This was what they wanted to hear him say.

"So we are faced with this choice, friends. To fight, or to hide? In considering, I ask you to remember your oaths. We swore to obey the *ona* in every command, but we also swore to give our lives for our brothers and sisters. Whatever we do, we break faith; we fail the *ona*.

"I for one, cannot obey the *ona* in this. I am going against her orders. I know in my heart I am right.

"I do not ask any of you to follow me. It is your choice, each of you."

It did not take long. One by one, the *Ëan* raised their weapons. The Tellorian guard saluted in unison. If he went into battle, they'd be right at his side. The *Reben* stepped forward, too.

Szera spoke for them. "We are yours, *kosatona*," she said quietly. "We will defy the *ona* to save her. We will follow you."

"Aye!" shouted the assembly.

Pride welled in him.

"Then we have work to do. We will have an army to wade through tomorrow. We need an army.

"Torhan, Szera, Ekata—are there any other warriors

among the Djorn?"

"No," Torhan replied. "But...we have other ways of fighting. I will go to them."

"Pat—can any of the *Reben* be mobilized quickly?"

The old foreman who'd once disliked him now answered smartly. "Per'aps two hundred, *kosatona*. But it'll take time."

"We have no time. We have until morning."

Pat nodded. "Yessir."

"Tiran—"

"The Guard is behind you, my lord," the captain said.

"Good. And...we need to rally every animal that will help us."

"We're still out-numbered—badly," Szera said.

"It'll be enough. Now, listen. This is what we will do."

Chapter 48

The day dawned cold and blustery. The wind howled fiercely with an angry voice. The sky was overcast with a hint of snow in the air, but as yet nothing had fallen.

In truth, it was not so bad for the Ëan's needs. The heavy cloaks they would be wearing to disguise themselves would not seem so out of place.

The Governor's men had spent most of the morning turning every man, woman, and child in Belond out of their homes and driving them to the square. The Governor wanted to use today to crush any future possibility of rebellion. The Ëan had joined the crowd, slowly and subtly filtering in. By ten o'clock, everyone was there.

William stood near the front of the crowd. The Governor's men had set up a platform that was practically on the dock, so the crowd faced the sea. It was shoulder to shoulder—there were *thousands* of people here. William stood beside Szera, Ovan, and Tiran.

The *ona* had not yet been brought out, but anyone could feel the distress of the crowd. The people were subdued, the fear in their hearts tangible. They knew what this victory of the Governor's would mean for them: no more protection, no more food—just oppression and death.

Then the crowd rippled at the back.

"She's coming," Ovan whispered.

The crowd parted. "Make way!" shouted Benjen, riding in first on a large horse. He was followed by Captain Zoc, about twenty soldiers, then the Governor, flanked by four men.

Following them was Baër, walking alone. Angry calls went up at the sight of him, but he looked only angry, as he ever had. William clenched his fists, but he kept his head down. Baër would give them away if he saw them.

Then Ria.

The crowd murmured in shock and anger. She was weak

with pain, and she could hardly walk. They'd been cruel to her; fresh welts had appeared on her skin. There seemed not an inch of her that was not bruised or bloody. She was surrounded by twenty guards, her hands tied in front of her. She would hardly have had the strength to fight off even one man.

Looking at her, William felt sick, his heart like lead.

Szera clenched her fists. "I'll kill them," she growled softly. "I'll kill every one of those—" She used a word William would not have repeated.

"Wait," William whispered. "On the signal, you can."

The crowd was of like mind with Szera. Their voices rose to shouts, and they pushed against the barrier of the soldiers, shaking their fists. For a moment, William worried that they would riot—and that was not what he would have planned. Then the *ona* shouted, her rough voice carrying above the clamor. "Peace!" she cried to the crowd. One of the guards in front of her turned back and struck her across the face. The crowd shouted louder, but the *ona* ignored the blow and shouted again, "Stand down!" The guard struck her again, this time with the end of his spear. But her voice carried enough authority that the people drew back from the soldiers at her command.

The Governor walked up the platform steps. He took a seat imperiously in a chair on the right side. Zoc stood behind him to the left, hand on his sword. The soldiers took up positions around the platform. The entire crowd was surrounded by rows of soldiers. Every one of *them* was there, too. William grimaced. It would be hard to get through their ranks.

"They suspect we'll make an attempt at a rescue," Ovan whispered.

"Of course they do. It's the *ona*! They know we visited her. We couldn't get her out of prison."

"They heard the rumors about *you*," Ovan said.

"Me?"

"A dozen people saw you kill those soldiers and rescue

the *ona* during the fire. They know there's a *kosatona* out here somewhere. He's nervous."

"Then we'll give him good reason to be," William said.

Ovan nodded.

They dragged Ria up. William was close enough to see her face. The only expression she showed was defiance, but he knew her better. He could see the fatigue and pain behind her eyes. They tied her hands to a pole in the middle of the platform, forcing her to kneel. They would beat her to death, as they tried to do a decade ago.

The crowd murmured angrily, but they could do nothing against the hundreds of soldiers amassed against them.

"C'mon," William muttered. "Where are they? We need the signal."

"Be patient," Tiran urged. "Don't ruin your plan by rushing into things."

The Governor rose.

The hair on the back of William's neck stood up. He hadn't seen the Governor this close in months. The usurper wore a malicious, triumphant smile. This was the best day of his life. He'd fought this woman as long as he'd been in Belond, and lost at every turn. Today was the first time he had defeated her—their last fight.

"Good people—loyal citizens!" the Governor shouted. The crowd quieted immediately, dwindling to the silence of fear.

"Save your breath, snake," Szera snarled. "Liar. As if they were loyal to *him*."

"Shh," William told her.

"We come together today on a day of victory!"

William watched him, repulsed, but also fascinated. The Governor had the sort of charisma that held a crowd. Despite his obvious evil, the way he made his speech reminded William of... Ria.

How had this Whitefeld, Lis's brother, fallen so far?

"Today is a blessed day! We are now near the end of lawlessness and rebellion in Belond. Be at ease, citizens.

Today, we make you safe from the predation of outlaws like this *Auria*. The insurrection of this woman is today at an end."

A few brave souls cried aloud in protest, unable to keep silent. It was impossible to tell who it was. Zoc's eyes narrowed. William put a hand on his sword, hidden beneath his cloak, but no soldiers moved into the rebellious crowd.

"Silence!" the Governor cried, anger tinging his voice, but it smoothed almost instantly. "We will no more allow any rebellion against the justice of the government. Let today serve as an example to you, citizens, of what befalls those who challenge the established authority of Edenia! Justice must be served!"

He raised a hand. "So be it! Long live Edenia, and long live the King!"

Lord Whitefeld's inclusion of the King sickened William. It was the most disgusting lie he had ever heard. He dared dishonor the name of the King?

The Governor sat down.

"C'mon," William murmured desperately. His companions looked nervous, too.

"Let us begin the—" he stopped.

"Yes," William whispered.

He looked to the sky.

The Governor stared.

Every bird in Belond, from eagle to sparrow, was descending upon them in a dense black cloud. They were led by the king of them all, Talon. The birds hovered above them, blocking out the sky.

The Governor gestured frantically to his executioner. He looked fearful now, losing the confidence he'd had a moment ago. The executioner just stared, holding his whip. The Governor stood up again, waving his arm angrily at the executioner.

"Stop!" William shouted, his voice loud in his own ears.

The birds went silent. Every whisper of the crowd disappeared. All eyes roved for the source of his voice.

He saw Ria. Just a glimpse. Time slowed down.

Her eyes found him. She pleaded with him silently, her mouth moving without sound. *No. Please, no.* She shook her head, just the tiniest movement.

He had one last chance to turn back.

"Get me up," he said to Tiran and Ovan. They raised him wordlessly and set him standing upon their shoulders. He threw back his cloak and hood, revealing who he was.

"Lord William!" the crowd gasped.

The Governor looked right at him, fixing him with a glare of absolute hatred. They were on the same level now, scarcely thirty feet apart. William met his gaze with sterner eyes.

"I am William Tellor, *Ëa kosatona*," he cried aloud to the crowd. "And I will stand aside no more."

"William Tellor," the Governor spat. "I knew it would come to this, you traitor."

William did not answer. He gestured to Tiran and Ovan, and they turned him so he faced the crowd.

"Belond!" he shouted. "How long will you suffer oppression? How long will you stand by and watch as your freedom is stolen? No more, I say! *Justice?* There is no *justice* here! Belond will never have justice unless we rise up and take it! Stand up, Belond! Fight! We must fight!"

The crowd roared. The common people were already charged. This was as far as they could be pushed. They had had enough. A fight was what they wanted.

"Fight!" William repeated. "For the *ona*, for Belond, for Edenia!"

The response was deafening. It was working!

"My lord!" Tiran cried. A moment later, he found himself falling from their shoulders. Tiran caught him. The arrow aimed for his head sailed uselessly over the crowd.

"Thanks," he mumbled to the captain.

"To arms, men!" Zoc was shouting. All around, the hundreds of soldiers drew their weapons.

"Ëan!" William cried. The Ëan, the *Reben*, and the Guard drew theirs. The common people drew pitchforks, staffs, knives, anything they had. A surprising number had swords—

the work of the Governor's traitorous smiths.

A dreadful stand-off followed. Silence reigned, neither side sure.

Then William began to sing the battle song of the Ëan. Slowly, slowly, the people joined in. A minute later, every voice willing to stand for freedom was singing. The air reverberated with the sound.

Then Zoc shouted, and battle was joined.

It was unlike anything William had ever experienced. He'd planned everything, but it went beyond anything he could have pictured.

Time seemed to slow down again as he moved through the battlefield. He looked around him.

Who said they had no army?

From the sides, the Ëan and the commoners were taking the soldiers. The *Reben* cut a path through to the south, holding it open for a stream of women and children to escape. From above, the birds descended. From the west, flying down from the mountain, dozens of forest creatures attacked the outside of the ring, led by Luna the wolf. Then the strangest thing: the Djorn.

There were about a dozen, standing empty-handed far on the fringes. They had joined the song, but in their own language, which had curious effects. Any plant nearby sprang up with violence, some appearing out of nowhere. Vines and branches strangled the soldiers as they fought. It was the strangest thing he'd ever beheld, and one of the most terrifying.

Only one thing was out of place.

The Tellorian Guard, instead of aiding the Ëan as ordered, surged to the front, flanking *him*.

"Tiran!" he protested.

"You cannot die," Tiran said simply. "That is our duty."

William had no time to argue. "*Kosatona!*" Szera called, pointing. She was trapped in battle on the outside, now, fighting beside Dero. Most of the guards surrounding the platform had joined the battle, Baër beside them. He saw

Szera rush at the traitorous *Ëa*, then he turned to where she'd pointed.

He had no time to waste. They still had to save the *ona*.

He pushed through to the platform. The soldiers left had formed a wall of men around it, impenetrable.

"No," William growled to himself. Nothing was going to stop him reaching her, not now.

He rejoined the song, his voice swelling with the strength of the words. Then he rushed at the enemy.

He fought like a madman. He *had* to reach her. There was no room for failure.

He used knives, saving the sword until he had more room. He plowed through a crowd of soldiers, fighting his way up the steps. "Hold on, Ria!" he called when he got a glimpse of her. He shoved aside a soldier, and Tiran dispatched him. In the brief space he'd gained, he threw both knives toward Ria, one splitting her bonds and the other thudding into the pole. Now she would not be entirely defenseless.

The gap closed. He drew his sword, growling with frustration. There were too many! He couldn't get through fast enough.

Then, as he watched, the tide shifted.

His guards, faithful as always, stormed to his rescue. They pressed against the men on the platform, throwing themselves heedlessly into the fight.

It was beautiful but terrible to watch. William couldn't look around without seeing one of them fall. But they were moving forward. He reached the top of the platform, Tiran and Ovan on his heels.

Their way to Ria was barred by Zoc. "I don't think so," the grim captain growled.

William lifted his sword to engage him, but he had no time. Ovan and Tiran, captains themselves, placed themselves in front. The brothers took on Zoc, calling to William, "Go!"

He ran for Ria, leaving them. He knew even the two of them would have a hard time with Zoc, but he had no choice.

"Ria!" He rushed to her. She was on the ground, holding

his knives, but she couldn't rise. He reached for her.

Her eyes widened suddenly, fixed somewhere behind him. He had no time to turn.

"No!" she screamed, shoving him sideways before he could react. The movement cost her a groan of agony. He landed hard on his back on the platform, his head smacking against the boards with an audible crack.

He shook his head, dazed. Spots danced before his eyes. He had trouble thinking clearly, and he knew he was close to blacking out.

Ria had found the strength to stand, and now she stood over him, arms upraised, knives crossed to block the Governor's sword.

He'd have died if she hadn't pushed him aside.

He moaned, trying to clear the fog from his mind. He had to get up. He had to get up.

The Governor taunted her. "I should've known you'd be sweet on him," he sneered. "And what good has it done either of you? You can't save him, sweetheart, and he can't save you. You're done for, girl," he gloated. "Your hero has fallen. Your Eagles failed to save you."

"I'm not finished yet," she growled. It was amazing she could even stand. How long could she resist him? William made another effort to rise and nearly blacked out.

"You've failed. All this—did you think it would do any good? It's a massacre, *ona*." He spat her title. "You're just a child. Belond is mine—and always will be. You're all going to die."

"*Some things never die*," she said quietly.

Then she attacked him.

Get up! his mind screamed at him. But he couldn't. His vision was still spotty. His head throbbed.

They fought. The *ona* put everything she had into the fight, ignoring her wounded leg and bruises. She needed every bit of her skill. The Governor was the best swordsman he'd ever seen, easily. But this was Auria. She'd slaved for eleven years to be the best—for right now, when she was hurt and weak.

She led the Governor away from William. They fought in the corner of the platform, metal clanging against metal.

She needed help. She couldn't hold out long. *Get up!* He *couldn't*. His head wouldn't stop spinning, and his vision flashed in and out.

She was singing.

The Governor screamed with rage. He pressed her hard.

Then he punched her on her wounded leg. She screamed—a horrible, wrenching sound. He threw her to the ground, but she kept a grip on her knives. She blocked his next blow and rolled up into a kneeling position, but she had no time to stand before she had to block his knives again. He put all his force into pushing past her crossed knives, their blades trapped together. Ria's arms shook, but she did not yield.

"No!" William whispered. He sat up, but he had to stop there, clutching his spinning head as he nearly passed out again.

The Governor's face knotted with anger. "What now, Karia?" he snarled, still pushing his sword against her knives with every ounce of his strength. "I should have killed you sixteen years ago when I had the chance. Now I will remedy that."

William groped for his sword. He couldn't reach it. He pulled out the dagger in his belt, the one he'd carried that night they'd rescued Dero.

"I win, after all," he said to her. "I killed your father. Now I will kill you."

Her face was twisted in pain, but she looked him in the eye. "I am not afraid. I spent my whole life hating you. Enough. Let it be over. Kill me. It doesn't matter. You can't kill what I've created. You *will* fail.

"You took my father from me, and I've never been able to forgive you. I don't forgive, Governor. But if I die, I want to die free. So, I forgive you. And I pray El forgives you, too."

He growled at her. "Save it, girl," he replied. "El means

nothing. *He* won't save you, either."

"Yes, he has."

He screamed at her. "You will rot in hell, child, like all of us!" he shouted.

He kicked her in the stomach, breaking the stand-off as she reeled backward. With a gleeful laugh, he moved to stab her through the chest.

"No!" screamed William. He summoned every ounce of his willpower.

He threw the dagger like he'd done it a thousand times before.

It landed with a sickening crunch in the Governor's back. He gasped. He looked down at the blade's tip, protruding from his chest. Blood spurted from the wound.

He turned around, looking at William in stunned amazement. Then his face hardened into a cruel smile. "I… still… won," he wheezed. Then he collapsed, dead.

Elation flooded William. It was over! They'd won! Without the Governor, the usurpation was over.

Then it faded away, replaced by horror.

Before he'd died, the Governor had thrust his sword into Ria's chest.

Chapter 49

"Ria!" he screamed. He stumbled to her side, heedless of anything else.

The sword had missed her heart, but it had pierced all the way through her shoulder just beneath her collarbone. It still stood there, an awful shadow. He left the horrible thing untouched, knowing better than to try to remove it himself.

He leaned over her. "Ria!"

Her eyes fluttered, and she moaned.

Alive.

"Ria! Can you hear me?"

"I can hear you, love," she whispered.

"I'm sorry—I'm an idiot. This is all my fault!"

She reached a hand up to touch his face.

"Can you forgive me? I disobeyed you—and you were right! I failed! I'm so, so sorry!"

She smiled faintly. "No... *You* were right. That's why I love you—you always do... the right thing in the end."

"But... I failed you."

"No. I fought, William. I fought him. We all fought. You were right. It worked."

"I disobeyed you."

"I knew you would."

"You did?"

"Yes. It was written plain as day on your face last night." She was smiling at him. He smiled weakly back through his tears. "I forgive you—all of you. Tell them for me." Her eyes were fastened on his, but her voice was fading. "I love you," she said softly. He was losing her. She'd lost too much blood.

"No! No, stay with me! Just hold on. You *can't* die."

She lost consciousness.

He looked up, wildly searching for help. From anyone.

Then he realized.

The battle was over.

The dead lay everywhere. Peasants, *Reben*, guards, *Ëan*, soldiers. It was a blood-bath. Ria had predicted it.

Not even half of those he'd brought were alive.

The soldiers, those few left, had surrendered. They knew they had lost. With the Governor dead, they were finished. The deception was over. Their weapons were thrown to the ground, their hands over their heads. They stood ranged about the square, perhaps a hundred of them only.

Everyone was utterly silent, staring toward the platform, in shock and horror. They all saw that the *ona* had fallen.

William looked from face to face, from distant to near. There were too few! He felt his heart would break.

"Dero!" he screamed when he found his friend. A twinge of relief surged through him at seeing Dero alive, but it could not completely alleviate his panic. "I need help!"

Dero was jarred from his shock. He sprinted for the platform. Szera ran too. Somewhere, a horse bolted for the outskirts of Belo—he thought it might have been Blazer.

Dero reached him. He took some herbs from his belt and forced them down her throat. "She's too weak," he choked in frustration. He pointed to her leg, adding, "And her leg's already infected."

The wound was red and swollen. How could she have stood on it? Szera cursed, a tear tracing her cheek. "Come on, *Vitha*," her voice whispered.

El, please. Please.

Ekata reached them. She had a scrape on her forehead but was otherwise unhurt. "Dero, go to the others," she said to him. "You might save some." Her voice was steely calm, but her lip was trembling. Dero touched her shoulder, then he ran off reluctantly.

Ekata examined Ria. Her hands shook, which William had never seen from her.

She flexed her hands to still the tremor. She moved to pull the sword, but her eyes spelled clearly that she could not save her.

"Wait," a voice said.

Yewul walked quickly to them, followed by Hlein. Blazer stood by the steps.

"Grandfather," Ekata said with relief.

"Go, now, child. Hlein and I will tend her. Save the others."

Ekata ran back into the square.

"Can you save her?" William asked desperately.

Yewul looked very grave. "I can only hope, my son. Now stand aside. The Ëan need you, *kosatona*. The people need you. You can do no more for *Vitha*."

He knew Yewul was right, but it was hard to tear himself from her. Now, of all times.

"Come," Szera said, pulling him up. "Leave her to Yewul."

He nearly fell, dizzy. The back of his head throbbed.

Szera caught him. "Steady there, *kosatona*."

"Thanks." His head cleared, if slowly. He managed to stumble away.

He did not go far.

"Tiran," he breathed. He rushed to the captain's side.

Zoc lay dead, but Tiran was dying beside him. Ovan sat at his brother's side, holding his hand and talking softly to him.

"You must finish your duty," Tiran told Ovan weakly. "I have done mine, brother. Are you... did I make you proud?"

"Yes, Tiran. No man was ever prouder of his brother. You've done well," Ovan replied firmly.

"Tiran," William said, kneeling beside Ovan.

"My lord! You are safe?"

"Yes, Tiran, I'm fine," William assured him.

Tiran smiled through bloody lips. "Good," he murmured. "Then I have not... dishonored my King."

"No—no! You can't die for me!"

"That was my duty," Tiran reminded him. He smiled wider, his eyes warm.

Then he was gone.

Ovan crossed his brother's arms over his chest, sword in his hand. "Be at peace, Captain of the Guard," he murmured.

William felt numb with horror.

Ovan slung an arm around William's shoulder. "He died with honor, William," he said thickly, his voice shaky. "They all did. They knew what this would mean."

"The Guard—they're *all* dead?"

"I am the only one," Ovan said sadly. "My duty is yet unfinished."

William stared in shock.

Ovan touched his shoulder. "There will be a time to grieve, *kosatona*. Now we must do our duty."

He rose and went wordlessly down to the square.

It was horrible. He knew these faces, staring blankly up at him. Guards. Elix. Hart. Pharin. Pav. *Reben*. Pat. Cob. Peasants. Lam. Lath. Robairt and Ellairt. And the *Ëan*.

Perhaps twenty *Ëan* had been killed. Just what the *ona* hadn't wanted. She'd have died a thousand times rather than let one of them come to harm.

Lagan. Ennor. Grayem. Joff. Allain. Kerran.

Kerran! He'd just married his sweetheart! They'd had only days!

He felt like collapsing again. He couldn't face this.

But he kept going. The *Ëan* who were living needed him more than those who were dead.

If this was victory, they could not celebrate it.

He touched those he passed with a gesture of sympathy. They were grieving, too. "Courage," he told them, though he could hardly muster the strength to comfort them. "Honor their sacrifice."

A group of the *Ëan* were guarding those who had surrendered. They looked to him for direction. "Take them to the prison," William told them.

Then began the flurry of the aftermath. The *ona* was gone. He was the leader. Everyone came to him with questions. Where to take the wounded. What to do with the dead. Food and water. How to root out civilians loyal to the Governor. Where to house displaced families. How to return stolen property to its old owners. When the *Reben* could come back to Belo. He labored tirelessly, though he'd had no sleep or food. He kept at it, though the whole while, his heart was with Ria.

That night, Ovan came to find him. "*Kosatona.*"

"What? Is the—"

"You need to rest, William."

"We're not done; I have to—"

"We won't be done for weeks, William. Most of us have had a rest—but you've been going all day, and you should see a healer, anyway. Come, now."

William let Ovan persuade him. He gave in. "All right. Where are we going?"

"To the Felds. It's where you sent the wounded. Plenty of room."

He voiced the question he was so afraid to ask, but was burning in his mind. "Do you know how the *ona* is?"

"I don't know. I haven't seen her."

A new energy took over William. "Will you take me to her?"

"You go. I'll take over for you."

He nodded gratefully. "Thank you, Ovan."

Ovan nodded back. He called to William's horse. Blazer picked his way over to them carefully. William pulled himself wearily into the saddle. He knew now how the *ona* must have felt at times as their leader. He hadn't slept since yesterday morning, and he felt more tired than he had in his entire life.

He left Ovan and rode for the Felds.

It was strange to enter the house again—at least, through the door. It was a bustle of activity. Every healer on the island was in this house. It was a place transformed. He hardly recognized it.

He found Lis running bandages to someone's room. "Mother!" he called.

"William!" She forgot her errand and slammed into him with a hug. "Oh, my darling!" She kissed his cheek, clinging to him with relief.

"Mother, where's Ria?" he asked urgently.

Lis looked sadly at him. "She's not good, dear—they

won't even let *me* see her."

"Who's 'they'?"

"Yewul and Hlein. They've been with her all day. They moved her here a few hours ago. I'm worried. I'm really worried."

"Where is she?" he repeated.

Before Lis could answer, Dero saw him. "William! Are you all right?"

William nodded. "Have *you* gotten rest?"

"I slept a little, but I'm okay." He didn't look it. He looked tired and sad.

"What about Ekata?"

"She won't rest."

"Tell her I said to. We need her well."

Dero nodded. He paused, studying William, then he said, "I'll take you to the *ona*."

"Thank you."

She was upstairs, away from most of the others, where it was quieter. "In here," Dero said softly.

He knocked lightly.

"Who is it?" Hlein's voice asked.

"Let William in," Yewul said unhesitatingly. He sounded calm and unwearied.

Dero nodded to him. William gripped his arm briefly, then stepped inside.

What he saw made him want to cry.

She lay on her side, wearing a plain, loose dress that went to her knees. They were changing the bandage on her leg, which was angry, red, and swollen. Her shoulder was wrapped all around with white bandages. Her body was covered all over with bruises. Her skin was deathly pale, and she was sweating. She was turning her head restlessly, but she was not awake.

"How bad?" he asked.

Yewul looked gravely at him. "We were able to pull the sword without her bleeding to death, but now it is the other wound that is giving the trouble. The infection has spread into her blood, and after she has lost so much of it. She is very weak to be fighting such a fever. Dero did well to stitch her leg—she would have died otherwise—but it has made things difficult now. She will probably still die, *kosatona*."

He sat forlornly beside her bed. He took her hand. "C'mon, Ria," he whispered.

She sighed in her sleep. She relaxed, just a little, not tossing her head anymore.

"You calm her," Yewul commented. "It is good you are here."

William nodded weakly.

"Hlein," Yewul said, "ask one of the helpers to bring the *kosatona* some food, please."

William spent the whole night there, falling asleep still holding her hand, slumped over the bed.

This became his pattern. During the day, he labored to restore Belond. Each night, he came to Ria and sat with her. She did not wake, fighting a losing battle with her illness. They saw no improvement from her, just the same burning fever, gray skin, and restless sleep. Every day, the people asked him how she was, and each day, he answered, "I don't know."

They only needed time, and then they would know.

Chapter 50

The days after the battle passed in a blurry frenzy. William worked himself to exhaustion, but it all seemed unreal to him. All his thoughts were bent on the Felds and the occupant of that house. Honestly, despite all they did, he remembered very little of the restoration of Belond.

The *Ëan*, together with any that could fight, led the search for the traitors who served the Governor amongst the people, the overseers and usurpers. These joined the soldiers in the prison. The property they'd stolen was returned to those it had originally belonged to, but he was not declaring judgments on the offenders. That needed the authority of an Edenian-appointed Governor.

Despite the snowfall, the *Reben* came pouring back into Belo. Many took back homes from the ousted traitors, or began planning new houses to build. Before long, the Nest was completely empty.

The healers worked busily day and night to save those they could, but all too many lay dead. Every person who'd died in the battle—man, woman, or child, *Ëa*, guard, *Rebe*, or commoner—was laid in a new plot outside Belo. Stoneworkers had been asked to make headstones for all of them as well as a monument commemorating the battle.

Each funeral rent William's heart unlike anything he'd ever felt. He fought with feelings of guilt, but he knew that dishonored them. They hadn't died for his sake. They'd made a decision and died for the *ona*, and for Belond, and for themselves. Though he wept each time they buried one of his brothers, he knew what they'd done was right.

In his heartsick state of mind, he later remembered only three things clearly.

The first was Betta and Dero.

She came with the other *Reben*, after the battle was well over. She was with Elénne and Hope.

They came to the Felds the night after the battle was over. William had just come back to see Ria, but he saw them come in.

Elénne ran for Dero, calling his name. He turned from his task to embrace her. "Hi, Énne," he said to her.

William just watched, not wanting to intrude.

Dero hugged Betta, too. "Dero, where's Kerran?" she asked. "I haven't found him yet."

For El's sake, had no one told her?

Dero couldn't speak. His mouth worked, but no sound came out. His sad eyes told the whole story.

A half-gasp, half-sob came from Betta's throat. Her hands flew to her mouth. "No," she groaned. Dero tried to hug her, to comfort her, but she flew at him, suddenly hysterical. "You promised me! You said he'd be all right!"

"I couldn't, I...he—"

Her hands flailed, and she punched his chest, shrieking and crying.

Elénne tried to pull her away. "Betta!" she scolded, none too gently. William started toward them, but Lis was there first.

"Easy, child," she said gently. She and Elénne pulled the hysterical Betta away from Dero. They took her away, casting sad glances back at Dero.

William hugged his friend. There was nothing else he could do.

"I wasn't ever to stop singing—that's what he told me," Dero said. "How do I sing now, William? I can't."

"I don't know, Dero. I don't know."

"I'm grateful," he said, but he sounded as if he was trying to convince himself. "I'm alive. Ekata's alive, you're alive. Belond is free, and it will soon be as it ought to be. Once the *ona* is well, we will all heal."

William smiled at him. "You always were the optimist."

Dero managed to smile. A tiny spark came back into his tired eyes. He nodded.

"Go see her," Dero told him, with a pat on the back. "I'll

be all right—and she needs you."

"Thank you," he replied. Dero smiled and left him.

A night later, as he sat by Ria's bedside, a sound drew his attention. He pricked up his ears.

It came from outside. He got up and looked out the window.

A whole crowd of people had assembled in the yard, beneath Ria's window. *Ëan*, *Reben*, villagers. They waved when they saw him. He waved back, smiling incredulously.

Dero was leading them. He beamed up at William.

William cracked the window, trying not to let a massive burst of cold air in.

"Sing for the *ona*!" Dero shouted to the crowd. They cheered.

They sang the song of the Ëan, the *ona*'s song.

It gave William hope, just a little.

He looked at Ria. She sighed in her sleep. Who could tell if she heard? But William's heart told him she did.

"Thank you," he mouthed to Dero. Dero just smiled.

They came every night to sing below her window. She never woke, but they prayed for her and believed in her, hoping beyond hope she would recover.

The second thing he remembered was Baër.

They'd captured him that first day. Szera had knocked the blackguard unconscious. Despite her bluster, she was reluctant to kill someone she'd fought beside for years.

When William had gone to inspect the prison, he inadvertently walked past Baër's cell.

He stopped, looking Baër in the eye. He thought of all the graves they'd made. He thought of Ria, lying in a fever, maybe never to wake up.

He wanted to fly at Baër, to hit him until he bled.

He walked away.

"I won, you know," Baër called after him.

William stopped but did not turn back.

"Now you can't have her, either. And I have revenge."

His voice was eerily like Zoc's.

"It's not me you hate, Baër," William growled without turning. "It's her. It's a good thing she's a better person than me—she might actually forgive you."

"She doesn't forgive."

"She does now."

"It doesn't matter. She's dying. You couldn't save her. Some *kosatona* you are."

William couldn't affirm or deny it. He just walked away.

The third thing he remembered afterward was, oddly enough, Anjalia.

She'd stayed safely at home during the fighting, but soon enough, the Felds was no safe place. The healers ousted any protectors she might have retained, including Bailan, the late Governor's steward. The servants, for the most part, had happily given way for the Ëan's conquest. After a few days, almost none of them remained in the Felds, leaving it to the healers.

The only person who did not clear the house was Anjalia.

She locked herself into her room and barricaded the entrance. Whenever anyone tried to get in, she screamed like a madwoman, forcing them to give up or risk disturbing the sick. It was Lis that brought the situation to his attention. Ever kind-hearted, she was worried about the girl. Anjalia *was* her niece, and Lis had practically raised her, but she'd never received anything but condescension and rudeness from the girl.

Still.

"She must be starving in there—it's been days! Please, William, she's Seyenne's daughter, whatever else she may be."

"A person determines his own merit, not his parents, Mother. But all right, I'll see to her."

"Thank you."

Seeing to her meant breaking into her room one morning through the vents, carrying a sack of food.

When he emerged in her room, she was sitting in a chair staring out the window. He tapped her on the shoulder.

She screamed loud enough to raise the roof. He winced. She clawed at him like an animal.

He held her down. "Enough, Anjalia! I won't hurt you!"

Slowly, she stopped struggling, but she shook with fear. He began to actually feel sorry for her. It wasn't her fault she'd been caught up in her father's schemes.

"I brought you some food." She snatched the bag and tore into it with unladylike haste.

"You know," he told her while she ate, "you don't have to hide up here. No one will hurt you. You can come downstairs."

She shook her head. "Killers. Outlaws. Barbarians," she hissed. She looked small and timid. She was just a child.

"Do I look like a killer? I promise, Anjalia, no one will harm you. They're good people, all of them. You've lived a selfish life, but if you stop pretending you're better than everyone they might accept you. Come on." He extended his arm.

She wouldn't take it.

"Trust me."

Her eyes were wide with trepidation, but she put a hand on his arm. He cleared her pitiful barricade and led her out.

People stared at them downstairs. He saw Szera sneer with disdain and Anjalia quivered, but he delivered Lady Whitefeld straight to Lis.

Lis welcomed her with open arms. "Thank you, dear. I'll take care of her."

"You sure? Aren't you looking after Betta?" Lis had been struggling to help the grief-stricken young woman.

"I'll manage. Thank you."

As he walked away, he glanced back to see Anjalia's eyes linger on him, as if he was her protector. There wasn't an ounce of superiority in them at that moment.

Maybe nobles *could* change.

A week after the battle, William was in the village helping

organize food supplies when he heard someone shout his name.

"William!" It was Dero. He ran up breathlessly.

"What is it?" William asked urgently. Fear rose in him.

"The *ona*," Dero wheezed, bending over to catch his breath. Gasps and looks of horror appeared on the people nearby. Ovan's face fell. "She's—"

William didn't wait to hear more. He took off running for the Fields.

"No, wait!" Dero called after him, but he didn't stop. "Ah!" Dero cried in frustration, running after him, but William left him far behind.

If she was dead, he couldn't do this anymore. He couldn't face losing her.

He sprinted all the way to the house, drawing concerned looks from observers. He didn't care.

Up the stairs. To her room.

He didn't even knock.

He burst in, panting heavily. He expected the worst.

Ria laughed at him.

She was awake!

All the breath left him in one huge sigh of relief.

"Ria!" He rushed to her.

She was sitting up a little, propped up by pillows. She still looked feverish, but some of her color was back. Her shoulder and leg were still immobilized in bandages, but her bruises looked much better.

"Well, hello," she said to him. Her throat sounded hoarse, but she was smiling, and there was the old spark in her eye.

Right then, he knew she would heal. She was going to live.

He really did cry. "Ria," he repeated.

"She is doing much better," a tired Yewul said, with a twinkle in his eye. "But she will not be mended for a long while yet."

"Yewul is always cheerful," Ria said wryly. Her voice was faint, but it was relieving just to hear it.

William laughed, wiping his eyes. "I've been so worried about you," he confessed. "I'm sorry—if I'd been faster—"

"I still would have taken fever," she countered. "It's all right, William."

He kissed her forehead. She didn't resist him.

"Yewul won't tell me anything that's been happening," she complained.

"Oh, now I know you're better. For heaven's sake, you're not supposed to worry about it! You just woke up."

"Please? I'm dying of curiosity! I need to know what's been happening!"

"No," Yewul said firmly. "Let others bear the grief and toil. You've earned a rest, *ona*."

"A thousand times over," William agreed.

She sighed. "But...I want to see them. I'm the leader—I want to see them."

Dero interrupted by poking his head in. A huge grin was on his face, though he was breathing hard. "Hi, *ona*," he said. "You look wonderful! Now you're getting better, everything will be perfect!"

She just laughed hoarsely.

"I tried to tell you," Dero scolded William playfully, but his grin never wavered. "You didn't wait to listen. There was no need to panic."

"Sorry," he apologized.

"Anyway," he continued, still beaming, "you might want to look outside."

William tore himself reluctantly away from Ria and moved to the window.

The Felds no longer had a lawn.

A massive crowd had assembled, whispering and looking concerned. William's rush for the house had likely worried them.

He waved to them, and they all started pointing. He opened the window. "She's awake!" he yelled down. A huge cheer went up. William grinned.

He looked back at Ria. She was smiling wistfully.

"How are they?" she asked when he came back to her.

"They will be happy now that we have you back. But it has been hard."

She nodded. "Can I see them?" she asked.

"You are not getting up, *Vitha*," Yewul said firmly.

"Just to the window?"

"You cannot walk on that leg. Not for a long time yet, *Vitha*. And you need to rest! Your fever is down, not gone."

She sighed, looking to William. He couldn't deny her. He'd nearly lost her. He'd do anything for her now, and this was so small.

"Could I just carry her to the window?" William asked.

Yewul wavered. "You might hurt her," he protested weakly.

"I'll be careful. Please?"

"All right," the old Djor relented.

It was hard to find a way to lift her without straining either of her wounds, but they did their best. William picked her up with more care than he'd ever handled anything. She was lighter than she had once been weakened by her illness.

She squeezed her eyes tight shut a moment. She leaned her head weakly against his shoulder.

"You okay?" he asked, concerned. He nearly put her down.

"Dizzy," she explained, opening them again. "I'm okay now."

He brought her to the still open window. "The *ona!*" shrieked one villager when he saw her.

Pandemonium.

William thought he would go deaf.

She smiled weakly, waving her hand. They began to chant. "Ona, ona, ona."

"Thank you, William," she whispered in his ear. He kissed her lightly on top of her head.

After a minute or two, he brought her back to her bed and laid her down. Yewul replaced her blankets.

"Will you stay with me a while, William?" she asked.

"Of course," he agreed immediately.

"I know you're busy—covering for me."

"There's nowhere I'd rather be than here, Ria."

She smiled playfully. "You promised not to be sentimental, William. Remember?"

"Right. Sorry."

She laughed lightly.

Chapter 51

After she woke, William spent several hours each day with Ria. During those times he felt happiest, just being with her. She improved steadily, each day looking a little better. She started to be engaged in things again, giving him advice or instructions, but there were also times she'd relapse back into fatigue. Still, William knew she would be all right.

"I've been thinking," she told him when he came in one day.

"Uh-oh. You're not supposed to be doing that."

She made a face at him. "I've been thinking about the future."

"What a dreary subject," he joked. He couldn't help feeling cheerful.

"I'm serious! William, the sea opens in just a few weeks. The King still knows nothing about what's happened."

A twinge of guilt passed through William. Quite honestly, he'd forgotten about his father, even about Ossia. He hadn't been lying to Ria. All his thoughts were with her, and he didn't want to be anywhere else.

"He'll be worried sick about me," William realized. "And he needs to know Mother's alive."

"There is that, yes. But we also need to reestablish the Empire's presence in Belond. We need a new Governor."

"You—they'll choose you."

"I'm the *ona*—I'm not sure I'm suitable to be an Edenian Governor. I'm not qualified."

"They wouldn't follow anyone but you."

"There's you."

He looked more carefully at her. She was serious.

"No. I can't."

"*You* saved me, William. *You* killed the Governor. *You* overthrew the traitors. This was *your* victory, not mine. *You* did it."

"We did it. I'd have died if not for you. And do you honestly think they'd have followed me if it weren't for you?"

She nodded.

"No. *You're* the *ona*. I'm just the *kosatona*, Ria."

She sighed. "Well, I don't know, then. It's the King's decision, in the end. The people just approve his choice."

"Yes."

"William?"

"Yes?"

"You're going to have to go to him."

He'd been dreading leaving since he'd joined the *Ëan*. He looked away.

"He still needs to know what's happened. I'd trust no one better than you to tell him. And... he's your father. He needs to see his son."

He sighed. "I can't leave, Ria. I can't leave Belond. I can't leave you."

"By the time the ship sails, I will be well enough. And..." she looked him in the eye, "you'll come back."

"I'm not sure he'll let me," William confessed. "I can't bear the idea of going back to Ossia. Please, Ria, let Ovan take Lis."

"You need to go," she said firmly.

"This is my home," he pleaded. "Please!"

She touched his face. "I know, William." She sighed. "I don't want you to go, either."

"Then—"

"But it's the only choice. Think of your father, William. Don't throw away your family."

"The *Ëan* are my family. So are you."

"And we always will be. But your parents and your brother are, too."

He couldn't argue.

"We have time, William. Several weeks."

"That's not enough time."

"Just think about it, all right? That ship has to sail to the King as soon as possible, and I want you on it."

He nodded in resignation, but the thought of leaving weighed on him like a millstone.

"Can you teach me how to write?" Ria asked abruptly one day.

He was surprised. She hated asking people for help, let alone instruction.

"I guess—if you behave."

She grinned. "I will."

"Why do you want to learn?"

"Um... Well, I'm not an outlaw anymore, you know? I need to be more *civilized*, if I'm going to deal with Edenia."

"Mm-hm. You'll always be a vagabond at heart, *ona*. But all right."

He scavenged a slate and a piece of chalk from Lis's old school supplies. He brought them up to Ria's room.

He sat on the bed beside her. He couldn't help teasing her a little. "It seems you've learned to appreciate feather beds and pillows." He laughed and leaned back against her cushions.

She made a face at him. "I have no choice," she grumbled.

He laughed and pulled out the slate. "Okay," he began. "All the letters in the alphabet represent sounds, you know? And put together they make words."

She glared.

"Hey, I'm trying! Okay, fine. Moving on." He drew on the slate. "This is the letter a. It can be upper- or lower-case, but it's the same letter." He glanced at her. She was staring at him, not the slate. He blushed, fidgeting. "Do you want to do this or not?"

"Yes," she answered, shifting her eyes to his drawings.

"Okay. Next is b."

He went through each of the letters then had her copy them. She wasn't actually that bad, but she clearly was unfamiliar with the art.

"It just looks like meaningless lines," she complained.

"Now, maybe, but it'll get better."

She sighed, continuing to copy.

"No, not that way. Around, up, then down. Better."

They worked for a long time, then William had to leave. "Keep practicing if you want. I'll teach you more later."

"Okay." She gave him a quick kiss on the cheek before he left, to his surprise.

She laughed. "Go on, *kosatona*," she told him.

"But now I want to stay."

"Mm-mm. Go."

He laughed and left her.

She was practicing when he returned.

"Hey, not bad," he complimented.

She smiled. "Can I learn to write words, now?"

"We can try." He sat beside her and erased the slate.

"Let's try your name," he said.

"Which one?"

He laughed. "I don't know—which do you want?"

She shrugged her free shoulder. "Let's do your name," she countered.

"Okay," he agreed, smiling. "What does it start with?"

She considered. He loved that thoughtful expression of hers. "W," she decided.

"Right."

She wrote a 'w' on the slate.

"Then... i... l... y?"

"Two ls. No y."

She sighed. "Spelling."

"Mm-hm. I always hated spelling."

"I?" she asked. He nodded. "U?"

"A." That one sounds weird."

She wrote it. "M," she concluded.

"Right! Good."

She examined her work with a smile, retracing it lightly with her finger.

"More?"

She nodded.

"Can I go outside?"

"No, *Vitha!*" Yewul scolded. "It has just..." he thought for the word, "snowed." Another late spring snowfall. "You will be much too cold."

"No, I won't. Please?"

"You have not even left your bed yet."

"And I'm suffocating! It's been over two weeks, Yewul! I need air!"

"You cannot walk, *Vitha*. You must not overtax yourself."

"William can take me. Please, *ona*? Please?"

He sighed. Even he had a hard time saying no to her. Hlein stifled a smile.

"Yes!" she crowed before Yewul answered.

"Only a few minutes, *Vitha*." He gave William a warning look.

"Yes, sir," William replied quickly, blushing.

They enveloped Ria in warm garments that left only her face exposed. "Honestly," she complained, but Yewul wasn't letting her get cold.

William pulled his own winter cloak on and then picked her up, very carefully. "That all right?"

She nodded.

He took her downstairs, following a back route so as to avoid a commotion. A few people did see them, though, and they exclaimed their excitement. She was a bit embarrassed, but pleased, too. On the whole, though, William got her to the back gardens with little enough trouble.

"You don't mind carrying me, do you? I mean... I wouldn't want to ask anyone else."

"No, I don't mind, Ria. Of course not."

She smiled.

He cleared the snow from a bench with his foot and set her down on it, keeping her leg elevated.

"Mm," she sighed appreciatively. "I've missed the outside air."

He sat on the ground beside the bench, then leaned back

in the snow, looking up at the gray-blue sky. He remembered how much she'd hated the underground. No wonder she was itching for the outdoors.

"Is winter like this in Ossia?" she asked a little dreamily.

"Pretty close climate, actually. But the air is smokier in a city. I never liked being outside there."

"I remember," she laughed. "You and the forest didn't get along."

He gave a mock groan. "Don't remind me."

They were quiet a while, just enjoying the snow. The trees sparkled with ice, and the extensive gardens of the house glittered with snow cover. It *was* beautiful. He could hardly remember a time when he'd thought this island wasn't. Dangerous it may have seemed, but not an Isle of Death. Not anymore.

William was there the first time she walked.

Actually, she didn't have permission. Yewul was taking some rest, leaving her alone for a while. William came in as she was attempting to pull herself up.

"Ria!" he exclaimed, rushing toward her.

"Oh, come on," she grumbled. "Spoilsport."

"What on earth do you think you're doing?"

"Shh. You'll get Yewul back in here. I'm sick of lying in bed. Come on, help me up."

"No! You're not supposed to—"

She grabbed his arm for support and stood up. She winced, putting most of her weight on her good leg.

"Ria!" He held both her arms to steady her. "You okay?"

"Just fine, love. Just weak, is all. My muscles aren't used to this anymore. Doesn't hurt."

He gave a half-laugh, half-sigh. "You are the most stubborn woman I know."

"Is that why you like me?" she teased.

"I don't *like* you. I love you."

"Mm-hm. Come on, help me move."

"You shouldn't be—"

"Don't care. I'm done being ill, William. I'm getting up."

He had little choice but to help her. Leaning heavily on him, she hobbled around the room. She beamed, and he couldn't help smiling back.

A week later, she was walking without help. She retained a brace and a sling, but other than that, she was practically normal.

And, of course, back to work.

She and William worked together. He had to admit, it was better that way. She had qualities and insights he never would, while he balanced her ruthless practicality. Before long, Belo was completely free of its old oppressive system.

But they knew it was only temporary. They were an Edenian province. They needed Edenia.

Ria ordered preparations for a message to be sent to the King on their ship. The *ona* and *kosatona* didn't talk about it much, but it weighed on both of them.

Time ran out. Soon enough, it was time to sail.

Chapter 52

William couldn't believe he was leaving.
Lis could hardly wait to go. She was practically dizzy with excitement. She restrained her enthusiasm only because she knew William was feeling depressed.

There were to be quite a few passengers on this voyage. All the surviving sailors (about two dozen, including the captain) would, of course, have to attend them. William and Lis were to be accompanied by Ovan, who would not have had it any other way. Escorting Lis home safely had been the duty he'd been charged with sixteen years ago. Lis was also determined to take Anjalia with them. Honestly, William didn't want to deal with her simpering, girlish ways on this journey, but there was nowhere else for her to go. Lis planned to reform her character and make her into a lady. Personally, William did not think Ossia was the best place for that—Belond was a less comfortable environment. Besides, if anyone could transform a spoiled noble, it was Ria. Her firm hand had fixed *him* up. But Lis wanted the job, so that was that. In addition, she was taking charge of Betta. Lis had become a mentor for her and was trying to help her through her loss. It was actually Dero's idea for Betta to go with Lis. Much as he loved her, he wanted her to be happy. She'd lost too much in Belond to ever be happy there again. Maybe someday, he hoped. For her part, she was grateful for his understanding, and they made things right between them before parting. To complete the party, a few of the *Ëan* were coming along as well. They were the ship's protection: Rosie, Shac, and Winna (who was coming partly because of her niece). They were excited to go, if only for adventure's sake, as Rosie put it. Any of the *Ëan* would have gladly attended them, but no more could have been spared by the *ona*.

In short, William was the only one who didn't want to go.
Practically everyone turned out on the morning of their

departure to see them off. The main square was crowded to its limits. The day dawned cool but clear. The captain pronounced *The War Goddess*, as they had named the ship, ready to sail. They'd brought the ship over to the east side so they could weigh anchor from the town.

William was leading Blazer up the street to the dock. Everything was packed and ready, but he still couldn't believe this was happening. Now. He was out of time. This was the end.

"Goodbye, *kosatona*!" voices called from the crowd. "Thank you! Don't forget us! Safe journey! El be with you!" They made it sound as if he was never coming back. His heart felt like lead. He barely managed a weak smile in response to their shouts.

His feet dragged as slowly as they could, but too soon, he found himself on the dock. A sailor took Blazer's reins and brought the horse on board.

William alone was left of the passengers to say goodbye.

All the Ëan stood there on the dock. It was one of the hardest things he'd ever had to do, but he said goodbye to each of them. His family.

Elénne and Fred were there, with Hope, having just parted with Winna and Betta. William said a brief word to each of them, and he gave the crying Hope a quick kiss on the forehead.

Dero and Ekata. They'd just parted from Betta, too, so Dero was already emotional. "Take care of her, would you?" Dero asked.

"Of course."

"Thanks." Dero looked him in the eye, a weak smile on his face. Then Dero hugged him tight. "I know you'll come back, William," Dero told him. "Just make it soon. I'll miss you."

William almost smiled. "I will."

"We'll be waiting."

There was nothing else to say. They parted. William kissed Ekata quickly on the cheek, and then he moved on.

Szera. "Don't stay away too long, *kosatona*," she told him

gruffly. High praise from the normally taciturn woman. He nodded.

Then the worst.

The *ona* turned to look at him.

He stepped forward to meet her.

He took in the sight of her, trying to fix her in his mind. As if she could ever be erased.

Her hair was braided down one side. She wore a clean white tunic and brown pants, a green cloak over it—as drab as her clothes had ever been. Her old knives were belted as ever at her waist, though she couldn't have used them in any case due to the sling that remained on her arm to keep her shoulder immobilized. She wore the blue paint of the Ëan smeared on each cheek. She was still, and always would be, Auria.

"Well, love," she said, her tone forcibly light, "this is it."

He nodded with difficulty, unable to tear his eyes from her face. Then he burst out, "I can't do it, Ria."

Her answer belied the look in her eyes. "It's your duty. You *have* to go."

He hugged her, squeezing her hard. "Please, Ria?"

"No."

He kissed her, ignoring the appreciative murmurs of the crowd. She laughed. "Still no, love. Just... promise you'll come back."

"I will," he said firmly. "I'll come back if I have to row the boat myself. I'll come back if I have to swim the whole way."

She really laughed now. "At least you'll be able to tell the sharks not to eat you," she teased. "Honestly, love. Don't be silly."

"Well, I *will* come back," he said defensively.

She nodded. "I know, William." She hugged him again briefly. "I'll be expecting you."

He couldn't leave her.

She turned to the crowd. She raised William's hand over their heads like the champion of a match. "People of Belond! Our messenger to the King: William Tellor, *Ëa kosatona*, hero of Belond!"

They didn't cheer, like they usually did in response to the *ona*'s speeches.

They knelt.

Even the Ëan.

Not because of who he was. Not because it was required.

He hardly knew how to react. He stood there blankly.

Then Ria pulled an Ëa salute. "Elé!" The rest of the Ëan echoed her, then the whole crowd did the same.

He raised a hand to the crowd in a feeble wave.

"Goodbye, William," she said quietly.

He stared into her eyes again. He could think of nothing to say. He could not bring himself to say goodbye. The word stung him.

"Go," she told him, gentle, but unyielding. She was braver than he was. It would have to be enough resolve for both of them.

He turned away and walked up the ramp. They pulled it up after him.

He stood at the rail beside Lis, watching as the ship pulled away. The crowd waved and cheered, but William was not watching them. His eyes were fixed.

He watched until he couldn't see her. He watched until he couldn't see the town. He watched until the island was just a smudge on the horizon.

Then it disappeared.

"Mother," he said. It was nearly two weeks later. "May I come in?"

"Sure, dear."

The cabins were smaller than the ones in his last voyage—but the size didn't oppress him the way it used to.

"Hello, Anjalia," he said to appease politeness.

"Hi."

"Honestly, William, you look completely miserable," Lis scolded. "Cheer up! We're going *home*, not to your funeral!"

"We'll arrive today."

"I know," she said, beaming. She was a bit giddy. "Ovan told me." She fussed with her hair in front of the tiny mirror. She'd been nervously fidgeting with her appearance for hours, as had Anjalia. "Do you think I look all right?" she asked.

"Mother!"

"No, I mean it. I didn't really have anything to wear, so I altered one of Anjalia's dresses." (Meaning the dress no longer looked ridiculous and actually flattered her well.)

"Mother, really! What does it matter? Besides, you're beautiful no matter what you wear."

She tucked back a stray curl. "But… I'm going to see him today." She flushed. "I can hardly believe it. It's been years, William. He might not even recognize me. You didn't."

"I wasn't looking for you. I didn't recognize you because I didn't expect to see you. Honestly, Mother. He won't care what you *look like*. He's been pining for you for sixteen years. He'll just be happy to see you at all."

"I know I'm being silly—I'm a vain woman," she sighed. "What if I've changed? What if things are different between us? It's been a long time."

"Do you still love him?"

"Of course! But it's been *years*."

"It won't matter. You'll see."

She smiled. "Thanks, dear."

He smiled back, or tried to. Happy as he was for her, his heart wasn't in his homecoming. He couldn't shake his depression. He tried to put his own feelings aside.

"Listen to me now, okay? I need to tell you what we're going to do."

She stopped fiddling with her hair. "What do you mean?"

"I mean, I don't want to draw a lot of attention when we first get there. Father should be the first to know we're here, not a bunch of meddling gossips."

"You mean *sneak* in?" Lis asked with a frown.

He actually laughed. "I'd love to give it a shot, honestly. That *would* be fun. But no. I doubt anyone but Ria could get past the King's guard without getting caught."

"So..." she prompted.

"Captain Wood will get us to the docks. He'll be in charge of settling the harbormaster—confirming we're legal and not pirates. He has the necessary seals and connections to pass us off as merchants. No one knows this ship, and it's pretty small. If we're lucky, no one will notice us. Then you, Ovan, Rosie, and I will go to the palace. I'll handle it from there."

"Aww," complained Anjalia. "I want to come!"

"Why all this secrecy?" Lis asked, ignoring her outburst.

"This is going to shock him badly, Mother. I want to make sure he takes it all right and hears it from the right people."

She nodded. "I see your point. Very well, then."

"Good."

An hour later, they were in sight of the city.

Truly a city. He'd forgotten how vast this place was. The most modern, civilized metropolis in the world.

He hated the very sight of it.

Lis shed a few tears. "Home. Home, William! Just look at it! It's so much bigger than I remember. It's beautiful! How I've dreamed of seeing it again!"

The Belondians were awed. They stared with wide eyes. Only Ovan and William remained unmoved.

"The palace!" cried Anjalia.

There it was. Practically a city in itself, rising floor upon floor. It sparkled in the highest part of Ossia, overlooking the bay. The center of the Empire's government. Noblemen's houses and the dwellings of the rich sprawled around it. The poor quarter lay cleverly hidden in the pockets of the city, especially the outskirts.

The wharves. Commerce of all kinds, the most thriving trade in the world. All William saw were greedy merchants vying for wealth. And what was the point, anyway?

Captain Wood spoke to the harbormaster. It took a little time, but they were eventually allowed to land.

They pulled up to the dock.

"Captain!" William called.

"Sire?"

William winced at the now unfamiliar word. "Buy a cargo if anyone gets suspicious, but it shouldn't be necessary. We'll be back soon enough."

"Yes, sire."

William rolled his eyes surreptitiously. "Right."

They disembarked. William led Blazer off, too.

"You all right?" William asked Lis.

"Yes," she answered, wiping her eyes and laughing sheepishly. "I'm just so *happy*."

He smiled. "Up you get, Mother." The future Queen of Edenia was not trudging through the muddy streets of the capital. He helped her mount, still holding the reins. He pulled his hood over his head and his two followers did likewise.

"Let's go."

They slogged through the busy streets. The crowd felt oppressive: merchants, tradesmen, vendors, all clamoring. They pushed through, though William had to stare down more than one shady-looking character.

They reached the wealthier district of the city, where the nobles resided, and then they found themselves outside the palace walls. William approached the gate and challenged the guards. "We need admission to the palace," he said boldly.

The leader laughed derisively. "*You?* Clear off, riff-raff. Entrance to the palace! Ha! This entrance is for noblemen and government officials only. You'd need a pass. Move along." He eyed William with a disdainful glance at his clothes. Rosie drew his stare, too, with a bow slung over her shoulder and men's clothes. Belatedly, William thought perhaps he should have brought Shac instead—he would have drawn less attention in a world where women weren't fighters. But the man faltered when he saw Lis, a woman whose dignity was undisguised, clearly recognizable as a noblewoman.

"No," William said calmly. "We need to get into the palace."

"No?" the captain repeated with surprise, affronted. He

drew his sword. Ovan set a hand on his own.

"Easy," William told him. He stepped forward. He took off his glove and flashed his ring at the soldier.

Shock and a trace of fear transformed his face as he realized what the sign on the ring was. "Not possible." He examined William more closely. "The prince is missing. You must be an imposter."

William jerked his head at Ovan. Ovan stepped forward and bared his tattoo.

The soldier's jaw dropped as he realized his mistake. "Forgive me, sire. I crave your pardon! I didn't know—I wasn't expecting—" He broke off abruptly at William's expression. "Get that gate open!" he called to his men. "Right this way. Might I escort you, sire?"

"No. Forget it. Forget you saw us—for a while."

He looked confused, but, bowing low, he said, "Yes. Yes, sire, of course."

William proceeded past him.

Once in the gate, it was a little easier. Ovan took the lead when they were challenged to save William the trouble of declaring who he was, since he preferred to avoid it for now. As a Tellorian Guard, Ovan commanded a fair measure of respect in the palace and could get nearly anywhere.

They left Blazer with Rosie and continued into the royal apartments alone. It felt strange to be back here. He knew this place so well, but it wasn't the same. Not at all.

Lis grew increasingly nervous and excited. She remembered it, too.

Finally.

The King's apartment. His office, in a sense—the place where he worked each day.

Lis looked a little faint. "Ovan will catch you if you pass out," William teased her.

"Very funny."

The King was in there, just behind that door. The dozen guards outside confirmed it.

"Halt!" the leader said. "Who are you?" the captain asked,

suspicious and surprised, taking in their appearance. "How did you get in here?"

"I need to see the King," William said quietly.

The captain scoffed. "Have you no respect! You cannot demand an audience with the King! And even if you were not... *riff-raff*... you could not possible enter! Only Lord Arthos is allowed in at this hour. His Majesty is busy. The likes of you could never be let in. You'll have to leave. You should not be wandering the King's private hall." He waved forward two of his men.

William lowered his hood.

That was all it took. All the soldiers froze. These were Tellorian guards. They knew him.

"My lord!" The captain sank quickly to his knees. "You... you were... we didn't know you'd—"

"May I pass, Captain Bernan? I need to see my father."

"Yes—yes, sire."

"Wait here for me," he said to Lis and Ovan. "One surprise at a time."

"Let me announce you," Bernan said.

"I don't need an introduction. It's been long enough."

"But, sir—"

He turned the doorknob and walked in.

The King sat at his desk, poring over a stack of papers with Arthos beside him. They were quite focused and didn't even look up.

"What is it, Bernan?" the King asked, a little trace of annoyance in his voice.

William hadn't realized how much he'd missed them. Hearing his father's voice again nearly brought him to tears.

He said nothing, though his mouth worked, trying to find words. *Hello* didn't quite cover it.

King Eduar looked up with a sigh. His face froze. He stared. William's older brother looked up, too, and his jaw dropped.

"William?" his father asked incredulously.

William smiled almost without realizing it, his face

breaking into a broad grin.

The King bounded out of his chair, gasping with relief. "William! I can scarcely believe... I've been so worried!" He nearly suffocated William in a tremendous hug. "There was no word—nothing! None of the embassy came back. You've been gone a year! I was sure something terrible had happened—I thought you'd been killed!" He laughed with the extent of his relief, the sound edged with a trace of hysteria, betraying the depth of his anxiety. "And now you're home! I had no word the ship had returned—how is that possible? I ordered the watch on the harbor tripled for any sign. All Ossia—no, all Edenia—should be heralding your safe return. You are well? Yes, look at you!" He held William at arm's length. "You're so *different*!" He squeezed William's now thick arm. "What happened? Where have you been? Why didn't you come home? Not knowing has tormented me! There was nothing we could do!"

Ria had been right. He needed to come back.

Why was that woman always right?

"I'm sorry," he replied quietly. Then he laughed. "It's good to see you again. I missed you." He realized now how true it was.

Eduar hugged him again. "But explain! Tell me what happened to you!"

"I will—I promise I will. But I brought someone with me, father. She's outside the door. May I bring her in to meet you?"

The King looked a little confused, but then a twinkle burst into his eyes. "Ah," he said, as if the mention of a "she" explained everything. "Lady Whitefeld, perhaps?"

"Uh... uh, yeah." Technically, that was true.

"Bring her in, then—you shouldn't keep a lady waiting."

William grinned again. He couldn't help a little triumph. He had, after all, been waiting for this since he was seven years old.

"Yes, sir," he answered.

He poked his head back out the door. "You can come in,

Ovan," he said.

Lis took her guard's arm.

William ducked back inside.

Ovan and Lis walked in. William glued his eyes to his father's face, the grin still dancing on his face.

A smile of welcome froze on the King's lips. Arthos stared. She stopped, looking hesitantly at him.

Eduar's face went flat. "I'm dreaming," he said stiffly. "I've had this dream too many times. This isn't real."

"I *am* real," she responded gently, looking a bit pained.

He sighed, closing his eyes. "Her voice," he mused. "Her very voice." He opened his eyes again, and they were wide with shock. "It can't be. You're dead. They told me you were dead. This is a dream."

"I'm not a dream," she promised, her voice cracking a little. A tear slid from her eye. "I was never dead."

"You're... You're really Elissana?" he breathed, still unable to believe it.

William wondered for a moment whether this had been too much for him.

"It's really me," she assured. "I've come home."

A tear slid down his face. "Lis," he whispered. He was still frozen in shock.

Then they both rushed for each other at the same time.

A smile spread on William's face. He couldn't help one tear. Sixteen years, and now, finally, this.

Eduar kissed her long enough to embarrass both his sons. He couldn't seem to let her go. Finally, he said, "I never dared hope—my beautiful, beautiful Elissana."

She gave a happy laugh. "I thought of you every day, every minute. I never thought I'd see you again."

"How is this possible?" he demanded. "Your brother told me you were dead!"

"It was a lie, Eduar."

He spluttered with indignation and shock.

"We will tell you everything—William and I." She beamed proudly at her son. "We would not be here if not for William."

"Yes—yes," the King said. But he wasn't ready to hear it, not yet. "I cannot believe it, Lis—I cannot!"

"Nor can I... It's been so long."

"I shouldn't have waited," he berated himself. "I should've married you all those years ago. This wouldn't have happened if I did."

"It's not your fault."

He shook his head. "I'm through waiting, Lis." He went down on one knee. She covered her mouth with her hands, beaming.

William's grin widened.

"I'm not the same man I was sixteen years ago. I'm older, wiser, and wearier. You may not wish to have me anymore—"

"No, don't say that!"

"Will you marry me, Elissana Whitefeld?"

She glowed, but first she said, "I may not be the same, either, Eduar. I'm a careworn woman—but I've learned that people are worth fighting for. If you still want me, of course I will marry you."

He laughed and rose to his feet to kiss her again.

William looked over at Ovan. "For Tiran," the guard mouthed to the prince. Ovan looked happy for the first time since his brother died.

Eduar turned to his son and extended his arms. Lis moved toward Arthos.

"Thank you," Eduar said, hugging William.

"Don't thank me; thank the Ëan," William countered.

"Ëan?" The King asked, the word confusing him.

William indicated Ovan. "There's the first of them. I have three more in the city. But Ovan's been her best protector."

Eduar shook Ovan's hand vigorously. "Thank you," he said sincerely.

Ovan pulled a Tellorian guard's salute. "My duty, sire."

Eduar's eyebrows rose. "You're a guard?"

Ovan displayed his tattoo.

"He was with us on the ship, Eduar—you sent us with some of your guard," Lis explained from a few feet away.

Arthos had an arm around her, grinning happily.

Eduar gave Ovan a second look. "Yes, I think I remember you. I sent your brother with William last year. He was the only captain willing to volunteer for the job, without me assigning someone. He told me about you."

"Tiran died protecting me," William said quietly.

Eduar's face fell. "I'm sorry," he said to Ovan.

"He did his duty," Ovan replied with a nod. "He was happy to die in your service."

Eduar nodded, a sad look on his face. Then he turned to William. "Tell me—William, Lis, Ovan. Tell me everything that's happened."

They did.

It took hours. They sat together, taking turns speaking. Eduar kept an arm around Lis the whole time, but he listened intently.

He was all outrage. William had never seen him so angry.

"So *Andel* is dead?" he asked.

"Yes, my love," Lis answered sadly. "And Seyenne. That much was true. But not Ria."

"Karia? Andel's daughter is still alive? But she was just a child!"

They went on to tell him all about Ria, the *Ëan*, and the Governor. Ovan narrated this, pride in his voice.

Then it was William's turn.

He stressed less his own doings, and more the people he'd met. He told the King about Lam, about Dero, about Kerran and Winna and Allain, on and on. Then Ria. He talked a lot about Ria.

They finally finished.

Eduar considered what he'd heard. Then he said, "I owe them all a great debt. All of Belond—but especially Andel's daughter." He sighed. He added, almost to himself, "He was my best friend. I should have been a father to her, when she lost hers."

"You will repay it," Lis comforted.

"I will," he agreed, almost defiantly. Then he smiled. "Look at us—a real family again. It hardly seems possible."

Lis beamed. She looked at William with a smile. He'd once said the same.

He smiled back at her.

Chapter 53

The King really was tired of waiting.

He sent a mass proclamation through the city that his son and his bride had returned. He was hosting a feast that very night to celebrate—and in exactly one week, he would marry Elissana Whitefeld.

He was determined to make it up to her. He abandoned his work to spend every possible moment with her. He showered her with jewels, dresses, and comforts of every kind. He made her feel like a Queen, and no one could deny that she enjoyed it.

Eduar was a changed man.

Arthos confided as much to William one night. Arthos and William had never been close. Arthos always kept himself detached, being more the smooth, charming, unfazable sort, but even he could not fail to be affected. "He was a mess when the ship didn't return last spring. He was depressed for months; he even wanted to try the passage before the sea opened again. He wasn't eating. We were all worried he'd waste away with grief. But now, he's like he used to be."

Even Betta warmed up a little. The King met her as Lis's special friend, and he took good care of her. He was one of the few people who could understand her. He knew what it felt like to lose the person he loved and to be lost in regret. He knew exactly how Betta felt.

The Ëan were awed, but they stuck carefully to William. Rosie admitted to him when he questioned this behavior that the *ona* had given them strict orders to keep him safe—though he had a new posse of Tellorian guards following him around. The new guards weren't the same as Tiran, though, and they definitely didn't comfort him the way the Ëan's presence did.

Anjalia was in heaven. As Lis's niece, she enjoyed special treatment, of course. Lis was going to have difficulty curing her spoiled temperament.

William was the only one who was dissatisfied, though he knew he should be as blissfully happy as his family. He *was* happy, but not perfectly so. He missed home.

The big day of the wedding arrived quickly.

Lis asked William to give her away. William was only too pleased.

It was perfect. Lis looked immaculate, flushed with happiness. The whole crowd—nearly all of Ossia—whispered what a beauty she was, and how lucky their King was.

Then came the feast.

He'd never before felt out of place in Ossian society. Now he did.

Rosie and Shac enjoyed the party, dancing and having a good time. People were only too interested in hearing their stories. Winna and Betta stayed together. Anjalia flitted from person to person. She soon had a gaggle of simpering girls who set out to flirt with any handsome noblemen they could find. Ovan stuck close to the Queen, as always.

He knew nearly all these people. But at the same time, he didn't know them at all. They weren't his friends. They were strangers.

He wandered over toward Arthos. His brother, always a ladies' man, had a string of women on his arm, all beguilingly hidden behind make-up and costly clothes.

"Ah, William! We were just talking about you!"

"Is that so?"

"Yes," gushed one pretty, dark-eyed girl in a red dress. Lady Dayeida. "We were just talking about your *dreadful* ordeal. Is it true you were captured by *barbarians*?"

"Not exactly, and they're not barbarians. They're Djorn."

"Ooh, the word just *sounds* vulgar! So uncivilized!"

He frowned, but he said nothing.

"It must have been terrifying," another girl put in. She pressed close to him with a sigh. "All alone. But I suppose you were very brave. Arthos says you fought the mad usurper yourself."

He gently distanced himself from her. She looked affronted.

Arthos laughed. "Don't bother, Maidale. His heart's taken already."

William reddened. He hadn't mentioned his feelings for Ria to anyone.

The girls cooed with interest. "Oh, yes," Arthos tantalized them. "He's left his heart behind, I daresay."

"Who is she?" they demanded.

"No one you'd know," William said calmly, forcing his voice to remain cordial. He'd grown better at controlling his temper, but he wasn't sure how long he could hold out. He remembered the *ona*'s dignity and he forced himself to live up to her standard.

"A noblewoman we don't know? But there aren't any in Belond—Arthos, you'd better not be teasing us. William, where'd you meet her?"

"In Belond."

"I knew it," said Arthos triumphantly.

"Ooh, is she beautiful?" sighed one young woman.

He hated talking about her like this, as if the *ona*, who was far superior to any of these girls, was just another piece of juicy gossip. It felt like a betrayal.

"How did you meet?" asked Dayeida.

"She ambushed me, knocked me out, and took me prisoner," said William, just for shock value.

He got it. Arthos laughed, but the women looked aghast. "She's a barbarian?" they gasped.

"No. She's Edenian."

Arthos smirked. William forced himself not to glare at his brother. He looked for a way to extricate himself, but the girls were too interested now. "But *fighting*?" one asked. "That's scandalous! No lady would ever *dare* presume to pick up a sword. No, you're teasing."

William laughed. "Have you met Rosie?" he asked.

"We thought she was just an oddity! We never knew there

were other women like her—let alone that you'd fallen for one! What possesses her to behave so?"

"She's a good warrior. She'd make mincemeat of the Guard. Best fighter in the whole Empire, I reckon. And others have said the same."

Now they really *were* scandalized. "It's disgusting! She must have been a common vagabond! A dirty little peasant, wasn't she? And you a prince! You deserve better—a lady. No, you wouldn't fall for some little provincial hooligan!"

"The *ona*," William corrected, then added, "and she's much better than a lady."

"*Ona*? So she *is* a barbarian!"

"Karia Whitefeld, if you like that better," William said, his voice beginning to sound strained. He could barely hold back his anger, and he knew he shouldn't rise to these weak-minded gossips.

The girls gaped, but Arthos said, "As I guessed. He's dead set on her. Probably spent this whole year chasing her. Face still burning from your kiss goodbye, William? Ha! See, look, I'm right!"

He was near losing his temper.

"Oh, that's *so* sweet! That girl that awful pirate exiled. And you rescued her! Oh, that's so romantic!"

He actually laughed. "*She* saved *my* life. Call that romantic if you like." He grew serious again. "Don't you go gossiping about the *ona*. I'd like to see one of you survive a minute of her life. She's the bravest person I know, and nobler than *any* of you. Plus it's none of your business. No more talk, understand?"

They looked shocked.

"Excuse me," he said darkly, and he turned on his heel and left.

"There you are," the King said.

William looked up.

He was downstairs in the guards' training room. He'd spent half an hour ripping apart a dummy with a sword, and now he was taking furious punches at a bag in the corner. He'd ditched his tunic (fine clothes felt uncomfortable now) and he was drenched in sweat.

"Hello," he said in response. He threw another punch then wiped the sweat out of his eyes.

"What are you doing down here?"

"Practicing. Didn't—have—much—of—a—chance—on—the—ship." He punctuated each word with a punch.

"Why did you leave the party?"

William abandoned his efforts and started doing push-ups. "I'm sorry...I know I shouldn't have left. It's your wedding day. I just...couldn't stay in there anymore. You didn't have to come down to find me. You should be enjoying yourself."

Eduar laughed. "I don't mind. You're my son. So...why did you come down here?"

"I don't know. This just feels...normal."

"By 'normal', you mean, 'like Belond.'"

William didn't respond. He got to his feet and went back to the disheveled dummy. Eduar watched him. After a moment, he said, "I've never seen that sword before."

"Ria gave it to me. From the Djorn."

"It's a beautiful weapon. May I see it?"

William stopped reluctantly. "Sure."

The King swung it experimentally in his hand. *He was a master swordsman, too.* "Excellent weapon."

William sighed, taking it back. "Look—you should be with Mother. I don't want you to be missing your own wedding celebration. I'll go back in if you like."

"I don't think you need to. But no need to worry. I like being with my son. Unless you'd rather I go?"

"No—no, that's not what I meant."

"I thought not."

William, unsure what to say, resumed his push-ups.

"Look, William," the King began. "Your mother and I have been talking about you."

Oh, boy. What did that mean?

"What about me?"

"She's worried about you. And so am I. You're not happy; anyone can see that."

"I *am* happy." He grunted as he continued to push his weight away from the floor. His muscles burned, but it felt good. Familiar.

"No, you're not. You're not the same boy I sent to Belond a year ago. Your skill with a sword is one thing, but I can see it in your face. Look at me, William."

William stood reluctantly.

"You don't want to stay here."

It was a moment he'd been dreading.

He sighed. "I miss Belond. I miss what I am there. I miss my family."

"Your family is here."

"Yes—but the Ëan are my family, too. I *belong* with them."

"Don't you belong in Ossia? You're the prince of Edenia."

"That's just it. Here, people see a name. There, they see *me*. I don't want to be respected for an empty title, Father. I'm the *kosatona*. I *earned* that name. That's what I want. No one here understands that. I can't talk to them, I can't even understand them. The Ëan are different. "

"And Karia Whitefeld?"

"Ria? What about her?"

"Do you deny you love her?"

"How'd you know that? Did Mother—"

"It was all over your face when you talked about her, son, no matter what you glossed over in telling me your story." Eduar laughed softly. "You were never good at hiding your feelings."

"Oh."

"So you do."

"Yes."

Eduar nodded slowly. "So you're going back."

William nodded. "Yes. I'm going back," he said firmly, though he was reluctant to say it. "As soon as I see you and

Mother happily settled, I'm going back. I'd rather go with your blessing, but I'll go without it if I have to."

Eduar's eyes shone. "Oh, William. You've grown up." He smiled. "Do you know why I sent you to Belond, son?"

"To figure out why things didn't feel right to you. To make peace with Mother's death for you."

"I was worried about *you*, not me."

William arched an eyebrow.

"You hadn't gotten over her. You were going through life aimlessly, not caring about anything. I wanted you to heal. I wanted you to be happy, to find some meaning again. You did that, and much more. You're a strong, confident young man. You know how to fight for what you believe in—and your beliefs are powerful, William; anyone can see that. You know what's right. I'm so, so very proud of you. And I love you. I want you with me, but I know how it feels to be separated from the woman you love. I would never, ever force you to stay away from her. If that means letting you go—" he sighed, "—so be it."

"Thank you," William responded fervently. He couldn't even begin to describe his relief. He hugged his father, making Eduar laugh.

"There's one more thing."

"What?"

"If you're going to marry this girl—"

"Who said anything about that?"

"You haven't asked her to marry you yet?"

"No."

"Well, what are you waiting for? You shouldn't keep a Whitefeld woman waiting, William. Believe me, it isn't a good idea."

William laughed.

"So if you're going to marry this girl, I want to meet her."

"Impossible. She won't leave Belond. You'll just have to trust me, name her Governor from here."

"We weren't talking about *that*! I mean my best friend's daughter, the girl who's going to become my daughter-in-law.

And I know she won't leave Belond. Lis told me that much."

"So…"

"So I talked to your mother, and we decided we are going to sail back with you—just for a short visit. I want to meet your new family, William—and, of course, I'll have to choose a Governor. I owe Belond some personal attention. El knows I've shortchanged them for years! How does that sound to you?"

William just grinned.

Chapter 54

The preparations for the voyage could not take place fast enough for William.

Honestly, Ossian society was appalled by the idea that their King, who had not left Ossian territory to visit any province, let alone the most obscure, in their recent memory, was sailing to Belond. But he declared it a holiday for himself and his wife, and no one could deny he had earned it. He hadn't taken a vacation from his duties since Lis had left. He planned to leave the capable Arthos in charge during his absence.

Anjalia and Betta were staying behind. Neither wished to return so soon, though for quite different reasons. Lis debated staying behind, most particularly for Betta, but neither she nor Eduar could stomach the idea of parting so soon.

Ovan, newly honored with a title and property for his services, though it hardly mattered to him, was accompanying them, having requested the honor of continuing to protect the Queen. The *Ëan* would return to the *ona*.

An entire fleet would be sailing. The *Ëan* had routed the worst band of one-time pirates, but the other islands might still harbor other unknown gangs. They were taking absolutely no chances this time.

The War Goddess would sail, too, though Captain Wood would not be piloting it. He wished to see no more of Belond. The King had rewarded him handsomely for his service, and he was settled comfortably in Ossia. Some of the sailors, however, were returning—mostly for Belondian sweethearts. They would be retained on the island for *The War Goddess*, which the King declared as belonging to the Belondian government.

A whole troop of Tellorian guards was joining them. Despite the protection of the *Ëan*, the King intended to leave his son well-defended. He also wished to bolster the now scarce military presence to aid the new Governor.

And, of course, an endless number of retainers and servants were coming along, too. William refused to let them near him.

In all, it took forever to get the voyage ready. Two weeks, in other words.

He spent the whole trip pacing the deck impatiently, chafing in the stiff, formal atmosphere and longing to arrive.

"Honestly, dear, relax," the Queen scolded.

He couldn't. Time crawled.

Then, the day arrived.

"We'll be there in a few hours," announced the captain one morning.

"Excellent," said the King, standing at the rail beside his son. He'd finally recovered from his initial few days of seasickness and was looking back to normal again.

William could hardly contain his excitement. She knew they were coming. He'd gotten up early and had a nice chat with her dolphin friends, albeit one-sided.

"I can't wait to meet her," Eduar offered, smiling.

"She may seem strange to you. She's not exactly traditional."

"If you love her, then that's enough for me. And she's Andel's daughter, remember. I couldn't be more pleased about whom you chose to fall in love with."

William smiled. He looked up, staring into the clouds. Then a speck drew his attention.

"Is that a bird?" the King asked. "It's awfully high."

A grin spread irresistibly over William's face.

"*Leianá teno*, Talon!" he shouted up as loud as he could, startling his father. An eagle's distant cry wafted down in reply.

The King looked strangely at him. The sailors and servants on deck looked at him like he'd gone mad. "Did you just talk to that bird?"

The *Ëan* strode up, along with Lis and her maidens. Rosie

beamed. "Talon!" she exclaimed brightly. "The *ona*'s on the watch for us."

"The bird?" asked the King's attendant.

"Eagle," corrected Queen Elissana lightly. "Ria's bird—er, friend. What's he doing out here, William?"

William grinned.

Just then, the eagle plummeted into a dive. The servants all gasped in surprise, which soon changed to alarm as the eagle sped toward the ship. The Ëan were unmoved.

Talon alighted with a scream and a flurry of wings in front of William. The servants all shrieked and backed away. Even the King looked nervous, and Lis unsure.

William faced him without a trace of alarm.

Talon made a few long croaks and pecked at a piece of cloth clenched his left claw. Then he soared upward and left the scrap behind.

William picked it up.

A few tentative, messy lines were scribbled in ink.

His grin widened.

"A message?" the King asked.

"What does the *ona* say?" Winna asked.

He just smiled and looked to the sky.

Talon wheeled away, still calling through the air. Then he disappeared.

Two more specks materialized, flying toward them.

"Yes!" shouted William loudly.

He leapt onto the railing.

"William!" Lis cried.

"Get down! You'll fall!" the King shouted.

Hands moved to pluck him off, but the Ëan prevented them. They seemed to understand, and from their grins, it appeared they appreciated the joke quite well.

"See you soon!" William called back over his shoulder. Then he jumped from the rail.

Screams.

He laughed as he fell, the sea air whooshing past him.

Pearl and Dragon snatched him out of the air by the wrists

and he went soaring upward.

"Show-off!" said Rosie merrily in Djoran as he flew right past them. He just laughed, whooping with delight.

His heart rose still higher when he heard the crowd. They saw him, and they were cheering up a storm. He had scarcely felt so happy in his whole life. "Ko-sa-to-na," they chanted enthusiastically.

He saw the Ëan. They were standing in a half circle in the very front of the crowd, a little apart. And the figure they surrounded...

The eagles dropped him on the dock. The crowd roared.

He came up running.

He looked for Ria. He found her easily. She looked how she always had. No bandages, no bruises. Healthy. Strong. Beautiful. Her war paint adorned her cheeks. Her knives hung at her belt. Her hair was braided into a knot at the base of her neck. She wore her same old tunic and breeches, weather-stained and dingy. She was the same old *ona* he loved and remembered.

She was smiling. No, she was beaming.

He ran right for her and kissed her. The crowd clapped enthusiastically.

"I take it you missed me," she said dryly.

"*Yes* I did! It's been almost two months!"

She laughed. "I'm glad you're back, William," she replied.

"Well, I'm back for good. I'm not ever leaving again."

She nodded. After pausing a moment, she said, "Welcome home, *kosatona*."

She waved the waiting Ëan forward, and they surged around him. Dero was first, tackling him with a hug. William nearly fell backward, but he laughed. "I *knew* you'd be back!" Dero exclaimed. "I *told* you!" He bobbed up and down with excitement.

William was still laughing. "Yes, you did," he agreed.

Before Dero could talk his ear off, Ekata moved forward. "Hello, *kosatona*," she said warmly. Then Szera shouldered past her to say, "It's about time, William," but her expression belied her tone. He smiled at the two women, but the rest of the Ëan and his other friends were each coming forward in turn, patting him on the back, wringing his hand.

Not even King Eduar could expect a welcome like this when he returned to Ossia. He felt like a hero.

By the time he found Ria again, the ship was pulling in. Or ships.

"Your father's here," she informed him, jerking her head at the largest and foremost.

"As I'm sure you knew ages ago."

"It's not as if he was subtle. Is that every ship you *have* in Ossia?"

"Pretty close," he laughed.

The tall ship pulled up to the long dock. The people cheered ecstatically. None of them had ever seen the King land on their island. The Ëan reformed their half-circle around the ona, but this time, with the kosatona standing beside her.

The three Ëan were the first to disembark from the ship, leaping over the railing before the gangplank was even lowered and jumping straight onto the dock. (William imagined the attendants were having a fit about the impropriety of their action, but the Ëan hardly cared.) They got as warm a welcome as William had, and they joined the ring of Ëan.

The retainers on board blew trumpets. The crowd hushed, eager with anticipation. A line of Tellorian Guards filed off and formed two lines on either side of the dock. They drew swords and held them pointed straight up.

A herald followed.

"People of Belond!" he cried. "I present to you His Majesty King Eduar Tellor, Emperor of Edenia, Supreme Ruler of the Seven Provinces, Lord of Ossia; and Her Majesty Queen Elissana Tellor, his newly wedded bride."

The King, splendid in his fine clothes, long cloak, and crown, descended regally from the ship, his lovely wife on his arm. The crowd sighed appreciatively, staring.

Ria whispered to William. "Lis was right. You do look just like him." He smiled at this. "She looks wonderful," Ria added fondly. But he had no time to respond.

The King and Queen halted at the end of the dock, trailed by guards, attendants, and the herald: a grand royal procession. The King looked at all of the crowd, but he had immediately spotted Ria as the leader. It was hard not to.

There was a moment's pause. Then Ria went down on one knee.

The effect was immediate. Every person in the crowd followed her example, as did the Ëan. William reacted the same way they did.

"Please, rise," the King said. Only the *ona* rose to her feet, but everyone else looked up.

The *ona* motioned for William to stand, and he did so. He turned to his father, looking him full in the face—though the King looked only at the *ona*. "My lord," he said formally, "may I present to you *Ëa ona* Auria, *Vitha Inkosa*, Karia Whitefeld, leader of Belond."

There were a few murmurs in the crowd that repeated the name Whitefeld in surprise. But she owned it now. There was no longer any dishonor in the name, nor any need to hide who she was.

"Welcome, Your Majesty," the *ona* said clearly. She, too, looked him in the eye, undaunted by any display of power.

The ruler of Edenia seemed to have trouble finding words. From the look of him, he had forgotten his station and authority. Finally, he said, "You are so like him—your father." Lis smiled.

Ria nodded with a genuine smile, but said nothing.

The King held out a hand to her.

She crossed the space between them. She took his hand, but he pulled her forward into a hug. "I'm sorry, Karia," he said to her. Only those nearest could hear, but the whole crowd murmured with surprise at his gesture. "You can't know how sorry I am."

She moved away to look him in the eye. "I don't blame

you. None of what has happened is your fault."

"I must share the blame," he insisted. "It was negligence on my part which led to your suffering."

"I have had a hard life," she admitted. "But I have many things now I would never have had without those hardships. I am content—no, I count myself blessed."

"All the same, I ask you to forgive me," the King pressed on.

"For my part, I forgave you some time ago," she said. "I was angry for years, yes, but I understand better now."

He smiled. "Thank you," he replied sincerely. "Now it is only for me to make amends, and to reward you for what you have done."

The *ona* indicated the circle behind her. "The *Ëan* are responsible for the liberation of Belond, my lord," she countered. She waved them forward and named each one to the King. Then she indicated the people and said, "The *Reben* have also fought, my lord." The crowd rose to its feet at her mention of them. He looked at them, surveying the faces. Then he raised his voice to speak.

"You are the truest citizens in Edenia," he said. "The Empire has wronged you—our negligence led to the gross injustice you have suffered these past years—yet you remain loyal. You have earned reward beyond measure for your actions, and I intend to do my best to see you receive it. I cannot pretend to undo the wrong that was done—to bring back your families and friends. I am truly sorry for their loss, and I know nothing can replace them. I can only mourn with you, as a King ought. But I wish to help you to rebuild this island to be even greater than it was before. Even without the Empire's help, you have gained your freedom, but now I wish to do all I can to honor and aid you in your victory."

The people cheered this little speech. It was well considered, clearly. It had been weighing on the King's mind what to say to these people. But they understood. And if the *ona* forgave him, they would.

The *ona* resumed charge of her crowd. "Let us show our

King a Belondian welcome!" she called to them. They cheered again, and she led the royal party forward into their midst.

The people had planned a huge feast and party for them in the square, attesting to the *ona*'s foreknowledge of their arrival. The town looked more festive than William had ever seen it. Far, far superior to any Ossian party, these people were here to have fun.

William joined them. He ate, danced, laughed, and sang with the Ëan. He and Dero stayed together the whole party, recounting what each of them had been doing. Dero had more news than William, telling him all about what the Ëan had been up to. Dero was more cheerful than the rest of the town combined. William laughed more than he had in months.

His only disappointment was that he saw little of Ria. She was wrapped up with the King, talking to him and introducing him to various people. In truth, at one point, he caught sight of them off in a corner, talking just between themselves. He was partly pleased that his father was spending time with her. (It had been the thing Eduar was most looking forward to.) He couldn't help but be a bit annoyed she wasn't alone talking with *him*, but he had little time to dwell on it.

They celebrated all day and well into the night. Only when it got very late, the square lit by a string of lanterns, did the *ona* jump up onto a table and shout that it was time to return home to sleep. Though disappointed, the yawning people did as she asked, and the crowd began to slowly dissolve, retreating with cheery waves and calls of farewell.

The *ona* brought the King's household to the Felds. It was the only place large enough to house them all, and even so many of them stayed aboard the ship. The house had changed again since William had left. The highest floor, now, was devoted to the healers, so as to give any patients that remained the most possible quiet. The Ëan lived on the bottom floor, now, but it was stripped of most of its frivolous decorations. It was still a handsome house, but it looked less like the old Governor's home and more like the Nest had. William liked the feeling of the place.

Ria herself showed her guests to their rooms. She ducked away only a moment to say to William, "Good night, love—I'll see you in the morning."

He felt again a stab of disappointment. "Where are you going?"

"When everyone is settled in, the King wishes to see me."

"You've been with him all day!"

"We have a... certain matter to discuss. I'll tell you later."

"But—"

"I promise, love." She darted away again.

"Tough luck," Dero consoled. "She's always busy, though."

"I know."

"Come on—your room's this way. Right next to mine!"

William started awake, clutching at the hand on his shoulder.

Ria laughed hysterically.

"Ria!" he scolded. "Honestly! It's *your* house now. You don't have to sneak around anymore! Just knock, for heaven's sake!"

"Come on, love, what's the fun of having your own house if you can't sneak around in it! Oh, you should've seen your face!"

"Mm-hmm. Thanks a lot." He got out of bed, already dressed. Those months as an *Ëa* had groomed the habit. "What are you doing here? It's the middle of the night!"

"No—it's about four-thirty."

"Same thing. I've finally gone back to *normal* sleeping. I don't do four anymore. And don't you *ever* sleep?"

"I haven't got the time." She winked at him. "I was talking to your father," she explained.

"All this time?"

"No. But I figured I'd better let you get a few hours of sleep or you'd be a grumpy boy."

He grunted.

"Can I talk to you for a bit? I know we haven't had much time, and I'm sorry about that."

He abandoned his annoyance at once, jumping at the opportunity. "Sure."

"Let's go outside," she proposed.

"Can we go through the door?"

"No, what fun is that? Besides, your silly guards would yell at me."

He'd forgotten the new captain had insisted on posting a pair of guards outside William's door. Lot of good it did. "Right. Okay."

"Talon's outside," she said with a grin. She opened the window and whistled softly. Three eagles flew in. He laughed.

"I think you miss having to break into places all the time," he said.

"Whatever gave you that idea?"

He laughed. "Hello," he said to the birds in Djoran.

"I imagine your father liked that little stunt you pulled earlier?" she asked teasingly.

"Your idea," he said defensively, then he laughed. "Scared him half to death, and I think most of his attendants think I'm mad. It was fantastic!"

She laughed. "Nothing beats flying," she said. Then she jumped out of window to be caught by Talon, and he followed.

They didn't go very far, just to the expansive grounds of the Felds. It was chilly, but he'd braved far colder weather than this. They thanked the eagles and they flew away, but only to the treetops above them. They seemed to be feeling especially friendly. He could hear them cawing continually from the branches overhead.

"I used to sneak out to the garden when I was little," she said. "I figured out I could understand animals, but I couldn't really talk back because I didn't know Djoran. I used to come and listen to the birds." She smiled at him. "Come on. There's a bench over there. Let's sit down."

He sat down next to her. "So you seem back to normal."

She nodded.

"No more pain in your shoulder?"

"No."

"All healed?"

"Yes."

He hesitated, then asked, "Can I see?"

She paused, then pulled aside her tunic enough for him to see the ugly red scar beneath her collarbone. He remembered how it had once looked. It was indeed healed, but the sight still made him wince.

"It's okay," she said, seeming to understand what he was thinking.

"I know... it's just..."

"Behind us. I survived. That's all there is to it. Don't dwell on it any more."

"I know. You're right."

They were quiet a moment, then Ria said abruptly, "So when are you going to ask me?"

"Ask you what?"

"You *know*... to marry you."

He gaped. "Uh... what?"

"You *are* going to ask me, aren't you?"

"Uh..."

"Oh, come on. The dolphins told me you stood on the deck all night the last couple days of your trip and practiced asking the question to thin air."

"What? Ria!"

"No, that's really sweet."

"You were spying on me?"

"No... I mean, yes, but not you in particular. Just the ship." She didn't look at all repentant, though she blushed a little. "So?"

"You're unbelievable," he muttered.

"*Are* you going to ask me?" she repeated.

"I don't know. What would you say if I did?"

"What do you think I'd say?"

He mimicked her voice. "*No. Don't be silly, love. Why would I do something as ridiculous as that?*"

She laughed so hard she was close to tears. "Am I that mean?" she wheezed through her amusement.

"You tell me."

"Well, you haven't actually put the question to me yet. I'm not going to answer until you ask."

"Aw, come on," he complained. It was true he had practiced framing the question. His father had put the issue into his mind, and it had been in his thoughts for days. But he couldn't say it to her face. He wasn't brave enough.

"Look me in the eye and ask me to marry you," she said.

He really did try. His mouth formed the words, but he just couldn't make his voice work. He groaned and looked away. "It's not that easy."

"Isn't it? Fine. I'll help you," she said in a schoolteacher voice. "Repeat after me. Ready? Will..."

"Will," he repeated, a bit sullenly, but half-amused and still more than a bit nervous.

"You..."

"You."

"Marry..."

"Marry me?" he forced out in a hurry.

"No. Why would I do something as ridiculous as that?"

"Ria!"

"Oh, come on, love, of course I will!"

He gave a relieved laugh. "You could've just said so." He gave her a hug, feeling elated.

"Well, good that's settled," she said, beaming. "Now your father is out of arguments."

"Wait, what?"

"I've been convincing him not to make me Governor."

"*What?* Ria, why? You're the only choice—"

"I want him to make both of us Governor."

He stopped short. "What? Is that possible?"

"He said it's never been done before. But I don't want to be Governor. I'm the *ona*. I would be able to manage Belond no problem, but not Edenia. You can manage both. In theory, it should be you. But you shouldn't do it by yourself, either. Sorry, love, but as long as I'm around I'd undermine your authority. So the only solution is for both of us to be Governor, together."

He'd been considering the matter himself, and honestly, this idea sounded perfect to him. Except... "Can we do that? Are we allowed?"

"Well, love, it helps that your father is the King of Edenia," she teased. "But, seriously, I think I convinced him it's the best idea. Both of us acting together as Governor, so neither of us are. We'll still be *ona* and *kosatona*. And if we married, it would only make sense, right?"

He smiled. "And you think you're not a politician."

"It's not just politics," she said. She looked at him. "I never said it yesterday," she said quietly. "But... I missed you, too, William."

His smile broadened. He didn't respond, but he kissed her.

Epilogue

The King lavished his blessings upon Belond. He gave all the gifts and treasures he could muster to the heroes of Belond for their reward. He cancelled the province's tribute for that year, and out of his own treasury he paid enough money for the Governors to rebuild the shattered Belond into a place even better than it had once been.

He lavished particular generosity upon the Ëan, and they became the elite of Belond's regular military, bolstered by fresh Edenian troops to be stationed there as in all the other provinces. Their ranks slowly swelled again, but they remained not an army, but a brotherhood. It was accounted the highest honor to become an Ëa and to serve the *ona* and *kosatona*. They were revered in Belond all their lives, and the tradition would be passed down to future generations.

As for those of the present, their best years were before them. Dero married Ekata, who, with Szera and Torhan, lived in Belo with the other Ëan. The pair continued to practice their healing art even in peacetime, and they passed their gift and their knowledge down after them.

Elénne married Aeric, several years after the liberation of Belond. Aeric was good to both her and her adopted daughter, but Hope always adored William. When she grew older, she followed in his footsteps to join the Ëan.

In Ossia, Lis and Eduar remained content in their reign. The Queen was loved by her subjects, and she worked hard to serve them, particularly advocating the cause of the children in all the provinces. Betta, serving as her second, aided her in all her efforts. She never returned to Belond, and she never remarried. Anjalia, however, married at the young age of eighteen to a handsome, high-born nobleman. She never fully reformed her spoiled ways, but she became a decent enough lady for Lis's satisfaction. Ovan remained with the Queen, but once a year he traveled with the Ossian embassy as ambassador to the Governors of Belond.

Never before had there been two Governors of a Province, but the *ona* and *kosatona* took up the role together as partners, and, married, they were an even better team than before. Belond remembered them afterward as the greatest leaders the island had ever known, and the memory of their deeds was treasured long after in stories and in the song which recalled their struggles, the Song of the Ëan.

About the Author

With this, her first book, Emily brings her faith and imagination into a story that has germinated in her mind since she was young. After she finishes college at Gardner-Webb University (and then grad school), Emily plans a career in physical therapy. In the meantime she offers this story of fantasy, faith, romance and coming of age as a different sort of therapy to her readers. The triumph of good over evil in an engaging and original story is a quintessential boost to the reader as well as to the writer.

Emily is an athlete (college swimmer) as well as a successful scholar. This novel, begun in high school at Grace Preparatory School and brought to completion in a gap year before starting college is now put forth for readers beyond those who know her well and have directly encouraged her multiple talents.

Emily calls northern Virginia home though she was born in Michigan. Her quiet determination has been most closely admired by two sisters, father and mother, and one black lab. If there are Ëan in Emily's "real" life, they are fellow swimmers at Gardner Webb who benefit from her friendship and her guidance in the academic side of their teamwork.

As far as we know there have never been Gnomi building tunnels under Dale City, Virginia or Boiling Springs, North Carolina, but perhaps they will continue to play a part in Emily's future endeavors.

About the Cover

The front cover photo was taken by Suey Nordberg in a glen near a family cottage on Keuka Lake in upstate New York.

Made in the USA
Middletown, DE
15 July 2019